Tiny House, Big Mountain

A NOVEL

Patrick Gillespie

Raw Earth Ink

2023

First paperback edition June 2023

Cover and interior design by tara caribou

ISBN 978-1-960991-05-8 (paperback)

Published by Raw Earth Ink
PO Box 39332
Ninilchik, AK 99639
www.raw-earth-ink.com

To all those who chose to come back.

Chapter 1

There's nothing so disquiets me
As snow new fallen on a tree—
Autumn when the leaves have fallen
And all beneath's turned cold and sullen.

I've seen the dogwood petals bring
Such beauty to the tree in spring
But there's another beauty, hidden,
As long in coming and unbidden—

Not in the clarion-gold of trees,
The loveliest pitch of autumn, these
Are not its colors, not the row
Of bales whitening in the field—no,

Not these. I've seen in darkening hours
A few final radiant flowers
Before they do not so much fall
As fade and close; but these are all

Another beauty. Later still
When frost slips through the windowsill
And I have had to scrape the glaze
Of ice as though some crystalline haze

Had covered up the world, then
I've seen such beauty—only then,
That for an instant veiled my sight,
That blinded me to all—that light.

1

About two dozen miles south of Burlington, where the Green Mountains shoulder southward, one of the half dozen Vermont roads crossing them begins its eastward climb. It was there that Virginia Fleetman pulled alongside East Brookway's gas station and grocery store. She idled the car, headlights scudding over the pavement, and unfolded a map between herself and the steering wheel. The store was dark but an old lamppost arching over the gas pumps made a flickering light. The concrete under them was stained with rust. The station itself was a clapboarded building with a dusty porch across the front. Sap buckets hung from the posts, a nearby birch, and a telephone pole. Virginia didn't notice.

If she had, she might have wondered why sap buckets were hanging from the posts. The joke had long since run its course among the locals, but the earnest inquiries of out-of-staters kept the buckets sugaring. Instead, Virginia wearily brushed aside some loose strands of graying red hair, brought the map to her nose, then tossed it onto the passenger seat. She steered the SUV back onto the start of the twisting climb. The roadside glittered with black-eyed Susan, goldenrod, and Queen Anne's lace. She rolled down the windows to breathe the moisture, grateful to be out of an airplane. After a few miles she almost missed the faded red bandana hung from a dead slip of white pine, marking the road to a property she had only visited years ago. She held her breath. The dirt road dipped into a copse of hemlock and poplar, straightened, climbed, turned again.

She quickly braked. Two green eyes peered into the headlights. She saw a long snout, a white muzzle and a mottled brown and gray coat—a coyote; she'd seen coyotes in New Mexico and none were as large. The coywolf stared as if it could see past the headlights, then turned and unhurriedly disappeared into the darkness of the scrub and trees.

She steered over a berm, stopping her SUV in the high grass next to a truck. Her headlights glanced over a foundation, a green tarp and into the dark nothing of Brookway Valley, but not a house. She stepped into the grass, engine running, headlights on. She took out her cell phone, stepped nervously toward a wedge of light beneath the foundation's tarp, almost stumbling in her high heels. "Hello?" she called. "Hello? Who's there!"

The green tarp was pulled tight over the deck that covered the foundation. Below the deck, darkly facing the overlook, there should have been the doors of a walkout basement. Virginia tripped down the weedy slope and called again. She stumbled backward when a younger woman stood out from the darkness.

She wore a white, sleeveless shirt and carpenter pants. She was lean and wiry with long black hair in a braid, clean eyebrows, lips and a straight nose. Her eyes were dark and her steps short and purposeful. "What do you want?"

"What?"

"I said, what do you want!"

"I live here!" said Virginia.

"No you don't."

"No. I mean– I don't live here. This– You– This is my property!"

"Did Daryl send you?"

"I don't know who you're talking about," Virginia insisted. "This is my property! I want to know where my house is!"

The younger woman lowered the flashlight. "What's your name?"

"Virginia Fleetman."

"I don't believe it," said the woman. "You've got no idea."

"What's your name?" Virginia asked.

"Drew Tippet."

"Well," Virginia collected herself. "Hello Miss Tippet. Now can you please tell me where my house is and why you're living here?"

"Mom?" A girl pushed aside the tarp. She looked eleven or twelve, hair shorter than her mother's, somewhere between a dark brown and black.

"Just a minute, babe."

"Who– Your daughter? Is there anyone else in there? Your husband? Your dog?"

"Don't have a dog."

"Well," Virginia sputtered. "I just saw one. I was pulling up and saw it. Whose dog is that if it's not yours?"

"What'd it look like?"

"Like—like a big dog!"

"Prob'ly a coywolf. We got 'em up here; and since you asked, this is my daughter, Cody."

"And you're the builder?"

Drew glanced up the embankment. "You alone?"

"I–"

"Nevermind." Drew sighed. "Come in. Not much of a house, but you get what you pay for."

"That son of a bitch!" Virginia hissed. She followed Drew through the flaps of the tarp and into the makeshift basement. Light bulbs were strung from joist to joist. Lanterns made from colored paper covered bare bulbs. There were two beds. One was a mattress kept off the damp concrete with boards on the flat. There was a small refrigerator, a pressure tank, a makeshift boiler, a utility sink, a claw foot tub and a toilet hidden by a paisley curtain. "Want somethin' to drink?" Drew asked.

"No. I don't want anything to drink."

"You should."

"What did you do?" Virginia asked. "Did you pocket the money?"

"Excuse me?" Drew's voice was strong for such a wiry woman. "What's wrong with you? Wanna know where your house is? I returned it. It was a pile of lumber. You think I'd be living here if I took your money? You think I'd live like this? You know where the money is? It's in the foundation. I paid for it. You want some water? I paid for that too."

"We sent you money."

"We?" Drew sat. "Yeah. Okay. Who's we?"

Virginia looked away, wanting to look at anything other than the younger woman's exasperated stare. "How much did he send you?"

"Six thousand eight hundred and thirty-four dollars and sixty-three cents."

Virginia rapped her knuckles just above her knee, a habit that left bruises. "Will you excuse me?" She didn't go far. She stood just a little way beyond the tarp, somewhere in the dark and the high grass. The girl, Cody, began to ask questions but Drew silenced her.

Drew could just hear the older woman's voice. *Yes...* she said. *Yes, I know what time it is... No, I don't care...* Then she blurted: *Well, what am I supposed to do? ...Yes, I have reservations... No. I wasn't– No... There is no house! Where am I supposed to live? I don't– No, I don't– I don't know. Drew Tippet. She says she's the builder and that she was never paid. How do I– because she's living in the foundation for God's sake! Alright– No, I won't calm down! ...No! I'll talk to you tomorrow. Tomorrow morning.*

"So is this your place or isn't it?" Drew asked when Virginia returned.

"Yes it's mine!"

"Then you owe me money."

"Look. I don't know if you're who you say you are. But if you are–" Virginia gazed upward, silently mouthing words, testing them. "Okay, I don't want you living here. I don't care–why–for whatever reason. I don't want you living here. This is my property."

"Okay."

"If you're who you say you are, then I'm sorry. I'll make sure you're paid what you're owed."

"I've got a little girl–"

"Maybe she should be with her father."

"Yeah—" Drew pursed her lips. "I'll start movin' out tomorrow."

Virginia looked like she might have had something to say, then abruptly turned, impatiently pushing aside the tarp of the doorway.

"So are we gonna live with Dad?" the girl asked.

"You really wanna live with Dad, babe?"

2

The next morning was a Wednesday. Virginia made several calls from Brookway's only inn, the Apple House. The farmhouse had a south facing view of the same valley Virginia's property overlooked. The valley was broad by Vermont standards, but narrow and introverted by New Mexico's – Virginia's home for four decades. The U-shaped course of the north-south valley stretched and undulated. Fields and mostly forest, houses and steeples were framed by the inn's lace curtain and the window's muntins.

Virginia learned several facts that morning. The first was that Brookway didn't have a police department or sheriff. The sheriff was two towns removed. Brookway had a constable named Warren Tinsdale but Virginia didn't talk to Warren. Warren was tedding hay. Virginia talked to Warren's wife, Lindsey. Virginia also learned the weather forecast and was told by Lindsey that a good rain was coming and that a good rain made bad hay. She also told Virginia that she knew Drew Tippet. She had done good work for Sage Patchel, among others, and by the way could use the money she was owed. That ended the conversation with Lindsey Tinsdale.

Virginia also learned that inmates at the New Mexico State Corrections Department can't receive calls at five-twenty in the morning. At ten-thirty, Vermont time, Virginia was reminded by her New York lawyer that her husband had been convicted, among other crimes, of embezzlement, theft by false pretenses, lying under oath, and impeding investigation; and that she should consider herself lucky to have a poured foundation, a drilled well, and a smartphone. That ended the conversation with her lawyer.

At eleven-thirty, Virginia learned that the Apple House Bed & Breakfast was six and a half miles from the house site. At a quarter to twelve she learned that she'd forgotten to cancel the delivery of a queen size bed frame and mattress, a writing desk, a chair, a couch, and a bookshelf. Virginia saw the delivery truck before she reached the berm. The two delivery men, with Drew, were already unloading. Virginia raced from the SUV without closing the door. "What are you doing?"

"Afternoon." The older of the two men glanced at the foundation. "Which room did you want these in?"

"I can't accept this!"

"Can't put it back. We got two more after this. Yours loaded last. Yours comes off first."

"I can't–" Virginia flailed at the foundation. "Look!"

"We'll put it on the deck. Keep it covered. And be back tomorrow, first thing."

"Help me!" Virginia turned to Drew, but Drew gestured at her pickup, packed since morning and that suited Drew just as well.

"Then I have no choice," Virginia said mostly to herself. The furniture was carried to the green tarp-covered deck overlooking the valley. Glittering fields and the mountain sides were spotted with the green shadows of clouds. They moved lazily in the sunning breeze. Drew's daughter, Cody, climbed into view. She came carrying a handful of daisies. "I owe you money," said Virginia to Drew "How much?"

"Just over sixteen thousand."

"That much?"

"A drilled well, a buried power line, two room septic, landscaping, and labor." Drew pulled an envelope from the back pocket of her jeans. "These are copies of the bills. "

"I—well—I don't have—I'll see what I can do."

"I'd like that." Drew took her daughter's hand. They went to the pickup truck, loaded with tools, mattresses, crates, and a refrigerator.

"I'm sorry, Drew."

"I have a lien on your property." Drew opened the truck door. Her daughter climbed in. Drew followed.

"When?"

"Small claims. Nobody showed up."

"Wait!"

"I guess there was a lot you didn't know." Drew pulled shut the truck door. She turned the key. There was a click and a pop. "Fuck!"

Virginia jumped.

"You know," Drew stared out the windshield, "I'm sorry your ex screwed you. Sorry you don't have a place to live. Sorry it's supposed to rain tonight. Sorry you never had a fucking clue! And sorry I don't want to talk about this right now."

"I just–"

"Pro'bly need a new starter."

"Maybe I can help."

"So I can get off your property?" Drew slammed the door then walked to the front of her truck and popped the hood.

"That's not what I meant."

"What do you want then?"

The delivery truck loudly started behind them. The younger of the two men yanked down the truck's overhead door. "Call the office!" he shouted before rounding the far side.

"Maybe they could help?" said Virginia.

Drew shook her head. "Like I said: needs a starter. Maybe a bad solenoid."

"Do you have Triple-A?"

"I've got a phone," Drew answered flatly. She dug it from her canvas dungarees. "Daryl? Yeah. I need you to get something. No. I know. Just later today. I need the starter. For the Dodge. No, I didn't put it— When was I supposed to put it in, Daryl? I know we're supposed to meet. Daryl. Damn it. Just get the part. Can you do that? Just one last thing— it's in the shed." Drew sighed, shook her head, shoved the phone back in her pocket. "Might as well get out," she said to Cody.

"I'm so sorry but I could use your help," said Virginia.

"Yeah—" Drew answered reluctantly. "Okay. My truck's goin' nowhere. What do you need help with?"

"It's supposed to rain tonight and—"

"Why didn't you just have 'em put the furniture in the basement?"

"I was panicked."

"Come on." Drew sighed. "Do you have somethin' to wear besides heels?" She pulled a folded blue tarp from the back of the pickup and walked with it toward the foundation.

"Yes," Virginia hurried after her, then veered to her SUV. She kicked off her high heels and pulled tennis shoes from the back seat. She hurried back where Drew was already throwing down the tarp.

"So— what happened?" Drew asked. "If you don't mind. Got nothin' else to do."

"I don't think you really want to hear how I ended up here, do you?"

"Daryl's not in any hurry." Drew tossed an edge of the tarp to Virginia, "Give me the long version."

"Well my whole life has been turned upside down." Virginia exhaled. "My husband is in prison. I've lost everything. I thought, at least, that I had a house here. Then finding you and your daughter living here— well—"

"What did your husband do?"

"He was a mortgage broker."

"And you?"

Virginia scowled. "I had a short career as a nurse. My mother never approved. She used to say that medicine was a man's world. I quit when I married and lived in a mansion. I had a swimming pool and dinner parties. All I had to do was obey my husband. Be a good wife."

"Was it worth it? Havin' all those things? Livin' like that?"

"Well, I got what I wanted, didn't I?"

"What about children?"

"No children."

"You didn't want 'em or couldn't have 'em?" Drew asked.

"Yes. No. I don't know."

"You gotta tuck the tarp under the furniture," said Drew. "Don't want wind under it."

"Yes. Of course."

"So what happened? Did you get a divorce?"

"Yes. My husband— My ex– He's in the New Mexico State Corrections Department."

"Sorry."

"Don't be sorry. He deserved it. He embezzled from me; he embezzled from everyone." Virginia's voice hardened. "Everything we owned was stolen. After criminal forfeiture, the only thing they let me keep was this property—inherited it from my mother."

"He embezzled from you?"

"Yes!" Virginia answered emphatically. "He took my money! He was supposed to be building our vacation home! The son of a bitch!" Virginia's shook her head with embarrassment. "Excuse me. I'm sorry."

"No. It's okay. I'd be mad as hell. So what are you gonna do?"

"I don't know."

"Why don't you finish the house," said Drew.

"I don't have enough money."

"Build a smaller house."

"I don't have anywhere to stay."

"Stay here."

"Stay?" Virginia incredulously gazed at the foundation. "I can't stay here! I can't live here. There's not even a door for God's sake!"

"I stayed here."

"I need a house. I can't live like this."

"You know where I'm goin' this afternoon?"

"No."

"To sign divorce papers. Waited over half a year for this. If you've gotta get divorced in Vermont— don't. You can't get there from here."

"Daryl?"

"That's right."

"Here." Virginia untucked the tarp and lifted it over the furniture. She began to speak again but hesitated. "Why don't you sit down while you wait."

They sat on the plastic wrapped, upholstered chairs, looking out over the valley's increasing haze. The breeze had deadened. The grasses and leaves simmered with the smell of humidity. Virginia's lips were thin and white with wanting to speak. The leaves showed their white undersides as a cloud moved over. Had there been a house, she might have liked the view. "I don't know what to do," she finally said. "I don't have enough money and it's been years since I was in nursing. Years. I'm not even sure I'd want to go back to that. Maybe I could find another husband to honor and obey. I'm good at that."

"You can get good at things."

"God, is there anything worse than listening to a woman feel sorry for herself?"

"Maybe you've got reason."

"How old is your daughter?"

"She's twelve. Gonna be thirteen soon," said Drew. "She's small but don't mess with her."

"Like you then."

"Yeah," Drew nodded. "A failed builder in a failed marriage livin' in a failed house for a failed customer."

Virginia continued to gaze into the valley. "Well– that's honest."

"So you got any more deliveries needin' canceled?"

Virginia thought about that, then with a panicked exclamation rooted for her phone.

3

The rattle of Daryl's truck came first and then the Ford's black grill crackling over the rise. He pulled next to Drew's truck, paused to cup a cigarette, and tossed a match underfoot. He was a stocky and powerfully built man. His black hair was cut short and his skin was weathered. He wore a white, button down shirt with rolled cuffs and approached the women, smiling. A cigarette was notched between the shrunken fingers of his right hand, stiff and claw-like.

Daryl nodded at Virginia. "Afternoon."

"Did you bring the part?" asked Drew.

He leaned with a foot on the tarp. "Not like you'd have time to put it in."

"Then how—"

"I'll take you and Cody down."

"Daryl." Drew sighed and shook her head. "No."

"We'll get the starter after," he said curtly. "I'll bring you back and help you put it in— one last favor." He glanced at Virginia. "You the owner?"

"Yes."

"You treat Drew right and you'll get your house." When he turned to Drew his temples shimmered with sweat. "Do you want to cancel?"

"Cancel?" said Drew.

"Yeah. All this. Everything. The divorce."

"Cody!" Drew shook her head with disbelief. "Get in Dad's car. We're all goin' down. Gonna sign some papers."

"She can stay," said Virginia.

"No she can't."

"She's comin' with us," said Daryl. "I'm treatin' her. I'm treatin' you both. Last time Mom and Pop are together. You want ice cream, Cody? I'll get you some."

"For fuck's sake, Daryl."

"Hey, it's a good thing," he said. "We'll just try to make it a good thing. Right, Drew? One last time together. No harm in a friendly good-bye. We'll get lunch, maybe, and then I'll get you some ice cream."

"After that the starter," said Drew, "and then we come back up here."

"Done."

"You gonna be okay with that?" Drew asked Virginia. "Leavin' my truck here. You gonna be okay havin' it on your property?"

"Yes. Of course. Leave it."

"Cody!" Drew shouted again. "Get in Dad's truck!"

Cody finally opened the door of her mother's truck and paused when a crow settled on the hood. Cody looked at Drew and Daryl, then at the crow.

"Cody!" Daryl snapped impatiently.

"There's a crow!" said Cody.

"Then honk the horn for Christ's sake, if you're scared of it!"

Cody hesitated, then slid out of the truck and slammed the door, causing the crow to fly off. She went to Daryl's truck, hands in her pocket and eyes downcast. Drew climbed in behind her.

"You have a good afternoon," said Daryl, winking at Virginia.

But Virginia didn't trust Daryl. She started toward the truck just as Daryl swung shut the door. The engine snarled to life. "Wait!" she shouted.

Daryl lowered the window.

"You don't have to go," she said to Drew. She leaned with one hand against the truck and dug a stone from the left heel of her sneaker. "I mean, tonight. If it doesn't work, whatever you're fixing, you can stay tonight."

Drew's eyes widened with exasperation.

"Go," she said to Daryl. "Just fuckin' go." He threw his cigarette at Virginia's feet. He backed up, tires popping in dirt and gravel, then swung away and over the rise of the driveway. That decided it. Virginia didn't like Daryl and worse than that she didn't like herself.

Chapter 2

1

For the first half hour Virginia didn't know what to do. She sat in her chair, on her deck, and imagined selling the property; then imagined having nothing, not so much as a job; and then watched the sky roll over the mountains. There were places that looked like this in New Mexico, where mountains were smooth and green, but there were no towns or valleys between, only a handful of long roads with a lone gas station.

She hated Vermont.

She wanted roads, or just one, that she could drive to nowhere. The quaint houses and tidy fields were insipid. She wondered how she ever imagined being happy here. She would sell the property with its view. Land was worth more in Vermont. She would take the money, buy cheaper land or a foreclosed house, and have enough to remodel or build something better. She would call a realtor tomorrow.

The phone rang and the number wasn't one she recognized.

"I'm trying to reach a Mrs. Fleetman," said a woman flatly. "Is this Mrs. Fleetman?"

"Yes. Who is this?"

"This is Dr. Brown from the Green Mountain Medical Center. I've got a problem. Ms. Tippet has been in an accident and can't be treated at the medical center. She's going to Fletcher Allen. The helicopter will be here in twenty minutes. Mrs. Fleetman, she's asked you to be her daughter's temporary guardian."

"What?"

"She wants you to be a temporary guardian for her daughter."

"But– she has a father!"

"Are you a family friend, Mrs. Fleetman?"

"No– I just–"

"Mr. Tippet is deceased."

"Do you– Oh! What?"

"Can you assume guardianship of the girl? If you can assume guardianship then we need you to come to the hospital as soon as possible."

"Yes, but where? I've never been there."

She heard a curt statement forwarding her to a receptionist. She stared blankly then jumped out of her chair. She hurried to her car with the awkward, broad-hipped gait of women unused to running. Within a step of the driver side door, she leaned, hipways, against the car, continued to hold the phone against her ear and dug another pebble from the heel of her sneaker. She flung open the door and scribbled directions on a dog-eared road map.

Then she was in the car and driving. Four miles down the road she was stopped by a flagman before a bridge. She immediately knew why. Five state patrol cars, two together and three on the other side of the bridge lit the darkening road with blue flashes. She smelled diesel, rubber, and gasoline. She saw a fire truck midway along the bridge and a crane was already moving into place. A black Ford pickup truck lay on its driver side, half buried in Sly's Brook. The name of the brook, on a slender green sign, was bent almost to breaking. The broken lip of the truck's hood caught the foaming water in its mouth. Water gurgled out of a windshield. The front passenger wheel was twisted and jammed into the bottom gut of the truck.

The nearest patrolman impatiently waved her across the bridge. After that Virginia remembered the directions without having to stop. The hospital was a small place, one building, three stories, that took up about a baseball field's worth of land. The side was a dull brown brick highlighted with lighter stone. She hurried through the emergency room entrance. She was hustled into a curtained space where she saw Drew, a lawyer, the doctor, a short woman with shoulder length gray hair, two nurses, and the papers she needed to sign.

Drew struggled to breathe, but spoke when she saw Virginia. "Thank you." Her voice was barely a strained whisper. She breathed again. "Ribs–"

"Why?" Virginia asked as she took the offered clipboard and signed. "I hardly–"

"Dad–" Drew's fingers twisted the sheets in pain. "I don't know— I don't know where— Mom. Don't trust– Daryl's parents– Assholes. In Georgia." Each word was a short, painful exhalation. "Cody– Okay?"

"What happened?"

"Bastard–" She began to sob and grimaced with pain. "Son of a bitch!"

The doctor gripped Drew's hand, silencing her, then guided Virginia out of the curtained enclosure while three men quickly wheeled a collapsible gurney to the other side of Drew's bed. She guided Virginia by the elbow, speaking quietly and firmly. "Cody is doing okay. It's a miracle the girl survived but she's doing okay. The worst is ahead. You need to know: Both the girl and the mother have told us that the father tried to kill them. I'm not here to confirm what happened but I think you need to assume what they're saying is true. That's a hell of a thing. Take her home. Don't leave her alone tonight and call us any time."

"She wasn't hurt?"

"When they found her, she was in the water. She wasn't breathing and wasn't responsive. We don't know how long she was under the water but she's awake and responsive now. She's better off than she has a right to be."

"But she's talking?"

"She's had a concussion. Wake her every hour. Make sure she wakes up. Talk to her. Ask her how she's doing. Make sure she's responsive. If anything seems wrong, call us."

The doctor rounded a corner and pulled aside another curtain. Cody sat upright with her legs outstretched. Virginia noticed her for the first time. Her hair was a dark silky brown and would have been smooth and straight if not for the blood. Her eyes were green, unlike her mother's. Gauze was taped to her forehead, just above her swollen left eye. Her cheek was bruised and her left arm was scraped and splotched with black and purple. Virginia didn't know what to say. She sat on the bed next to the girl, hands fidgeting in her lap. "I'm so sorry."

That was all Cody needed. Tears welled and she leaned forward. Virginia took her in her arms. The girl's small frame shook as she sobbed. Virginia held her with a fierceness she'd never felt before, and the emotion stunned her. She held Cody until the shuddering sobs became smooth and deep breaths. "She's going to be okay," she finally said. "Your mom's going to be okay. You're going to be with me until she comes home."

And then Virginia considered how all her decisions had put the girl and her mother in the truck. She angrily drove the thoughts away–too close to self-pity. When it was time, when the breathing was slow and measured, Virginia helped Cody off the bed. The girl limped and held Virginia's hand as they found their way back to the Admissions Desk. The doctor saw them and knelt.

"I'm not going to ask you how you're doing, Cody," she said. "We all know how you must be feeling. Before you go, look at me again. That's it. Look left. Right. Up. Down." She smiled. "You're going to be okay. Right? And your mom's going to be okay. She's going to the best hospital with the best doctors. She's got some broken ribs–"

"She almost broke her back."

"Who told you that?"

"I was there."

"Yes, that's right, but did your mom tell you?"

"No. I saw it."

"You saw it? How did you see it?"

"Saw it when they pulled me out of the truck, but they didn't know I was there. I tried to tell the woman who was helpin' to make me breathe again, but she couldn't hear me."

"Somebody must have said something."

"Nobody," Cody answered. "I wasn't in my body when I saw 'em. I was watchin' them and watchin' myself, but they didn't know that I was. Mommy didn't break her back. But she's hurt pretty bad."

The doctor held Cody's hands in both of hers then sighed and turned to Virginia. "You have my number?"

"Yes," Virginia answered. "Have they flown Drew out?"

"Twenty minutes ago," said the doctor.

There was nothing more to be said. Virginia wasn't the praying kind and wasn't going to say it. She thanked the doctor, then led Cody out into the unexpectedly cool night. The air was fresh with the smell of a quick rain. They walked silently to the car, then once inside the girl asked: "Where are we going?"

"To the Apple House, hon."

"Never been."

"You'll like it. We're going to wash your hair, get you into something clean, and put you in a good bed." The girl didn't answer at first. Street lights intermittently lit her features until the road stretched into a scattering of dark fields and distant farmhouses.

"What kind of car is this?"

"It's a Navigator, sweetie."

"It's nice."

"It's a gas guzzler."

"Why d'ya own it then?"

"All good things in life are guzzlers."

"What d' ya mean?"

"I've got to buy something more my size," said Virginia with a long exhalation.

"So are you gonna stay?"

"Think I should?"

"Yeah. Mom was really mad at you, but said it wasn't your fault, that she kind of liked you anyhow."

Virginia finally nosed the SUV onto the blacktop and dirt lot of the inn. The house was fronted by a large porch. A Victorian turret with a conical roof marked one corner and black shutters decorated the windows. The gable eaves were chased by a filigree of turns and corbels. The inn was well looked after, freshly painted, and catered to tourists, weddings and the occasional passer-through.

The owners of the Apple House were a couple in their 50s. She was short and stout; he was thin and tall. The short and stout woman was named Meredith and wasn't chatty and kept the inn officiously. She wore small, wire rim glasses that, when she wasn't wearing them, hung over her breasts. Her hair was short and gray.

She and her family, and her family's family, had lived in Vermont since the state was New Hampshire. Her husband, on the other hand, was a flatlander from Ohio, typical of garrulous men from the Midwest. His work was to welcome the guests and hers to welcome their money. They were the perfect couple to run an inn, and had been running it for close to thirty years.

Both usually knew the goings-on in town but, for whatever reason, didn't know that Virginia, an uninteresting woman who had only just arrived in Brookway, would walk into the entryway with Drew Tippet's daughter, bloodied and limping; and that furthermore the uninteresting woman had been made the girl's temporary guardian.

Before the evening was out, the reasons, whereofs and wherebys would spread like a drought-fire through the little town; but presently Meredith gaped at Virginia and Cody, her small eyes shifting back and forth between the two. "Cody!" she said, and then didn't know what else to say.

"She'll be staying with me," said Virginia.

"She will?"

"Yes, is that extra?"

"No." Meredith answered. "No, not tonight, or any other night." She busily tried to piece together the puzzle. She had heard the sirens. She had heard the fire truck. There had been an accident at Sly's Brook, and Daryl's truck had been pulled out. "If you don't mind. Cody's mother and my daughter were best friends growing up. Is she alright?"

"She was just flown to Burlington."

"She's gonna be okay," added the girl.

"Yes, of course she'll be okay." Meredith agreed but the pieces didn't fit. She was already plotting calls; but first she pressed the digits of one hand through the other's, then turned and led Virginia and Cody up the stairs. She pulled an extra cot from a hallway closet, brought it into the room and opened it.

She wanted to say more, turned to Virginia, then to Cody, then back to Virginia, then awkwardly wished them a good night.

"Well. That was strange," said Virginia.

"I just wanna sleep," said the girl.

"I think we should clean you up." And by that, Virginia didn't mean a shower or bath. She was exhausted with worry. She offered her hand. Cody followed into the bathroom with its lace curtains, white walls, and floral trim. They sat on the edge of the claw foot tub and Virginia used a damp washcloth, hands, and shampoo to rinse the clotted blood from Cody's hair.

She dropped the bloodied washcloths into a mop bucket of water, one that she found tucked between the end of the claw foot tub and wall. Cody leaned against the elder woman. Unlike Cody's mother, Virginia was soft and comfortable and the older woman's kindness and gentleness reminded her of the day's terrible cruelty. Her eyes welled and she wailed. "Daddy tried to kill me!" Her fingers tightly clutched Virginia and she sobbed again. "Daddy tried to kill me!"

2

The next morning was fruitful for Meredith.

Suicide and attempted murder are infrequent events in any town and the ugliness of what had happened lit gossip's tinder like a struck match. After more than one conversation, Meredith learned that Drew had called Jessie Aymes looking for a spare bedroom until she could find an apartment, or, at most, until she could move in with her father.

Jessie Aymes was Brookway's self-appointed matriarch, a tall and thin woman with a thin face and long white hair. Jessie was purposeful and didn't indulge distraction; and whatever she did for the community unfailingly impressed on others what they hadn't.

Jessie had at first wondered why Drew didn't call, then had discovered, through calls of her own, that she had been in an accident that hadn't been an accident at all. What a terrible thing to do, she said. What a horrible thing. One thing for a husband to kill a wife or a wife a husband – who hasn't wanted to? – but to kill a child and one's own? As far as excuses, there's none and never will be; and she wouldn't comment on a man who was dead, but she didn't have to.

"And who's this looking after Cody?" she asked.

"Nice enough woman," answered Meredith. "Sal Darby's granddaughter."

"Oh, that's going back."

"Had more kids than a flight of stairs."

"And not one of 'em took after him," said Jessie. "I'll bet she's the only grandchild with anything of the Darby Farm."

"Well– he was a tough ol' cud."

"You say she's up from Arizona?"

"New Mexico."

"I'll bet she's Fred's daughter. He went southwest to lawyer and be an oil man."

"Looks a bit like him—red hair and all."

"And owes Drew a bit of money by what I hear."

"Now you make sense of that," Meredith said flatly. "Why would Drew put Cody in that woman's hands?"

"How's she seem?"

"Nice enough gal but Jessie, she could've asked you? Or her mother or father?"

"Well, Drew's father left her when she was just a girl and her mother's a lush and ne'er-do-well who lives in Monkton. As for me, suppose she had her reasons."

"Do you know what she aims to do?"

"No, but want to know the strangest thing of all?"

"What's that?"

"It was Fred Telford who found them down the brook and called 911. But here's the thing, he said he never woulda seen it if it hadn't been for a crow, or raven, or some such bird, big and black as any he'd seen hopping back and forth. Wouldn't let a car go by unless to run over it. He reasoned something must've happened to one of its chicks and so he got out and he said the bird jumped right up to the guard rail. That's when he saw Daryl's truck down in the water. He never would have seen it otherwise. He figured just about anybody would of driven by and not seen 'em."

"You don't say!"

"No. That's what he said. If he'd decided to run over that bird, they'd probably still be down in that brook and dead, and that bird too."

And that was how the two women left it, for it was just that moment that Meredith's husband, John, interrupted her from the front desk. Virginia was checking out. Did she know of a place to buy a decent used car?

Meredith pushed up her bottom lip and her wire rim glasses as if expecting more. John sighed. "No, I didn't ask her where she planned on living. That's not any of our business, Meredith."

"Well, then what did you tell her about a car?"

"I told her to go to Barstowe's."

"Oh for God's sake, John! He's crooked as a dog's back leg. You know that." She pushed herself up out of the desk chair and brushed her husband out of the way. Her office was separated from the front desk by two doors. Between the two doors and on either side were floor to ceiling shelves filled with shoe boxes and paperwork. A slanted ceiling, the underside of the stairs going to the second floor, were on one side. She rushed through the two doors, around the front desk, and caught Virginia on the wide porch headed to the gravel parking lot.

"There's a Volvo you could buy, sold by the owner," she said, then added, "and if you tell us where you're staying–" She rested her hand on Virginia's. "Most the town knows what happened. We'd be happy to help you with something warm, cooked, and ready to eat."

From that kindness Meredith learned that Virginia didn't have a house; and for that tidbit, Meredith bartered the names of a dozen villagers before they parted. Cody was already in the passenger seat. The visor was down and she was looking in the lighted mirror, lifting the bandage above her eye.

"Cody!"

"I'm just lookin'."

"You looked already!"

"Never had stitches."

"So who were you talking to in the lobby?" Virginia asked.

"Somebody from New York. She said she worked for a newspaper. They're gonna do some sort of story about it bein' fall in Vermont."

"She looked familiar."

"I said she prob'ly shouldn't."

"Why?" Virginia backed the car out of the lot and onto the main road. A northerly breeze during the night had washed out yesterday's humidity. The road was a brilliant morning white and the mountains were crisp.

"Because there's a big storm comin'. Nobody's gonna be able to drive the roads. A lot of people are gonna be hurt. Some'll die for steppin' too close to the brooks."

Virginia glanced at Cody, then at the road, then at Cody again. "Honey, you can't say things like that."

"Why not?" Cody turned her attention to the older woman, still running her fingertips over the hard knots of the stitches. Virginia wasn't the kind of woman Cody was used to being with. She wore khaki knee-length skirts, jewelry, and her reddish-grey hair was drawn back tight. She wore makeup, eyeliner, and lipstick. She looked like a tourist from out of state. She wore high heels and that was nothing her mother ever wore. Not once. Being with Virginia was like being with a traveler from a foreign country. "They must be hard to walk in."

"What?"

"High heels."

"Well–" Virginia lifted her chin. "I think you might have a point – in Vermont."

"Do ya shave your legs?"

"What?"

"Do ya shave 'em? Your legs?"

"Well– Yes."

"You'll have to stop or you won't fit in."

Virginia laughed. "Any other tips, hon?"

"Let your hair down."

"That'll be the day."

"There's Barstowe's," Cody pointed to the right. "You still wanna go?"

Barstowe's Used Cars sparkled with eagerness. The owner, George Barstowe, had a desk hard against a red-trimmed front window. The used car lot abutted a small brook and the store was a former gas station sided with white tiles. Barstowe came from a long line of New England farmers who'd survived fitful summers and stubborn snow. With that kind of persuasive genius to draw on, Barstowe came to retail like a duck to the pond. When Virginia's Lincoln Navigator swung into the lot, his soft bulging eyes went to the tires first, saw they were new, then saw the plates and knew as much as needed. He rose with a hefty grunt, tugged at his pants and sidled out the door.

Barstowe had a knack. He knew before the customer what they wanted. He pretended not to know. He offered the car they didn't want. I'll give you a bargain, he'd say; and by this the buyer thought he and Barstowe drove the same ox. But Barstowe was never on the same side. He'd work up a story for whatever car the buyer wanted and always with the same ending: Can't lower the price on that one, he'd say, sure you don't want t'other?

But today something unexpected happened. He'd been thinking about his late cousin Ned Barstowe and three-fingered Bub Furnham and about all the clutter Ned Barstowe had left him with, when Cody knocked all his deliberations right out of him.

"You picked the wrong car."

George studied the girl, tongue stopped behind his lower lip, as if noticing her for the first time. "Oh–" He tucked his thumbs behind his belt. "You're that girl."

"Which one?"

"The one almost drowned in Sly's Brook. That was a terrible accident."

"It wasn't an accident."

"It should have been."

"You picked the wrong car," Cody repeated, sticking her hands in her oversized overalls. She looked over her shoulder, following the blacktop to where it broke apart and puzzled out into a fine grit of dirt and tufts of grass. The grass thickened into a break of high grass, then trees, both broken by a brook that flowed down next to the lot and under the road. Virginia was still changing her heels for sneakers in time to see Cody point to the cars, backed one beside the other to the edge of the blacktop, to the start of the brook slope. "All them," she said, "if you wanna keep 'em, you'd better move 'em."

George Barstowe guffawed. "How so?"

"That brook's gonna carry 'em up and off."

"We just have a couple minutes," Virginia said, briskly joining the girl and Barstowe.

"Good morning, ma'am," said George, but he'd turned back to the brook, there being nothing more interesting than the weather to a farmer-descended New Englander. "Why that brook don't have it in her. She can barely carry her own water."

"She will and I seen it."

"Honey," Virginia gripped the girl's shoulder to silence her. "We're here to look at cars."

"When did you say that storm was comin'," George asked, and not that he wanted that little girl to think he believed her, but he'd long ago decided all girls and women had a touch of the Grafton witch in them.

3

Ned, for no good reason, had died; but worse than that, had left George with the contents of a barn – hemp rope, cracked block and tackle, a tangle of barbed wire and worse yet, a whole other barn inside the barn: planks, timbers, posts, beams, floorboards, siding, old tin roofing, long rusted sheets sitting on top of the mess – because there's never knowing when a farmer might need another barn. There were axles, broken wheels, a busted baler, and tedder. There were buckets of nails, barn post nails, roofing nails: eights, tens, sixteens. Some of the buckets had filled with water and had drained and filled again until the nails were an aggrieved porcupine of rust – no good to anybody. Half a dozen chainsaws hung from collar ties, like gutted animals; but Ned, it was said, had a way with hoarding.

If a mower needed fixing, or a chainsaw, or tractor, he could do it. For a time, Barstowe looked as if he meant to put the mechanic's trade out of business. He never bought anything new. He'd take a bad part and replace it with a used one; but there was something supernatural about it. He wouldn't just replace one part with another, but would want to know where the used part came from. If it was a chainsaw: Who owned it? How long did he run it? What kind of cutting did he favor? Where did he keep the saw? He'd say the inanimate had past lives too; that a sprocket could have good karma or bad, depending on who owned it. And there might have been more than a few who scoffed at the notion, but Ned could start a mower that hadn't started in years. He pulled tools back from the afterlife; all until the Sunday three-fingered Bub Furnam visited.

Bub Furnam had lost the little finger and a ring finger of his right hand trying to drown a Maine coon in a barrel of water. He'd had enough of cats and meant to clear out the farmyard, but the kitten had other ideas. It clawed and bit so that Furnam, always a short-tempered man, decided to reward himself by killing the kitten twice over – shooting it in the barrel while it drowned; even if it meant killing the rain barrel with it.

The story goes like this: Bub leaned the rifle against the rain barrel and shoved the kitten in the water. The kitten gave Bub such a bite that he yanked his hand and kitten straight out of the water. He and the kitten reached for the rifle at the same time, the kitten to save itself from a fall, and Bub to stop the kitten from saving itself. That's when the gun went off. The little Maine coon lost its tail and Furnam lost two fingers. The barn roof had a new hole in it.

You can't make this stuff up.

Story has it that Flow Henderson, Bub's next door neighbor, found his fingers two days later weeding the garden. She offered them back to Bub, but Bub declined. She buried them, but she always liked to say she planted them. Bub formed a new respect for the kitten and the two of them lived in peace after that. The kitten turned into one of the meanest mousers Bub ever owned. She kept to her business and Bub kept to his. Their respect was mutual. Every so often, she would visit Bub's lap and spend an hour there while he rubbed and stroked her. She wouldn't let anyone else near her. It was a dour and gray day when that cat died and Bub followed her a week after.

Folks called him three-fingered Bub, but truth was, and despite the story, Bub had four fingers. And that's where Ned Barstowe got into it. Rumor got around that when Bub had visited Ned that the morning, he had three fingers and when he left that evening, he had four.

It's not that folk begrudged Bub the finger, but the thought of where that finger came from was like a nettle on the tongue of every gossip. Everyone knew that Barstowe liked to keep used parts about, but thinking on that kind of part was more than the imagination bargained for. Barstowe, who liked nothing better than to be the butt of gossip, never let on; and Bub didn't either until it got to be a little joke between them. The upshot was that folk quit visiting Ned; and that was alright by him. The one thorn in Ned's side, such that he felt it enough to confide in George, was that no one had ever come to him looking for a post, or beam, or some other part for a barn. Ned always prided himself on being a librarian of used parts, and not just parts but the useful kind.

4

Without having bought a car, Virginia drove the thirty eight miles to Burlington and to Fletcher Allen. She and Cody settled into Drew's hospital room a little after noon.

"Hey babe," said Drew groggily. "Come here! Just—no hugs. Squeeze my hand. I just wanna know you're okay." Cody hurried to her mother's side. Drew bit her lip and tried not to let the intake of breath hurt. "Okay. Maybe don't squeeze so hard. All of it hurts."

Virginia waited, hands together, rubbing the top of one thumb hard over the other. Drew gently freed her hand and pushed Cody backward so she could see and touch the bandage above her eye.

"I got stitches," Cody answered.

"How many?"

"Ten."

"I'm so sorry, babe. I saw you–" Her voice rose and broke with a little groan. "I saw you in the water and I couldn't – I couldn't help you. I was so scared. I'm so sorry."

"I know. I tried to tell you I was okay."

"You're alive. That's all I care about." She turned to Virginia. "Thank you."

"I don't know–"

"I broke two ribs, an ankle," she took a breath, "and I got a compression fracture."

"I don't have a home," answered Virginia.

"Yes you do."

"I can't take care of a little girl! You can't expect me to take care of her! How? I've got enough money for a month at the inn. That's it. Then what? Do you expect me to live– to live up in that– that cave?"

"She isn't so little and yeah."

"I can't," said Virginia.

"I don't know how you grew up but my mom would leave me alone–maybe a day, maybe a week." Drew took a painful breath. "She didn't tell me when she went. She didn't tell when she was coming back. I was eight years old, made my own meals, washed my own clothes. I kept Mom's gun under my mattress case of a stranger. You think I should let Cody live with her? My dad's a dreamer. He took a job in Maine when I was nine years old. Seein' him was like seeing a trapped animal. He'd drink like hell and tell me we'd all been better off if I'd never been born."

"I'm sorry."

"Or maybe you think Daryl's parents would be better?"

"No, I just–"

"I haven't talked to them," said Drew.

"Do they know?"

"Yeah."

"I'm so sorry." Virginia nervously rubbed her hands, each in the other.

"They're gonna want to take Cody."

"Well, I'm sure–"

"Don't!" Drew coughed and momentarily spasmed with pain. "Don't let 'em!"

"No, of course not!"

"I don't want Cody living with them. Ever."

"I can't make that promise."

Drew flinched, leaned back in her pillow and stared at the ceiling. "No, don't suppose you can."

"I'm sorry."

"Use my car. I called up Joe Standage. He's gonna put in a new starter. All you have to do is meet him at the rental."

"I really don't need–"

"Me. I need you," Drew closed her eyes with the effort of so much talking. "And Cody needs you. Until I'm through this. Please. Fix my truck. Drive it. Up at your land, I know it's not much. You got water. You got a bed. You got a stove and a sink–"

Virginia's hands continued to roll in and out of their own nervousness. "I can't live there. There's not even a door–"

"So what are you gonna do?" Drew flinched. "Huh? You're just gonna give up because you don't have a door? Then what? Sell your property? Do you own a car? Go ahead; sell the one thing you own–your home."

"How do you expect me to take care of her?" Virginia's voice rose.

"School's startin' in a week."

"Drew, I hardly know you and you hardly know me."

"Can you please, please take care of Cody until I get out? I just need you to help me and then I'll do whatever I can to pay you back."

"I don't know how to!" Virginia's voice cracked. "I couldn't even take care of myself. I don't deserve anyone's trust—let alone this child's. I don't. I just don't."

"Will you?"

Virginia closed her eyes and exhaled. "I'll do what I can."

"Thank you."

5

On the drive home, somewhere between Burlington and Brookway, Virginia pulled off the road to hold Cody. The girl shook and sobbed. The grief came on sudden. Virginia quietly held the girl, stroking her matted hair until the sobbing and shaking gradually stopped. Then she quietly said, "I promise, hon. I promise."

Chapter 3

1

"How long?" Meredith asked.

"I don't know," Jessie answered. "I suppose Virginia would know. Why don't you ask her?"

"I asked last night."

"What did she say?"

"Didn't answer. Cody said she'd be okay though. Don't know what that's worth."

"How's Cody?"

"Back from the dead, I hear."

"How'd she look?"

"She's got stitches over her eye—more like she fell out of a tree than the hereafter."

"Thank God."

John called back from the front desk. "Meredith, we have a check-out."

Meredith crooked the telephone at her shoulder and glared at her husband. "I've got to go," she said before hanging up the phone.

John came into the back office. "It's Virginia and Drew's girl. Thought you might want to see them off."

"She's checking out? "

"That's right, Meredith."

"Don't use that tone of voice." Meredith stood and brushed past him. Virginia waited at the desk. Meredith smiled. Cody was out on the porch's rocking chair. Meredith waved off Virginia's credit card and peered at her over her wire-rimmed glasses. "After what you've gone through, and what you're doing for Drew and Cody, it's the least I can do."

"Thank you."

"It's a small community. We try to help each other."

"I'm in your debt."

"You're no such thing. Take care of that girl and if you need anything at all, anything, just call."

2

An hour and a half later Virginia was on Route 7, south of Burlington, sitting in Drew's pickup truck. Joe Standage was standing next to the open driver side door.

"Now listen," he said. "There's nothing to it. You just gotta let up the clutch slow. Not all at once. Just do it slow and give it gas just the same."

Virginia let up the clutch. She glared at the steering wheel in defiance, but the truck lurched and stalled. She gave a short cry of surprise and kicked from sheer frustration. Cody sat next to her on the bench seat keeping one hand on the dash, with its dusty foot prints, to brace herself, and the other against the seat-back. She was turned so she could see what Virginia did wrong.

"You gotta push in the gas when you let up on the clutch! You gotta do 'em at the same time. En't you ever driven standard?"

"No!"

"How can you not-have? En't you ever driven a pickup?"

"Now c'mon, Cody," Joe said, shushing her, "not everybody's pickup is a shifter."

Virginia started the truck for the tenth time. She pinched her lips, rattled the stick, then let up on the clutch. The truck lurched forward. The tires squealed. The door almost clipped Joe. "Give it more gas!" he hollered. "Give it more!"

The truck stuttered smoothly into a coasting first gear. "I did it!" Virginia whooped. She drove a lazy circle around Joe, then, braking, lurched and stalled.

"You gotta put in the clutch when you stop," said Cody.

"Any other tips?"

"You got it now," Joe called out, his hands in his back pockets. Judy, Joe's wife, waited in their own pickup. Joe climbed in and she waved, then pulled out without so much as a fare-thee-well. That's considered friendly in Vermont.

"You've come a long way, baby," Virginia muttered.

"Where're we headed?" Cody asked.

"Home."

"You mean your place?"

"I mean our place."

"Good." Cody said evenly. She wiped her eye with a knuckle, straightened and looked out the passenger side window.

"I understand, hon."

"I don't care 'bout any of that stuff."

"Which way to a grocery store?"

"Kemp's store," Cody answered, still peering out the passenger side. "They got most everything we need."

"They have most everything we need."

"That's what I said."

"You said got."

"Same thing," Cody muttered.

The two sat in silence for a few miles. The western slopes of the Greens were a late summer's dark, the fields were a spoil of wheat, wildflower, and corn. Every so often the road rose high enough to overlook the blue scattered waters of Lake Champlain, an inland sea dotted with sailboats and backed by the see-saw and saw-toothed ridges of the Adirondacks. Virginia could almost imagine there was an unmarked road, if only she could find it—a way out of trouble and worry.

She left Route 7, took the left which crossed railroad tracks and headed eastward into the Greens and over the first ridge into Brookway. "What do you like to eat?"

"Hot dogs."

"What else?"

"Hot dogs, mac and cheese."

"How about Macadamia nuts?"

"Don't know 'em."

Some twenty minutes later, having avoided all but one red light, they'd pulled into Hugh Kemp's grocery store—the same that Virginia had stopped by a couple nights before. The red clapboarded building was at the meeting place of the east bound road and Sly's Brook, each following each into the Greens. The wood floor was so worn and buckled by the mid-summer's humidity that children liked to balance on the sprung edges.

Virginia went straight to the checkout, a smooth wooden counter where groceries were pulled along with a makeshift wooden draw. "Macadamia nuts" she said to Hugh's daughter Rachel, a good-looking teenager with straight red hair, skinny as a rail, and freckles. She was leaning against a waist-high backboard, reading Hemingway.

"You're gonna be flooded," added Cody.

Virginia sighed.

"We were almost flooded before," said the teen. "You hear there's a storm comin'?"

"I saw it."

"Where'd you see it."

"When they were pullin' me out of the car."

"Cody!" Virginia interrupted.

The teen lowered her book and studied the younger girl. "You mean, like – how?"

"Like I could fly."

"Fly?"

"Like a crow."

"A crow? Why like a crow?"

"'Cause I had wings like a crow."

"Oh wow," said Rachel slowly. "You had a vision!"

"Did you say whether you had Macadamia nuts?" Virginia asked, pointedly.

"Oh, you were bein' serious."

"I was asking if you had Macadamia nuts."

"Nope."

"Do you have pecans?"

"Nope."

Ten minutes later, and after only one stall, they were wheeling uphill with hot dogs and mac and cheese. Virginia decided she'd have to remove the red bandana in the morning. She made some lurching shifts through the turn and rise of the dirt road and finally stopped at the house site with a few select words—the likes she hadn't uttered since marriage and divorce. And then, for an instant, she felt half her age and better than she'd felt in years.

"You sure you've never done any carpentry, 'cause you sure swear like a carpenter." Cody pulled on the sneakers she'd kicked on and off for the better part of the ride.

"I was expressing gratitude."

"That's a funny way of expressin' it." Cody hopped out of the truck and was about half-way to the foundation before she turned. "You comin'?"

Virginia had dropped one foot out the car door. She stared at the dark green tarp that was the roof of her home and the blue tarps that covered the furniture atop the deck.

"You comin'?" Cody asked again.

"Just a minute."

"You okay?"

"Just give me—" Virginia tried to breath.

"You don't look so good."

"I'm having a panic attack!" Virginia blurted. She gripped the steering wheel in her right hand and the seat's edge with her left.

"What's that?"

"God almighty!" Virginia burst out laughing, and maybe half crying too. "It's– This! This!" She frantically waved at the foundation, the tarps, the covered furniture. Her exhalation was long and shaky.

Cody turned, trying to see what Virginia saw, then turned back. "Don't see it. But there's lots I'd trade if that's all your panic's about."

Virginia screwed her lips. She let go of the steering wheel. She elbowed shut the driver side door and yanked the second bag of groceries from the back of the pickup. She took two steps, breathed deeply, then walked, by God, down the short slope to the foundation's entry. Goldenrod and ox-eye daisies speckled the path with yellow. Hop clover smudged the fringes with purple and the broomsedge was beginning its umber turn. These were the colors and leafy smells that painted away the panic. Virginia would find a glass and pick some of the flowers, but first there was food to cook.

There was no stove, just a hot plate with a propane tank under it. She could cook the mac and cheese in the microwave but she needed a skillet for the hot dogs. Cody asked: "Why not just make a fire?"

That's how Virginia ended the evening—outside on the hillside. The few clouds hanging over the mountains had taken on the multicolored pitch of the sun's late-day slant. Virginia couldn't remember how long it had been since she'd cooked anything over a campfire, and the heat reminded her that the days weren't going to stay warm too much longer. "So, what was your mother planning?" she asked Cody.

"For what?"

"You weren't going to stay here, were you?"

"No."

"I shouldn't think so."

"She was saying she was gonna buy property, local; and build a house."

"A house?"

"This fall, on a trailer; once we built it we'd move the house wherever we wanted."

"That's a mobile home, hon."

"It's a tiny house."

And then the whole of the day seemed to settle on Virginia. "My God," she said, "but this isn't what I expected."

A man hello'd from the top of the slope. Virginia was startled but Cody recognized the voice–Virginia's neighbor. Hoyte and his father, Arvid, stood at the top of the slope. Hoyte was a year older than Cody and the two, being each other's only neighbor, had taken up being best friends.

"I only wanted to say hello," said Hoyte's father with a Dutch accent. He was a gangly man who walked carefully, navigating with a cane. "And I wanted to know if Cody and Drew were okay."

"I'm okay," said Cody.

"That was a terrible thing that happened to you."

Cody shrugged.

"No," said Arvid. "I can see you have lost a little piece of yourself, but I think you will be okay. You will make a larger, more beautiful piece than the one you've lost." Then he turned to Virginia. "You are the owner?"

"I am," she sighed.

"If you and Cody need a place to stay," he said, "I have a room. If not, then perhaps you would have dinner with me?"

She warmly thanked Arvid for the offer. Unexpectedly, and with an insight which creeps up on one, Virginia suddenly saw the unfinished house as something like her life after a lost illusion. Maybe this was a second chance to build her life the way she should have. Here was a new foundation, a starting place, and her old life returned to begin again. There was a little refrigerator in the foundation, she said, and she had already made plans; though she had none at all, and though she was terrified.

When Arvid asked after Cody's mother, Hoyte joined Cody and the two moved up slope out of the fire's light—back along the driveway to the road. Hoyte was a head taller than Cody, plus some, and the tallest in his class. His brown eyes were thoughtful and his hair fell straight until it almost, but didn't quite, curl at his ears.

"So," he said, "you're stayin' here?"

"Yeah."

"I mean, you're not gonna be stayin' with your family or anything like that? Like your Gramma?"

"Mom says we're better off we don't."

"She gonna be okay?"

"Yeah." Cody stuck her hands in the overalls. "I got ten stitches."

"Ten!" Hoyte studied her appreciatively and with something like admiration. "Most I've ever had was seven. Ever read *Red Badge of Courage*?"

"No."

"Tie the bandage 'round your head and it'll look like you were in a fight."

"I was."

"Prob'ly so," said Hoyte thoughtfully.

Cody didn't answer. She and Hoyte walked out of all but starlight. The noise of leaves spread up the mountainside off and on again, as if the weather meant to change but was of two minds.

"Hoyte, you believe in God?"

"Dunno. Maybe. I mean, I went to church once, with Gramma and Grandpa. Don't know if I believe in an old man sittin' on a throne or anything like that."

"You ever had a dream?" Cody persisted.

"Sure."

"'Bout God?"

"No, nothing like that. Just dreams."

"'Bout the future?"

"No, just dreams where soon as you try and tell anybody 'bout 'em you can't remember why you bothered."

"So what do you think God would be like?"

"Suppose he'd be nice."

"Yeah," said Cody. "Me too. Nice."

"Why'd you ask?"

Cody was silent for a step or two. She kicked a couple of the larger stones in the gravel driveway. "Just something I been thinkin' 'bout."

"Fox came through yesterday, killed three of our ducks."

"Nice for the fox."

"Wonder what those ducks think of God."

"Maybe they think they're the lucky ones," answered Cody.

"Bet the fox would differ."

"How would the fox know?"

"What's not to know?" asked Hoyte. "He's alive. Ducks aren't."

"What if you knew something terrible was gonna happen and nobody believed you?"

"How would you know?"

"Maybe God showed you."

"Yeah," said Hoyte, "but I mean, how would you know whether or not somebody believed you?"

"What if nobody did?"

"Then there'd be no reason for God to tell you," Hoyte answered. "Seems to me. I s'pect God wouldn't tell you 'bout the future 'less he knew someone was gonna listen."

"What if I said there was a big flood comin'; that a lotta' houses were gonna go under, and cars, and there was gonna be bridges knocked down and roads so torn up nobody could get in or out but by flyin'; that the only way to school would be hikin' through the woods; and there'd be no way to get from one side of the state to the other there was so much flood comin'."

"First I'd wanna know if I was s'posed to live or die."

"What if ya didn't see anythin' like that, just that there was gonna be a big flood."

"How big?"

"Turn brooks into rivers and rivers into lakes – brooks that was never meant to wet a toe."

Hoyte looked up at the trees. "So, what're you sayin'? Are you sayin' God showed you the future?"

"God didn't show me anything," Cody answered. "I just saw it."

"When?"

"When I was in the truck."

"Today?"

"No, Hoyte. You know, down by the bridge." Cody tucked her fists in her overalls.

"So, you're bein' serious?"

"Yeah."

"Who've you told?"

"Some woman from New York doin' a show on Vermont, Barstowe, Virginia, you."

"What'd they say?"

"Nothin'."

"Suppose I wouldn't know what t' say, myself."

"Virginia says I shouldn't be tellin' people 'bout what I saw."

"But how'd you see it?"

"Like I was a bird, like a crow, like the wind didn't touch me; like I could look down and see it all."

"You believe it?"

"Don't know. When people look at you all funny, you start thinkin' 'bout yourself the same way."

"You gonna tell anybody else?"

"Would you?"

"Guess I don't know."

Chapter 4

1

"Hi, I'm Cody's grandmother. Marjorie." Daryl's mother extended her hand. She and Virginia shook. A slow smile stretched the tight skin at the corners of Marjorie's lips. She spoke with a heavy southern drawl. "Thank you so much for looking after her."

They'd pulled up in a Malibu. The older woman had hurried ahead of her slower husband. He walked old and stiffly, swinging his right leg to join the two women.

"I'm so sorry," said Virginia.

"So sad. So sad. Daryl was a troubled child, you understand, but we never expected anything like this."

Cody appeared, climbing the short slope from the basement.

"The owner of the little inn, such a nice woman, said you were living up here with hardly a roof over your head."

"The house is unfinished," said Virginia.

"This is my husband, Wayne." Marjorie gestured.

"Glad to meet you," he said.

Virginia shook his hand in turn. Cody, in the meantime, stood uncertainly behind Virginia just as Marjorie stooped and held her hands toward Cody. Bracelets jangled at her wrists. "Give Gramma a hug."

Cody did, but Virginia didn't miss who hugged who. "Let me see you." Marjorie studied Cody's face and the bandage above her eye. "Oh sweetheart. I'm so sorry." The older woman stood. "It'll be hard to live here, won't it? What with school just around the corner, fall coming and winter. I imagine there won't be a moment's peace with all the construction."

"Well, I don't think Drew will be in the hospital too much longer."

"I wouldn't know," Marjorie answered.

"Oh," Virginia hesitated. "Well. Maybe another week but I don't know what she's planned."

"Cody, honey, would you like to stay with Gramma and Grandpa?—just until this all gets sorted out?"

Virginia rested her hands on Cody's shoulders. "I think... I'm sorry, that's not up to Cody."

"Honey, I'm her grandmother," Marjorie smiled.

"Cody's mother appointed me her guardian." Virginia straightened.

"Can they do that?" Marjorie turned quickly to her husband. "Just like that?" She turned back to Virginia. "Drew's a dear. What's your church, Virginia?"

"I'm sorry, I don't go."

"It's so different up here." She turned to Cody. "We're going to be having a little service on Tuesday. I think."

"I'm sorry for your loss," Virginia interrupted. "Thank you for informing us."

"Informing Cody," the older woman coolly corrected.

"Honey," said her husband, "That's enough." His voice was soft, a tenor voice. He turned to Virginia. "We just come to see how she was and tell her. That's all. If Drew appointed you Cody's guardian, then we'll respect her wishes."

Marjorie cocked her jaw before speaking. "Please send our best wishes to Drew. If there's anything we could have done. It's just we don't want her to hold it against us—"

"Marjorie," her husband interrupted, "come on, honey. I'm sure Virginia understands."

"You prob'ly don't wanna stay too long, there's a flood comin'," Cody blurted.

Virginia inhaled.

"A what, sugar?" asked the older woman. "A flood?"

"You and Grampa'll get stuck."

"Really? Who told you there was gonna be a flood?"

"I saw it."

"You mean like Noah's flood?"

Cody shook her head. "There's just gonna be a lot. I just saw a lot of water in the brooks, more than I've seen or anybody's seen. There's gonna be bridges knocked down and houses turned upside down."

Marjorie knelt. "Cody honey, there's lots you don't understand about this world. There's a war going on and you need to be mighty sure you know which angel's whisperin' in your ear. God would never lead a little girl astray, but Lucifer— Lucifer means light. The Angel of Light, is that what you saw?"

"Marjorie," said her husband plaintively. "Let's not have this discussion now."

The older woman pursed her lips, as though to speak again, then reluctantly stood. She smiled awkwardly before turning with her husband back to their car. When he reached for her elbow, she shoved his hand away. Virginia said nothing. The car doors closed. Then and there Virginia made a decision. As long as she was Cody's guardian, hell was going to freeze over before she handed over any child to that woman.

"You don't like her," said Cody.

"I didn't say that."

"You don't have to."

"It's not my business to like or dislike your grandmother."

Cody shoved her fists tight into her overalls. "I don't either."

"Hon, do you want to go?—to the service?"

Cody fixed her gaze and shook her head. "School's startin'."

"When's school starting, hon?"

"Couple weeks."

"Well." Virginia nodded. "That would be a good place to start. How about the name of the school. And what do you kids wear nowadays besides overalls? How about some notepads? Pencils? A backpack? I never had any kids, hon. You're going to have to help me out."

"There's local and a place down Middlebury."

"Middlebury?"

"Middlebury."

2

In the middle of the second night, Virginia woke with a scream. She leapt out of bed, throwing off covers, batting at her face, shaking her hair until her hair was too flustered to be shaken. Cody hid her face half under the lip of a blanket.

"I'm okay," said Virginia, breathless, hands at her scalp.

"Okay."

"Something ran over my face. Something. I felt its fucking feet on my— oh God, I'm so sorry," Virginia let out a little whoop of hysterical laughter. "I shouldn't have. I didn't say that. I don't—"

"It was a mouse."

"A mouse?"

"Mom was gonna get a cat."

"What's that?" Virginia abruptly interrupted.

Cody heard cries that were something like laughter and cackling howls. She smiled in the darkness. "That's a coywolf."

"A what?"

"A coywolf. They talk to each other at night. I think they get lonely; and then sometimes I think they hoot and holler eatin' mice."

"Is that what I saw when I pulled in?"

"Prob'ly."

"Dear God!"

"They eat mice."

"I can't live here."

"They don't bother or nothin'; and they eat mice."

"It ran across my face!"

"Didn't bite, did it?"

"That's hardly reassuring. Do they run across your face too?"

"Never have."

"We need a cat."

"Soot Tabor's got kittens she's tryin' to give way," said Cody. "We were gonna get one."

"Tomorrow."

Virginia couldn't go back to sleep. A little while later Cody crawled into bed with her, sobbing; the kind that made her double up and that hurt her stomach; that only ebbed as she fell back to sleep, intermittently shuddering like a small child. Virginia held her tightly, her own tears unraveling in the bed sheets.

The next morning Virginia awoke to Cody sitting upright and cross-legged next to her. She looked quietly out the window next to the door's tarp-draped rough opening. "Is Lucifer the devil?" she asked without turning.

"Well," said Virginia, "if you believe that sort of thing. Yes."

"You don't?"

"Not in that kind of devil." Virginia blinked, still waking up. "I believe in the kind that goes to church on Sunday and sins on Monday, the kind who loves you on Tuesday and cheats you on a Wednesday, who's all your joy and happiness on Thursday and all your grief and sorrow on Friday."

"I know all about that kind," said Cody.

"I suppose so."

"So why did Grandma say the devil was the angel of light?"

"Well," Virginia rolled onto her side, "I can tell you why, because a long time ago, when everyone spoke Latin, Lucifer meant morning star. And when everyone spoke Latin, they even called Jesus Lucifer—the bringer of light."

Cody sat with that for a time, then unfolded her legs. The mattress being so close to the floor, she only had to slide sideways and stand. She pulled aside the tarps and looped them over hooks to either side of the rough opening.

Light poured into the basement.

3

First thing was to drive to the hospital, where Drew reached for Cody the moment she stepped into the room. "C'mere, babe" she said, words dulled by morphine. Cody half crawled onto the bed, hugged her mother without hugging. "They can't operate on my ankle 'til next week."

"Why haven't they already?"

Drew glanced ruefully at the cast. "That's just to hold it still."

"But next week?"

"That's when the surgeon's available."

"There isn't one surgeon available?"

"Not for this," Drew exhaled painfully. "The talus is broken, joint's crushed, and there's bone fragments."

"Well, what are they giving you for the pain?"

"Morphine."

"Well, but—" Virginia's hands fell to her side as if she were dissatisfied with the answer. "Oh, this is awful!"

"Thanks."

"I mean," Virginia stuttered. "There's just a basement—That's no place for you to stay. For any of us!"

"Are you offering?"

"Well," Virginia hesitated again, "I don't know. Yes. What choice do I have?"

"The old house," said Drew, "Daryl was supposed to buy me out but it's all a mess now." She grimaced. "I s'pose it's mine." She turned to Cody. "You wanna go back there, babe? Back to the old place?"

"No," Cody shook her head, "storm's gonna flood it anyhow."

"What storm?"

"I saw it when I was in the water."

"Babe—"

"I saw it and tried to tell you."

"Babe!" said Drew. "I don't see how! You were drownin'. You drowned. Who wouldn't think the world was floodin'?"

"It wasn't like that."

"What was it like?"

"Like nothing mattered. I saw you. I saw myself. I saw the whole world like I was flyin' and none of it mattered."

4

"Where are we going now?" Cody asked.

"Well," Virginia shoved the truck into third gear, "seems like none of us have a proper home. We're going to need another bed.

How can your mother expect to be comfortable in that makeshift bed? She needs a real bed."

"I know a place sells beds." Cody squinted at the side mirror, lifting the bandage over her eye.

"You shouldn't play with that."

"Wanna see what my scar's gonna look like."

"What makes you think you'll have a scar?"

"Don't you have a scar?"

"Why would I?"

"Well, weren't you scarred when you lost all your stuff?"

"No," she slowly shook her head, "I was scarred when my husband betrayed me. Stuff is stuff."

"Don't you wish you had a scar everybody could see? It'd be a warning. The next time anybody saw that scar they'd know better."

Virginia smiled a wry, lopsided smile. "I suppose so."

Cody touched the stitches above her blackened eyebrow. "This scar's gonna be a warning—to everybody."

"Well, that's not something you're going through again."

"Right, I'm not." Cody lowered the bandage and pressed herself back into the seat. "You gotta turn right up here."

Virginia took the right into Brookway's downtown, an old mill village; like so many in Vermont, built where a dependable run of water turned wood and metal. The buildings remained, and so did the brook, but neither any longer paid mind to the other. Whether the brook considered the buildings to be passing through, or the buildings the brook, depended on the weather. Though the nights were coming in earlier, the days remained humid and the water went from stone to stone with an idle indifference.

Gnats worked above the brook and butterflies eddied above the gnats. Brookway's brief sidewalk was a dust of heat and sunlight. Once over the bridge, hardly having the look of a bridge, Brookway's main street broke into a tributary of streets, alleys, and diversions; reverting from the brick buildings downtown to clapboarded houses that had long since become a restaurant, a bookstore, or gift shop. Off the side street that followed the brook downward and out of Brookway was a store built into what must have been part of a textile mill—selling futons and furniture.

Cody took straight to trying out the futons, going to each, falling straight back and dreamily gazing at the girdered ceiling. There were lanterns and many colored prayer flags hanging from the girders. She turned her gaze to the side, looking out the nearest street level mill-window when something made her rise from the futon.

A couple were arguing on the sidewalk, only they weren't like a couple but more like animated paper cutouts, and the woman's pioneer dress and the man's olden days clothes were like paper; and when the couple argued they spoke words typed on the paper—of dirt roads long since paved and of neighbors long since gone.

"Cody?"

Cody sat up. Startled.

"Cody," Virginia said again, "I'm sure you shouldn't be frolicking on the beds."

Lydia Peacham walked quickly into the little showroom, glasses at the end of her nose. She glanced at Cody with a moment's recognition, then offered her hand to Virginia. "Are you—" she paused. "You must be Virginia! Fred's daughter."

"I am," Virginia sighed.

"I'm Lydia Peacham," she said, speaking sharply and clearly. She wore a tight dress over a figure ten years younger than what it deserved to be. "You know, that whole accident—but you can't call it that—was the headline this morning. All anyone's been talking about. What you're doing for Drew's little girl—" Lydia held Virginia's hand between hers and squeezed before abruptly letting go. "How can I help you?"

Lydia Peacham was a little younger than Virginia. When she was a teenager in high school, she was considered the most beautiful. She had had the foresight to marry Tanner Peacham, a high school sweetheart voted most likely to succeed—though that wasn't how the vote was phrased. Shortly after the vote, when the runners up went to colleges and universities, Tanner stayed in town and worked as a landscaper. That was accounted a tragedy by nearly everyone who had assumed the tall, dark-haired, athletic youth would study law and eventually run for Vermont's governancy. Instead, Tanner spent his first year out of high school freshly married to Lydia and digging ditches. Lydia's peers, who had had their own designs on Tanner, took some satisfaction in the ordinariness of the couple's downfall. But it wasn't long before Tanner turned ditch digging into landscaping and landscaping into a business, a house, barn, horses, an apple orchard, and four children.

Lydia's first great ambition had been to marry Tanner; after that, to have a family with half a dozen children, white Christmases, and a wood-burning stove. Tanner provided her what she wanted, including children; but after all but one of her children had moved on, Lydia was dissatisfied. All she had to show after so much ambition were letters addressed to Mrs. Tanner Peacham; and Lydia's peers, who considered her marriage little more than an act of seduction, took satisfaction in referring to her as Mrs. Tanner.

Lydia was aware of the gossip but took some pride in the accusations. Deciding to make a name for herself, she parlayed her reputation into the two businesses she had a right to know something about—mattresses and romance.

She started a business selling futons and did well enough to pursue her second ambition—writing romance novels. Success as a romance novelist still eluded her, but she had put together a select group of like-minded women with an ambition to write. The quality of her rough drafts were debated but the consensus was that romance was best written by those for whom it was an impossibility—and that put Lydia at a disadvantage. When Virginia and Cody walked in, Lydia had been several defiant pages into a third draft. She was about to answer Virginia's question when Cody seemed taken with a sudden realization.

"You'd better get your futons upstairs if you got one."

Lydia looked over her glasses. "Why?"

"Cause there's a storm comin' and it's gonna flood your whole place."

"You know, I don't think this building's ever been flooded."

Cody shrugged.

"What else do you know?"

"Sometimes I know what people are thinkin'." Cody gripped the futon as if to steady herself. "I hear 'em like they were talkin' to themselves and sometimes what they're thinkin' shows up like a picture book."

"Like a picture book?"

"Sometimes."

"Cody," Virginia nervously fidgeted with the purse she had slung over her shoulder, "we're here to buy a mattress."

"So," Lydia turned from Virginia back to Cody. "I'll make you a deal. If you can tell me just now what I was just thinking, I'll move all my mattresses before this storm. Will I know there's a storm coming?"

"Everybody'll know, but there's most won't take it seriously til it's too late."

"Then what was I thinking?"

Cody said to her that she didn't know what she was thinking right here and now because it didn't work that way, but just a minute ago she'd seen and heard an argument. Then she told Lydia what she'd seen and that left Lydia speechless for a good minute or so. Virginia made to object but Lydia laid a hand on Virginia's forearm. "That's straight from the story I was writing."

Virginia glanced at Cody, then at Lydia, wondering if a game were being played. But Lydia merely patted Virginia's arm. "I'll show you what I have in stock."

Some fifteen minutes later the new futon, rolled tight in plastic, was in the back of the truck along with a bed frame. Virginia didn't say anything at first. She was unnerved.

"It's not like I want to," said Cody.

"Want what?"

"To hear what you're thinking; and mostly I don't. It's like there's a wind and it depends on which way it's blowin'."

But even that was more than Virginia was willing to concede. She decided she'd call the doctor in the evening.

5

Though Virginia stopped by Kemp's for more groceries, a warm dinner was already in the offing, cooked and brought over by Hoyte's father. Virginia uncovered the furniture atop the deck. She and the other adults took the furniture while Hoyte and Cody sat on the deck's edge, feet dangling above the basement's tarp-covered entrance.

"So," said Hoyte, "did ya tell anybody else about the storm?"

"Yeah."

"Anybody listen?"

Cody shrugged.

"There's a hurricane just got started," said Hoyte. "They're callin' it Irene, first one. Named it yesterday, I think. You suppose that's it?"

"I didn't get a name."

Hoyte considered his next line of conversation. "So are you gonna keep livin' here?"

"We're pickin' Mom up next week. Friday. Her ankle's hurt pretty bad and isn't anybody 'til Friday can operate on it."

"Bringin' her here?"

"Don't see as we have a choice."

"Why not? Didn't you used to live in town?" Cody didn't answer and so Hoyte leaned back and added. "Was just askin'. So how is she?"

"Broke her ankle, back, and broke some ribs."

"That's some kind of goin' over," then Hoyte faltered. "I mean—"

"I know."

Then Hoyte sat quiet until he judged the moment was right to begin again. "School's startin' soon."

"Jesus, Hoyte. Ya tryin' to make me cry?"

"There's gotta be somethin' you can be upbeat about?"

Cody studied the way the valley's lights slowly emerged from the humid flood of darkness. "Suppose we got it upside down," she said. "When you look at all those lights in the valley you think that's where home is and when you look at the stars you think that's where your dreams are, but maybe that's upside down. Maybe the stars are where we're from and the world is where we do our dreamin'."

"How would you ever know?"

"Because—" Cody paused. "Because I didn't want to come back."

"To here?"

"No. To life. But then I saw just a little of what was gonna happen—"

"Like what?"

"I don't remember what but remember knowin'."

"Ever hear of the one-eyed witch?"

"No."

"My pa told me about her."

"Wanna tell it?"

"Yeah, so, there was a really beautiful girl who had everything she wanted. And learnin' came easy to her. She learned everything she wanted and she travelled 'round the world pickin' up languages, art, music, math, science. But there was one secret she couldn't find the answer to—and that was when was she gonna die. And so she travelled all the way 'round the world until she ended up where she started.

"Just about when she was gonna give up she heard about the one-eyed sailor. She heard that the one-eyed sailor could tell anybody when they was gonna die. All they had to do was give him the one thing worth more to them than anything else. And if they didn't know what that was then they'd die right there on the spot. That was the price. But the girl wasn't afraid. She went lookin' for the one-eyed sailor and found him. He had one eye just like everybody said and he was lookin' out over the ocean like he was waitin' for a boat that never came.

"Then she showed up and she said to him. I hear you can tell a man when he's gonna die and how and where.

"That I can, he says.

"And can you tell a girl when she's gonna die?

"That I can, he says.

"Then I want you to tell me when I'm gonna die and how and where; and no secrets, no shadin' the truth, no hidin' anything. If ya do I'll know it, One-eyed Sailor.

"I'll do all that and first you give me the one thing you love more than anything else.

"Now the girl knew exactly what that was and thought nothin' of it 'cause she'd always known. So, there's a reason we're born with two eyes. With one eye we can see what's most valuable to us. With the other eye we see that we en't gonna live forever. As long as you have both eyes, neither sees perfect. But each helps the other. It's knowin' that we don't have forever that makes us look harder with the other eye, to look for what we want the most. And the one-eyed sailor knew that if you wanted to see when you were gonna die, you had to blind the other eye. But he didn't tell this to the girl.

"All he said was: Look at me. I'm gonna take what you're offerin' and it en't gonna hurt one bit.

"So he took the girl's eye, the one that let her see what was most valuable in life, and before she could say anything contrary, he'd put her eye where his own was missin'. Then both of them was quiet a moment—too shocked to speak. Then the sailor begins to laugh and laugh. Tears are runnin' down his face 'cause now, after livin' for a hundred years and more, he can see what really matters—and it was such a simple thing, such a small and trivial thing that he turned into a twirl of dust right then and there.

"Now the girl saw when she was gonna die clear as day and when and how. But now that her other eye was gone she couldn't remember why it mattered. She couldn't remember what it was so important that she needed to know when she was gonna die. 'Cause if you know when you're gonna die, then all you can think about is what a terrible waste life is—and then nothin' at all matters to you. So the girl became the one-eyed witch.

"Nobody knows where she lives, but you don't have t'know. You only need to know you want to find her and you will. But the hardest part to findin' her is knowin' what's most valuable to you before you find her 'cause if you're wrong, you'll die right then and there. And that's the funny thing isn't it? You think you know what you'd give everything to have, but are ya willing to stake your life on it? Some people, says Papa, will spend their whole life lookin' and never find it—but then maybe it was that lookin' that made them happiest.

"So anyway—'bout everything you were tellin' me. It sounds like maybe you met the one-eyed witch. She showed you everything that was gonna happen right down to the day you were gonna die, when and how. But you were smart enough not to give her your eye so you don't remember any of it, just that you knew and forgot."

Chapter 5

1

Doctor Latham sat across from Cody, fingers laced at her knees. In the waiting room there were chairs, a flat screen TV, a microwave, a little table for children, coloring books, and toys.

"So, tell me," said Latham, "how are you doing?"

"My bruise looked better before it turned yellow," said Cody.

"I think you look better. Are you sleeping well?"

"Long as I'm not sleepin' on my stitches."

"How's the rest of you?"

"Like I been tripped, punched, and shook hard."

"You're sore."

Cody agreed and shrugged.

"Anything else I should know?"

Cody shifted and glanced to the side. "Virginia told you 'bout what I've been tellin' people; 'bout the storm comin'; 'bout sometimes hearin' and seein' what people think."

"Did that start after the accident?"

Cody paused again then turned to the older woman with a defiant gaze. "I saw myself like I wasn't myself. Like I was floatin' above myself. I was tryin' to tell mom I was okay, that I wasn't hurt, but she couldn't see or hear me. Then I was flyin'."

"Anything else?"

Cody was silent again, looking away.

"Anything you can tell me?"

Cody slowly shook her head. "I don't wanna be called crazy."

"I know stranger stories than yours."

"Like what?"

Latham smiled. "If I told you, you wouldn't believe me."

Cody moved to the edge of her seat. "I would."

"I started my practice in a small town in Maine and used to go on house calls. One night I got a call from a woman named Maggie O'Hara. She was a superstitious woman. She and her husband had come from Ireland years and years ago. Maggie was frantic. She told me her husband was going to die that very evening. I asked her why and she said the banshee was wailing."

"What's a banshee?" asked Cody.

"Some say it's an old woman, a spirit, who wails when death is expected."

"Like a warning?"

"Like a warning. I almost said no; but when I showed up, poor Maggie was pale as a ghost, wringing her hands." Latham imitated the woman's Irish accent: "'Last night a spell came over him. He was reelin' like a drunken sailor, slurrin' his words, all out of sorts and could barely keep his feet under him. I'd have called already but he'd have none of it. Then it was the teakettle this mornin'. Here I was, out in the garden, and with it a'whistlin' and a'whistlin'! He didn't hear it! How can ya not hear such a thing? Soon as I get the teakettle sorted, he goes out to drive into town. Such a keenin' and a wailin' you've never heard.'"

"Bet it was the alternator belt," said Cody.

"You like cars?"

"Daddy used to let me—" Cody looked away, expression stoney.

"It's okay, hon."

"I like fixin' things," Cody said flatly, "engines and fixin' up cars. Bet it was the alternator belt."

"'It's the banshee,' said Maggie. Her husband waved me off. 'I'm fit as a fiddle,' he said. 'Fit as a fiddle!' And he wouldn't let me touch him.

"Maggie begged me to take him to the hospital. Then she said: 'Oh, it won't matter. There's nothin' to be done. Why does he have to be stubborn? It's the banshee. Wailin' at every turn! She's come to tell us; and once she starts wailin' there's no undoin' it.

"Who would believe such a thing? But that very night her husband died."

"What if I warn people," said Cody, "but nobody listens?"

"Don't be a doctor," the older woman sighed. "We doctors can all tell the future."

"How's that?"

"Well, if you take up drinking, smoking, and don't exercise, you won't like what I have to say."

"That's different."

"Not when I'm right."

2

After their hospital visit, Virginia stopped by the bank. She withdrew enough money to buy more furniture, lights, bedding, a refrigerator, cookstove, groceries, and chocolate. At each stop Cody carefully weighed whether the owners wouldn't mind knowing about the future. At Dale Trembly's Appliances, also gas and propane, she began her inquiry subtly.

"Do ya smoke?"

"No ma'am, I don't," answered Dale, a slender man with a quick and businesslike manner.

"If ya did smoke, would you want to know if you were gonna die from it?"

"Cody!" Virginia interrupted.

"Well," said Dale, taken by the proposal, "I suppose I'd also want to know what was gonna kill me if I didn't smoke."

Cody's eyes narrowed and she rocked from heel to toe. "Why's it matter?"

"Suppose you told me that if I smoked and kept smokin' I'd have twenty-six years, three months, and two days to live. And that on that day I'd drop dead of a heart attack because of my smokin'. Now knowin' that, you might think I oughta quit smokin'. But supposin' I do, and one day, instead of lightin' a cigarette to consider the inequities of fate, I decide on a walk. Now it just so happens that as I'm takin' my stroll I'm run dead over by a driver lightin' a cigarette. And that's the end of it. So. You might fairly concede that if I'd kept smoking I'd of lived a longer and happier life."

Cody considered the travesty of an early death caused by the curtailment of a bad habit. She settled on a different strategy. "What if there was a flood comin'? A big one. Would you want to know?"

"S'pose I would."

"There is; and it's gonna make it so we can't get in nor out."

Ten minutes later Virginia handed Cody a box. Cody stood in the back of the pickup. "Must you announce to everyone the end of the world? What if you're wrong? What if there isn't a flood? Then what?"

"I saw it."

"Cody," Virginia sputtered, "Take it from me. We can fool ourselves. I loved a man who turned out to be a sociopath!"

"So wouldn't ya have appreciated somebody warnin' ya?"

"Yes, but—"

"Would you have believed me?"

"No," said Virginia. "No, I don't think I would have."

"But I woulda been right."

"Yes. I suppose so."

Cody went for the kill. "Well why don't ya believe me about the flood then?"

"Because," said Virginia, aghast, "it's a hypothetical! You weren't there!"

"Bet you wish I had been."

"Oh for God's sake! Good thing you don't know what I'm thinking!"

"Wind's not blowin' right or I would."

"Back into the cab."

Once they were under way, Cody put her feet on the dashboard and fretted with her stitches. "Do ya have a nickname?"

"Not since I was married." said Virginia flatly. "My husband never liked it."

"Just wonderin'."

"Ginger."

"I like that. Easier than Virginia." Cody stuck her hand out the window, riding the air. "Have you ever heard of the one-eyed witch?"

"The one-eyed witch? No."

"If you could go back to before you was married, would you rather know when you was gonna die and what's gonna matter most in your life?"

"Oh, that's easy: What matters; because when you're young you think you know but it takes a mean life to teach you what it really is."

"So do ya know now?"

"I know better than when I was twenty."

"What is it?"

"Well—" Virginia thrummed the steering wheel. "There's nobody who's going to make you happy if you aren't happy with yourself."

"I know that," said Cody. "Took you a whole lifetime to figure that out?"

"Sounds easy, doesn't it?"

"I'd pick knowin' when I was gonna die."

In a fit of pique Virginia regretted quick as it came over her, she said: "Didn't you already?"

"—Again," Cody added.

3

By August, though the cloud tops sail in a hazy late summer's light, the undersides brim with the dark weight of autumn. Vermont's nights come earlier. The maples, here and there, trade their sunburnt green for the first flickers of change. The birds are silent. Crickets come into the house when they can and hide under the stove where cats can't go. The waters of the pond, brook, and river give up their warmth with icy exhalations. The mists don't burn off until mid-morning and sometimes noon the next day. Cody and Virginia arrived at Virginia's lot with the afternoon just slipping out of the valley. Cody jumped into the back of the pickup and pushed boxes to the tailgate with her feet.

Hoyte came over.

Only a copse of hemlock and birch separated his back yard from Virginia's lot, the second of two houses on a short stretch of dirt road. He'd grown accustomed to having a friend his own age next door and whenever he heard the pop of gravel, he quit his projects to trade in conversation. He adjusted his baseball cap, sidled up to the truck, and leaned on the bed's rim. "Need help?"

"Yes," said Virginia, "Yes, I do."

Cody crab walked to the tailgate and hopped out. Then she and Hoyte started with the rails of the bed frame, each carrying an end.

"What'd you do today?"

"Visited Mom."

"Still gonna get her Friday?"

"Yeah."

"How long you gonna keep livin' here when she comes back?"

Cody shrugged. "Don't know."

Hoyte backed down the slope, almost stumbling before finding his footing at the basement's entrance. "Seems like it's gonna be a while."

Virginia followed, still buoyed by the little bit of purpose and direction shopping had given her. Despair descended as soon as she stepped into the foundation. With a box in her lap, she collapsed in the nearest chair, the straight-backed wooden chair of her writing desk.

"Are ya havin' another panic attack?" Cody asked.

"I just—" Virginia stuttered. "I just need to sit. Why don't you two put the bed together. Put it—" She paused again, seeing the small foundation, only half the square footage of the planned house, there being nothing but the concrete walls, damp with humidity, and not even the forms ties broken off. "Put it by the window. And then why don't you two bring in the rest. I'm just going to sit."

Hoyte and Cody were almost to the truck when Cody's grandparents' nosed their car over the driveway's rise. The low lying sunlight flashed in the grill. Cody waited, hands in her overalls, Hoyte behind her. The car ground to a gravelly halt. Cody's grandmother stepped out with short and precise steps. She offered Cody a nervous smile. She glanced at the pickup's unpacked boxes, then over the children's heads.

"Where's Virginia?"

"She's havin' a panic attack," Cody offered factually.

"My, you do always say what's on your mind, don't you."

Cody shrugged.

"We're burying your daddy," said the older woman. "We're burying him tomorrow."

Cody's grandfather ambled up behind her.

"Why are ya tellin' me?" asked Cody.

"He was your daddy," said her grandmother, "and my son."

Cody's eyes welled. "He tried to kill Mommy."

"I just—" Her grandmother faltered. "I just find that hard to believe. He wouldn't— I'm sure it must have been an accident."

"I saw it," said Cody flatly.

"Marjorie." Cody's grandfather put a hand on his wife's shoulder. "Maybe this isn't the time."

Cody's grandmother turned. "Well, when is it ever? Do you think Daryl was a murderer? You're just going to let them think that?"

Cody took a step back, eyes narrowing. "I saw him do it."

"Are you sure, hon? Maybe there was a deer. Did he swerve to miss a deer?"

"No. He just swerved. Wasn't any reason. He just did it."

"Maybe there was something you didn't see."

"He tried to kill me!" Cody shouted, bursting into tears, fists clenched. "He kept goin' faster and faster. You weren't there. There was nothin'— nothin' he did but try and kill us!"

Cody turned and ran. Virginia was already climbing the bank.

"There she is," said Cody's grandmother.

Virginia stopped Hoyte. "What on earth is going on?"

"It's Cody's grandparents," he said. "They were tryin' to make her think her dad goin' off the road was by mistake."

"Oh for God's sake!"

"Virginia." Cody's grandmother unsteadily walked the path down to Virginia.

"Well," Virginia demanded, "what do you want?"

"We're burying Daryl tomorrow," said Cody's grandfather.

"Did you tell her it was an accident?"

"We just don't think Daryl would have done that," said Cody's grandmother.

"You are not entitled to debate that with a twelve year old girl! She almost died!"

"We lost our son!" said Wayne.

"So you did!" Virginia stepped closer, voice lowering. "And that little girl lost her father; and not only her father but everything a father stands for. I know what that's like; and that will scar her for life. What father tries to murder his own child?"

"We don't think he was capable of that," said Marjorie icily. "Is that what Drew told the police? Do the police think our son was capable of murdering his own child?"

"I wouldn't know," said Virginia, "but what I do know is that it's up to Cody whether she goes."

"Who are you to decide that?"

"We're her grandparents," added Wayne.

"Until that girl's mother is out of the hospital, I am her guardian."

"You?" Cody's grandmother snorted. "What kind of guardian lives in a hole in the ground? Our granddaughter has no business here. You mean nothing to her and I don't know how Drew got mixed up with you but Cody should be with kin until her mother's out of the hospital; and, frankly, I don't see how she'll care for that child until she can walk again, if she does. I wouldn't know."

"Her mother wouldn't be in the hospital if not for your son."

"How dare you!"

"This is my property," Virginia snapped. "And I am Cody's guardian."

"We'll see about that."

"We're contacting our lawyer," added Wayne.

"I'll be calling the sheriff."

"You don't know who you're dealing with," warned Cody's grandmother, turning, yanking her husband after her. Virginia stayed put until they had backed out of the driveway. Then, with an exasperated exclamation, she hurried down the bank and back into the foundation. Cody was sitting on her mother's unmade mattress, knees drawn up, forehead hiding between them, and arms around them. Hoyte sat next to Cody, hands in his pockets, staring at his feet.

"We'll have to—" But Virginia didn't know what to say.

"I wanna stay with Mom tonight," said Cody.

"I don't blame you."

4

The hospital made an exception when they pushed a reclining chair next to Drew's bed. Cody fell asleep holding Drew's hand. Virginia returned to the Apple House instead of the unfinished foundation and took a long bath. She imagined all the ways she might escape her predicament, but she had no brothers or sisters. She had no parents, aunts, or uncles. She could sell her little piece of property but the dread of the unforeseen terrified her. She would find a way to build something on the little foundation—something before the onset of winter.

5

There were two chairs and a little table in the inn's room. Virginia's put her phone on the table and the window spilled light across it.

"They're the grandparents?" asked her lawyer.

"Yes."

"But the mother is cognizant?"

"Yes."

"Ignore them."

"But—"

"Ignore them."

"But if they hire a lawyer—"

"They won't. The mother appointed you a temporary guardian. Period. End of discussion."

"But they're the grandparents!"

"So what?"

"Well I just thought—"

"You're in Vermont. A grandparent has no intrinsic right to a grandchild unless the parent is deceased, incompetent, or abandoned."

"That won't stop them—"

"No lawyer would represent them."

"Well—" Virginia shifted in her seat. "Then I suppose that's that."

"Yes."

"Well. Thank you, Alex."

"How are you?"

"I have no house."

"You have a foundation. Didn't you say you had a foundation? Hire somebody to finish it."

"You make it sound easy."

"Either finish it or sell it."

"Oh Alex, what a mess I'm in."

"I don't envy you."

A few minutes later Virginia reluctantly checked out of the inn. Meredith asked after Cody and Drew but Virginia had little to say: Cody was with Drew and Drew's ankle would be set on Friday. When Virginia arrived at the hospital, Cody was sitting next to her mother watching TV.

"The service is today," said Virginia.

"You don't need to go, babe." Drew's hand was on Cody's knee.

"Okay."

"Babe, we were gettin' divorced for a reason. If you hadn't made it out of that river— I'd of blamed myself, Cody. But I'll tell you somethin'. The day Daddy decided to drive us off that bridge was the day he died. You understand?"

Cody nodded.

"You don't owe that man's parents anything; and you bein' there isn't gonna undo what he did. You don't owe them that. Whatever good Daddy left behind is in you, babe. It's not anywhere else; and you don't need to pretend like it is—not for anybody."

Cody nodded again and carefully hugged her mother before she went with Virginia. Walking down the corridor she made her decision. "Let's go get one of Soot Tabor's kittens. Then we won't have mice runnin' over us."

"Do you think Hoyte would help us unpack?"

"I can get 'im. And he'll want to see the kitten anyways."

6

Soot Tabor had one eye, a chimeric eye patch, and a quixotically painted house—the latter being a useful corrective to lost tourists. The clapboards were purple, the shutters and trim were orange, and the standing seam roof was red. The leaded front door had once belonged to a Victorian mansion but to live in Vermont is to live in houses full of exhausted borrowings. Soot was toiling in the flower garden fronting her porch when Virginia and Cody pulled up. She gazed at them with her one eye then stood when she saw Cody. "Oh!" she said. "There you are!"

"Do ya still have any kittens?"

"I do," she answered. "I saved the best one for you." She pushed her glasses up her nose and it was a strange thing to see glasses with an eyepatch. "Follow me."

Soot led them into the house. Old couches were covered in paisley sheets. Pillows of every color were scattered on the couch and upholstered chairs. The scent of incense hung in the air along with paper lanterns, spider plants, and glinting crystals. Each wall was painted a different color and jalapeño lights were strung over the doorways, along with philodendrons.

Cody instantly liked the house and liked Soot. "It's amazing in here."

"It's 'cause of my one eye," Soot answered. "When you only see half the world, you make the good half do twice the work." She took them through the kitchen, a florid combustion of yellow chairs, a red table, and purple cabinets.

The cat and her kitten were napping in the pantry. Cody instantly scooped up the kitten.

"What do we owe you?" Virginia asked.

"Nothing." Soot touched Virginia's hand. "I'm just glad she'll find a good home. Would either of you like some tea? Some milk and honey?"

The kitten crawled onto Cody's shoulder.

"Are you sure?"

"You're Sal Darby's granddaughter, aren't you? The Tabors and Darbys go back. Our grandfather's lands abutted. If Cody wants to trade me a little help cleaning 'round the house this fall, I wouldn't mind that at all."

Several minutes later they sat at the red table. Cody played with the kitten in her lap. Soot refilled everyone's cups. She had listened to Virginia's woes and had added a little extra cream and sugar to Virginia's cup. "Just last year I inherited my father's hunting cabin. Not any place you'd want to be. Saving it for my niece, Fiona. She doesn't know it yet but she's going to be living there. She'll have her hands full just like you."

"What am I going to do?" sighed Virginia.

"Virginia—" Soot patted Virginia's hand. "Life's full of fieldstones—some big and round as a mule's hind end. That doesn't mean you quit plowing. In New England it means you build a stone wall so as you don't have to listen to your neighbor's advice giving."

Cody guided the cat from one shoulder to the other. "I'm gonna go outside." She stood with the kitten on her shoulder and went out the back door. The screen door creaked on rusty hinges. Soot watched her go. "How has she been?"

"It's been hard," said Virginia.

"How's Drew?"

"She's coming home— Hardly a home. Honestly. She has a house. It was the father's house. Cody doesn't want to live there but are we all going to live in my basement?"

"If I know Drew—"

"And Cody!" Virginia interrupted. "She's told half the town they're going to be underwater! You can be sure I wouldn't give a hoot if God drowned my ex-husband and the state of New Mexico with him."

"A flood?" asked Soot.

"I don't know what to do with her!"

Soot considered that with satisfaction. "That explains it."

"No child deserves what that man did to her."

"I don't know if I should even mention it." Soot's voice lowered to a whisper. "It's like there's starlight in her hair." She put her hand back on Virginia's. "It's blinding."

7

Once home, Cody put the kitten safely in the bottom of a cardboard box. She named it Ratter. Then she ran to find Hoyte, returning with both Hoyte and Arvid. Hoyte and Cody unpacked and put furniture together. Virginia organized. Two makeshift rooms were made with blankets hanging from the overhead floor joists. There were two beds on one side for Drew and Cody and one for Virginia. Arvid awkwardly sat in a chair as Virginia organized the kitchen. "This is very kind of you," he said.

"Not it's not. It's guilt is what it is."

"What do you have to be guilty for?"

"If I hadn't ordered that girl and her mother off my property— What did it matter? Why should I have cared? God knows I didn't need to be here. I could have hired her to finish the house!"

"But you can't blame yourself for what Cody's father did."

"Yes I can."

"Then that's a responsibility I don't envy," said Arvid. "But what you do, Virginia, is very kind."

"It's temporary."

"I expect so. And Drew will return to the house in Brookway?"

"Where, honestly, they should be. But everything about that house reminds Cody of her father. I can't blame her." She smiled wryly. "You know, she tells everyone she meets that Vermont's going to be flooded. You don't need to be Sigmund Freud to understand what she's saying. She's been through a horrible experience. If being here, if you can call it a house, gives her a place to restart her life then that's the least I can do."

"I can make room."

"It's still August. We have running water, beds, and a roof. We can make do for a little while; and then surely Drew will decide to move back to Brookway. I don't know what choice she has?"

"What will you do when the weather turns?"

"Well, I don't know."

"You strike me as an interesting woman, Virginia, I hope you stay."

"Interesting?"

"Yes."

"Hardly."

"And I like your sense of humor."

"Inherited. The lawyers let me keep it."

"No, you have more than that. I can see why Cody likes you and why Drew made you Cody's guardian."

Virginia put her hand on Arvid's. "You're a very nice man."

Chapter 6

1

After the morning's hospital visit, Virginia brought Cody back to spend the day with Hoyte. Virginia left for Brookway, saying she would be back with dinner. After she left, Cody and Hoyte uncovered the couch, the last piece of furniture still sitting on the deck. The rest had been moved below.

They turned the couch so that it faced the valley, as if the long valley, mountains, the slope's clovers and asters, hemlocks and the spindly birches were all their living room. Hoyte leaned back, his long legs stretched and crossed at the ankles. Cody watched his lanky unfolding, then copied him exactly, crossing her hands behind her head with her elbows wide.

"Do you think Virginia would sell this to your mom?" he asked.

"Hasn't offered."

"Seems like she doesn't like it much here."

"She would if there'd been a house."

"She ought to hire your mom to finish it."

"Don't see how she can," said Cody. "She's all broken up. Not much use for buildin'."

"You still think there's a storm comin'?"

"I saw it."

"Then I bet it's Irene."

"Where's it at?"

"They think it's headed up our way." Hoyte took satisfaction in his interpretive acumen while considering the humidity's bluish haze. The distant mountain sides nearly traded their color with the sky and the nearest had lost their distinction. The wind momentarily shook in the sunburnt shrubs. "Wanna get Ratter?" he asked.

"Yeah."

Hoyte followed Cody down the slope to the basement doorway. They were just out of sight when they heard the pop of rubber on gravel. Cody decided it must be Virginia but she'd only just looked over the slope's verge when she saw her grandparents. She slid back down the slope.

"Hoyte!" she hissed. "Get down!"

Hoyte crouched. Cody shot off slantways along the slope, on knees and elbows until she was under the heavy shade of a hemlock. Hoyte followed close behind and turned when she turned, watching. "Did they see you?"

Cody shook her head.

"What do you suppose they want?"

Marjorie had stepped out of the car, sunglasses flashing. She wore white pants, white sandals, and a floral blouse. "Hello!" she cried. She waited for a response. She glanced at Cody's grandfather, still standing behind the driver's side door. She called again, looking over the slope, not once in the children's direction. When she didn't hear an answer she walked back to the car with quick and wiry steps. She reached through the open window and held up a smartphone.

"She's takin' pictures," said Hoyte. "That can't be good."

"She doesn't like me living here."

"How's it their say?"

"I wanna throw a stone at 'em."

"Best you din't," said Hoyte. "You suppose Virginia knows they're up here?"

"I'm gonna throw a stone."

"You will not," said Hoyte. "What if you hit 'em."

"I'll throw another before my luck wear's off."

Cody's grandmother descended the slope. She pushed uncertainly at the tarp covering the basement doorway then haphazardly fastened it to one side. She took more photos, let the tarp fall, then hurried up the slope.

"What did you see?" asked Cody's grandfather.

"Much as I needed."

She opened the door matter-of-factly. Climbed in. "Let's go."

The car backed over the berm. Hoyte stood and pushed through the shrubs.

"What are ya doin?" hissed Cody.

"What d'ya mean what am I doin? What are you doin'?"

"Hidin'!"

"From what?"

"What if they come back?"

Hoyte picked up a stone and weighed it like he was going to throw it. "I got better aim than you."

"Do not."

"I do." He lifted his chin defiantly. "Bet I can hit that birch over there?"

"Why'd you want to hit a tree?" She squinted.

"Why not?"

"En't a reason to throw a rock at a tree."

"There is," said Hoyte, "and it's 'cause a tree won't throw back."

"They're alive aren't they?"

Hoyte let the branch fall with a kind of exasperation. "Are you comin' out from under there or not?"

"Fine." Cody brushed off her knees. She followed Hoyte back up to the foundation, hands stuffed in the pockets of her overalls.

"What makes you so hot-headed?" Hoyte asked.

"Got a right to be."

"You're gonna get yourself in a fix you can't get out of."

"No such thing."

"You gonna tell Virginia 'bout your grandparents bein' up here?"

"Think I should?"

"May make more trouble than it's worth."

"No such thing."

2

That day and the next passed by. Cody and Hoyte introduced the kitten to her new home. When Cody later rode into town with Virginia, she warned a few more of Brookway's folks that the easy water in their backyard, along the dirt road, or rambling under the covered bridge was about to change into something mighty and terrible.

But for all her warnings, late August seemed as it should, taking on the tarnished yellows of exhausted fields. The clouds that had blossomed with a white intensity early in the summer now towered heavily in the slumberous air. The cicadas' shimmering calls rose and fell—autumn's harbingers.

Friday afternoon Virginia and Cody went to the hospital to pick up Drew with a rented SUV. The little pickup truck wasn't any sort of ride for the wounded, but that was still no comfort for Drew. She moaned in the back seat and grimaced. Some ways south of Burlington, she vomited. Cody jumped out just in time to open the back door.

Every turn and bump was a knife's edge. She began to shiver and her teeth clattered. Virginia's jaw clenched and she glanced at Drew in the rear view mirror. "What did they give you?"

"When?"

"For the ride home?"

"I don't know."

"Was it Tramadol?"

"Yes."

"Can you make it another twenty miles?"

"I'm gonna throw up again!"

Virginia stopped and stopped once more before they reached home. Climbing out, Drew's knuckles whitened on the crutches. "Christ, almighty!" She slowly made her way down the slope, down the little bit of ledge, soil, and burnt stubble that was the path worn between the scrub of grass, ox-eye daisies, and milkweed. She rounded the foundation's corner and hobbled awkwardly inside. "Hey," she winced, "looks nice." She let out a relieved exhalation as she lowered herself into bed.

Virginia carefully arranged pillows, then said "I'll be back."

Cody balanced back and forth on the crutches. "Virginia bought all kinds of furniture," she said, "and we divided up the basement."

"She did?"

"We used the sheets to make the rooms."

"Do you like, Virginia?" Drew asked.

"She's not too smart 'bout practical things."

"It's why builders make a livin', hon."

"We ate out last night."

Drew experimentally shifted her foot. "What did you eat, babe?"

"Had a hamburger."

"Hamburger?"

"And french fries."

"No vegetables?"

"Why didn't you wanna get out of the car?"

"I was stallin'."

"Seems a car's the last place you'd wanna stall, much as you threw up."

"You should try a broken ankle, babe."

Virginia returned with Drew's hospital bag. "It's withdrawal," she said. "It's why you were throwing up."

"Jesus, fine," said Drew dismissively. "It's withdrawal."

"Wanna see Ratter?" asked Cody.

Drew laughed ruefully. "Babe, get me some painkiller."

"Aspirin?"

"Jesus, no. Morphine."

Virginia told Cody to stay put and returned with a glass of water and medicine. "It's withdrawal and the sooner you're off these drugs the better."

"Ever use crutches with broken ribs," Drew asked, taking the pills, then added "Mom visited. Yesterday. She was mad. She was mad I didn't call. Mad Virginia's looking after us. Mad the nurses were rude to her." Drew paused, as if telling a joke. "Jesus. You'd have thought she was the one run over and left for dead."

"So is Gramma in town?"

"And how."

"Is she comin' up tonight?"

"Probably. You wanna show me Ratter, babe?"

3

By noon the following day there was talk that hurricane Irene would make landfall in New Jersey and was likely to move up the coast. Vermont and New Hampshire had been scoured by hurricanes before, had lost trees, but always the sort one expected to lose, shallow rooted, at a field's edge, or clumped together so that any falling took the neighbors. Here and there a barn roof, left to rust, might be peeled like the lid of a sardine can, one or both corners wrapped over the ridge, and all the hoarded store fingered by the wind. And here and there a splitting gust might pry the clapboards from the house, but there was seldom anything lost not already discarded by man or nature. By and large, the residents of Brookway, like most residents in northern New England, anticipated the storm's landfall with the admired stoicism of those whose tree, as they say, leans over the other man's roof.

4

Drew woke early. She haltingly made her way out of the basement, up the slope, and atop the deck. Drew expected her mother's landfall at any moment. She slipped the tarp off the couch and carefully sat. There were strips of cloud and blue sky, moments when the westward mountaintops were lit by the sun, only to disappear again in a smoke of cloud and shadow. And then, because there was no one to ask why, she cried.

After half an hour or so Cody came carrying a banana and a bowl of granola to dip it in. She was careful of her mother's ribs, hips, and leg, but sat close enough to touch.

"How are ya doin', babe?"

"Okay," said Cody.

"Did you sleep good?"

"Uh-huh."

"How's your head feel?"

"Like I wanna pull the stitches out."

"You will not."

"It's been five days."

"Let me see 'em."

Cody turned her head. Drew carefully lifted the bandage above Cody's left eye. The bruised cut travelled from the top middle of the girl's forehead diagonally to the left side of her left eyebrow. "Oh baby," Drew sighed. "I don't know but that's gonna leave a scar."

"S'okay if it does. I want it. I wanna scar."

"Why?"

"You got tattoos, right?"

"Yeah, babe, but I wanted those."

"But they're scars, aren't they? Only difference is you got to pick what they looked like."

Drew smiled and nodded. "Yeah. I suppose. I guess you could say that."

"Well, this is my tattoo and it's a warning."

Drew studied Cody and sighed again. "So we gotta get those stitches out."

"I'll do it." Cody brightened. "There's a mirror and all I need's some scissors."

"If you poke your eye out I'm not helpin' you look for it."

"I en't gonna poke my eye out," said Cody flatly. She set down her bowl and banana. She was down and back in a minute. She put the mirror on the couch cushion next to Drew, knelt and leaned over the mirror. With the sudden calm and concentration of a surgeon, she moved the tip of the scissors under the stitch closest to her eyebrow and snipped.

"Don't you think you oughta snip each one?"

"I'm gonna!"

Cody slipped the tip beneath the next stitch and snipped, and then each one after that.

"Good to see your brains haven't fallen out."

Cody lay the scissors between her knees, then pinched the first knot between her fingernails. The skin lifted with the stitch before slipping free. After the last stitch, Cody ran her fingers over the strangely smooth skin, admiring the scar.

"What do you think?" asked her mother.

"Don't like the stitch marks."

"They're gonna go away."

Cody turned her head to one side. "I like the scar."

"Scars run in the family."

Cody collected the stitches in the palm of her hand and studied them with a kind of satisfaction—the little bit of crusted blood, the glistening serous, then tossed them over the edge of the deck.

"You ready for school?" Drew asked.

And then it was Cody's turn to cry. She twisted into Drew's arm, her head on her mother's breast, and tried to speak but couldn't. Drew held her shuddering daughter, grimacing against the painful embrace. "You're gonna be alright." She touched the scar on Cody's forehead. "You wanna know somethin? Grandpa used to take me to Pow Wows, and he'd say the red face paint was a fighting color—for strength, success, and beauty. The worst a human can do was done to you. You're gonna feel that wound for the rest of your life, but it's gonna make you strong, beautiful, and powerful."

"I don't see how," Cody finally whispered.

5

It was a little before noon when Cody's grandmother, Kati, arrived at Virginia's tarp-covered basement. The long strips of cloud had merged and dropped their mists over the mountaintops. The rain was steady. The drops tapped at the deck's tarp trying a thousand prying ways to get into the basement. Kati shrugged off her raincoat. Her hair was longer than Drew's, but graying. Loose strands dripped over her eyes and lips. She looked wild and disheveled. She wore turquoise bracelets, a lapis-beaded necklace, hempen dress, and a sleeveless top. "Where's Virginia?"

"I'm here," said Virginia, standing in the background.

"Thank you for looking after Cody," said Kati, condemning Virginia in the thanking.

"Well," Virginia hesitated, "okay. If you'd like anything to drink? I could make—"

"Some tea if you have it." Kati swept the hair from her face.

Drew had folded the futon frame of her bed into a couch. Her foot was propped on a pillow. She half sat up and carefully hugged her mother, a delicate hug—more touch than hug. "It's a hell of a place to live," said her mother.

"Be nice, Mom."

"Okay, but that house belongs to you."

"I know, Mom."

"If there's nothing else that SOB left you."

"I know."

"Just like a man, isn't it? Never enough for a man to kill himself. Never is. Cowards. They find out the world doesn't need them, not one of them—"

"Mom!" Drew's jaw clenched. "Stop."

"I'll stay. I'll help settle you in. I'm sure Virginia has enough on her plate. She doesn't need an invalid to take care of and Cody shouldn't be so far from school. Straight after the weather I'll clean the house out and we'll move you down there."

"Mom, just give it rest. A couple of days. Next week, alright, we'll take a look."

"Do you have the keys?"

"No, I don't have the keys. They're probably still in Daryl's truck, wherever that is."

"Find out. I'll get them."

"Mom!"

And then Kati's demeanor abruptly changed. "How are you feeling, hon?"

"If you don't mind," said Drew after a moment's pause, "another pillow under my ankle?"

Virginia handed out the tea. Cody took a cup with dollops of milk and sugar. There was nothing more but to settle in. The rain didn't let up. There was more and more dripping as the water found its way through the tarp. The ground outside the slab's entry turned into a widening pool. By mid-afternoon Kati went home. By evening, when the whole of the basement floor was black with pools of water, Virginia, Cody, Drew, and Ratter took up with Hoyte's father. Hoyte and Cody slept side by side in sleeping bags. Virginia slept on the couch and Drew gratefully slept on Hoyte's bed. The rain that had begun at noon thrummed until even the relentless drumbeat of the cicadas was put out. Nightfall descended. Then well into the night Cody shook Hoyte awake. She was sitting up. The rain was an unremitting flood of noise, sheets that drummed and somersaulted from the metal roof, that thudded the back deck, that cracked against the window panes with an endless splashing.

"This is it," said Cody.

"What is?"

"This is it." She glanced at Hoyte. "The storm. The one I saw when I drowned. I remember lookin' out the window just like this."

Hoyte sat up. "So what now?"

"I dunno."

"Bet your basement floods."

"It's already flooded." Cody crawled out of the sleeping bag. She walked to the porch door and pressed her hands against the glass, face between her hands. "It's too dark to see."

Hoyte turned the spotlight's switch but the electricity was out. A muddy stream of water, barely visible through the flashing rainfall trundled down the door yard's swale. "Wanna go out?" he asked.

Cody shook her head.

Chapter 7

The rain was like a river that flowed above rivers, cloud-carried over the sea, fields, and mountains; over-filling its banks, spilling billowing waters earthward. There was neither ebb nor increase, but a steady cascade. At first the cracked soil absorbed the deluge, then the congregating waters tilted seaward, finding out old channels, carrying new-fallen leaves, limbs, and whole trees. Brooks and rivers, long abiding by their beds, re-authored themselves, trading old turns for new discourse. Livestock swam to higher ground in low-lying pasture. Weed and brush snarled in barbed wire fences, chasing the current that ran before them. The clear waters turned brown and incurious. Rocks and boulders were overturned under the surface and their knuckling and thumps were a thunderous shudder in the fields.

1

Through Sunday afternoon torrents washed the sky with pulsing sheets of water, fitfully subsiding only to increase again with a full-throated deluge that sent the brooks cascading down the hillsides. When the rain subsided, so did the brooks, and when the rain engulfed the landscape, brooks and rivers rose by the foot. When the hurricane's end finally came, that mid-afternoon, the abatement was sudden, as if the watery tail end of a serpent had finally found its way through the mountains. Here and there a sliver of blue broke through and the sunlight beaded the bedraggled leaves.

Cody and Hoyte stepped out onto the back porch. The swale still kept a diminishing stream. To either side the grasses had been rolled flat. The white trunks of the birch glistened. A hemlock had lost its footing and fallen; its roots branched nakedly into the washed air. A tussled crow shook itself, its feathers momentarily raking the barbed air before it shifted from one foot to the other and closed its wings around itself.

"Wanna go take a look?" asked Hoyte.

"Where to?"

"Down the road," he said, "and where the road circles back."

"Let's go over my place first," said Cody.

Cody skipped back to the half-opened French door. "We're gonna go check out our place then go down the road."

Drew experimentally inhaled and slowly let out a breath.

"Mom?"

"Just give me a minute, babe."

"Can we go?"

"Think the ribs are gettin' better. Try usin' crutches with broken ribs. I dare you."

Cody bit her lip impatiently.

"Fine. Don't do anything stupid," said Drew.

"Not goin' swimmin' or anything," Cody muttered.

"Get goin'. If you're not back in an hour I will embarrass you: me, the sheriff, the National Guard. Got it, kid?"

Cody stalked out of the room and headed off the porch. "You comin' or what?" she asked Hoyte without turning.

Between Hoyte's property and Virginia's there was a streamlet running through the roots of the hemlock and birch, and not one they'd ever seen before. The tarp covered deck mirrored the sky with pools of water. While the concrete was drenched with moisture, only the feet of the beds, drawers, table and chairs were wet. Satisfied that their makeshift home had survived, Cody hurried back up the driveway and to the road. Hoyte matched her smaller steps.

"Is that the first time water's come through?" Hoyte asked.

"Like that it is."

Out on the main road, they walked downhill round the first bend. The road descended into a tight, wooded valley; the bank on the left steeply alternated between ledge and pine. The right side fell away and the roar of the brook sounded through the trees. Not far along, a spruce had fallen across the road, rain having washed the earth out from under it.

"Notice somethin' strange?" Hoyte asked.

"Besides the tree?"

"The whole time we've been walkin' there hasn't been one car."

They stopped round the next bend. In the narrow granite straight where the tight valley opened, the powerful flood was impatient. The modest falls were transformed into a shouting roar. The downslope trees were gone, their black trunks crosshatched and half-submerged below the pounding turmoil. Where the brook collected again, the earth had slipped away and the road was gone on the opposite side. Only the twisted guardrail, like a ruined vine, lay twisted and pulled beneath the waters, telling where the road had gone.

"How are we gonna get out?"

Cody stuffed her hands into her pockets. Her army green pants were soaked below the hem of her raincoat. "Not drivin'."

"What do you think's happened in Brookway?"

Cody's green eyes searched as if out beyond the valley. "Bet it's bad."

"You think it's what you saw in your dream?"

"It wasn't a dream."

"You think there's anything left of Brookway?"

"Nothin' next the river."

"That's about the whole town, Cody."

"I know."

"You know this is gonna change everything."

"I know."

"And I don't mean this flood. I mean everybody you told. It's come true, what you said. If there were people didn't believe you, they do now. And everybody's gonna wanna know what happens next. They're gonna expect you know what else is in the future."

"I don't."

2

Virginia had visited the sodden foundation when Cody and Hoyte returned. Arvid was balanced on the edge of Drew's couch with a sandwich and cider. The cast of Drew's broken ankle rested on the arm of the couch. "Is it flooded?" she asked.

Virginia collapsed on a chair next to the couch. "Nobody can live there. I won't have it. Cody can't start school living in that basement. I'm sorry. But surely as awful as it would be— We can't. I'm sorry. I'll go back to the inn. I'm sure Arvid wouldn't mind—"

"The road's gone." Hoyte said matter-of-factly, bumping the door open with a shoulder.

"The road's gone?" said Arvid. "How is it gone?"

"It's gone," confirmed Cody. "Brook took it out. It's gone. There's nothin' left."

"The brook?" asked Drew.

"You'd drown if you fell in," said Hoyte.

"The whole time we were walking there wasn't one car," Cody added breathlessly. "And there's a tree 'cross the road."

"Jesus, babe."

Cody shrank. "No. You should see."

"The house!"

"Some rain got through the tarp but nothin'—"

"No, babe, our house!"

"It's not ours." Cody locked her fists in her pockets. "It's Dad's."

"Well, but what does that mean," Virginia looked from Arvid to Drew. "Are we trapped here then?"

"You're not trapped," said Arvid gently. "You are guests for as long as it takes."

"No," Virginia objected petulantly. "No. There's no electricity. Good God—but what about the road. It can't be gone?"

"We have a generator," said Arvid evenly. "If you need a refrigerator, then bring your food over. We can make room. Hoyte, the generator should be full with gas. You remember how to start it?"

"C'mon Cody," said Hoyte; and he led her to the backside of the one car garage where there was an old generator sitting under a little tin roof.

"Cool, that's an old one," said Cody.

"What do you know about generators?"

"Me and Dad used to fix 'em—" And as soon as she spoke she jammed her fists in her pocket.

"You okay?"

"I don't wanna talk about 'im."

"You don't have to."

There was a key hanging from a rusted wire just above the generator. Hoyte opened the gas line, slid the throttle to choke, put in the key and turned. The starter clicked but the engine didn't turn.

"Bet the battery's dead," said Cody.

Hoyte followed the red and black wire to the car battery tucked between the generator and the clapboards. "Nothin' wrong with the wires."

"Try pullin' it," said Cody.

Hoyte stood to the side, braced himself, and yanked at the pull-cord. After the fourth try the motor turned over, coughed, and stopped.

"When's the last time you cleaned the carburetor?"

"Dunno. Sometimes it won't start and sometimes it'll start and not stay runnin'. Dad said it probably needed more oil."

"You put more in?" Cody asked.

"Yeah I did."

"And gas too, and probl'y overfilled it with gas and oil," said Cody, "and gas got into the carburetor; got into the engine and into the crankcase. Prob'ly oughta pull the carburetor and clean it out."

"You done?"

"Got some carb cleaner?" Cody asked.

"The carb doesn't need cleanin'."

"Well they get all gunked up with shellac if you use ethanol."

"We're not cleanin' the carburetor."

"Gotta be flammable is all."

Hoyte glared at Cody again then rooted through a crate under the generator. He popped the lid from a spray and Cody took it, priming the carburetor. This time the old generator fired up. "You're pretty smart for a girl."

"And you're not that dumb for a boy," she answered over the noise of the little motor. She gave him a shove that left him with a corkscrew smile, like he'd pulled a string he wanted to pull again.

3

"Hey babe, wanna take a drive?" asked Drew.

"How are you gonna drive?" said Cody.

"Arvid's gonna drive us. Gotta see what's left in town."

"Isn't it gonna hurt?"

"Not as much as needin' to know. You comin' or not?"

Cody shrugged. "Don't think you're gonna be able to get there."

Cody and Hoyte piled into Arvid's old Saab with Drew in back, her cast balanced on Cody's lap. Her forehead was a sheen of sweat but she impatiently waved at Arvid. The drive to the first washout didn't take long. Arvid turned sharply left in the middle of the road, before the fallen spruce so that Drew could look out the window. "Jesus," she said, "you weren't kiddin'."

"It's bad," echoed Cody.

"You should see down further," said Hoyte eagerly, "there's not even road left. It's all gone. Nothin' even to walk on. You'd have to hike the hill to get 'round it."

"So then, let's see if we can get down Peterson's Road," said Arvid.

They went uphill to the Peterson pull-off but only drove a mile or so before the first washout. There was a gully on the uphill side, scoured two or three feet down to the ledge and field stone. The torrent had fatally crossed the road, landing the culvert some ten yards downstream, crushed and bent around a tree in a mix of mud, limbs, and brush. Arvid turned the car and decided they'd try the other side of the mountain. They got further downhill than before but where the valley had narrowed, the furious waters had undercut and lifted the blacktop like fractured sheets. Orange and white barrels, the town constable, and a road crew were on the other side. Arvid climbed out and stretched. Hoyte followed.

"Hey!" said Cody.

"We're not goin' anywhere," said Hoyte.

"Everybody all right?" hollered the constable.

"We can't get out," Arvid answered.

"It's bad all over."

"What's it like down in Rockford?"

"Carried the old Newcomb house downriver and we lost the covered bridge," answered the constable.

"How do we get out?"

"Can't get down to Brookway?"

"No," said Arvid, "same thing. The road is washed out."

The constable turned, talked to one of the road crew. Arvid couldn't hear. Then he hollered back, "Soon as the water's down. Could be a day or two. Any emergencies?"

"None that I know," said Arvid.

"Arvid!" Drew leaned forward so she could be heard through the open door. "Hoyte! Arvid! What about Brookway? Ask 'em if they know anything about Brookway."

Hoyte passed on the question and was answered that it was bad all over. There was nothing to do but go home. They might have called but the landlines and cell signal were dead too, the latter always iffy to start with. Once home, Drew settled onto the couch and propped up her ankle. Her skin was pale and damp, and despite Virginia's misgivings, she quickly took the codeine-laced acetaminophen.

Cody found a place to sit outside.

The world after the storm seemed as if it too, like Cody, had woken from a terrible collision. Yet when Cody saw where a nearby white pine had toppled, its ruined halo of roots lifted out of the earth, she also saw the valley filled with a blinding exhalation of sunlight. The dissolving mists fell from the leaves and evergreens as evening receded into darkness. The light was like a benediction and the trees standing over the broken pine washed it with their waters.

4

The roads still weren't passable on Monday and no road crews had come to repair the washouts. Virginia, Cody, and Hoyte worked to dry the foundation. They moved futons outside, sheets and clothes to keep them from mildewing. They untied and rolled back the tarp covering the deck.

Come Tuesday Drew decided she was ready to take another look and this time George Barstowe was on the other side of the washout, smoking next to his excavator. Drew would be damned if she stayed put. With maybe just a little less pain, she pulled herself out of the car and crutched to the edge of the washout. The flood had left a stony gulch with just a trickle of water running through it.

"George!" she called.

"Why hell!" He threw down his cigarette, walked to the opposite edge of the gulch and tugged at his trousers. "Town's got you listed as missing! Your daughter there with ya? And Virginia?"

"Yeah!"

"Well, after your place got washed downstream nobody knew. Thought maybe Middlebury finished what Sly's Brook didn't. Hell of a thing that woulda been; your girl and all, no bigger than a pint of half drunk cider. Figured that'd be the last we'd ever see of her."

"Shit." Drew shook her head as if she might have flown into a rage if not for the crutches. "Shit!"

"You and a lot of other folks," said Barstowe.

"Downstream?" she asked again as if in disbelief.

"Yeah," Barstowe answered earnestly. "Sittin' downriver and topsy-turvy like a box with the wind knocked out of it—weathervane nose down in the river. Waves got under, in it, and swallowed it. And a few more houses too. Had a crew down there just today pokin' 'round, seein' if anybody was in 'em."

"My place?"

"Sure as rust. And damn lucky you weren't."

"What's downhill of here?" asked Drew. "I want to go down."

"'Nother washout. Fixed that one so you could get by if you wanted. You'd have to move the tape out of the way. Don't tell nobody if you do, Drew. Hell of a storm. Took out 'bout a hundred yards of road, I'd say."

Drew slumped. "What are we supposed to do? Is school startin'? How soon are we gonna be able to get into town?"

"Was supposed to fix it but the town's sendin' rigs t'other way. Should be back tomorrow, next day latest. And there's some out-of-towners asking 'bout your daughter."

"Cody?"

"Yup. Cody. She saw all this was gonna happen."

On the drive back to Arvid's. Hoyte leaned into Cody and whispered, "You were right."

Drew, sitting in the front this time, turned the rear view mirror so she could see Cody. "Anything else of ours headed downriver?"

Cody shook her head.

Virginia and Hoyte were folding sheets dried in the heat of the mid-morning's sun. Drew wouldn't let anybody help her out of the car. She grimaced, made her way to the front of the car, and sat on the hood.

"You still can't get through?" asked Virginia.

Drew gave a short, sharp laugh. "Our place is gone. Storm took it."

"Gone?" said Virginia. "What are you going to do?"

Drew shrugged. "What are you gonna do?"

"I don't know."

"Gonna kick us out?" she asked.

"No!" said Virginia. "You—No. No, I'm not kicking you out. No!"

Drew turned to Cody. "Get me some codeine."

"Didn't you—"

"Just do what I tell you."

Chapter 8

1

"School?" said Cody.

Cody and Hoyte were both wrapped in blankets.

Drew held up her flip phone with a little wave. "Yeah, phone works again. Life sucks, huh babe?"

Cody threw herself onto her back. "Wait," she said, gazing at the ceiling. "How are we supposed to get there."

"Gonna have to hoof it."

"Really?" Cody sat up.

"Yeah, you and Hoyte. You remember that trail we took? Goes to the Appalachian Trail? You're gonna go down instead of up. The school bus is gonna pick you up on Jezebel Road."

"That's, like, a mile!"

"Yeah, just you and Hoyte, 'cause, you know, Arvid's got a bum knee, I'm a cripple, and if you take Virginia with you you're gonna have to carry her out."

"Cool," said Cody.

"So when are we supposed to meet the bus?" asked Hoyte.

Drew checked her phone. "You got an hour and a half. So get up. Eat. Go. And Cody, take Virginia's phone with you and get a picture of our old place."

2

Hoyte took the lead. Cody followed, guarding his back as though it needed guarding. The trail they took was part of a shortcut from the ridge of the mountain to a pull-off alongside a dirt road. The trail descended through ledge, dirt gullies, under hemlock, ailing beech and maple. The flood of rain had cut a new waterway through the years-old floor of leaves, secreting them under fallen limbs, alongside the moss-covered lengths of fallen trees, in sandy swirls that had been little whirlpools.

Hoyte pushed aside a fir's dead limb. Cody ducked. "Hey!"

"Sorry."

"I'm right behind you!"

"Watch out," said Hoyte, "or you're gonna be famous."

"What?"

"'Cause of your predictions."

Cody's thoughts just as quickly diverted elsewhere. "They thought we were in the house when the river took it."

"Who did?"

"Rescuers."

"You coulda been." They both jumped over a moss covered log.

"How?"

"I mean, supposin' you'd still lived there with your mom and dad."

"So what are you sayin'?"

"Just—" Hoyte paused. "Things work out."

"You call that workin' out?"

"Maybe your dad sort of saved your life."

Cody gave Hoyte a sharp push from behind. "Not true and you know it."

"Just sayin'."

"So stop sayin' it."

They were both silent for a moment.

"There's a woman I talked to, a reporter," said Cody. "She's trying to find me."

Hoyte turned, his smile a skeptical slant. "I told you!"

"Told me what?"

"You're gonna be famous."

"I don't wanna be famous, Hoyte."

"Then you better not talk to that reporter."

"Why not?"

"You don't think you saved a bunch of people's lives? People are gonna think you can see the future and they're gonna want you to keep tellin' it."

"So you think I shouldn't talk to her?"

"I'm not tellin' you your business."

"You do."

"Well I'm not now."

"It's not a power anyways," said Cody irritably, "and I can't see the future."

"What about the hurricane?"

"I didn't see anythin' else."

"Nothin' else?"

Cody hesitated. "Well, yeah, but it wasn't the future."

"Then what?"

Cody rolled her eyes. "I don't wanna talk about it anymore."

3

Drew lay back on the couch. Arvid and Virginia sat at the small dining table in Arvid's living room. Beyond the couch was the window that overlooked the deck and the valley. Arvid's house was a saltbox built in the sixties—a mix of opportunistic beams and half-hearted sheetrock, but the small house had a welcome lived-in feel. The wide pine floor was beaten and dark, never finished. A tall upright piano was backed into a nook with an old blanket and books piled on top, some in English, and some in Arvid's native Dutch. A small kitchen was around the corner and the sun stretched across the floor touching the cabinets. Arvid glanced at Drew, then Virginia. Virginia sat ramrod straight with her fingers clasped in her lap. "To be honest," said Arvid, "I do not think your situation is as hopeless as you believe."

Drew shook her head. "What have I got, Arvid? Until yesterday I could have sold the house. Now that's gone."

"But you must have flood insurance, yes?"

"We were two feet above the floodplain."

"I see." He turned Virginia. "And do you not have the means to complete your house?"

Virginia shook her head.

"You know," Arvid continued, "I used to work for the United Nations as a crisis negotiator. I have dealt with crises where there were many lives at risk. In just these few days you have worked and lived together and this has benefited both of you."

Drew pushed herself upright and carefully lowered her cast to the floor. "You know—" she started with a grimace. "You know, she could start by payin' me the sixteen thousand dollars she owes me."

"Ah. Could you pay her this amount," Arvid asked Virginia.

Virginia laughed. "Oh good God, if you only knew—" She paused. "After my husband was convicted—Well, there's forfeiture, restitution, clawback and—" She laughed again. "Do you know that embezzled funds are taxable? Well, you have to pay tax on theft too!"

"When it rains it pours," said Arvid. "So we must assume you have nothing?"

"No." said Virginia. "I have this property."

"Then perhaps—"

"I have to sell it."

"You do?"

"Yes. Obviously. I owe Drew sixteen thousand dollars. A week ago she at least had a house. And, well, now—what good does this place do me?"

"How much would it cost to finish the house?"

"I'll talk to Alex, my lawyer," she answered before turning to Drew. "I'll have him—I'll just tell him you need to be paid and that's that."

"But is this money in dispute?" asked Arvid.

"That's my problem isn't it? It's Drew's money. Whatever they do to me is my problem."

Drew gingerly stood on one foot, picked up the crutches, then made her way to the window. She could just see the unfinished foundation through the dividing copse of evergreens.

"Well I have an idea," said Arvid.

4

Cody and Audrey sat across from each other, eating lunch. Audrey used to be Cody's next door neighbor. Her sandy hair was long and braided in a ponytail. She tried not to stare at the scar above Cody's eye but hoped Cody would talk about the accident. Cody only wanted to know if Audrey had watched the river take her old house. And so Audrey described what she had seen. There wasn't anything like a crashing wave that swept it away. The river rose and kept rising, consuming the bank with furious gulps of foaming water until there was nothing left for the house to stand on. One corner finally stuttered and collapsed like an animal that had lost its footing, then another corner followed, then the whole lumbering house turned as if in a giant eddy before the water took that too.

"So who's the letter from?" Audrey asked once she'd finished with her description.

"A reporter."

"A reporter?"

"I told her about the storm."

"And she wants to interview you?"

"I predicted it."

"Predicted what?"

Cody leaned forward. "I saw it happen before it happened."

"Was it a dream?"

"Sort of."

"Can you see the future?"

"That was all I saw, but sometimes I hear what people are thinkin'."

"You can read minds?" Audrey's eyes widened.

"Not on purpose. It just happens. I hear 'em thinkin' and it's like they're talkin'."

"So if your mom lets you, would you?"

"Lets me what?"

"Be interviewed!"

5

Drew studied the images on her phone. Where their house had been, half a stone foundation was filled with mud. Cody had taken pictures to the north and south. Some houses looked untouched, two more were gone. A barn still stood but with the supporting stones swept out from under one side. Propane tanks popped out of the rain-drenched ground like weather buoys and had collected in the river's tree-clogged bend.

"Is that it?" asked Drew.

"It's all I had time for," said Cody, "if I was gonna get the bus home."

"Jesus, babe. It's gone. It's really gone."

"'Cept the tool shed."

"Heard the water went right over the bridge downtown," Hoyte added.

"There's a reporter wants to interview me," said Cody abruptly.

"What for?"

"Cody's famous now," said Hoyte matter-of-factly. "Heard other kids talking about her at school, saying she saved a bunch of people's lives."

"I'm going to see if the road has been repaired yet," Arvid interrupted, returning from the garage. "We have run out of gasoline I'm afraid."

"Saved lives?" persisted Drew.

"Everybody listened 'cept George Barstowe."

"Figures Barstowe wouldn't listen."

"Flood took all the cars in his lot," said Hoyte, putting on his shoes. "They're all in a pile at the bottom of Boyle's Street."

Cody slipped into her sandals and followed Hoyte. Barstowe had nearly filled the washout with gravel. Arvid walked ahead. Hoyte and Cody followed. "Are we going to be able to drive the road tomorrow?" Arvid shouted over the excavator's noise. Barstowe motioned for him to wait, spread one more shovel full of gravel, then shut off the motor. He stepped out, tugged at his pants up, and made his way across the gravel. "Hell of a storm, wasn't it?"

"We're out of gasoline," said Arvid.

"I suppose so," answered Barstowe. "Lots of folk are."

"Will we be able to drive into town soon?"

"We'll open tonight. Just a lane. And there's another down the road from here."

"I saw all your cars piled up," said Hoyte.

George gave a sly smile. "I suppose I'll have to quit the business now."

"Aren't you sad?" asked Cody.

"I suppose I should be."

"How bad was the storm in Brookway?" Arvid interrupted.

"Some lost their houses. Joe Depthord's livin' in his tool shed. You know how that goes. All the houses down the flats were flooded but one. Joe's was flooded. Gonna have a lot of work to do. It's a funny thing how the water took up in some places and didn't others. But this was the right storm for livin' on a mountainside. Even then there's some houses were flooded. Some new brook got stirred to life and decided the shortest way down was through the kitchen. Are you and your ma livin' up here now?" Barstowe asked Cody.

"I think they ought to," said Hoyte. "If Virginia lets 'em."

"Virginia? Isn't she Sal Darby's relation? Back from down South is it?"

"That's her."

"Yeah, she was lookin' at some of my cars. You and her," he said to Cody. "Good thing you were up here when that storm come through. Is Virginia holdin' up?"

"I think, now, she has no choice but to stay here," said Arvid.

"So is your ma gonna buy some land up here then?" Barstowe asked Cody.

"We have to finish Virginia's house," said Cody.

"You all are gonna live in Virginia's place, then?"

"And first we gotta figure out where we're gonna get the stuff to build it."

"Suppose so," said Barstowe. "You oughta get that foundation closed and warm 'fore winter." Then put his hands on his hips and met Cody's gaze. "I might have somethin' for ya far as that goes. Times bein' what they are, buildin' supplies are gonna be in short supply." The heavy snarl of another dump truck sounded lower down the road. "Well, that's my next load. You tell Virginia I said hello. Better stop dubbin'."

"What're you gonna do with all those cars?" asked Hoyte.

"Collect insurance!" said Barstowe with a sly backward glance, as if the answer were obvious.

A red Jetta followed the dump truck. The reporter Cody had met at the inn stepped out, brown hair cut above her shoulders, wearing black cargo pants and a jacket. Someone else was driving, but Cody couldn't see through the windshield. The woman peered at Cody as if to be sure, smiled, waved, then crossed the rut on the uphill side of the road.

Cody waved uncertainly.

"Remember me?" said the woman. "I'm Kate Brenner. We talked at the inn."

"I remember."

"Are you her father?" she asked Arvid.

"I am not."

"I'd love to talk with you some more," the reporter said to Cody. "You're a celebrity in this little town."

Cody dug her hands in her pockets.

"You puttin' her in the news?" Hoyte asked.

"Maybe." The woman answered. She turned back to Cody. "What you did was very special. I'd like to share it."

"Do I have to be on TV?"

"No, I'd like to write an article."

"The road will be open tonight," said Arvid. "Perhaps if you return this evening you can speak to Cody's mother?"

"You know what?" she answered. "If your parents—"

"My mom," Cody corrected.

"Just in case the road's not ready tonight, I have time now. Do you think I could meet your mom and talk to you tonight?"

"You'll have to walk," said Cody.

"Deal."

6

A little while after the interview Cody sat with Hoyte on the deck's edge behind his house. Their legs swung under them and their shoulders almost touched. Cody leaned forward with the heels of her palms to either side. She gazed as though to peer further into the valley. Hoyte pushed a hand through his curly hair, glanced at Cody, then at the valley, then at Cody. "So," he finally said, "what'd she ask you?"

"First she wanted to know all about me, how old I was, what I liked to study in school. Then she wanted to know how I saw what was gonna happen?"

"What did you tell her?"

"About the wreck. How I saw it and I wasn't in my body. How everything sort of happened at once, even the future, and I saw everything that was gonna to happen like I was flying."

"Did she want you to tell any more about the future?"

"Yeah."

"What'd you say?"

"Said I didn't want to know any more."

"There's lots who'd like to know."

"No they wouldn't."

"Why not?"

"'Cause you have to die to see it."

"Who says you have to die?"

"Dunno. But I almost had to. It shoulda killed me, and I wouldn't wish it on anybody, but I wouldn't trade seein' what I did for anything. But even then it's sort of like apples fallin' on both sides of a stone wall. Even when you can see 'em on the other side, it's the same apples. Might as well just eat the ones you already got."

"You said all that in the interview?"

"No." Cody shrugged. "Just thinkin' about it."

A new feeling, a feathery confusion that hung in his lungs, knocked out of Hoyte whatever he meant to say next. All he knew was that if anybody ever said anything ill of Cody, he'd knock them flat.

7

Before heading down the trail with Hoyte, Cody stopped by the foundation, bringing jam, toast, and tea. Virginia had spent the night alone. She had mopped up the last water, put sheets up to dry, and had put back the furniture. From there, Cody and Hoyte hopped down the mountain's steep slope, from ledge to ledge, then took turns leading along the level stretches. "So," Hoyte finally said, "did you see the headline this morning?"

"Where?"

"New York Times."

"No."

"I went and looked on Dad's smartphone."

"What'd it say?"

"Girl's prediction saves lives in Vermont town."

Cody didn't answer, Hoyte caught up, feet noisily shuffling through the leaves. "I was gonna show it to you but you'd already gone off to Virginia's."

"Don't talk about it at school."

"I won't," said Hoyte, "But you think nobody's gonna know?"

Cody shrugged

"So—" Hoyte's stride matched Cody's, "why'd you let her interview you then?"

"Dunno."

"You know everybody's gonna be talkin' 'bout you."

Cody stopped, dug her hands in her coat pocket, eyes watering. "Well, maybe that's it. I just wanna prove— Just wanna— that I wasn't supposed to die— that he was wrong."

"Who?"

Cody pushed Hoyte out of the way. "My dad, okay." And what Cody meant by that took a moment to sink in. When it did Hoyte caught up again and this time let the matter rest. But when the school bus came, the talk and cross-talk dropped an octave. Cody didn't look at anyone but took her seat next to a window and stared through it. Hoyte sat next to her, if only to keep anyone else from sitting next to her.

An older girl in front of them, turned, glanced at Cody, then at Hoyte. "You two, like, girlfriend and boyfriend?"

Hoyte nervously glanced at Cody, but Cody, if she heard, didn't turn from the window.

"So what if we are?"

The girl smirked. Cody's lips may have turned just a little, but too late for the girl to see and too brief for Hoyte to notice.

In the afternoon, Audrey and three more of Cody's mutual classmates sat across from Cody. Audrey theatrically dropped her jaw and stared at Cody. "You're on the front page of the New York Times!"

"I know." Cody gazed down, turning a small portion of salad with her fork.

"So what's it like?" asked another girl.

"And sometimes you can read minds!" said Audrey.

"Not, like, when I want to," said Cody defensively.

"I bet the town gives you a medal," said another girl.

Cody leaned over, elbows on the table, covering her face.

8

By the afternoon, one lane over the mountain had opened. The school bus let Hoyte and Cody out by the driveway. When they walked over the rise descending to Virginia's property they saw George Barstowe's rig and Barstowe heaving lumber from his truck onto Virginia's deck. Virginia stood to the side, hands clasped together under her chin. Drew leaned on her crutches next to Virginia.

Both Hoyte and Cody broke into a run.

"Are you gonna build a house?" Hoyte hollered at Drew.

"Not today or tomorrow," she answered.

"So what are you doin'?"

"I don't know. George," Drew turned to Barstowe, "what're we doin'?"

Barstowe tossed the last piece of lumber on the pile, old timber, beams, doors, windows, barn boards, and an assortment of nails from his cousin Ned's barn. Barstowe wiped his brow. The afternoon's humidity had picked up and the sun had laid down a bare glaze of heat atop the deck. "I don't know about you, Drew, but maybe I'm feelin' neighborly. "

"When have you ever, George?"

"That, Drew, and for your kid. You know I've always had a knack for knowin' what people want before they know it themselves, but your little girl, there, she knew it before God knew it."

Drew glanced at Cody. "I'm afraid to ask. You gonna tell me, babe?"

"Nothin'," Cody shrunk. "Just about the storm comin'."

Drew turned back to Barstowe. "Heard all your cars went downriver."

"That's right," said Barstowe.

Drew considered that, then narrowed her eyes with a knowing nod. "You goddamn old snake."

Barstowe raised his eyebrows. "Now don't jump to any conclusions!"

"Tell me you didn't move those cars just a little closer to that water."

"Gossip and rumor don't befit you." Barstowe awkwardly climbed down from the deck, huffing and puffing, and ratcheted the truck's tie downs back in place. "Now how was I to know that little toehold of a brook was gonna take all my inventory?"

"You're damn right you owe Cody," said Drew.

"We're square," he said to Cody. "Ain't we?"

Cody grinned shyly, rocking on her heels. "We're square."

"When you get legs under you again," he said to Drew. "I wouldn't mind a little help with some siding. Gettin' old. God damn diet's gonna kill me before I have a chance to die. And I'm s'posed to stop smokin' on top of that." He took a red bandana from his back pocket and wiped his forehead.

"I thought we were square," objected Drew.

"Ayup. Me and you. You don't owe me nothin' 'cept don't be tellin' nobody Barstowe's giv'n such and such away."

"Old swindler."

"Of course," he answered, swinging himself up and into the cab of his truck. "Can't have you goin' 'round sayin' I wouldn't skin a mouse for hide and tallow. You know what happens when word gets out 'bout bein' a man of means. I need that like a lamp needs moths."

"Well," Virginia blurted, "surely I can pay you for some of this."

"Oh God," Drew muttered under her breath. "Don't."

"I'll think about that," he said, then cranked the truck's motor. "Now don't let that lumber sit too long."

"Yeah, old man," said Drew, "you just get on with your swindlin'."

Barstowe smiled graciously and doffed his Stihl baseball hat, "Thank you."

"Don't sit too long."

"Oh I got a little life left in me yet," he said, elbow out the window. He backed the truck up, turned, then rumbled out of the driveway.

"What a nice man!" said Virginia.

Drew stuck her tongue in her cheek, considered telling Virginia the obvious but thought better of it. She'd let Virginia find out on her own.

Virginia gazed at the lumber. "Now what?"

"Are we gonna build the house?" asked Cody.

"Me and Virginia gotta have a talk first," said Drew.

"So you're thinkin' 'bout it?"

"How?" objected Virginia. "I can't afford to pay you, let alone what I already owe you!"

"We'll help," said Hoyte.

Drew looked exasperated. "You build it."

"Ha!"

"Yeah, you build it. I'm gonna help you. I'll tell you how."

"I've never built anything in my life!"

"Well I wasn't born with a nail in my mouth," said Drew. "You can learn."

"I can't do it by myself. One person can't build a house!"

"Says who?"

"We'll help," said Hoyte again. "We can do it after school."

"Virginia," Drew said evenly. "We can do it. I'll help. What else are we gonna do. You think Daryl's parents are gonna help me? And how long are you gonna be your ex's wife?"

Chapter 9

1

At the end of the next school day, while waiting for the school bus, a parent found Cody and gave her a bowl inside a glittering plastic bag. The bowl was full of cookies. Cody took the bowl, suddenly shy, and offered an embarrassed thanks.

"I'm Emma Finch. My daughter's in second grade," she said. "You don't know me but you told Soot Tabor about this storm coming. I don't normally put stock in predictions like that, but hearing Soot talk about you, what could it hurt? I moved my goats and sure as certain they'd have drowned. So. Some cookies. The goats thank you."

A little while after that, while sitting in the school bus, a dozen older and younger children crowded around Hoyte and Cody. "What'd she give you?" asked a younger girl.

"Cookies," said Cody.

"Was that because of your prediction," asked an older boy.

"Yeah."

"Can you tell the future?" asked a younger girl.

Cody shook her head. "Do you want a cookie?"

"Yeah!" The girl held out her hands. Cody passed out the cookies until the school bus driver ordered the children back to their seats.

2

Back at Virginia's, the tarp had been pulled to the middle of the deck. The pile of lumber had been arranged according to which piece would be needed and when. Virginia and Drew both sat on the uphill edge, where the deck was only a foot or two from the ground. Virginia was flush, sweating, leaning back on her palms and face turned up. A water bottle was next to her. Her light blue sneakers were scuffed and dusty. Drew spoke to her, though neither Cody nor Hoyte were close enough to hear what she said.

Though the afternoon was just as hot as the day before, the night had rinsed the humidity from the air. The greens and blues of the further mountains were scrubbed clear. The clouds floated over the mountains with the towering indifference of late summer, leaving the memory of the weekend's hurricane to the scoured brooks and riverbeds. When Hoyte and Cody hurried to join Drew and Virginia, they saw that a wall, lying flat on the deck, only needed to be tipped up. The lumber wasn't clean, but hardened and twisted stuff from older buildings, probably from barns Ned Barstowe had taken down—and hard to drive a nail through. Virginia sat with her hands in her lap, palm up, studying them. "When I was a nurse, I used to see builders come in with terrible injuries!"

"Why don't you go back to nursing?" Drew asked.

"It's been so many years. I'd have to be recertified, and I never dreamt I'd have to work again. So much has changed. I'd be a dinosaur."

"How long has it been?"

"Thirty years."

"You should do it."

"Well, I'll think about it. I don't know how else I'm going to make a living."

"So how was school, babe?" Drew asked.

Cody shrugged.

"There was a parent gave her cookies 'cause Cody saved her goats," said Hoyte.

"Really?"

"I gave 'em away on the school bus."

"So you really are a hero."

"'Cept I heard there was some people sayin' it was the devil talked to Cody," said Hoyte as if he'd known it would happen all along.

"Yeah. Nothin' good goes unpunished," said Drew.

"I don't care," said Cody.

"And who was sayin' that anyways?"

"Another girl in Cody's class," said Hoyte. "Overheard her talkin' at lunch. I think she belongs to some church from out of town."

"Oh God," said Virginia. "Why are people like that? I hear so many sad stories about kids never vaccinated coming into emergency rooms and it's all hospitals can do to nurse them back to health. And it seems like so many of them are homeschooled."

"Just ignore them," said Drew to Cody.

"Let's tip up the wall!" said Cody hopefully.

"Nah. Tomorrow. I'm done, babe." Drew planted her crutches and awkwardly pushed herself to one foot. She was sweating and pale as she made her way to the basement. Virginia pursed her lips, watching Drew leave.

"Are we stayin' here tonight?" asked Cody.

"Yeah. We're stayin' here. We can't just keep livin' wherever's convenient."

"I don't mind."

Drew made her way to the couch they'd finally moved into the basement. She carefully let herself down, leaned back, and closed her eyes. "Get me some codeine, babe."

"Isn't it at Hoyte's house?"

"Yeah, go get it."

When Cody returned she looked for a glass. Stood on her tiptoes, leaning on the makeshift countertop of plywood and the stainless steel sink. She meant to wash the first glass she could reach, fogged with the storm's humidity.

"Babe, just give me the pill."

"I was just gonna—"

"Jesus, just give me the pill. I'll be fine."

Cody handed her the pill. Drew swallowed. "C'mere, babe. Sit next me. How are you doin'?"

"Fine."

"That's it? You're front page news, people callin' you from all over the country, givin' you cookies, and now you got some cranks sayin' the devil whispered in your ear? That's all you got to say?"

Cody shrugged.

"Hey." Drew pulled the girl into her ribs even as she winced. "Wanna hear a funny story 'bout the devil?"

"Sure."

"Grandpa said the devil and God were tricksters, like Coyote and Crow. Crow tricks us into making the right choices and Coyote the wrong ones. So, when Crow and Coyote were teaching our ancestors they argued over the best way.

"They divided a burning stick and Crow brought her stick to man and said: With fire you'll be immortal. But Crow has a way of saying things. Coyote brought his stick to woman and said: With fire you'll be immortal. But Coyote has a way of saying things.

"Man took his stick and set the world ablaze because being immortal means creating and destroying. But when smoke and darkness filled the world, he was lost and lonely.

"When woman saw the smoke and darkness, she was curious. She searched the dark because being immortal means bringing light to darkness. And when she found man she led him out of darkness.

"After that, humankind discovered the good and bad in fire."

"So?" asked Cody.

"So—" Drew gave Cody a squeeze and sighed. "I just build houses."

3

The story of a girl's prediction was retold and embellished until she'd saved the entire town. Drew, who only had a flip phone, turned it off when one call followed another—calls for interviews and invitations. Cody didn't want to interview again and Drew regretted having allowed the first but, with or without, the story would have been told.

A faulty generator canceled Friday's school and so Cody and Hoyte dedicated themselves to raising the first wall of Virginia's tiny house. But first to do was to find extra tools; then squaring the wall; then, because there wasn't plywood, they used the old barn-planking, nailing the planks across the bare frame while it still lay on the floor. Soon enough, Cody and Hoyte's fingers were blistered and sore with driving nails into the rough wood.

Drew laughed, maybe for the first time since the accident, watching the others aim at nails and miss. Nonetheless, by mid-morning the wall was ready to raise. Virginia took a deep breath, stood with her crutches, and ordered Virginia to one side, Hoyte and Cody to the other. "It'll start out heavy. Just go slow and stay slow."

At the ends of the wall were two notched boards. The two boards swung from the top and were meant to catch a barn nail before the wall leaned too far. They started with pry bars, putting blocks under the wall. Then pried again until the top of the wall was at waist height. Then the three of them spread out, wedged themselves under the top plate and pushed. And that was all it took.

The first wall of Virginia's tiny house was up.

"Check it for plumb," said Drew. To Virginia and Hoyte she said, "When the ends are plumb, nail the braces."

Once they'd done that, they nailed the bottom plate to the deck. Cody bounced on her tiptoes and Hoyte ran from one end to the other like an inspecting foreman. Virginia stood with her hands on her hip.

"See?" said Drew. "That wasn't so hard."

"The next one," said Cody.

Buoyed by the success of one wall, Hoyte and Cody hurriedly laid out the second. Hoyte measured and marked. Virginia used Drew's circular saw, her expression a mask of defiance. She expected the saw to lunge for her fingers at any moment but the saw was well-behaved. There were some respectable doublehungs Barstowe had left in the woodpile. Hoyte and Cody argued over where the rough opening should go, but Drew had already made plans.

An hour or two after they should have had lunch, a car pulled onto the gravel driveway. Jacqueline Jodi stepped out, or JJ as Drew called her. She had been a school friend of Drew's, worked as a realtor, and was a notary public. She carried a quitclaim deed and a pie. The pie she gave to Cody, then carefully hugged Drew before shaking Virginia's hand.

"Thanks for bringing this," said Drew.

"Like I was gonna make you drive to Brookway," JJ answered. She then turned to Virginia. "It's a nice thing you're doing for Cody and Drew." She lay the quitclaim deed next to the pie on the edge of the waist high deck. "So, all you have to do, Virginia, is to sign where it says Grantor, then you and Drew sign where it says Grantee. I'll notarize, and then you need to record the deed at the county clerk's office."

Cody studied the deed. "Are we buyin' the property?"

"Sort of, babe," said Drew. "This house is gonna belong to all of us until we can build ourselves a new place."

"Where's that gonna be?"

"She's dividin' the property, babe, givin' us half, thirty acres to build a house on."

"Up here?"

"Yup."

"So we're not goin' back to our old place!"

"What old place, babe? It's gone. We don't have money to build new and Virginia can't build by herself. First we're gonna build ourselves a new place where we can all live, and then build a place just for us."

4

Rather than blast the ledge, it had been cheaper to make half the foundation a slab and half a full basement. But when Virginia's husband stopped payments, only the basement had been poured. This meant that Drew and Virginia had half the planned footprint; and that meant building a house half the original size. Barstowe's donation only added up to something like half a house anyway; and that was good because smaller walls are quicker to build and easier to raise. By Sunday afternoon, the walls were up. The wall that faced the valley, over the basement's entry, was several feet taller than the other three walls. Though there was good weather ahead, and lucky for that, a shed roof was the quickest to build and quickest to cover. They decided they might have a week to do it.

School was a distracting torture for Cody and Hoyte—Cody in seventh grade and Hoyte in eighth. Audrey jumped from her desk to lean on Cody's. "So," she said, "there's like a church in town and they're passing out flyers about Jesus and God."

"Did you get one?"

"No!" Audrey glanced to both sides conspiratorially, "but I think it's 'cause of you predicting the storm."

Cody suppressed a smile. "No they're not."

"They are."

"How do you know?"

"'Cause they say things like, I don't know, like no prophecy was ever made by the will of man; then talk about being defiled by familiar spirits and looking for wizards."

Cody leaned back and covered her eyes with the palms of her hands, then pushed her fingers back and through her hair, eyes closed.

Then Audrey remarked, "The little stitch marks are going away."

"Where did you see them?"

"Like little dots on both sides of the scar."

"No," said Cody, "the people."

"They were outside Blaire's Grocery yesterday. I don't think anybody pays attention to 'em."

The first bell rang. Audrey and a few late stragglers found their desks. "So, how was summer?" asked Mr. Griggs, their science teacher, a tall and narrow man. The classroom answered with a combination of mumbling and some exclamations.

"This last week was memorable wasn't it?"

"I saw Stan Tremont's house washed right into the river!" offered a boy in the back.

"I heard the covered bridge go down and under the waves!" offered another.

"Our barn flooded and all the pigs had to swim until we let 'em out," said a girl. That was met with a burst of laughter and guffaws.

"Couldn't they just fly out?" cried a boy.

"So you guys know what kind of storm that was?"

"A hurricane," came the scattershot burst of answers.

"So let me ask you something," said Griggs. "How many of you were prepared?"

Most of the children raised their hands.

"Why is that?"

"'Cause we saw it on the internet," said a boy from the back. "Me and Dad were watchin' it the whole week as it was crossing the Atlantic."

"That's right," said Griggs, "and you know what made that possible?"

"Satellites," said a girl, then embarrassed at having been the first to answer, added, "I mean, maybe."

"But they all have one thing in common," said Griggs. "Anybody know what that is?"

"The internet," said a student.

"Not quite," said Griggs. "What field of knowledge makes things like the internet possible?"

"Math! Science!" came the scattershot answers.

"That's right. We predicted the path of the hurricane because of science. And lucky for us we're going to learn all about science this year: evolution, biology, what chemistry is, astronomy, cosmology."

"What about Cody?" Audrey spoke up.

Griggs glanced questioningly at Cody, then Audrey. "Did you want to say something?"

"Cody predicted it before even science knew," said Audrey.

"Was that you?" Griggs glanced at Cody.

Cody shrank, hands jammed in her pocket.

"And I'm hearing some amazing stories," said Griggs, then turned to the rest of the class. "I was just going to ask: What do you think human beings did before there was science?"

"Made things up," came an answer.

"Guess and got lucky," said another girl, Olivia.

"It wasn't luck," said Cody.

"What was it then?"

"It wasn't luck," she repeated.

And it might have ended there. Cody determinedly stared at her wooden desk as if she could will away the roomful of children. The window's curtain abruptly bellied into the room, plucked from its curtain rod by a gust. The sheet whirled between the children like a robed accusation before stopping at Cody's desk, pointing, and saying with Olivia's voice: 'So we're all supposed to worship you now?'

"No!"

Cody looked up as startled as the other children. The window was closed and the white curtain hadn't moved.

"I didn't say anything!" said Olivia.

"You did," said Cody. "I heard you. You said I act like you're supposed to worship me!"

Olivia was momentarily nonplussed. She turned to the teacher. "I didn't say it! I was just thinking it!" She looked at Cody with a combination of fear and rage, gathered up her books, and hurried out of the room.

Griggs called after her, then sighed. "Welcome back. Let's try this again. Let's talk about science, okay?"

Cody kept her hands stuffed in her pockets and slumped in her seat.

"So. Humans have always been scientists," Griggs continued. "Each one of you grew up being scientists. You made observations. You constructed ideas about how things work. Scientists call those ideas hypotheses. You tested your ideas. You experimented and learned from your experiments. For example, what makes the best skipping stone?"

"Flat ones!" came the universal response.

"And how do you know that?"

And the question was followed by a flood of answers; not just the size and shape of stones but with the method of throwing, stance, and the wind's direction. And that was how Mr. Grigg's science class began. If it was a declaration of disbelief, Cody couldn't tell. After class Audrey reassured Cody. She didn't think Cody's stories were just stories.

5

Kati showed up at noon. Drew was awkwardly making her way up the slope from the basement, a sandwich bag, and water bottle in opposite jacket pockets, crutches catching on them. Ratter followed, as kittens will, distracted by every nugget of motion. Kati swept her long hair behind her and hurried to meet her.

"Let me carry the sandwich."

"No. I'm good, Mom."

"You should see what's happened!"

"I've seen some of it."

"I don't know how anyone's supposed to get from one side of the state to the other. You know how long it took me to get here? I had to go almost fifty miles out of my way! A tree's down. A road is washed out. A bridge is gone." Kati gestured beyond them both. "I don't know how you can live here!"

"Where am I supposed to live?"

"The house. Your house. It belongs to you. I don't know why you thought Daryl should keep it. I'll live there with you, just to get you back on your feet."

"It's gone."

"No. It's yours!"

"It's gone, Mom. It's literally gone. The river took it."

"What? Really? You can't be serious!"

"Gone Mom, and half the foundation with it." Drew pushed past her stunned mother.

"You had insurance, right?"

"It wasn't supposed to be in the floodplain."

"But you had insurance. You had to have insurance! You can't have a mortgage without insurance."

"Not the same as flood insurance, Mom. We didn't have flood insurance."

"Well, what are you going to do?"

"Mom!" Drew turned awkwardly on her crutches. "All I know is that Cody's happy here. So for right now we're gonna live right here. We're buildin' a house, all of us together, where we can live."

"If I had room you could live with me."

"Sure, Mom."

"Don't say it like that. You know if I could, I would, but I have so little room."

Drew rounded the corner and carefully sat in the doorway's rough opening. She set her crutches to the side and pulled the water bottle and sandwich from her pockets.

"What else do you need?" Kati asked.

"Just the sun."

"No, that's not what I mean. Are you in pain? You must be in pain. Are they giving you enough medication? I can get you more if you need more. You look like you need more."

"Just let me eat."

"How's Cody?"

"Fame's more than she bargained for."

"What fame?"

"She saw the whole thing comin'."

"When?"

"When she near drowned in the brook."

"She had a vision. Your grandfather used to have visions. She saw there was going to be a hurricane?"

"Saw the weather, saw we were gonna lose our house, and told everybody who'd listen."

"I'd be grateful."

"Not everybody is."

"Why wouldn't they be grateful?"

"'Cause people are people."

6

By the end of the school day a rift had grown between Cody and Olivia, not the kind that divides a class, but one that invites discerning gossip. Olivia was blonde and taller than Cody. She maintained a self-possessed air of aloofness and was a straight-A student. If she had parents, no one had met them. What was not presumed was Olivia's knowledge of the Bible. She had already condemned several children to hell for infractions that included riding bicycles the wrong direction and indiscreet vocabulary. Olivia's judgment was a florid and prized event, deploying Biblical passages with irredeemable precision. But nature created Olivia's opposite in Jerry Adler—a boy in the same neighborhood and almost a year older. He had a way of provoking Olivia, listening to her theology, her fine-grained damnation of language, sidewalks, and church attendance, by saying nothing at all. He could walk away with a tip of his baseball cap and Olivia's towering condemnation would come crumbling down. After the loss of Olivia's usual classroom reserve, Jerry took an interest in Cody. "So," he said, leaning back in his chair, "heard you're supposed to be somethin' like a fortune teller."

"Not any kind of fortune teller," said Cody.

"Said the storm was comin' and it did, right?"

"Yeah."

"So how'd you know?"

"Just saw it."

"How? Like in a movie?"

"Yeah."

Jerry leaned forward, his thumbnail momentarily between his teeth. "Never seen Olivia so rattled."

"I've seen her mad before," said Audrey.

"Not like that," said Jerry. "How'd you rattle her?"

"Wasn't anything on purpose."

"You read her mind?" Jerry asked.

"I don't always like talkin' about it," Cody shrank and once more jammed her hands in her pockets.

"You don't have to."

"So what's up with Olivia anyway?" said Cody.

"Her parents," said Jerry. "Probably thinkin' you made a pact with Satan."

"Some pact," Cody mumbled.

7

Later that day Virginia returned to Lydia Peacham's store of futons, frames, and paper lanterns and saw that the first floor had been flooded to the height of her knees. Workmen were already inside stripping sheetrock. The front door was wide open. The carpeting had been stripped out. She saw it through the window and was about to leave when Lydia waved at her from a doorway inside the showroom. Lydia crossed the showroom and motioned for Virginia to join her at the entry doors.

"I'm so glad you stopped by," Lydia began at once. "I didn't know how to call you."

"I can't believe it!" said Virginia. "I can come back!"

"No, no!" Lydia gestured for Virginia to follow. She led Virginia through the showroom and up a set of stairs that doubled back to a floor above, a studio with four tall windows overlooking the street. Futons were stacked neatly on one side. There were boxes, assembled bed frames, folding couches, night stands, and floor lamps. A fan was in one of the windows.

"Almost all of this was downstairs."

"They weren't damaged by the water?"

"Cody was right."

"I can hardly believe it."

"I mean, it would have been covered by insurance, but as soon as I saw Irene was going to hit Vermont, I moved everything up here. Why take a chance? Are you her grandmother?"

"Oh no!"

"A friend?"

"Oh, it's a long story, but yes, we're friends."

"I want to give her something. Do you think she'd like a little lamp?"

"Oh God," Virginia slumped. "We don't even have a house to put it in!"

"Was it the flood?" Lydia put her hand on Virginia's arm.

"No. Well. I just returned to Vermont. I wasn't born here but Sal Darby was my grandfather. My husband and I were going to retire here but—well, my husband turned out to be a common criminal and then this awful accident—"

And that's as far Virginia got.

The rest of the story waited to be told until Virginia could sit down, Lydia next to her, and pour out all that had happened while dabbing at her eyes. Lydia sat with one hand on Virginia's knee. When Virginia described the house they were building Lydia stopped her. "You're building a tiny house!"

"Yes," Virginia nodded ruefully.

"You should film and blog it! Tiny houses are all the rage."

"Me? Watch an incompetent middle-aged woman build a house?"

"Who better?"

"A professional builder for one."

"Do you like to write?"

"Oh I remember writing stories when I was a teenager. Yes. I enjoyed it."

"Then you should write about it."

"I wouldn't know where to begin."

"I manage a writing group. Just women. It's half romance-writer's group and half an excuse to get together. You should meet Ada Byron. She's always looking for little stories and something local to write about."

"I suppose I could."

"Yes, why not?"

"I'll write my riches to rags story," said Virginia.

"I'm jealous."

"Of me?" said Virginia. "Why in God's name would you be jealous of me?"

"Because you get to start over."

"It's overrated."

"You know, I love my husband and my children and I don't regret a single choice, but I ask myself: What if I were young again? What if I could start over? What would I do differently? What kind of a man would I fall in love with? What if trying out a man was like borrowing books from a library?—a card catalog of men arranged by the dewey decimal system. I want a man conversant in the arts and recreation. A man of the 700's. But I get bored after a month. Now I want a man of science. Conversant in insects, flowers, stars and the universe. A man of the 500's. But what if I want to travel? Then he's one more belonging to schlep around. So I return him to the library and travel wherever I want."

"Why don't you?"

"I live vicariously in my romance novels," she smiled coquettishly. "Think of it as practice."

"There's still some little part of me wishes I had it all back."

"And your husband?"

Virginia stared at the unopened boxes on the opposite side of the room. "Is it wrong?"

"It's a scary time."

8

There's a saying goes around Vermont: "Just 'cause a cat has kittens in the oven, don't make 'em biscuits." To which any sensible kitten will answer: "A kitchen without a cat is a cupboard full of rats." To which any self-respecting rat will answer: "Well that suits rats just fine."

And that brings us to Soot Tabor's father. In his younger days, before he took up engineering, he painted houses, an occupation requiring nothing more than an excess of patience; a virtue that Malthus Tabor turned into a vice. More than a few women had shown interest in him, but in the way that seasons lead on to seasons, there's only so long to pick a berry.

It wasn't until Malthus was hired by Emma Willard to paint her kitchen that Malthus's mother, Chloe Tabor, took an interest. What needed sprucing up at Emma's, she suspected, wasn't the kitchen but Emma Willard's daughter. They're on the wrong side of the tracks, she said; but that was a common refrain from both sides. The Willard's are troublesome, she said. Don't expect them to pay you.

Malthus paid no mind. He threw a step stool, bucket, a handful of brushes, and paint into the back of his truck and took up Emma's job no different than any other. Mila Willard, Chloe's daughter was a year younger than Malthus. Her hair was raven black and long enough to brush to the small of her back. The first morning Malthus arrived, he saw straight away the kitchen was more than he bargained for.

Though the kitchen was neat and tidy, there was a touch of grease in every corner. That's not something can be painted over, so Malthus set to work cleaning. Mila, who had begun baking early in the morning, already had an armful of bread and buns to sell from the back of her hatchback. And though Mila was never known for friendliness, she offered Malthus a bun.

Now it just so happened that the harder Malthus worked to renovate, the busier Mila's oven became. Soon enough, Malthus was as involved in tinkering with Mila's oven as he was with painting. Some say that's how his interest in engineering started and others say that's how you make biscuits—or a kitten as the case may be. This strange congruence of events wasn't lost on Chloe Tabor. But if she hoped Malthus would be done with the Willards, or that the Willards would run out of money for paying Malthus, she was sorely disappointed.

Mila liked to give Malthus little gifts. She hid her gifts in whatever she baked for him; and Malthus would dutifully return them. It happened that Malthus's favorite surprise was a little blue marble. Malthus's mother, in a fit of pique or spite, hid the marble in an eggcup before Malthus could return it. And though Malthus looked all the next morning, he returned to Mila's without the blue marble. He might have suspected his mother, but she only replied that girls shouldn't be putting marbles in muffins.

Mila was despondent.

You might have thought a terrible trouble had befallen her, but then one morning Malthus arrived and there was a baby in the oven. Naturally enough, Malthus and Mila married. When Mila delicately took the baby out of the oven, showing her to Malthus, Malthus saw that one eye was missing just as neat and clean as if it had never been there. The other eye was a beautiful blue, as blue as the marble Malthus had lost.

That little baby was Soot Tabor, who got her name from being baked, as some liked to say, in that oven. Born two months too soon, small as a fresh-baked bun, old Doc Gillespie, the town doctor in those days, gave Malthus and Mila strict instructions. He had them put Soot in a shoebox and in the oven warmed by a pilot light, and told them how to feed and swaddle her. Soot grew up strong, happy, and one-eyed. But in the telling, folks preferred to add a touch of witchery to the girl baked in the oven, whose one eye was stolen by her stepmother.

9

Virginia returned late afternoon with the lamp for Cody and a nightstand for herself. Cody and Drew were sitting in the living room, still only four walls and roofless. The afternoon sun cut slantways through the rough opening that overlooked the valley. Cody had made a makeshift table on sawhorses and had brought up three chairs. Drew sat on one, her crutches leaning on the table, and Cody sat kitty-corner, working on her homework. Drew corrected her from time to time.

Virginia brought Cody's lamp to the table, a graceful and curving lamp meant for a nightstand. She asked if the third chair was for her and it was. Knowing that righted the see-saw of Virginia's troubles. Drew briefly smiled at Virginia before returning to Cody's scrawls. "No, babe, you carried the wrong amount."

Cody kicked at nothing under the table and glared at her homework.

"C'mon, babe."

"My head hurts," said Cody.

"It isn't that bad."

"No, really, it hurts."

"Hey," Drew cajoled. "Where does it hurt?"

"My whole head."

"Maybe you're just tired?"

Cody sat up, eyes moist, pushing her hands through her hair, then leaned back with her arms crossed over her eyes. "It's like the world keeps gettin' smaller and smaller 'til it hurts to breathe."

"I'll get you an aspirin."

"I was at the futon store today," said Virginia. "The whole first floor was flooded."

"You mean Lydia Peacham's place?" Drew asked.

"The lamp is for you, Cody." Then she added, "Because, well, you predicted a flood and there was a flood. She moved everything to the second floor because of you."

Chapter 10

1

Meredith held her pencil calmly in her lap as she considered Ada Byron's story. Ada liked to turn the history of Brookway into short stories, poems, and now a novel. She was waifish and excitable. She pressed her lips tight as she waited for comment. The women had gathered in the back office of the Apple House, Meredith's inn. Meredith gazed at Ada with the candor of resignation. "Soot was born in the oven?"

"Well of course she wasn't born in the oven," said Ada. "She was born prematurely. Granddad told Soot's parents to put her in the oven in a shoebox. Isn't that so, Soot?"

"I liked it," volunteered Soot.

"Of course you would," said Meredith.

"Ada's grandad was Doc Gillespie," said Lydia, in an aside to Virginia.

"Are you writing fiction or fantasy," Meredith asked.

Ada tilted her head the way one appraises a child who charmingly misapprehends the nature of the world. "Fiction is just another word for the truth."

"The truth?" scoffed Meredith. "What does a marble hidden in an egg cup have to do with Soot's missing eye?"

"Everything."

"I hardly think so," said Meredith. She turned to Soot. "You lost it in a hunting accident. With your father. Isn't that right? That's what I remember. The butt of the rifle kicked you in the eye."

"Oh no, my father never hunted," answered Soot.

"Well then, where did I hear that? " asked Meredith, taken aback and glancing at the other women.

"But," Soot added under her breath, "There's an element of truth to it."

"Oh for God's sake," said Meredith, "why don't you just tell us!"

"Where would be the fun in that," said Ada. "Don't you think there's more truth in a good story than in the minutes of a committee meeting?"

"A functional society doesn't run on good stories."

"They're the stitching that holds us together," said Ada. "Suppose a little girl goes to buy bread and decides to stray from the sidewalk. In the alleyway, the girl meets a strange man who asks where she's going; because little girls shouldn't be walking through dark alleys. The girl tells him. Later, when she arrives at the store, the strange man has murdered the storekeeper and taken his place. He invites the girl inside and tells her he knows where the freshest bread is baked; but the girl's suspicious and just then a policeman passes by—"

"I would say it's a poor imitation of Little Red Riding Hood," Meredith interrupted.

"Fairy tales tell the truth."

"Your pond's run out if you ask me," Meredith answered flatly.

"But haven't we all had that experience?" said Ada.

"It's a metaphorical truth," offered Lydia. "And sure, who among us hasn't felt like Little Red Riding Hood?"

"I wouldn't know," said Meredith, "not all of us go wandering in the metaphorical woods, do we?"

"Meredith!" said Lydia with a kind of exasperation, then turned to Virginia. "What do you think?"

"Well—" Virginia glanced at the other women almost apologetically. "Well, if you had asked me six months ago I might have agreed. Fanciful. I would have said that. But I don't know. I think, maybe, truth really is stranger than fiction."

"You've been helping Drew and her little girl," said Meredith.

"Yes," said Virginia.

Meredith considered Virginia, then as if satisfied with Virginia's answer, she turned to the other women. "We've gotten calls from reporters across the country looking for rooms and even a church group."

"A church group?" asked Lydia.

"Yes, I suppose it has something to do with Drew's little girl—"

"Why would a church group care?" Virginia interjected.

"It's anybody's guess with those people," said Meredith curtly, "but I assume you weren't here when that whole Civil Unions business was going on? You would have thought the world was going to end. It wasn't even marriage. I don't know but I had my fill of Bible thumping by the end of it. Better a skunk in hell with its back broke than sit through another sermon after all that spite and meanness. But anyhow, the surest way to ruin a relationship is to get married. No sooner did half those people marry than they filed for divorce."

"Meredith!" Lydia objected.

"As for the other half, the threat of marriage scared the relationship right out of them."

"You exaggerate," said Lydia flatly.

"I'm romanticizing the truth." Meredith glanced at Ada.

Virginia let out a whoop of laughter, then struggled to apologize.

"Anyhow," Meredith continued with dry pleasure, "now that we've been run over by a hurricane I suppose they're back to gloat, that and Drew's little girl taking instruction from the almighty."

"Well I wouldn't have believed it," said Virginia, "but everything she said was true."

"I'm guessing she has a vivid imagination," said Meredith. "Poor thing. What she's gone through. I can't blame her."

"She told the truth," said Soot.

"She made good guesses that turned out to be true," answered Meredith. "There's a difference."

"Virginia," Lydia abruptly turned the conversation, "did you write anything?"

"Therapy."

"Lydia told us you're building a tiny house!" said Ada. "I'd love to live in a tiny house. I love Soot and Soot loves me, but I think she's getting ready to kick me out."

"Why don't you read what you've written," said Lydia.

Virginia exhaled and reluctantly read the little bits of biography that were like confessionals: her husband's betrayal; her arrival in Vermont; a house that wasn't a house; the loss of all that had been her life. Afterward Meredith broke the silence as she usually did. "You know," she said, "you don't give yourself enough credit. That man meant to kill his daughter and wife and that had nothing to do with you."

"They wouldn't have gotten in that car if not for me!"

"And because of that," Meredith answered flatly, "they're alive. If he'd used a gun, they'd all be dead."

2

Cody woke to the dry and cooling air of an early September's morning. The turning of the trees had already begun among the variety of maples, and though the leaves of the poplar, cedar, oaks, and birch were still green, there was a brittleness that made the wind a dusty white.

Ratter poked a spider's web and the spider resentfully retreated to Cody's nightstand. The kitten's tail made a twitching question mark before she withdrew, shaking the sticky web from her paw as if the whole affair had been beneath her dignity. Cody shoved her bed sheets down, pulled on her overalls, and slipped between the sheets of their makeshift basement walls. Drew was at the table with a book and a cup of tea. Ratter ran beneath and sidled up against Drew's cast. "Morning, babe."

"Are we gonna work on the house today?" Cody asked.

"You bet."

"What're we gonna do?"

"Put on a roof."

"What do we have to eat?"

"Cereal."

"Can we make eggs or somethin'?"

"What do you mean *we*? How 'bout *you*, babe. How's your head?"

"It's fine."

"I heard rumors things got rough at school."

Cody shrugged.

"You wanna talk about it?"

"Not really."

"Hey, babe, I may be on crutches, but if anybody messes with you—"

"It's cool, Mom."

Cody cracked two eggs above the little camp stove. A few minutes later Cody heard the driveway's gravel pop with a car's arrival. "Who's that?"

"Virginia."

"Where was she?"

"Gettin' stuff from our tool shed."

Cody took a last bite of scrambled egg. "And Hoyte. Hoyte's comin' over."

A shelter is a burrow, a beaver's lodge, a woodpecker's hole, and a wolf's den. That mankind also wanted his own burrow; a place where a midnight's rain might not wake him or carnivores consume him leaves its traces painted on cave walls. Eventually man discovered that he too could shape mud, leaves, and wood into the makings of a shelter. The ancient footprints of these and whole towns still mark the earth, appearing unexpectedly like crop-circles on dry summer days.

The way to build a house hasn't changed all that much in thousands of years. Houses are still made of wood and stone and roofs still shed water like boats turned upside down. Building a small house or a large house is the same and once you've done it, like building anything, a sentence, poem, paragraph, or novel, the design of the smallest part builds the whole.

The lumber that George Barstowe had given to Drew and Virginia must have come from an old watermill—the long boards being up-down milled and rough. Wood that's seasoned for decades, even white pine that starts out soft and pliable, can turn hard as oak. By the end of the day, as with the prior day's wall raising, Cody and Hoyte's palms were sore and blistered.

The beams Drew picked for the roof were four by eight beams. They had mortises in some places, where a barn's braces used to be. The advantage to wood that's seasoned a hundred years is that it's given up its water. If it's rough and hard as knots, it's also light and easy to lift.

Drew wasn't content to sit. She impatiently circled the tiny house on crutches, giving advice, flinching as she shielded her eyes, cursing under her breath. One by one, and with Cody and Hoyte arguing over leverage, they set each beam in place. Long timber screws fastened them down. Virginia was like a leaf in flood waters. She moved helplessly from one task to the next. Midway through the day she cried out, "Stop!"

She put down the circular saw, stared at the newly installed roof joists, then went down the slope and into the basement. Drew followed after her.

"Mother used to drink rum and cokes," said Virginia. Her hands shook as she opened a bottle of rum, poured some into a glass and followed that with Coke. "She was never a drunk, but after she'd had her rum, she'd stop complaining about money, about Dad, about us. 'You'll like it when you grow up,' she'd say."

"Just get that?" Drew asked.

"This morning."

"Didn't know you were a drinker."

"Neither did I." Virginia closed her eyes and drank with a gratified sigh. "I'm terrified of saws. I was an Emergency Room nurse. Me! Emergency Nursing! That's what I did before I married money. How do you make sense of that? When did I turn into such a morose little violet?"

"Hey, you did good today."

"One of the worst," Virginia continued, "was a man who cut off his knee. Who uses a dangerous tool like that? On his lap? Well, he cut right through his kneecap. That was something."

Virginia poured another cup.

Drew closed her eyes, head back, leaning into the chair. "Every time I've ever sent myself to the hospital it was with a hand tool."

"You're lucky."

"Nah, when tools stop scarin' you, that's when you put 'em down. Daryl was like that. Bein' 'round him was like standin' knee-deep in water with a shorted saw. Nah, it's always been the hand tools. I get too comfortable with 'em."

"Insights come unexpectedly," said Virginia. "Dad used to say that if they weren't unexpected, they wouldn't be insights. The best insights, he'd say, come to you like stepping on a hoe. And emergency rooms are where insights go to recover. Well, here I am. This—" Virginia waved at the foundation, pointing with the glass and a lifted finger. "This is my emergency room: this house, this property, this state. I don't need any more insights. I've had my fill of insights. Honestly. I'll take my stitches and get back to living."

"Cody!" Drew called.

"She must have ran off with Hoyte," said Virginia

"Damn it."

"I'll find her. I'm going back up."

"I just need a med."

"Tylenol?"

"No, I want the oxycontin."

"Where is it?"

Drew gestured above her, toward the open shelves above the kitchen sink. "I wanna go into town tomorrow. Can you take me?"

"Of course! Where?"

"I wanna see the house."

3

Cody followed Hoyte through the narrow copse dividing their properties. He stopped. "Check it out," he said, showing her a diagonal row of blisters across his palm. Cody defiantly showed him her own.

"I got 'em too."

Hoyte poked at one of the blisters. "Are you gonna pop yours?"

"No."

"Why not?"

"Maybe."

"If you don't pop 'em they'll probably pop themselves." Hoyte just as quickly lost interest, then turned again. "You're lucky your mom can build."

"Why?"

"Don't you wanna build your own house someday?"

"Maybe."

"I'm buildin' my own."

Then it was Cody's turn to be distracted. "What happened to your dad's knee?"

"It wasn't his knee. He was in a helicopter crash."

"For real?"

"Yeah. He was peacekeeping in Bosnia."

"So what does he do now?"

"He's a translator."

"What's he translate?"

"Legal stuff from Dutch." Hoyte continued along the path. There was a washout where the water had scooped and carried the round stones of a resurrected streambed, leaving them in a comet-like trail over the grass. They were a good size to hold in the hand. Hoyte picked one up, eyed the down slope, and threw the stone out and over as if into the distant valley. There followed the smack of leaves and a crack as the stone struck limbs and returned to earth.

Cody tested two or three stones before throwing. Her own didn't make the treetops. Hoyte smiled. "You can't throw like that."

"Like what?"

"Like—" Hoyte hesitated. "Like a girl."

"How else am I supposed to throw?" Cody's eyes narrowed. "Or didn't ya notice I'm a girl? Throw another one."

Hoyte took measure of three more stones, picked the best, held the others in his right hand, and threw an arc that descended into the topmost leaves and limbs. Cody watched with lips pressed tight. Then as quick as that she knelt and sorted through a handful of stones without glancing at Hoyte. She stepped back, just like Hoyte, and this time threw with a swing in her slight frame. The stone didn't soar, but when the stone ricocheted through the lower leaves and limbs she glanced at Hoyte with a mix of defiance and competitiveness.

He grinned awkwardly.

"What?" she asked, breaking a smile like his.

"Nothing." He turned away, as if embarrassed, and threw another stone. "So—" he said. "What happened to not throwin' stones at trees?"

"They don't throw back," said Cody.

Hoyte grinned. He threw another. "So everybody's talkin' 'bout how you can read minds."

"I don't mean it to happen."

"What's it like?"

Cody threw another stone that this time crested in the crown of the trees. "It's like if you were talkin', just like you're talkin' right now. I mean, I think it's like that. It's not like I actually look at anybody when I hear 'em thinkin' or mean to. It just happens.

And sometimes it's like the world draws a picture of what they're thinkin'."

"I used to want to read people's minds."

"Why?"

He lobbed another stone and shrugged. "Don't know. Just thought it'd be cool—bein' able to do somethin' that nobody else can do."

"It's worse knowin' what people think."

"But saves you havin' to ask."

"I'd rather be saved from knowin'."

"I don't know," Hoyte answered defiantly. "It's not like it's ever gonna happen to me. Don't you ever not want to overthink somethin'?"

"I en't overthinkin' it," Cody turned on Hoyte. "I hear what people are thinkin'. For real. I hear 'em. And sometimes I see what they're thinkin'." Then she turned her gaze to the valley, adding almost resentfully. "I don't mean to."

4

Toward evening, and inasmuch as he could, Arvid helped Virginia pass the few remaining planks up to Hoyte and Cody. They nailed them across the roof joists and by evening they had pulled the tarp over the roof. The shell of the tiny house was finished. Sometime after that Drew's mother, Kati, showed up again. As quick as she saw Cody, she took the girl from her seat and knelt in front of her. "Let me see!" she said, and pushed aside Cody's hair to look at the scar on her forehead. "You'll have a scar."

"I know," said Cody.

Kati traced the scar with her fingertip. "As you grow older it won't be so noticeable."

"It's okay Gramma."

"It doesn't bother you? It doesn't make you sad?"

"No."

"Hey, Mom." Drew swung into the kitchen on crutches. "Thought you'd taken off?"

"I'm staying with Jessica until tomorrow." Kati stood. She glided to Drew, hesitated, unsure how to embrace her, then lightly placed her hands on Drew's shoulders. She lowered her voice. "Where's Virginia? Is she paying you to build her house? Has she paid you back?"

"She put my name on the deed."

"She gave you the property?"

"No, she added me to the deed, Mom. We're building the house together."

"But what about the money?" Kati asked almost plaintively. "What about building where your old house was?"

"With what, Mom?"

"She should just pay the money! If you can build a house here then you could build there."

"It's not like that Mom."

"You know I love you," said Kati. "Don't you think you would both be better off living in your own place?" Kati lowered her voice further. "Do you like Virginia? Why wouldn't you ask me to look after Cody?"

"Drop it, Mom."

"I'm just trying to understand why you wouldn't call your mother?"

"Drop it."

The older woman turned away, swiping at her hair with dissatisfaction. "If you let your hair grow out, it would be beautiful," she said to Cody. "It would look just like your great, great grandmother's hair. You have cheekbones like hers. You know you're not just descended from the Abenaki but the Iroquoi too."

Kati hoisted the shoulder bag she had carried with her onto the plywood kitchen counter. She opened the top, then turned to Drew. "I ran into Daryl's mother and father."

Drew maneuvered to the nearest chair. "Yeah, they stopped by, I wasn't here."

"I had to restrain myself," Kati said dramatically.

"Leave 'em alone, Mom."

"Leave them alone? I didn't have any interest in seeing either one of them, but there they were. What was I supposed to do? I told them you were recovering—and Cody; after what Daryl did to you both. You know they think you're lying. That man's mother—what's her name?"

"Marjorie," said Cody.

"Yes. Marjorie and Wayne." Kati echoed, exaggerating their names. "I suppose I'd expect more from her. I'm sure she knows better but does what her husband tells her to do. She's a good woman. Good women do what their men tell them to do, don't they Cody?"

"Jesus. Mom."

"If it was a good idea I'd do it," said Cody.

"Good for you," said Kati. "How else is a man supposed to know if he's got a good idea."

"Mom!"

"I'm sure Wayne would never suspect his son."

"It doesn't matter, Mom."

"Have they offered to help you? Have they done anything for Cody? No. Of course not." Then she abruptly asked, "How do you feel? Are you still in pain?"

"I'm okay," Drew answered.

"Yes. You're okay. You're on crutches, your ribs are broken and so is your back, but you're okay. You don't complain. I don't either. Your mother has her aches and pains but she doesn't complain. Why should we complain? We're women. Women never complain. But we take care of ourselves. I brought you some medication." Kati withdrew a tiny silk purse from her shoulder bag and put it on the counter. "I can get more."

"I don't want them, Mom."

"Drew," Kati lowered her voice, "of course you don't have to take them. I'm only leaving them here if you change your mind."

"You didn't tell Daryl's parents did you?"

"About what?"

"Mom!"

"Is that your rum?" Kati asked, noticing Virginia's rum next to the Coke cans.

"Mom, did you tell Daryl's parents?"

"Why shouldn't I?" Kati answered defiantly. "Why shouldn't I be allowed to take care of you?"

"For fuck's sake, Mom!" Drew awkwardly pushed herself upright and pulled her crutches under her.

Kati cinched her shoulder bag. "I think I shouldn't stay. But that's okay. You know I love you. And Cody, your great grandmother used to say: In life, you punch up or pinch down."

5

Drew sat on the edge of the bed, stroking Cody's forehead. "You put a roof on a house today."

"Almost."

"Nah. That was a roof, even if it was just a tarp. You're a good one."

"When did you know you wanted to be a carpenter?"

"First time I climbed a tree."

"Why then?"

"A tree builds its own house—living wood, babe. And you climb as high as you can go, until your heart's beating like crazy, and you see the world the way a tree sees it, bigger, deeper, windier; and it makes you want to fill up your little piece of earth like a tree, to make something beautiful, send down roots and live in it like you grew there."

"Did you ever build a house like that?"

"Not yet, babe."

"Why not?"

"Hey," Drew narrowed her eyes, "you think I'm gonna tell you dreams change? Nah. I'm gonna build us a house. When you're a kid, you're growin' up happens on the outside, but you never stop. You keep growin' on the inside once your outside is done. And you keep dreamin'."

"Did you have a lot of dreams?"

"More than I can count."

"D'ya think there are dreams you can't have?"

"Havin' a dream is like makin' a wish, babe. Be careful what you wish for. Sometimes havin' dreams is better than getting 'em."

"How do ya know which is which?"

"You don't."

Cody stared at the ceiling, dissatisfied. She crossed her hands behind her head. "Why'd you marry Dad?"

Drew sighed. "When I first met him, he was full of dreams. I liked that about him. Both of us were good with our hands. I was gonna be a builder and he was gonna be an engineer. My dad was always tinkerin' with cars and figured he and Daryl would go into business—start their own garage; but money was always burnin' a hole in your dad's pocket; and what he had wasn't good enough—not me, not you. That was why we were breakin' up." Drew gently wiped Cody's moist eyes with the back of her hand. "I'm sorry, babe. There's no sugar coatin' it. I could tell you he loved you but—" Drew swiped at her own eyes. "But that day— what he did—I can't square that with any kind of love."

Cody shook her head. "I'm okay."

"You're not okay. I know you're not. Not yet but you're gonna get better. And stronger too."

"So what's the point of dreamin' about something if it's something you can't have? If all it takes is somethin' happenin' and you can't ever have it?"

"I thought I was gonna make enough money to build a house for me and my little girl. Then we got stuck livin' in a basement. But then look what happened? My little girl's buildin' the house we're gonna live in. If you can't let your dreams change, then how are your dreams gonna change you?"

"Just wish everything wasn't always changin'."

"Safer not to have dreams, isn't it?"

Cody squinted at the ceiling. "Maybe."

"Wanna hear a story?"

Cody turned on her side, hands under her cheek. "Yeah."

"There was a little girl who dreamed of havin' the moon. She climbed on her roof, then climbed a mountain, but she couldn't ever reach the moon. She got all thin and hungry thinkin' 'bout the moon and thinner and thinner, just like the moon, until she was gonna disappear.

"One day when she was sittin' by the river she was visited by Coyote.

"'Coyote,' she said, 'you know the way to everything.'

"'I do, cousin.' Coyote circled the girl. 'What makes you out walkin' the world at midnight?'

"'I want the moon.'

"'The moon?'

"'But no matter how high I climb, I can't reach it.'

"'That's easy,' said Coyote, and sat on his haunches. 'That's 'cause you're lookin' in the wrong place.'

"'Coyote,' said the girl, 'don't tell me I can't have the moon. What's the moon good for, if you can't have it?'

"'Scratch my back,' he said, shaking his coat.

"The girl knelt and scratched Coyote and he was pleased. 'The trouble,' said Coyote, 'en't that you can't have it, but that you're lookin' in the wrong place. No matter how high you reach, you'll never reach the moon. That's 'cause the moon is a reflection. The real moon is in the river. Hold out your hands.'

"Having said that, he went to the river, opened his great jaws as wide as they would go, and carefully plucked the moon out of the river without breakin' it, and dropped it in the girl's hands. 'Now,' said Coyote, 'what are you gonna do with it?'

"'I don't know!' said the girl.

"'You always gotta know what you're gonna do with a dream once you catch it,' said Coyote, then he stretched the way coyotes stretch, rump first, then front legs as if already thinkin' on other things.

"The girl ran to her village. Once she was in her room, she hung the moon from the ceiling. All night she stared at it. But the next night she was bothered. No matter where she hung the moon, it didn't look right. She carried it on the end of a stick to light her way at night and she showed it off, but no one believed it was the moon. They just thought it was a lantern.

"The girl tried hangin' the moon in her window, but that wasn't right. She painted trees on her walls and gave them leaves. A cold wind blew through and carried off the leaves, blowin' them over her bed and under. The girl liked this and thought the moon was especially beautiful through the bare trees. She drew seeds on the trees and these were carried outside and into the world. They took root and the world was filled with trees, but she wasn't satisfied. She cut stars out of paper and hung them around the moon.

"Another wind blew through and carried off her stars, filling the whole sky with 'em, but the girl wasn't satisfied. She thought the moon oughta have more than a river, so she painted lakes on one side of her room and an ocean on the other. She hung the moon over the ocean and that very night the tide came in and poured out of her doors and windows until the world was full of ponds, lakes, and oceans.

"But this wasn't enough. One night she painted owls in the trees and their eyes were like two moons. She painted wolves and they sang songs to the moon. She painted toads and frogs on the floors and they plopped between her feet and hopped out the door. In the grasses between the trees she painted crickets. They crawled under her bed and sang all night. She folded pieces of paper into little white moths and they chased the moon until it was morning.

"And after all this she still wasn't happy."

"You'd think she'd be happy by now," said Cody.

"She wasn't. One night someone appeared in the trees of her wall, at first like a black smudge but that turned into a black bird with two black eyes. The girl looked closer, because she hadn't drawn it, and she said, 'Who are you?'

"Crow leapt from the wall with a hop and toss of wings. 'You oughtn't know what Coyote knows,' said Crow.

"'Who told you?'

"'Just know,' said Crow. 'Just know,' then flew off. The girl ran to the window, but Crow was too dark and too quick to see.

"And then what else could she do but hang the moon from her ceiling? Night after night she stared at it but havin' the moon didn't make her happy; not the trees, not the stars, the crickets, or the moths. She was lyin' in bed and she turned and made a black smudge on the wall, then gave it black eyes and black feet; and then just like that Crow hopped into her room."

"Crow hopped 'round lookin' at this and that and said to her: 'You aren't supposed to have the moon.'

"'How do you know?' asked the girl.

"'Just know.' said Crow. 'Just know'

"'So who is?'

"'Follow me and I'll show,' said Crow.

"And so the girl put the moon on the end of her stick and followed Crow to the top of a hill. And then Crow leapt into the air, plucked the moon from the girl's stick, and placed it like a button in the middle of the sky. At first the girl was very angry with Crow but gradually decided it looked more beautiful than ever. Crow said, 'Dreams are for sharing.'"

6

Drew had been wearing skirts and dresses since coming home with a cast. Today, wincing as she did so, she slipped on the most oversized carpenter pants she owned, slipped her hammer into a belt loop, and put on her black leather jacket. That suited her better. Her arms, armpits, shoulders, and hands were sore with using crutches, but she bit her lip and met Virginia outside at her old truck.

"Do you need help getting in?"

"Give me a minute." Drew backed against the high passenger seat, braced herself by the palms of her hand, and pushed herself up and inside. A needle of pain stabbed her ribs. "Jesus, fuck!" she grimaced. She gingerly swung into the seat. "I'm okay. Put the crutches in the back, can you?"

Virginia threw them in and they drove down to Brookway. Drew saw the damage for the first time: the gouged banks, the new-piled rocks, stones and boulders drying and bone-white in the brooks and riverbeds, the limbs of fallen trees dangling in the uppermost branches of other trees. As they descended from the tight meanderings of the mountain into the broader valley, the rivers had left behind swaths of white and yellow sand.

Here and there Drew asked Virginia to slow down, letting cars go by. "That's Joe Freyer's place," she said at one stretch of road and pointed to a barn where the brook had found a new bed to follow. But what Drew noticed most of all were dozens of excavators belly deep in brooks and waterways. The water had taken swipes out of embankments and had undermined bridges. It was decided that the quickest way to put the state back together was to let excavators in the water and then you might have thought every Vermonter's second car was an excavator. "He's been wantin' to do that for years," said Drew, seeing Freyer's own excavator up to its slew ring in water. "And up to no good."

Their first stop was Drew's old house. There were just three sides of the cellar hole. All that was left was the shed Drew and Cody had built. The lower two rows of clapboards showed the rise of the muddy waters. Drew turned in her seat and slid out onto her good foot. She made little hops toward the truck bed, tried to reach for her crutches, flinching when the truck's bedside pressed into her ribs.

Virginia got them for her. Then they both went to the shed's side door, white with layers of cracked and flaking paint. There was a padlock through a hasp and staple to keep it locked. Drew pulled the hammer from her pants and handed it to Virginia. "Do it."

"What?"

"I don't have a key. Fuck knows where the key is." Then she smiled. "Aim for the staple and lock both." Drew moved backwards three or four steps on her crutches. She laughed at Virginia's first swing. "Jesus, we're gonna be here all day."

"Well, I don't want to ruin it."

"Yeah ya do! You got a hammer, not a key."

"I've never broken into anything in my life!"

"Never too late to start."

"Well, I need more than a hammer, don't I?"

"That's all you need. All this stuff is just decorative anyway."

"Well, okay, stand back then."

"And hit it harder."

"Oh for God's sake, Drew." Virginia planted her feet and took another swing. The hammer glanced off the staple.

"Harder."

Virginia swung again, flinching as the hammer struck, but didn't stop until the rusty heads of the staple's screws began to tear from the wood.

"Now use the claws to pry it out," instructed Drew.

Bearing her weight on the hammer, she whooped with surprise when the staple abruptly gave way. Drew pivoted to the door and pulled it open. The inside, like the outside, showed flooding. That wasn't enough to damage the portable generator or any of the old power tools still hanging on a peg board above the work bench or arranged on shelves. There were buckets of nails and screws, wire, sandpaper, old boards and two-by-fours standing on end in the corner or stacked in the collar ties. Several boxes that had been left on the floor had peeled into collapsed shards of cardboard. Drew studied it all without saying a word or without going in, then finally, "Mind throwing some stuff in the back of the truck?"

"Well, do we have a wheelbarrow?"

Drew swung and gestured with a crutch toward the river. The wheelbarrow that had once leaned by the bulkhead doors of the vanished house was all that was left, nose first in the mud at the edge of the gouged earth, as though only a little more rain might topple it into the river.

7

"Before you go to class, we need you to stop by Principal Reynard's office." Mrs. Levitt's hand was on Cody's shoulder. She walked half behind Cody, stooping and smiling as if to put her at ease. Her high-heeled shoes clacked on the hallway's linoleum floor. Then Mrs. Levitt sailed past her on the way to another chore.

Cody turned back the way she'd come. Reynard's office was next to the school's main entrance. The first doorway led past Levitt's desk on the left and the second into Reynard's office, a room with one desk that faced the door, chairs, bookshelves, and dark wood paneling. He smiled, seeing her, leaned back in the desk chair and gestured for her to sit. He was a younger man with a round face and heavy jaw. His eyes and hair were brown and his habit was to stand with legs slightly apart, as though with a kind of impatient athleticism. Cody swung her satchel to the floor.

"How are you?" he asked.

"Okay."

"And your mom?"

"She's okay."

"I know you've been through a lot," he said, still leaning in his chair, "both of you."

Cody shrugged.

"Are you excited to be back in school?" He swiped at his forehead. Cody instinctively touched the scar above her eyebrow.

"It's okay."

"Okay," he straightened, elbows on the desk, hands clasped before him. "You probably know why I asked you in."

"Because of Olivia?"

"That's right."

Cody waited for the follow up.

"I read the article in the New York Times," he said, then waited again. When Cody still didn't volunteer anything he added: "That was quite the write-up."

"I didn't read it."

"So, funny thing is—I'll be honest with you Cody; you think about all the things that can happen in a school and you make plans and over the years you develop solutions. Mostly the problems are cliques and bullying. But a student who reads minds?" Reynard looked at Cody expectantly. "That's a first."

"I don't mean to."

"You don't mean to?" Reynard raised his eyebrows. He sniffed, rubbed his nose. "You know, normally, I would just check in, ask how things are going." Reynard paused again. "You've become a bit of a local celebrity. The New York Times says you predicted Irene would hit and it did."

"I didn't start it," said Cody, eyes welling.

"I'm not saying you did."

"And I didn't mean to read her mind, it just happened."

"Yeah, see, that's where I'm having trouble."

"With what?"

"Maybe you should tone that down."

"Tone what down?"

"Reading minds."

"I can't."

"Look," Reynard leaned forward, "I'm on your side. You're not being punished." He considered Cody for another moment. "Can you read my mind? I'll think of a number. Can you tell me what it is?"

"It doesn't work that way."

"How does it work?"

"When I don't expect it." Cody's heart raced. "It just happens when it happens. I don't mean it to."

"Did you tell her you read her mind?"

"No."

He spread his fingers as if disbelieving "She says you did. Cody, I'm not going to say I don't believe you—"

"But you don't."

"Cody, I'm not—"

"Why does she care anyway?"

"It disrupted the class."

"Did you tell her you didn't believe her too?"

"Cody—"

"Why not?"

Reynard's face reddened. "Cody, why we're here is to prevent another disruption like this. It's only the first week of school. We've all had a rough end of summer. Let's see how the next few days go, and if you need to talk about anything at all, I'd encourage you to visit Mrs. Santoff. Okay?"

"Okay," said Cody, her fists tight.

8

"You don't look so good," said Virginia.

"I'm okay," Drew answered, but she was pale and sweating. "Just carsick."

"Maybe we should go back?"

"I'll be okay." Drew rolled down the truck window and leaned into the wind. They pulled into the Brookway Co-op. Drew didn't get out at first though Virginia waited with Drew's crutches. When she finally slid out of the truck with one hand on the door, she immediately bent over as though she were going to throw up. Virginia wanted to speak but waited. Drew slowly straightened and took the crutches but they didn't make it to the store before a woman and a younger man stopped them, holding flowers.

"Do you believe in God?" asked the woman.

"Are you for real?" Drew almost laughed.

"Okay," the man smiled. "Okay, I'll take that for a yes. What kind of work do you do?"

"Who are you?"

"Friends," said the woman.

"Now's really not a good time for friends."

"There's no time that's not a good time for God," said the woman. "We'd just like to talk to you about God. Do you have a phone number?"

"Why? Is God on a plan?" Drew asked dryly.

"Okay, what do you think it takes for somebody to get to heaven?" asked the man.

"Jesus, I don't know," Drew rolled her eyes, "a full tank?"

"Where are you from?" asked Virginia.

"We're from Fayetteville, North Carolina, miss," answered the woman.

"Fayetteville?" asked Drew.

"That's right, ma'am."

"Why did you come up here?"

"To spread the word of God."

"No," Drew shook her head and skipped forward on her crutches. "Why *here*?"

"Well, because it seemed like our neighbors up north could use a hand."

"A hand with what?"

The woman touched Drew's hand. "Grace means God sending His only Son into hell to reconcile us with God in heaven. The true prophet puts Jesus at the center of his teachings. The false prophet keeps Him at the margins. The false prophet invents stories. He tells stories he's made up. The true prophet appeals to the scripture. The false prophet tells people what they want to hear; condemning them in their false believing."

"God damn you," Drew stiffened, knuckles turning white around the crutches. "She's just a girl!"

"Thank you," said Virginia nervously, placing herself between Drew and the couple but Drew hobbled around her. The man and woman backed away, smiling uncomfortably.

"I know where you're fucking from," Drew said without looking at Virginia. "You know Marjorie and Wayne? The fuck you don't! Tell them I don't ever want them anywhere near my daughter. You fucking tell them that!"

"Who?" asked the woman.

"You're from the same fucking church!"

"We're so sorry—" said the woman.

"The fuck you are," spat Drew.

"Drew—" Virginia tried to intercede, wanting to touch Drew, but hesitant.

"She's just a girl! God damnit. And you know what? Her daddy tried to murder her. Fucking murder her! He drove us off a goddamn bridge doin' eighty. And here you are—What the fuck are you doin' here? Prophets? What in fuck's name does my daughter have to do with prophets? She did the only thing that made sense. She wanted to help people."

"I'm sure it's only a misunderstanding," said the man. "We'd be happy to hear your testimony—"

"Fuck your testimony!" Drew shouted. She spun around, turning her back on the man and woman, her knuckles white on the crutches. She tried to catch her breath as if she were going to throw up.

"Maybe now's not a good time—" Virginia began.

Drew angrily turned. "No! No time is the best time. You tell Marjorie and Wayne, I swear to God, you tell Marjorie and Wayne to go fuck themselves. I will kick your asses! That's my daughter! I will fucking kick your asses—" Drew lost her balance. Virginia hurriedly stepped in.

The co-op's manager, having heard the shouting, rushed out and stood between them. "Look, I don't know what's going on here." He turned to the young man and woman. "We have a no soliciting policy here. I have to ask you to leave. Please." Then he turned to Drew, hesitating before he spoke. "Look— I'm so sorry but I can't have shouting like this right outside the store. So if I could—"

"Move!" Drew shoved past the manager and hurried to the adjacent bushes. She threw up in the mulch. She gave a sharp cry of pain as the heaving squeezed her ribs.

"Should I call 9-1-1?" he asked, glancing at Drew and then at Virginia. "Does she need a doctor?"

"No," said Drew, spitting into the mulch. "I just got carsick."

"You have goosebumps," said Virginia quietly.

"I'll be okay."

"It's not okay."

"I'm fine. Just help me up."

"Well I don't know, are you done?" Virginia asked.

"What do you mean, am I done?"

"I wasn't sure if you were going to attack those two?"

"What if I did?"

"You can't just go after people like that," said Virginia. "If you do, well, you're going to end up arrested and I'm going to end up looking after Cody again."

"At least I'm doing something."

"What does that mean?"

"All you do is mope and—and—moon and mope and for what? So you ran to Vermont and guess what?—there wasn't a vacation home waiting for you? Well cry me a goddamn river!"

"And what's this?" Virginia waved at the departing couple. "Pick a fight? Well you know, I was an emergency room nurse. Yes, me! I saw women just like you, terrible things done to them, picking fights with the world, and who do you think won? I just think—I think you're an angry woman. You have every right to be, but God knows don't we all? Cody doesn't need an angry mother—"

"Let me ask you something," Drew pressed forward on her crutches. "What has all this moping and mooning gotten you? Huh?"

"And what does feeling sorry for yourself get you?"

"Me?"

"Yes!" said Virginia. "Look at you! You're throwing up in a parking lot! You're pale as a ghost and—well—I've seen this. There's something you're not telling me!"

Drew jammed her lips together before hunching on her crutches. "I don't feel sorry for myself."

"If you had someone to talk to?"

"That was all about Cody!" Drew jabbed her crutches into the parking lot for emphasis. "I don't need a fucking shrink!"

"Well," Virginia answered dramatically, "all I can say is if you want to take care of Cody then maybe you'd better start taking care of yourself."

Drew's jaws clenched. She shouldered past Virginia and the manager. "I don't feel sorry for myself."

"Look, maybe now's not the day—"

"I didn't get your name?" Virginia asked, interrupting the manager.

"Phil Flannagan."

"We'll be fine, Phil," said Virginia.

"What she said," added Drew. "We'll be fine."

"Oh," remarked the flustered manager. "Oh! You're *that* girl's mother!"

"Yeah, I'm *that girl's* mother," said Drew, going into the store.

9

Cody and Hoyte walked to Soot Tabor's after school. Soot Tabor's house was several backyards away, a field, a dip through a copse of woods, a run along the river, then a steep slope up into Tabor's neighborhood. They had just started their walk between two houses, downhill along a barn, dragging their palms over the rough, dry, granite of the foundation. Autumn's early leaves, always the maple, were already cracking underfoot.

"I got called into the principal's office," said Cody.

"'Cause of Olivia?"

"Yeah."

"You didn't get into trouble for that, did you?"

"He wants me to see Mrs. Santoff."

"Did he say that?"

"No, but it's what he meant."

"She's like a psychiatrist or something."

"I don't know. Maybe."

"'Cause he thinks you're crazy."

"'Cause he thinks I'm hot-headed," said Cody under her breath.

"Hot-headed makes you crazy," Hoyte added with a smile. He jumped over a muddy divot in the path. Cody put her steps in his and jumped just the same. She didn't like to go this way. She used to have a friend that lived in the same neighborhood and this stretch of path that passed behind houses and was invisible to the street, was where the older boys liked to meet after school. She hadn't seen them here but knew they did. She had seen them elsewhere, lean, spitting, hands loosely in the pockets of their jeans, watching without being seen as watching, smiling at something said. She didn't know. The woods might as well have been theirs. But Hoyte paid no mind, even when they passed by three boys who'd stopped ahead of them, one with his back against a tree.

The boy gave a quick nod, jaw jutting, tongue sliding under his lip as if he'd packed snuff. "Hey, Hoyte. What's up?"

"Nothin'. You?"

The boy glanced at Cody, with a kind of nervousness, as if deciding how to answer, "Nothin'."

Hoyte glanced at Cody, then back at the boy. "What?"

"Nothin'," he said.

"I'm not gonna read your mind," said Cody.

The boy gazed at her. "Could ya?"

"Not on purpose."

"Could ya if you wanted to?"

"No."

The boy's stare turned into a crooked smile. "Heard you read Olivia's mind. Must not of been much to read." The other boys laughed. "Heard she went runnin'."

Cody glanced at Hoyte. "Yeah."

"Hey, that was messed up, what your dad did. That was really messed up." The other boys nodded in assent.

"I'm okay."

One of the other boys glanced at Cody's forehead. "That from the crash?"

"Yeah."

"How's your mom?"

"She's gotta use crutches and can't work."

The boy nodded as if with an exchange of earned understanding they had all tasted a bitterness which became a bond. Then another of the boys said something and the conversation moved on. Hoyte said 'Later' and the others answered likewise.

"C'mon," said Hoyte.

Cody followed and they took the path sidelong down a steep embankment that leveled off alongside the river.

"Do you know them?"

"Yeah, that was just Jerry, Roy, and Mike," Hoyte said almost indifferently, then asked: "So, could he make you?"

"Make me what?"

"See a shrink?"

Cody lifted the straps of her slipping backpack. "If it happens again I think he'd make me."

"Can he do that?"

"I don't know."

"I don't think he can; not unless your mom said it was okay."

When Cody didn't answer Hoyte turned and saw that tears streamed down her cheeks. He didn't know what to say, but to ask the question he already knew the answer to: "You okay?"

Cody didn't answer. She didn't look at him. She veered off the path, walking deliberately, then spun and abruptly sat with her back to a tree, in a nook that was like a seat—a root and leaves in a small bank. She stared straight ahead, the tears unabated. Hoyte shifted nervously, ill at ease, uncertain of what to do. He shrugged off his backpack and sat next to her without touching her. She began to sob and Hoyte fidgeted. "Olivia's not worth cryin' over," he said.

"I don't care about her," Cody said darkly, squeezing the words through clenched teeth.

Hoyte stared at his feet and then slowly, awkwardly, put his arm around her shoulder. She leaned against him, shaking as she recovered, then took a deep breath and straightened. She wiped at her tears with the back of her wrists. "My dad used to say that if anybody ever hurt me— Messed with me—" But she burst into tears again, stomach heaving before she could finish. She gripped her pants tightly, twisting them.

"What'd he say?"

"He tried to kill me, Hoyte!"

Hoyte wiped his own eyes and said nothing, letting Cody's sobbing ebb and her breathing and the intermittent shudders quiet. They sat that way for a while, saying nothing. Cody squeezed her eyes shut and leaned forward as though in pain.

"You gonna be okay?"

"My head hurts."

The wind every so often rattled through the tree's canopy. Momentary windows of daylight slipped across the forest floor. Cody's nose was running. She swiped it with the sleeve of her shirt, then her eyes with the same sleeve.

"I bet your mom would kick anybody's ass."

"She's on crutches, Hoyte."

"She'd kick their asses with crutches."

Cody leaned over and started to draw circles in the dirt between her feet. "Where's your mom?"

"I don't know."

"Did your parents get a divorce?"

"No."

"Did she just leave?"

"Wanna know somethin' I've never told anybody?"

"Sure."

"My dad's not my dad."

Cody turned, her wet hair falling over her eyes and lips. "Why do you call him your dad? Are you adopted?"

"Yeah."

"So—do you—do you, like, remember your mom and dad?"

Hoyte shook his head. "My dad thinks they were killed. He adopted me. He wasn't supposed to and they weren't supposed to let him, but he did it anyways. He says I was in an orphanage."

"Why'd he adopt you?"

Hoyte smiled, drawing circles between his feet too. "He said I smiled when I saw him. Said it was the first time they'd ever seen me smile."

"I bet you were pretty unhappy."

Hoyte shrugged. "I don't remember much."

"Have you ever wondered who your real parents were?"

"Yeah."

Both were silent again, then Cody took a deep breath, somehow comforted by Hoyte's story. "We should probably get goin'."

"You sure?"

"Yeah," she adjusted her backpack. The path was gone which used to go along the river. A bed of fine sand and silt, like a desert, paused under the trees, had buried or washed away the undergrowth. There were piles of stones elsewhere, sun-dried greys, whites, and browns, and rounded into ovals. The bank that used to be a thick hedge of undergrowth—fir, birch, and spindly white pine—was gone and a new bank was carved out in its place, making the river wider. Hoyte and Cody walked to the river's water, finally returned to a shallow meandering. An axle and hub, the rusted bones of a model-T, stuck out of the dredged bank. Cody hopped onto an island of stones where she could pick among them. She found a fist-sized piece of obsidian, the remnants of a long vanished iron mill.

"We should come back," said Hoyte.

"It musta' dug up stuff from a thousand years ago," said Cody, studying each find as if it hinted at a greater discovery. Finally she pocketed two stones and leapt back to the bank. From there the path wound through a brace of smaller ironwood trees, then up the steep slope to Soot's neighborhood. They found her kneeling in front of her house, pulling weeds from a flowerbed.

"There you are!" she said. She shook the dirt from her fingers and took Cody into a tight hug. "How are you, sweetie?"

"Okay," said Cody. "Everybody asks that."

"I suppose they do," said Soot. "Follow me," she said, then asked: "How's Ratter?"

"Hasn't caught any mice yet," said Cody.

"She will."

"I'll bet she's scared 'em off though," said Hoyte.

"Ever painted?" Soot asked as she rounded the back corner of the house. "All I need you two to do is to scrape the door and paint it."

"What color?" asked Cody.

"Whatever you want, sweetie."

Then Soot went inside, returned with two scrapers, a broom, and a washcloth. She knelt in front of Cody. "Hold still." She wiped Cody's face with the washcloth. If it had been her mother, Cody wouldn't have stood for it—wiping her face as if she were still five. But for Soot, Cody stood subdued until she set the washcloth aside. She brushed Cody's hair behind her ears with the tips of her fingers. "That's better. Now you don't look as if your heart was broken."

Cody touched her scar.

"Can't clean that up," said Soot. "Life is like that. The older you get, the more you wear your heartbreaks and joys like an old coat. You just got started a little early. You need your face wiped, Hoyte?"

"No, ma'am!"

Cody gave Hoyte a sidelong glance, then impatiently took one of the scrapers from Soot. She shrugged off her backpack. "You gonna help scrape or not?"

Some twenty minutes later, when they were just about done, George Barstowe rounded the corner. He adjusted his hat and tugged at his pants seeing Cody and Hoyte. "How are ya all comin' along up there, Cody?"

"We're startin' to build."

"That so? Good to hear it."

"Walls are up and we got a roof up," added Hoyte.

"A roof?" said Barstowe. "Already?"

"Just a tarp," said Cody.

"Is Drew already puttin' up that house?"

"No," said Cody, "she's tellin' us how to do it."

"That's the right way to do it," said Barstowe. "Puttin' other people to work. And how's 'bout Virginia. How's she takin' to housebuildin'? Hasn't given herself a black thumb has she?"

"Don't think she likes it," said Cody.

"Cody's mom would be doin' the buildin' if she could," said Hoyte.

"I don't doubt it," said Barstowe. "Say hello to Virginia for me and now you wouldn't know where Soot's got to?"

"I'm in here!" Soot called from the kitchen. She straightaway invited Barstowe, Hoyte, and Cody inside for lemonade. They sat at the kitchen table and talked about the flood. Seemed there were roads, houses, and bridges lost in every town. Talk of disaster inevitably led to man's ingratitude. Barstowe leaned back in his chair. The joinery creaked. He wiped his stubby fingers on his pants and considered Cody. "Don't you worry none 'bout what people think of you. You're not the first prognosticator that's lived in Brookway. There was a gal named Lavinia Farnagle when I was a youngster. Married to Umber Farnagle. How that came about is a hell of a story." And then, because Barstowe was in an expansive mood, he leaned forward, elbows on the table, and told the story of Lavinia and Umber Farnagle. It went something like this:

'Round about when Umber Farnagle was still a young man and the great orchard of life lay before him, he visited Lavinia Moody, a noted psychic, prognosticator, and palm reader. Lavinia's income had fallen off, though not because of her prognosticating. The trouble was that Lavinia never set out to be a fortune teller. Lavinia originally took her income from jams and preserves; wines made of apple and rhubarb; and from soaps she sold to tourists.

One morning, after grousing that hers was no way to make a living and that every choice she'd ever made was the wrong one, she announced that what the world sorely needed was competent fortune tellers. Any fool with hindsight can dice tomatoes, but tell the future and that's a dish worth serving. But Lavinia gave no quarter to fortune tellers. It was only when Pracilla Granger insisted on reading Lavinia's cards that Lavinia's future changed.

Pracilla got about halfway through the reading when Lavinia decided any fool could shuffle a deck. She scooped up the cards, shuffled them, and proceeded to tell Pracilla's fortune. Lavinia made no wild guesses but took her inspiration from whatever card turned up, the way a practiced swindler reads a mark. And yes, once Lavinia had sorted her last card, she took an authorial satisfaction in the elaborate narrative she had constructed.

Lavinia would have thought nothing more of the matter but that the events in Pracilla's life unfolded just as Lavinia predicted. Word spread and it wasn't a week before Lavinia helped to avert several delicate crises that might have tarnished the otherwise spotless moral fabric of her clientele.

Soon enough Lavinia no longer made wine or soap. And though Lavinia remained invincibly dismissive of fortune telling, she nevertheless generously raised her rates in recognition of her talents. The trouble was that she had a fabulist's gift for fortune telling which made her predictions recklessly accurate.

Fortune telling is the art of subterfuge. Call it a knot in human nature, but tell any man or woman how the future is going to sugar off and they'll make a point of doing the opposite. Of course, doing the opposite sometimes lands you in the very acre you were trying to avoid. The trouble, as always, is in knowing which contrary is the right one.

So it was that townspeople began to wonder if there was any point to avoiding the future if the future was unavoidable. Lavinia decided what she needed to do was make a prediction so outlandish it couldn't possibly come true. And it just so happened that this was the day Umber Farnagle arrived for his reading. Umber was not accounted a particularly handsome man. He was red-haired, with a nose like a carpenter's square, and an Adam's apple the size of a block plane.

But there's no accounting for taste. Lavinia was stricken by the sight of him. The same can't be said for Umber, who sat before a smallish woman his own age, her flat brunette hair parted in the middle and drawn back with puritan zeal. Lavinia's good sense fled the sprigs and forks of her reason like a rattled chickadee. She concocted a future for Umber that was as luridly unreasonable as it was hopeful.

Now it must be said that the love of fishing among boys is surely nature's way of preparing men for the conversation of women. A woman's conversation is a beautiful thing that begins in the smallest of rills, descends among lilies and cattails, and only gradually follows the course of cause and effect into the pond of her conclusion, where it grows into a magnificent fish if only the man is patient enough to keep his hook in the water. But if his mind impatiently wanders and if he misses the nibbling at his hook, he might as well reel in his line and fish another day for all the good casting will do.

Umber Farnagle was not that fisherman. His mind wandered. He fussed and fidgeted as Lavinia unraveled her prognostication so that all he heard was a description of a house, a carefully appointed and detailed description, and the promise that buried beneath it was a treasure beyond compare, beggaring description, such that Umber Farnagle would envy no man their riches.

Sure enough, in the months that followed, and much to Lavinia's despair, Umber found a house that matched her description to the last nail. The house had comfortably settled into its wooded acre and had been home to generations of men and women. And children too, whose toys had fallen into the nooks and crannies of its walls and floors like wistful treasures.

But the house had seen nothing like Umber Farnagle. Umber at once took to the cellar like an old maid poking under the bed. At first the house paid no mind. Each man had had his own peculiarities and no harm had come of it. The digging was on and off for the next month. Lavinia brought pies, jams, and preserves with freshly baked loaves of bread. She might have thought they were swinging on the same fence but Umber treated Lavinia's efforts as a selfless gesture.

Determined to save Umber from his own foolishness, Lavinia surprised him one morning by appearing in his basement, having put on her skimpiest and most fetching outfit, which in Vermont means taking off your coat. The great treasure for which Umber had been searching was revealed to him—a helpmate; and so he passed her a shovel.

Lavinia didn't complain. Some part of the atheist in her softened on the notion of karma, being that it was she who had put the fever in him. She helped him dig until, by day's end, she felt that whatever guilt she shared in the project had been expiated. A sweaty and besmirched woman, she thrust the business end of the shovel into the dirt and told him there was no treasure, that she'd only meant to make an example of him, and that if he meant to waste any more time plowing the cellar then good luck and good riddance.

Umber decided if that's the way she felt, then he'd take the treasure for himself. But by this time Umber had begun to undermine the patience of the house. Though he'd put up makeshift blocking, the old house let him know its tolerance was just about used up. Nails popped. Doors whined. Floors creaked.

The lantern in this or that room swung in warning. Umber paid no mind. He kept at his digging until, with a dusty and cobwebbed harumph, the old cape put its foot down. Umber's blocking toppled. One corner after another collapsed like stacked dominoes. The house sighed into a new and peaceful repose with Umber stuck beneath it.

It was about a week later that Lavinia discovered Umber howling like a masterless dog. She tried to open the trap door, the only way in and out, but it might as well have been fixed with barn nails. She hurried back to town and soon enough found a dozen or so men, far in excess of what was needed; but in light of what was considered a normal day, she could have emptied the town.

Umber was rescued—a poor, thinned, and bedraggled man. The next day's headline proclaimed: Umber Farnagle Discovered Buried Beneath his House. And it was in reading that headline that the truth of Lavinia's prognostication landed on Umber with all the weight of another house. He, Umber Farnagle, was the treasure that he'd been looking for, the treasure beyond compare, beggaring description, that, buried under the very house Lavinia predicted, was of greater worth to him than any of the riches possessed by man or woman.

Umber went straight to Lavinia and within the month they were married. Lavinia put her tarot cards in the attic and never looked at them again. She took up dowsing instead, despite considering the field fit only for shysters and swindlers. And as you'd expect, her skill at dowsing was legendary.

After Barstowe was done with his story, he leaned back, palms on thighs and elbows wide. "See," he said, "just 'cause you see the future don't mean you changed nothin'. But now we got folk runnin' 'round actin' like it's them and them alone knows what's in God's kitchen. See now, if you ask me, the whole problem started when we was told Man was made in God's image. And that got people thinkin' that if they looked like God, then God must look like them. Why if Joe Samley don't like ham on Tuesday, then God don't like ham on Tuesday. And if Fetter Hankins don't like the look of boys and girls kissin' each other, then God must not like it neither. And if Lucy Jenkins don't like gals runnin' 'round with their belly buttons showin' on a hot summer's day, why God must not like it neither. And when you get enough people thinkin' the same thing, then it must be 'cause God wanted 'em to make a religion of it. And what's worse than a buncha people thinkin' God looks and thinks like them? Now, see, I'll tell ya who God looks like. God looks like me, you, and every man or woman alive or who ever lived; and it don't matter what makes 'em dance, what color their skin is, who they kiss, or what religion they call themselves. You want to know what God looks like, then you gotta look at everybody, not just the good-lookin' ones, or the ones whose got money, but the ones who's been burnt, ain't doin' so well, could use a hand; and it isn't just what's on the outside. You want to know what God thinks, then it isn't just the ones preachin', or them physicists, or any of 'em that talk loudest, but along comes a little girl from Brookway and she's in God's image and God's in her image. Now," Barstowe surveyed the table magisterially, "I'll tell ya somethin' just between us all, bein' baked proper in the local oven, as the sayin' goes. God's a New Englander. You ask me how I know? I'll tell ya. God don't mind nobody's business but his own. When's the last time you saw God walkin' 'round mindin' other people's business? Tellin 'em when to shut their cows in, when to cut the grass, and what not. Don't mind His and He won't mind yours. That's what makes God a good Vermonter. He's got a wall between us and Him and makes us good neighbors. And as for mindin' God's business—" Barstowe's bulk leaned toward Cody with a creaking of wood. "If God didn't want ya to know what you know'd, then God knows ya wouldn'ta know'd it."

10

After Virginia picked up Cody, and after Hoyte had gone off, she made Cody a grilled cheese sandwich and poured her a glass of orange juice. Not wanting to offend, Cody drank the orange juice and then a second glass full before mentioning that her mother didn't let her drink orange juice.

"Why on earth not?" asked Virginia.

"She says it's mostly sugar."

"What about apple juice?"

"Same."

"Grape juice?"

"She let me have wine once."

"Well if you can't have juices, then what?"

"Cider."

"Well, cider is full of sugar just like apple juice!"

Cody shrugged.

"Well I don't dare give you any more."

"I won't tell."

"With your mother's temper I should hope not."

"Why?" Cody perked up.

"She said I'm mopey."

"That's nothin'. You should hear things she says 'bout other people."

"Do you think I'm mopey? Have I been mopey? She said I moon and I mope."

"Yeah, you have been kinda mopin' sometimes."

Virginia sighed. "Am I really that bad?"

"Seems like more often than not you wanna be anywhere but here."

Virginia leaned with an elbow on the table, her chin on the heel of her palm, and gazed at Cody. "Fine."

"It's just Mom." Cody grinned despite herself. "Stuff works her up sometimes."

"I'd say."

"What'd she do?" Cody leaned forward.

"Well, I don't know if I should say, but there was a couple from a church, I don't know which church, and I don't know if it's what they meant, I mean—they weren't being awful about it— but they were handing out flyers and your mother thought the flyers were about you."

"Prob'ly. What'd she do?"

"As much as crutches let her."

"She get mad?"

"And how—the store manager had to come out to put a stop to it."

"It was about me."

"Well I don't know," said Virginia. "All I can tell you is that they were handing out flyers and warning about false prophets—"

Cody thrust herself back in her seat, then leaned forward again. "What'd Mom say?"

"Well, as you Vermonters like to say: some women aren't all maple sugar."

Another smile, too shy for Virginia to notice, visited Cody's expression. When it was time for bed, she found Ratter and took the kitten with her to her mother's bed. Then, without waking her, Cody quietly crawled into bed, under the sheets, and under her mother's arm. Drew let Cody think that she hadn't woken her.

Chapter 11

September is at ease with the loss of summer. Cooler winds descend from the north and rain rinses the humidity from the air. The see-saw calls of the chickadees are up and gone. The highway medians that were riotous with wildflower have been mown, and the wild grasses make no hurry to return. The tassels left standing take their color from the sun's yellow decline. If because there aren't that many choices a tree can make, their colors arrive in a colloquy of disagreement—first to wayward limbs, then by disparate opinion to one tree or another, and then before long by brittle winds descending into the valley's quilt-work fields, rivers, and towns. Agreement may last just a day or two before a northerly gale sends the season scattered earthward. The vines of the roadside farm lose their vigor, and the fattened pumpkins float above them. Sunning bales of hay dust the air with the odor of their cutting while the tractors that barked and thrummed shine quietly. On days like these, afloat with clouds in their blue theater, the laborer working in the weather thinks there's no better work. September is the month for apples, bees crowding the cider press, and the slow procession of stars who visit evening earlier and earlier.

1

There are disagreements that rise above mere words. Drew and Virginia were having such a disagreement. Cody moved between them like a mouse. Virginia had gone outside, up the slope, and sat with a book and tea in the wide room of the tiny house. Drew was in the makeshift kitchen and when Cody had finally woken, stretching and rubbing her eyes, her mother pushed herself upright onto her crutches and offered to fry her some eggs. Her balance was still precarious.

"I can do it."

"I'll do it," said Drew with a menacing generosity.

"Just trying to help."

"Hey. That's really sweet but right now I don't need anybody feelin' sorry for me. I can manage two eggs. Over easy or hard?"

"I wasn't feelin' sorry for you."

"Good." Drew turned with one egg still in her hand. "And you know what else I don't like?"

"Cookin' eggs?"

"People wastin' their time feelin' sorry for themselves."

"I'm not," Cody shrank. "I don't."

Drew exhaled with frustration. "Not you. Jesus. Not you, Cody. Me. You think I feel sorry for myself?"

Cody shrugged. "It's not like you don't have reason."

"It doesn't matter if I have reason." Drew turned and cracked an egg over the pan and hot plate. "Everybody's got reason to feel sorry for themselves. What good does it do?" She turned again. "I don't feel sorry for myself."

"Didn't say you did."

"I know you didn't." Drew turned. "But do I act like I've been feelin' sorry for myself?"

"No."

"Don't be so defensive."

"Can't help it."

"Do you want salt?"

"Okay."

"Yes or no."

"Yes."

"If anybody ever tried to make a living out of self-pity, it was my dad. There was nothing wasn't a cross for him to bear. He used to joke it was me who made him a whiskey drinker. He'd drink and start kickin' my ass 'cause he was drinkin'."

"Least he didn't try to kill you," said Cody under her breath. But Drew heard her. She turned off the hot plate and swung to the chair opposite Cody. She winced as she sat, leaning back with a long exhalation.

"Yeah," she said. "Maybe I am feelin' sorry for myself."

Cody leaned, elbows on the table, arms crossed and balanced on the edge of the chair. "Does it still hurt a lot?"

"Yeah."

"I still get headaches."

"You were banged up pretty good, babe."

"Mostly 'cause I'm hungry."

"Smartass. Get your own fucking egg."

Cody popped out of her seat, stood on her tiptoes for a plate, and returned with the fried egg and a fork.

"But I'm nothin' like Virginia," said Drew. "Jesus, all she does is moon and mope. Like, how can you have no clue? Did she never wonder where all that money came from? Fuck it." Drew leaned back, glaring at the ceiling. "I suppose I should have seen it comin', right? I mean, what the fuck? What the hell was I thinkin' when we got into that truck?"

"The crow tried to warn us."

Drew straightened. "The crow? What crow?"

Cody took a bite of egg. "It was on the hood. I think it was tryin' to tell me not to go."

"What hood?"

"Right on the hood when Dad—" Cody paused. "When Dad told me to ignore it."

"Yeah, I don't remember that."

Cody shrugged.

Drew leaned back in the chair, now looking out the basement door. "Well, if you see that crow again, listen to what it says, will you?"

"I see it all the time."

Drew sighed. "This is bullshit. Soon as I get off these crutches everything's gonna change. We're gonna figure this out. We're gonna make this work. We're gonna build ourselves a home, get some money for our old place, and figure it all out. I swear, kid, this is a turning point. There's nothing worse life can throw at us. We make it through this and we're gonna be okay." Cody finished her fried egg, rinsed the dish, then made two more for her mother.

"I need you to go down with Virginia to get some stuff from our old tool shed."

"Didn't we go already?"

"Last trip." Drew turned up a piece of paper and pushed it across the table. "I wrote a list 'cause she doesn't know half of what she's supposed to be gettin'."

"Are we gonna work on the house today?"

"Yeah, so don't take long."

2

The list wasn't long, mostly fasteners and a medley of tools Virginia had never heard of. After Cody safely stowed them in the bed of the truck, Virginia announced they would be stopping by Brookway's outdoor store. She wouldn't need long.

"What for?"

"Well," said Virginia, "I'm not a rich man's wife anymore."

Cody watched the neighborhood pass by as they drove into town, as if considering what Virginia had said. "So—why's that make you want to go shopping?"

"'Cause maybe it's time I stopped dressing like I was."

"How's that?"

"Weren't you the one telling me to stop shaving my legs?"

"That's if you wanna fit in Vermont."

"That's a start."

"In Vermont, the richer you are, the poorer you dress." And Cody said it so flatly that Virginia glanced at the girl, distracted from her driving. "George Barstowe," said Cody, "he's rich."

"How do you know?"

"'Cause he's always complainin' 'bout how poor he is."

"Well maybe he is," said Virginia.

"'Cause people who are poor," continued Cody, "don't wanna look poor. They wanna look rich 'cause that's what they wanna be, and the rich dress poor because they don't want poor people envyin' them or thinkin' they're too rich for 'em. That's how you tell who's rich and who's poor in Vermont."

"Am I mopey?"

"Sometimes."

"I don't want to look mopey."

"So that's why you're buyin' new clothes?"

"I'm building a house with your mother, for God's sake! What am I doing wearing high-heels and oxfords? Good God!"

"So what are you gonna get?"

"It won't be slacks. Or a skirt. Or a blouse. Whatever will I do? I'll just have to throw out my petticoats."

"You oughta just wear carpenter pants."

"I'm going to be my own woman, Cody. No more moping. No more mooning."

"If ya want to fit in you should start wavin' at people when they wave at ya from other cars."

"I don't know them!"

"Don't have to."

"Nobody waves at anybody in Arizona."

"Ever?"

"Well, no honey, we call that road rage in Arizona."

Cody let that sit for a spell. Then as Virginia parked, she asked if she could wait in the car.

"You're going to help me pick them out."

Cody tried not to let too much of a smile break through. "Really?"

"You New Englanders don't smile much, do you?"

"Only when we're gettin' away with somethin'."

3

Drew was sitting in the front door's rough opening when Virginia returned. And when she saw Virginia's carpenter pants, t-shirt, and baseball hat, her eyes narrowed. Virginia uneasily sidled by. "Cody picked them out."

"That explains it."

"Well," said Virginia. "I think it's time I dressed the part."

Drew glanced at Cody but Cody frowned earnestly as she walked by.

"Hey," Drew stopped her.

"What?"

"Get my baseball cap."

After that, work on their tiny house resumed. The two women took to working as though for pay and it was only Hoyte's joining them that saved Cody from the misery of their company. Drew laid out the plans for a loft and had them snap chalk lines for the bathroom walls, door, and the kitchen cabinets. That way Virginia could begin to see what the inside of the house would look like—a sleeping loft, a tiny bathroom, bedroom, mudroom, and a kitchen with room for a table and chairs.

Once that was done, measurements were taken for the loft and because they didn't have a beam, Drew decided they'd find a sapling strong and straight enough instead. For Cody and Hoyte, the thought of cutting down a tree was just the thing to bring some joy back into the project. It was no small feat for Drew to do so much and by noon her forehead was beaded with sweat and her skin pale. She sat on the lumber she'd readied for the next cut and leaned the two crutches next to her. The ghost of them were two angry bruises under her arms. "Run and get me a couple painkillers, babe. The good ones."

Virginia made sandwiches and lemonade. She brought them to the table in the roughed-out living room. They had framed up the walls of the bathroom and had lain the bottom plates for the other walls. The floor that had at first seemed spacious to Virginia was steadily divided up. Just yesterday she might have sat glumly remembering her spacious house in Arizona, its floor to ceiling glass overlooking miles of scrub, grit and sun-burnt clay. "Well," she said instead, "I had no idea we'd have room for a mudroom."

"Is anybody gonna sleep in the loft?" asked Cody.

"You will, babe."

"When are we cuttin' the tree down?" asked Hoyte.

"Hey," Drew glanced at Cody. "You know what I'm lookin' for, right?"

Cody nodded hesitantly.

Drew made a circle, about six inches, thumb to thumb and forefinger to forefinger. "About that thick and straight. No popple."

Hoyte and Cody hurried through their sandwiches and took off for the woods. They both theorized as to where they could find a sapling and each, showing the beginnings of maturity, agreed on nothing. But, as it turns out, the straightest saplings grow in the shadow of other trees. An old field pine, drunk on too much sunlight, is the worst for timber. Gluttonous limbs spread indiscriminately. The same breed of pine, growing in tight competition, will shoot straight as an arrow in its skyward race. Cody and Hoyte found such a tree in a clump of competing hemlock and maple—a white pine.

They waited until early evening to cut the tree down. Hoyte was eager but Cody's on-and-off-again headache had returned. She lay on her back with an arm over her eyes. Drew rested on a saw horse. The pain killers had done her some good but Cody wasn't having it. "Let's wait 'til tomorrow," she said.

"Let's just knock it down, babe."

"Why?"

"Last job of the day."

"My head hurts?"

"Bad?"

"No."

"Been drinkin' enough water?"

"I have Ibuprofen," Virginia volunteered, "can she have Ibuprofen?"

"You want some Ibuprofen, babe?"

"No."

"We don't have all year to build this," said Drew.

"What's one day gonna matter," said Cody, her arm still over her eyes.

"Between school and weather, we gotta take the days we get. C'mon. Get up. If I can drag my ass into the woods so can you."

Cody sat up and pressed the butt of her palms against her forehead. Hoyte jumped to the ground, glanced at Cody expectantly. She stood and followed, the weight of weariness in her stride and shoulders. It wasn't easy for Drew to navigate the waist-deep grass, but once under the trees, the going was easier. Virginia followed with a bow saw and Hoyte led the way with a felling axe. The pine was straight and eight inches at the bottom.

"Notch the tree," said Drew. "You want the notch the side that's falling." Cody took the saw from Virginia and knelt in the leaves and dirt. Hoyte offered to take a turn but Cody had a point to make, and not just with the tree. The end of the cut was a struggle, the saw's aggressive teeth snagged and stuttered.

"Babe, why don't you let Hoyte finish?"

"I can do it, Mom." Cody then threw the saw behind her and took the axe from Hoyte. It took three swings but the notch popped out. She handed the axe back to Hoyte, walked half a dozen steps out of the small circle and sat with her forehead in her palms.

Hoyte took his turn. There is a satisfaction to swinging an axe that Hoyte didn't want to pass up. After only a few swings he discovered an easy rhythm and accuracy that soon had the tree leaning on the increasingly slender hinge of wood between the two cuts.

"Push on it," said Drew.

Hoyte and Virginia threw their weight against it. The tree was caught by the dry limb of an intervening spruce.

"Cody!" Drew snapped impatiently. Hoyte stepped aside as though making way for a stranger. Virginia was apprehensive but when all three pushed, the recalcitrant limb gave way with a sharp crack of wood. Hoyte and Virginia moved to the side but Cody, between them, stumbled forward. The butt bounced upwards, and gave Cody a glancing blow that sent her reeling to the side.

When she rose to her knees, her face in her hands which were covered in blood. Virginia carefully pulled them away. Tears streamed from Cody's eyes. Drew tried to kneel next to Cody but Cody was having none of it. She quickly stood, wiping the blood from her lips with the back of her hand and left without saying a word.

"I should have said something," said Virginia.

"It was my fault," said Drew.

Hoyte awkwardly guessed he should probably go home. Drew found Cody back at the house, cross-leggèd on the couch, and persuaded Cody to let her have a look. The damage was less than the blood. Cody had already cleaned up most of it with a washcloth. Drew finished cleaning up in that way that one asks for forgiveness. "Hey kid," she said, "How are ya doin'?"

"I'm okay." Cody's headache had given way to the bearable ache of a bruised cheek and split lip. She gingerly touched it.

"I'm sorry."

Cody shrugged. "Wasn't your fault."

"We don't have to work tomorrow."

"I want to."

"You sure?"

"I wanna build the loft; I wanna sleep in it."

"So then," said Drew, "we gotta pull that tree out tomorrow, peel it, and put it up."

Cody pushed her bottom lip out with her tongue, testing the cut.

"You're making it bleed, kid."

Cody touched her lip and looked at the little bit of blood on her finger's tip. "How long are we gonna have to work on the house?"

"Not long. It's a small place. We're not buildin' a house for the ages, just somethin' for the cold."

"I like it here."

"You wanna tell me 'bout those headaches?"

"It went away."

"They come and go?"

"Yeah."

"You'll be okay, babe." Drew kissed Cody on the forehead; and when she later took her codeine, hands shaking, she swallowed one and broke another in half.

4

The next day was splendid. Drew and Virginia put away their resentments. Drew made pancakes. Virginia drove the four short miles to Hugh Kemp's and returned with a quart of maple syrup and ice cream to be paid out at day's end. The day's project was to build a loft for Cody. Hoyte didn't visit until the afternoon, but when he did he was full of admiration for Cody's bruised cheek and lip. He told her there wasn't a boy in Brookway could rival her.

"They'd all be dead by now," she answered.

"So are you okay then?"

"First I'm gonna build the loft, then I'm gonna eat ice cream, and then I'll decide if I'm okay."

"So what made you so mad last night?

"Headache."

"Hope ya don't get another one."

In short order the rest of the studs were put up and they only had to drag the tree out of the woods, peel it and set it in place with timber screws. That might have been enough work for one day, but Cody was determined to put floorboards down. She meant to sleep in the loft that night and every night thereafter.

After nailing down the last board, Cody and Hoyte put up a ladder, climbed into the loft and lay on their bellies. Ratter purred between them. Barn windows were planned—two by two foot windows among George Barstowe's hodge-podge, but for now there were two rough openings. If the children could have floated, they might have crawled through and into the evening's bluish air, floating above the valley, slowly turning head over heels as they learned to give their flight direction. This is what they imagined and they discussed where they would go and how they would go about it.

Sometime later Cody and Hoyte, Virginia and Drew ate ice cream, and after that, Cody officially made the loft her new room with a bed, books, lamp, and Ratter.

5

The next morning Cody arrived at school in a buoyant mood but was stopped in the hallway and told to go to Mrs. Santoff's office by Mrs. Levitt who, as before, stopped her with a hand on her shoulder. She glanced at Cody's new bruise with a mix of pity and concern. Cody didn't know what she had done or whether Reynard had changed his mind. She sat in the little waiting room with a ready resentment and diffidence.

A younger woman stepped in from the hallway. Her thick black hair was box-braided with beads and almost the shade of her skin. She wore a colorful dress and necklace and looked like no creature that had ever inhabited Brookway, Vermont. She smiled, disarming whatever resentments Cody had been rehearsing. "Hi," she said, "are you Cody Tippet?"

"Yeah."

"I'm Tisha." The lithe young woman, still smiling, sat across from Cody, put her messenger bag at her feet, and leaned forward with her elbows on closed knees. "How are you doing?"

"Okay."

"You can call me Tisha, I'm from the Family Services Division of the Department for Children and Families."

"Hi."

"Hi, Cody. I'm here to ask you some questions. Do you know what the Family Services Division is?"

"Yeah." And then to clarify, Cody added: "No."

"Okay. Our job is to make sure all children, no matter their age, live in a safe, supportive, and healthy environment. We received a call from someone expressing concern over your wellbeing."

"Okay."

"And one of the ways we make sure children stay safe and healthy is to talk to children and their parents."

"Okay."

"And that's what I'd like to do this morning. I just want to ask you some questions."

Cody's stomach tumbled in that weightless way that's fear and the desire to flee. "I'm okay."

"Can I ask you a few questions?"

"Okay."

The young woman drew a clipboard, pen, and papers from her messenger bag. "What's your birthday?"

"November second, nineteen ninety-eight."

"Oh," the young woman smiled, "you're a Scorpio. My sister was a Scorpio. I learned not to mess with Scorpios. How's school? Are you enjoying school?"

"Yeah."

"Good. And how's homework?"

"We're buildin' our house right now, so I don't have much time."

"That sounds like a lot of work."

"It's not too bad on the weekdays."

"Not too bad?"

"No, we really gotta get it done before it's cold so we work on the weekend."

"Do you have a room?"

"We just built my loft but it doesn't have any windows yet."

"And a kitchen?"

"My mom had somethin' up before—" Cody paused. "Before she broke her ankle and her back. We got a sink, a fridge, and a couple hot plates."

"Is it cold in the mornings?"

"Just startin' to be."

"Do you have any brothers and sisters?"

"No."

"Is it just you and your mother living in the house?"

"No. There's the woman who owns the place—Virginia. She came up and when she found out the house wasn't finished she tried to throw us off her property, then—" Cody paused again. "Then my mom was in the hospital and we didn't have a place to stay and Mom asked Virginia if she could look after me. Now we're friends and are buildin' the house together."

"How did your mom get hurt?"

Cody shrank and pressed her lips together. After a long pause she forced herself to say the words. "My dad tried—" Her voice rose, throat tight, and she wiped the tears from her eyes. "—tried to kill me." She didn't want to look at the woman but looked out the window.

"I'm so sorry," the young woman's voice was gentle. "You just take as much time as you need. I'll wait."

But Cody wasn't having it. She turned on Tisha: "What's it matter to you? Why do you want to know?"

"Just so that I can help you if you need help."

"Why would I?"

"How does your cheek feel?"

"Fine."

"Can I ask how that happened?"

"My mom."

"Your mom?"

"I don't know—" Cody pressed herself back into her seat. "We were cuttin' down a tree for my loft. I had a headache. I didn't wanna do anything."

"What happened?"

"The tree got hung up in a branch and the harder it hung up the madder she got."

"You had a headache?"

"Sometimes."

"Have you always had headaches?"

"No."

"When did they start?"

"After bein' almost killed," Cody answered. "After bein' driven off into the river."

"Okay." The young woman nodded. "There are some notes about that here—about what happened. Let's talk about the tree. Why was your mom angry?"

"She was mad 'cause the tree was takin' too long to fall. So I got on it and pushed and when it fell it came up and hit me in the face."

"Was it just you and your mom?"

"No, Virginia and Hoyte were pushin' too."

"Virginia is the woman with whom you're building the house; and who is Hoyte?"

"He's my best—" Cody stopped herself. "He's my friend."

"Okay. What happened then?"

"We quit."

"Did she take you to the doctor's?"

"No."

"Did she give you any pain medication?"

"No."

"Did you ask for any?"

"No."

"I'm going to need to take a picture of your bruise, Cody."

"Why?"

"Because my job is to assess your welfare; and there are some things for which a description isn't enough." The young woman took a smartphone from her messenger bag. "So, Cody, if you want to hold onto your knees like that, that's okay, but I just need you to move your hair out of your face. And are there any other bruises I need to know about?"

"No."

"You're sure? Nobody's in this room but you and me." Then she emphasized every word. "You are safe. If there's anything else you want to tell me, or show me, you are safe."

Cody shook her head.

"Okay," Tisha put away the phone. "What about your mom? You said she broke her ankle and back. How is she doing?"

"She's fine so long she takes her painkillers."

"What happens if she doesn't?"

"She gets cross."

"Just cross?"

"She's in a lot of pain if she doesn't take 'em."

"Does she drink?"

"Not much, especially now as she's not s'posed to 'cause of all the medicine."

"Can I ask you about your dad?"

Cody paused, arms around her knees. "Okay."

"Did he ever touch you inappropriately?

Cody shook her head.

"Do you know what I'm asking?"

Cody nodded.

"Sexually."

"No."

"Did he ever hurt you in any way?"

If Cody could have hidden behind her knees, she would have. She nodded instead, then wiped the tears from her eyes. "He'd get mad."

"What did he do?"

"My stomach. My ribs. My back."

"What does that mean?"

"He hit me."

"How about your mother?"

Cody shook her head. "He told me not to tell her. He said it'd be my fault if anything bad happened to her."

"You know that wasn't true," said the young woman.

"It was when he said it," Cody answered.

"Yeah." Tisha nodded, concerned, then said gently, "I hear you. Just one more question."

"Okay."

"Do you want to tell me about any unusual experiences you've had?"

Cody shook her head.

"You don't see or hear anything that nobody else can see or hear?"

Cody twisted in her chair, impatient with the question. "Sometimes I know what people are thinkin'."

"Does this happen often?"

"Can't control it if that's what you're askin'."

"Is it ever scary?"

"No."

"Is there anything else that happens during these episodes?"

"No." Cody shook her head.

"You don't faint or black out?"

"No."

"Anything else?"

"When I drowned I saw what was gonna happen to the town."

"When you drowned?"

Cody frowned, angry at how the memory of it, in this little room, and with this woman, made her tremble. She answered with a quiet "Yes."

"That was when your father drove you and mother into the river?"

"Yes."

"Thank you, Cody," the young woman smiled in a way that was meant to comfort. "Is there anything else you'd like to say, to know, or ask me?"

Cody shook her head again.

6

That same morning Drew and Virginia set to work on their tiny house. They had only just begun sorting when a middle-aged woman, square reading glasses attached to a cord at her neck, stepped from a Land Rover. She approached the two women while gazing at the tiny house. "What a lovely spot!" she said, then addressed Drew. "Are you Drew Tippet?"

"I am."

"I'm Nora Spellman from family services."

"From where?"

"Child protective services," she offered.

"What?"

"The Family Services Division of Vermont."

"Why?"

"We were contacted concerning the welfare of your daughter, Cody."

"By who?"

"I'm sorry but I can't divulge that."

"So what do you want?"

"I'd like to discuss the allegations and assess Cody's living conditions.

"Assess her living conditions?"

"Yes, ma'am."

"Are you threatening to take her away from me?" Drew hobbled forward on her crutches, her hands and shoulders shaking. "Who the hell made the allegation?"

"Ma'am—"

"What did they say?"

"Ma'am," the woman held out her hand as if to calm Drew, "I understand you might feel threatened. I apologize. That's not my intention and I don't want to take your daughter away. But an allegation has been made, and by law, I'm required to assess the merits of the allegation."

"God damn—" Drew leapt forward, or just so much as the crutches let her. She stumbled and would have altogether fallen if Virginia hadn't caught her.

"I'm sorry," Virginia stammered. "What did you say your name was?"

"Nora Spellman."

"Nora," Virginia steadied Drew and drew the crutches back under her arms. "Could you— I'm a nurse. Just—please—could I have a moment alone with Drew?"

"Yes—" The woman hesitated. "Yes, if you need a moment."

"I don't need to fucking—"

"I know," Virginia cut her off, turning Drew, encouraging her to return to the tiny house. Drew shook but kept by Virginia's side until she leaned on the wall next to the door. "Listen to me—"

"She wants to take Cody away!" Drew furiously wiped her eyes with the palm of a hand. "God damnit, she wants to take my girl away!"

"Stop!"

"You're not a nurse." Drew glared at Virginia. "Why did you tell her you were a nurse?"

"Do you think I haven't seen the terrible things a parent can do? I saw awful things and I saw good people trying to help. But you haven't done anything wrong. So what are you going to do?"

"Tell her to stay the hell away from my daughter!"

"She can't do that."

"Then I'm not lettin' her go on some fucking fishing expedition. I know what they're like. I en't lettin' her— Hell, we don't even have a house. What's she gonna think if she goes lookin' around? I can't lose Cody, not now; not after everything! I can't. Jesus Christ. That'd kill us both!"

"Drew." Virginia placed her hands on Drew's shoulders. "You asked me to be your daughter's guardian."

Drew didn't answer.

"So you trusted me. You had to trust me. You asked me to look after her."

Drew nodded, glaring at the dirt underfoot.

"Okay," said Virginia. "You're going to be polite. You haven't done anything wrong. You're going to ask her to read the complaint. You're going to answer her questions. Don't make excuses or apologies. She's going to ask to see, well—our house. If you say no, she might think you're hiding something; and then she'll have to come back with a warrant and she'll have policemen with—"

"Have you seen how we live?"

"They won't take your child for building a house!"

"Sure. What's she gonna think? What does she fuckin' care if Cody's dad tried to kill her—"

"Her job is to make sure Cody isn't being abused or neglected. If she asks about medication, you tell her you have a prescription. That's all." Then it was Virginia's turn to pause, summoning the courage to say more. "You shouldn't be taking that many painkillers, Drew. I don't know where you're getting them but you have to stop. I've seen drug dependency and this is what it looks like."

Drew's voice was dark but even. "I need 'em."

If Virginia meant to argue, Drew ignored her and went to speak with Nora. She asked to hear the complaints and the woman read them: that the living conditions were unsanitary; that Drew was addicted to painkillers; that she was obtaining painkillers illegally and neglecting Cody; that Cody suffered from hallucinations; that Cody was being denied medical treatment.

Drew listened, white-knuckled. The child care worker asked what Virginia and Drew's relationship was, then asked to inspect the tiny house. She went into each of the three basement rooms with their makeshift walls of hanging sheets. She went into the newly started tiny house, taking off her reading glasses to awkwardly climb into Cody's loft. She asked why there were no windows in the openings, asked when they were going to finish the house and wanted to know what medications Drew was taking.

"You don't have to answer that," said Virginia to Drew, then to the woman. "She doesn't have to answer that."

"Excuse me?"

"Well," Virginia hesitated, "no, I've worked with child protective services before. I understand the procedure. If you have an allegation of abuse or neglect, then you should investigate that; but whether or not this woman is taking prescribed medication?—or how often?— or her prescription? This has nothing to do with abuse or neglect."

"Are you her lawyer?"

"She's my friend," Drew corrected. "She had custody of Cody when I was in the hospital."

The woman lowered her reading glasses. "As I read before, the allegation is that your mother is supplying you, illegally, with prescription drugs."

"That's not an allegation of abuse or neglect," said Virginia.

"Parental substance abuse is a risk factor and Cody's hallucinations—"

"She's not having hallucinations," said Drew.

"She claims to read minds," said the woman. "And that she has episodes out of her body. If you've worked with child protective services before then you know that parents who abuse alcohol or drugs are a risk factor."

"That's a reason to be concerned," said Virginia. "But that's not abuse or neglect."

"Okay." The woman spoke crisply, cleanly. "But we might revisit this."

"What else?" Drew asked. Her black hair fell over her face like two black curtains.

"Cody's hallucinations," the woman answered. "Has she seen a doctor?"

"Yes," Drew finally spoke.

"About the hallucinations?"

"Yes," Virginia interjected. "I had Dr. Latham speak to her."

"Has Cody spoken with a therapist, psychologist, psychiatrist?"

"No," said Virginia, "I wasn't told that was needed."

The woman noted Virginia's answers, leaving only with the promise that the investigation would be finalized within sixty days.

7

Cody gazed out of the bus's window. Hoyte looked past her. "So, what are you gonna do?" he asked.

"I dunno."

"Why do you suppose they talked to you?"

"I know why."

"'Cause of your readin' minds?"

Cody shook her head. "It was Grandad and Gramma."

"Why?"

"'Cause they think— I don't know what they think. They think Mom's lying about Dad."

"They must think you are too."

The bus rolled to a stop before Hoyte and Cody's drive. Cody winced as she stepped out, the voices of children suddenly flooding her thoughts, thoughts that weren't her own, and she stopped, shoulders hunched, eyes closed tight.

"You okay?"

She pressed her palm between her eyebrows and the cacophony subsided. "Yeah."

"So your gramma and grandad can just make stuff up?"

"Probably."

"Your mom should talk to my dad."

"I guess," said Cody.

"You okay?"

Cody walked quickly away from the departing bus. "Yeah."

"You sure?"

"Yeah. C'mon."

Halfway to the fork in the driveway leading right to her own house and straight to Hoyte's, they saw Drew and Virginia walking to meet them. Drew fixed her crutches under her and held out her arms. They embraced.

"There was somebody interviewed me at school," said Cody.

"I know."

"They wanted to know if you were doin' drugs."

"I know, babe."

"I told 'em it was just for killin' the pain."

8

Cody gratefully climbed into her loft that night. There wasn't yet a staircase out of the basement. A rough opening had been framed but was plywooded over; left to be cut out once the deck was closed in. The only way to get to Drew's loft was to walk outside, up the bank, and in from the driveway. Cody heard none of the conversation downstairs. She peered at the stars and dreamed.

"I know who it was," said Drew. "It was Daryl's parents."

"And you think they spoke to your mother?" asked Arvid.

"Mom was braggin' about it."

"And does your mother bring you prescription drugs?" he asked.

"Yeah."

"So you know that I am not a lawyer in America and I've never been involved in anything like this—not even in the Netherlands. But I did a little research before coming over this evening. I think maybe, if your mother is providing you prescription drugs, this is not a good thing. It is very easy to become dependent on pain medication. It happened to me. But this is not a reason to take a child from their parents. If you are not abusing or neglecting her, if you are not producing or selling drugs, and if it is not impairing your ability to parent, then it cannot be considered."

"Okay," Drew nodded, eyes welling.

"Can you afford an attorney?"

"No."

"I cannot legally represent you."

"I know."

"But I don't think it will come to that."

"I swear to God—" Drew didn't finish her promise.

"I expect you are angry? That you want to confront your ex-husband's parents?"

Drew didn't answer.

"You must remember that whatever you do can affect the outcome of an investigation. Confronting your ex-husband's parents will not benefit you in any way. It is only for you to demonstrate that you are the parent Cody already knows, trusts and loves."

Chapter 12

This time of year when I go out
Winter is like an inland sea—
Waves halfway up the gutter spout
And ripples lapping at the tree.

You'd think the swelling tide of snow
Claimed memory of an ancient shore
And with a melting undertow
Would turn the stone to shells once more.

But only once when I'd come to
Half-wakened from a fitful dream
Did something like a tide slip through
The bedroom window's broken seam.

The snow seemed finally come for good,
An icy shore beneath my bed,
And yet I think that if I'd stood
I would have stepped on sand instead.

The taste of salt was in the air
And though the frost had licked the hinge
I saw, at midnight, something there—
Sunlight skirting the doorway's fringe.

I only had to go outside
To see the ocean at my sill—
I only had to—but that tide
Will come again. Someday, I will.

1

Cody sat on the playground bench with her hands over her ears. A book was on her knees. She read until she was tapped on her shoulder. Olivia stood behind her. An older girl and a boy, from the grade above, were standing with her.

"There was an article," said Olivia. "It was in a science magazine and it says you're a liar."

"Leave me alone, Olivia."

Olivia held up a paper torn from a magazine, the other hand on her hip. "You want to know what else I think?"

"No."

"I think you're lying about reading people's minds."

"Fine. I don't care."

"So why did you do it? Why did you lie?"

"I didn't lie."

Olive dangled the article between a thumb and forefinger. "Want to read it?"

"No."

"Then I'll read it: In a recent New York Times article it was claimed that a young girl living in Vermont predicted that a storm would sweep through the state, causing extensive flooding and even loss of life. Does that sound like Hurricane Irene? The girl's 'predictions' are said to have saved lives and preserved what property was moved to safety; and since then psychics have been touting this young girl's predictions as proof of psychic ability and the supernatural, but are they?"

"I don't care," said Cody."

But Olivia triumphantly continued. "Let's examine: First, let's provisionally accept the claim that this girl's predictions were made prior to any knowledge of Hurricane Irene. The known facts argue that making such a prediction already entailed a considerable likelihood of success. In the midst of a hurricane season, the likelihood of a hurricane striking the Eastern United States is almost a certainty. But the girl specifically predicted that a storm would strike Vermont—"

Cody stood up, walking away.

Olivia followed, still reading. "Was that a daring prediction? Not at all. Heavy rains associated with tropical storms sweeping up from the Gulf and Atlantic coasts are a nearly annual event. In the three years preceding Hurricane Irene, New England was visited by seven tropical storms including three in 2007 and three in 2008.

"But how likely is it that she would predict a storm—"

Cody rounded on Olivia, fists tight, then stopped, startled, glaring at the boy.

"What," she said.

"I didn't say anything," he answered, equally taken aback. He blushed and so did Cody.

"Hey—" began Olivia.

"Hey, why don't we just leave her alone," said the boy.

Olivia stared at him, dumbfounded. "Why?"

"She wasn't doin' anything."

Cody opened and closed her fists. She stepped toward the boy as if to push or punch him. He raised his hands, backing away, half smiling. "Hey, c'mon, I'm on your side!"

"Jesus." Cody turned.

"Look," the boy followed after her, "I don't know what her problem is—"

"Because you think I'm pretty?" Cody rounded on him.

He stopped, perplexed, words like barbs on his tongue, the kind that tear out pieces of childhood. He made as though to speak, hesitated. "I mean. I dunno. Not that you aren't—"

"Just leave me alone." Cody turned.

"Did you read my mind?" The boy followed after her.

"No!" Cody stopped, turned. "I didn't read your mind. It was obvious."

"I just wanted— I mean, I didn't mean anything by it."

Cody nervously glanced at Olivia behind the bench. "Whatever. I don't care."

By now Jerry had joined them, having noticed the altercation. "What's up, Owen?"

"Nothin'," the boy answered and then said to Cody: "We're cool, right?"

"Sure. Whatever."

Jerry turned a shoot of grass in his mouth. "Is Owen botherin' you?"

"No, I'm fine."

"Somebody take after you?" he asked.

Cody self-consciously touched her lip, then wiped her hair out of her eyes. "Tree hit me when I was pushin' it down."

Jerry smiled. "I bet the tree took it worse than you did." Jerry's friends, two other boys, joined them. "Hey, you and Hoyte should come down and hang out. You know, down by the river."

2

Meredith put her hand over the phone. She still preferred the old corded phone, refusing to give it up; and tourists always remarked that they couldn't imagine a Vermont inn without one. She mouthed the name 'Drew Tippet' to John, and directed him to take the front desk with a sharp nod. "I have to take a call," she said to the guests at the counter. "My husband will look after you."

"Drew," she said, once she'd pulled herself and the phone into a corner. "What can I do for you?"

"I'm lookin' for Daryl's parents," said Drew. "Are they still there?"

"Well I don't know," Meredith answered, "why don't you tell me their names."

"Marjorie and Wayne Tippet."

Meredith held her hand over the phone and counted to ten. "No. Not anymore. They checked out two days ago."

There was a moment's silence before Drew thanked her and hung up. When John was done at the front desk, he stood by Meredith's side, cleaning his glasses with a handkerchief. "You know," he said, "that's a first. Congratulations. You've lied. What's it like to walk among the mortal?"

"Oh for God's sake, John."

"I won't hold it against you, dear."

"They'll be gone in two more days."

"That's still a lie."

"It was a white lie and I'd have been a fool not to."

"Oh, I know: Caesar did never wrong but with just cause."

"Seems that Virginia inherited some of her grandfather's good sense."

"Did she call to warn us?"

"She did."

"And if they decide to extend their stay?"

"They can do it elsewhere."

"What should I tell them?"

'Oh for God's sake, John. Tell them we're booked. Tell them there's a wedding. Tell them we're remodeling."

"Involve me in your deception?"

"If that girl's mother finds out those two are down here, we'll have the police and fire department next. They refuse to accept their son was murderer. I wouldn't be surprised if they thought the mother was behind it."

"If they complain?"

"Well of course you're going to lie, John."

3

Shortly after midday, when in mid-September the sun dusts Vermont's fields with a summer's heat, Drew and Virginia took lunch on the tailgate of Drew's pickup. They sat in the shade of one of the hemlocks growing between their house and Arvid's.

They sat quietly side by side at first. "You know," said Drew finally, "I don't think it's gonna look half bad."

"No," said Virginia. "It's not what I expected but—" She stopped herself and straightened. "I think it's the most beautiful house in Vermont."

"Uh-huh."

"Well, I'm building it."

"Have you never built anything?" asked Drew.

"Not so much as a bird house."

"Why'd you tell her you were a nurse?"

Virginia didn't answer at first. She looked past the house and the blue-tinged mountains. "I wanted to be taken seriously."

Drew nodded.

"That was something I was building," Virginia continued. "My nursing career."

"You think I should keep buildin' after this?"

Virginia looked at Drew quizzically. "Well of course, if you enjoy it."

"Have you looked at me lately?"

"You were in a horrible—well, it wasn't an accident! Your husband tried to kill you!"

"What if it doesn't stop hurting?"

"I don't know if pain like that ever goes away."

Drew shoved the crutches under her arms and stood. "But you think I'm gonna get back to work?"

"For Cody's sake if for no one else's!"

"And not for mine?"

"For your sake too!" said Virginia. "Of course! For your sake too!"

"Then what's your excuse?" The dark curtains of Drew's hair fell over her eyes.

"Well— I—"

"You got some right that I don't?"

"No," said Virginia, "No I don't suppose I do."

Drew swung her hair out of her face. "You should go back to school and be a nurse."

It was Virginia's turn to pause thoughtfully. "I had that coming."

"Sure as hell did." Drew gingerly backed up to the tailgate and sat again. She was pale and sweating.

"Oh, hon," Virginia shook her head. "We've got to get you off those painkillers."

Drew closed her eyes and exhaled.

4

There's a burl in human nature that's best explained with the help of the woodchuck. The woodchuck is also called a groundhog, whistle-pig, or land beaver. That such a lowly creature has earned so many names tells us that it speaks to something we recognize in ourselves; something observable even in the youngest child. We all have our own burrow and we all have it in us to suss out whatever secret is in the burrow next door. Olivia had twice been thwarted; and as she saw it, she only needed a stick long enough and she could poke into the open whatever was hidden in Cody's burrow; and whatever that was, she was sure, would vindicate her.

If you had asked, she wouldn't have known what to expect; but Olivia's world was ruled by a God who reviled sin, who tormented the damned in the melting heat of the earth, while the faithful were rewarded with eternal righteousness. Olivia experienced a rage she couldn't articulate. She wanted a confession. She wanted to expose Cody's deception. Olivia knew, without knowing why, there could be no compromise—she was made in God's image and God in hers.

But even this was more than Olivia could articulate. She only knew, instinctively, that she must make Cody too small for anything like God. She was one of the dozens of crowded children waiting for the school buses to arrive at the curb, spilled from the double doors and the concrete stairs that descended to the wide sidewalk, and when she saw Cody ahead of her she raised her voice. "Can you read my mind?"

Cody turned.

"What's the matter?" Olivia prodded.

"I didn't say anything."

"I thought liars were always good at talking."

"I'm not a liar," said Cody.

"So why don't you tell the future," said Olivia while the nearest children lowered their voices with cautious optimism. "What am I gonna say next?" Olivia dared.

"I don't care."

"Because you're a liar." Olivia smiled but she didn't have the right stick. It wasn't long enough. She would find the right stick. She would force Cody out of her burrow.

"Why do you care anyway?" said Cody.

Olivia stepped forward. The gathered children, older and younger, gave room. "Because I think a nobody would say anything to be important."

"I'm not a nobody!" Cody's fists tightened and her black hair fell forward. She tried to ignore the burgeoning ache behind her eyes, voices that weren't voices, thoughts that weren't her own but like a flood of burning leaves .

Olivia almost had the right stick, she could feel it. She remembered a second or third grade class project—family trees. "I bet you're not even Indian."

"I am."

"What are you?" said Olivia. She could see Cody shrinking—too small for anything like God. "Abenaki? You think that makes you special? You don't look like an Indian. You're too white."

"Shut-up, Olivia."

"Hey, I know. You're a mutt. Why would God ever talk to a mutt?"

Cody was pushed from behind, pushing her toward Olivia and Olivia laughed. "Oh, you want to fight, little mutt? Does the little mutt want to fight?"

Cody shoved her backwards. Then Olivia saw it. She saw how to make Cody disappear. She almost laughed at the obviousness of it. "How did you get your face beat up? Was it your mom? Was it for lying? If I'd been your dad, I would have tried to kill you too!"

What happened next was classroom lore. Cody had never thrown a punch. And after she'd thrown it, after Olivia sat on the concrete, one hand behind her and the other under her bloodied nose, Cody was stunned by the ease of it, that the muscle and cartilage of the face could be so fragile; that she didn't shake or cry; that she wanted Olivia to stand up so that she could hit her again; but Hoyte had appeared and already stood between her and Olivia, and the screaming of the enthralled children had already attracted the attention of the adults.

5

Cody sat next to the small table in the tiny house's first floor. Drew had drawn her own chair next to Cody's and turned hers to face Cody. She laid her crutches on the floor next to both of them. "Let me see your hand."

Cody held out her hand and Drew turned it in hers, studying Cody's knuckles. They were bruised and one knuckle was scarred, cut it on Olivia's tooth. Drew sat back. "Jesus Christ, babe."

"She called me a nobody," Cody's eyes grew moist.

"What?"

"And a liar."

"So you hauled off and decked her?"

"I pinched down."

Drew pushed her fingers through her hair. "How about you don't haul off and break any more noses?"

"I didn't break her nose."

"How about you don't try? How does that sound? C'mon, Cody. I'm doin' my best. What do you think's gonna happen when the state finds out about this? I mean, Jesus, what were you thinkin'? Don't you know? Your grandparents want to take you away, babe." Drew's voice cracked. "I can't lose you. I don't know what I'd do without you. Jesus, the last thing you need to be doin' is sendin' some girl home with a bloody nose."

"That's not all she said," Cody began to shake.

"Okay, what else did she say?"

"She called me a mutt."

"Wait," Drew leaned in, "why did she call you a mutt?"

"She said I was too white."

"Too white for what?"

"To be Indian."

"Oh." Drew momentarily considered that. "Oh. Okay. So she's hittin' below the belt. Why? What gives?"

"I dunno."

"You didn't set her off—"

"No!" Cody answered forcefully, eyes welling.

"Yeah, that's tough, babe."

"She said more."

"Okay. What else did she say?"

"She said—" Cody's voice rose. She sobbed. Her hands twisted in her pants. "She said—she said if she'd been Daddy she would have tried to kill—kill me too!"

Drew leaned forward and took her daughter in her arms. She held the girl sobbing against her breasts, stroking her hair until the hiccups and sudden tremors were intermittent. "Is that when you hit her?" she asked softly.

"Yeah," Cody convulsed.

"How hard?"

"Hard."

"That's my girl."

"So you're not still mad at me?"

"I was never mad at you—just scared."

"I hit—" Cody hiccupped. "Hit her really hard."

"What your daddy did to you— It's gonna take a long time for that to stop hurtin'; that pain's never gonna go away, babe. And it's okay to feel it. That's okay."

"I know."

Drew gently pushed Cody back to the edge of her seat. "Let me take a look at you." She shook her head. "You get any more banged up and they're gonna run out of places to put bandages."

"I don't care."

Drew laughed; she once more brushed Cody's dark hair out of her eyes. "Babe, I care. You know I'd do anything in the world for you, but if you're gonna be just like me then we both gotta find a better way of gettin' on in the world." Drew curled Cody's hair over her fingers. "Your hair's gettin' long."

"I don't mind."

"You want me to braid it?"

"I like it straight."

"No bangs?"

"No bangs!"

"That's my girl."

6

Raccoon is a vain and intemperate animal. He thinks he's exceptionally beautiful. "You see the rings on my tail?" asked Raccoon rhetorically. He waddled through the hemlocks and chestnut trees. "There is no other tail like it."

The birds were as watchful as ever. Raccoon likes nothing more than eggs, but there was a bounty of acorns, chestnuts and walnuts. Luckily for the birds, Raccoon was fat and ready for the snow.

The squirrel didn't like that Raccoon was stealing its acorns, but was grateful not to be an acorn. The rat, fish, snake, and frog were also grateful. Raccoon had many friends and knew just how each one tasted. But then a terrible thing happened. It rained and all of Raccoon's friends made fun of him until Raccoon went to the old oak to complain.

"There was water on my pelt!" cried Raccoon.

"I see no water."

Raccoon turned, studied his pelt, rolled onto his back, plucked at his belly, but here was no water. Raccoon stood on his hind legs, pointing. "There was mud on my tail!"

"Was there?"

Raccoon chased his tail until he caught it, but it was bushy as ever. "They insulted me!"

"They did?"

"Again and again!"

"That's funny," said the oak, "but I don't see any."

"I will prove it," said Raccoon, and so the next time it rained, and the next time his friends laughed at him, he didn't shake the mud from his tail, he didn't pluck the cockleburs from his belly, and said to himself: "This will show that old oak!" He huffed and puffed. The wild grape tangled in his feet. The sun on his back made him itch. The thorns poked and prodded.

It's hard work carrying so many insults.

By the time Raccoon reached Old Oak he was skinny as a squirrel, hoarse as a frog, and his tail was as bedraggled as a rat's. "You see?" said Raccoon.

Old Oak laughed so hard that half his acorns dropped straight on top of poor Raccoon. That was when Raccoon decided that maybe it wasn't so wise to cling to insults. They're like thorns and thistles, like mud and cockleburs, and they itch and there is no end to the scratching. Raccoon shook himself off, rubbed his bruised noggin, and didn't let any insults stick to him after that.

7

That was the story that Drew told Cody. Cody nuzzled next to her and fell asleep before she felt her mother's goosebumps, her shaking, or the cold sweat that made Drew rise from bed, break her mother's pills into thirds before swallowing one of the fragments.

Chapter 13

1

The next morning before Cody went to school, Cody asked her mother: "Do you believe me?"

"Always, babe."

"About what happened to me in the river?"

"Yeah. I do. Is there anything else you wanna know, babe?"

"No." A flicker of a smile turned Cody's lips as she slipped her backpack over her shoulders. "Has anything like that ever happened to you?"

"Sort of."

"When?" Cody stopped.

"Nah. Not enough time. You gotta get to school. And you still wanna go to Soot Tabor's?"

"If they let me."

"Nah. We're gonna talk about what happened after school and then you're gonna go to Soot's."

Hoyte was waiting for Cody where their driveways joined. "So what's happening? They gonna suspend you?"

"I don't think so."

"She started it," he said.

"I think they want me to talk to a counselor."

"Aren't you already?"

"I don't want to," Cody groused.

"Yeah. Probably wasn't the best plan to punch Olivia's lights out."

"Not like I planned it, Hoyte."

"Glad it wasn't me you punched."

"I'd of punched a lot harder if it'd been you."

"So just talk to 'em and figure out what they want to hear."

"Doesn't matter," said Cody. "They don't believe me when I'm tellin' the truth and think I'm bein' honest when I'm lyin'. Not sure it's worth bein' an adult. If you punch somebody there en't any confusion as to what's true."

They stopped at the roadside. Both of them drew hoods over their heads under a soft rain. Hoyte rocked back and forth from heel to toe. "So are you full Indian?"

Cody shoved her hands in her overalls. "I'm quarter Irish, quarter Cherokee, and half Abenaki—or something like that."

"So where's your Abenaki come from?"

"Mom."

"I wish I knew what I was." Cody didn't answer, so Hoyte went on: "Don't you like knowin'? I don't even know who my mom and dad were."

Cody still said nothing but absent-mindedly moved a hand to the scar on her forehead.

"She wasn't saying it because you're Indian," said Hoyte. "She was just figurin' a way under your skin."

"If you knew your mom and dad's last name would you change yours?"

That stopped Hoyte. "I don't know. I don't think so. I mean, my dad's my dad now."

"I wanna change mine."

"Why?"

"'Cause wouldn't you if your dad did the same as mine?"

"Guess I would."

2

Later in the afternoon, Drew took the long way to Arvid's. The shortcut through the copse of trees was too soft and wet for crutches. The long way went down her own driveway and then Y'd onto his. The rain picked up, dripped over the hood of her raincoat, ran down the sleeves and crutches. She looked down to keep the downpour out of her eyes and when she looked up again she inhaled sharply. A coywolf blocked the gravel drive, its pelt bristling with rain, the color of a leaf-strewn woods, and its muzzle white with age. Its green eyes were fixed on hers. Slowly, crutches still under her arms, she lifted her hood. Her voice shook. "Hey."

The coywolf lowered its snout.

"You have something to tell me?"

The fur of the animal's powerful shoulders twitched and its right paw moved forward just a little, claws disturbing the granite stones. It turned its head the other direction then back to Drew.

"Just you and me."

The animal made her feel like a little girl again—fear, wonder, and fearlessness—and that finally made her smile. By now her long dark hair was soaked and matted to her cheeks and throat. The animal turned its head again, as if hearing another voice, and smoothly disappeared into the woods.

Ten minutes later she rode with Arvid down the winding road to Brookway with its gravel washouts and single lane detours. She had asked Arvid to drive her to the after-school meeting with the principal. Arvid didn't ask why. Then Drew told Arvid that her ex-husband's parents were staying at the Apple House.

"Are you sure?" he asked.

"I'm not an idiot."

"But, I mean, you are sure it is wise to confront them?"

"They're tryin' to take Cody away."

"Yes, but what do you hope to accomplish by confronting them?"

Drew didn't answer

They pulled into the inn's parking lot. Drew pushed open the door, leaning her crutches against it as she maneuvered to her feet.

"Do you need my help?" Arvid asked.

Drew turned up her palm, fingers wide. "Five minutes."

"That doesn't seem like enough time if you really want to talk with them."

"I'll be back," said Drew, the twisting in her gut like a rusted knife. The rain had let up. There were puddles in the inn's gravel lot and Drew swung through them. The sun was half out. She saw their car and plates before she saw Daryl's parents. They were on the way to the car and when they saw Drew. They stopped. Drew's fingers tightened. She blew the damp hair from her lips. No one spoke. The older woman gripped her husband's arm. If the older woman had meant to speak, the words slipped away. Drew turned around. She returned to Arvid's car, yanked the crutches onto her lap, and slammed the door.

"Is that it?" Arvid asked.

"Let's go."

"What happened?"

Drew stared straight ahead. "There's a coywolf up at our place."

"And you saw it?"

Drew nodded but didn't add anything more. Arvid pulled out of the lot and neither he nor Drew looked back. "To the school?" he asked. "We will be a bit early."

"To the bookstore."

"The bookstore?"

"Yeah."

For the next five minutes neither spoke, then Drew: "I think he's an old one."

"You mean the coywolf?"

"Yeah."

"I haven't seen it."

"I saw it on the road to your place," she said, "crossin' the road in the rain."

"As you were walking?"

"Yeah."

"So close?"

"Yeah," said Drew with a flickering smile. "Right in front of me. Like life itself."

"And terrifying, yes?"

"Yeah, and beautiful too."

"Yes." Arvid glanced at Drew as though seeing some part of her for the first time. "Yes, I know what you mean."

3

Before her last class Reynard met with Cody and Drew. They sat in undersized wooden chairs while Reynard leaned on his desk with both elbows and hands together. "So let's start by asking how you're doing Cody?"

"I'm okay." Cody shrunk, fingers nervously between her knees.

"I understand you injured your hand?"

"It's okay."

"And are you curious about Olivia?"

Cody didn't answer at first. "She got a bloody nose."

"You could have broken it."

"She called me a liar and said if she'd been my dad—" Cody paused. She was giving the pain a sharp tip, a wounding tip, something for her enemies and the careless to be wary of. She wasn't going to give way to tears again. "She'd of killed me."

"And do you think hitting her was the answer?"

Cody paused again. With the beginnings of adulthood, she knew there were two answers in the room. "I suppose you're gonna tell me I shouldn't of?" she said defiantly, quietly, voice low.

Reynard leaned back in his chair, elbows moving to the armrests, fingers lifted in a temple. "No, you're right," he said confidently. "And why do you think I'd say that?"

"'Cause your dad never tried to kill you."

The tip struck. Cody saw it. Reynard's face reddened, his jaw set, his eyes became rheumy. Cody had seen that look in her father. She hated it. She despised it. She felt her mother's glance but didn't turn. She heard the tick tack of the blinds in the opened window.

"She's a twelve year old kid," said Drew. "And she's been through a hell of a lot."

Reynard nodded gravely. "I get that. I spoke to Olivia and her parents this morning. I'm not singling out your daughter and I don't want to minimize the seriousness of Olivia's comments. I do consider her behavior bullying. What I'd prefer in the future, however, is that Cody contact a teacher or administrator if the bullying continues. I can't have students getting into fist fights."

"Does the racist comment fall under bullying?"

"Yes."

"And what if the bullying doesn't stop?"

"Cody needs to come to us first."

"Okay." Drew glanced at Cody. "You can do that. Right, babe?"

"Yeah." Cody kicked at the carpet.

"So," Drew turned back to Reynard. "If Cody comes to me, tellin' me this other girl is still bullying her and you're not doin' anything about it, I'll be the next one talking to Olivia's parents."

"It won't come to that."

"Just make sure she leaves Cody alone."

"I will," said Reynard, "and if you don't mind I'd like to talk to you privately." He turned to Cody but he didn't have to say anything. She pushed herself off her seat and left the room.

"Okay, what?" asked Drew.

"Cody has gone through an extremely traumatic experience. You both have. I think she might benefit from counseling. Mrs. Santoff could work around Cody's schedule. I strongly recommend it."

"Why?"

"Some of the staff are concerned by her behavior—statements she's made to other children. Speaking to a counselor would be cautionary, but given the kind of trauma Cody has experienced, we want to be sure there isn't something more serious wrong."

"Like what?"

"Sometimes when a child has experienced severe trauma—Let me put it this way, we're concerned that Cody's behavior could be signs of delusions or hallucinations."

"For example?"

"She claims that she can read minds."

"What if she can?" Drew's question was like a dare.

"I know you're doing everything you can—"

"So let me ask you something," Drew interrupted. "When kids come to school talking about Jesus this and Jesus that, do you recommend they see the school psychologist?"

Reynard's face reddened. "I don't think you can really compare—"

"Why not? Cody had a spiritual experience. How is that any different? I'm supposed to let her be counseled out of those experiences but believing in Jesus is okay?"

"I'm not suggesting that—"

"Good."

Drew stood, goosebumps pricking her arms, maneuvering her crutches under her. Reynard rose from his desk. "Family services interviewed Cody's teachers this morning." He opened the door for her.

Drew's fists tightened around the crutches. "Thanks."

"Just thought you should know."

She bumped the door as she shouldered past him. "Yeah, I get it."

Cody followed her mother into the hallway.

"You okay, Mom?" Cody stuffed her hands in her jacket pockets.

"Hey, I saw a coywolf this morning."

"Where was he?"

"Right up our driveway. Where it meets Arvid's."

"Did ya see the crow too?"

"Just the coywolf, babe. Seein' him. I don't know. Seein' him," Drew paused and smiled. "My aunt always used to talk about the animals bein' our ancestors." She nodded and shrugged. "Seein' him changed my plans. That's all I can tell ya."

"What were you gonna do?"

"I'm just tired of bein' angry. Just tired."

4

"So what happened?" Hoyte asked.

Cody led the way this time, down into the scrub and shorter trees of the river bank. "He just said not to punch anybody again and if Olivia was still bullyin' me, I should tell somebody."

"I thought maybe you'd get suspended."

"They couldn't of without suspendin' Olivia," said Cody. "She's the one who started it."

"Why wouldn't they suspend Olivia?"

Cody didn't answer. She walked faster and Hoyte had to skip a step or two to catch up. The dry odor of autumn leaves fretted the air and the last cicadas sipped the fraying sunlight. Any other year, the waters of the river would have pooled and eddied between dry stones but the hurricane-soaked earth fed the tributaries and kept the basins full. Cody almost slipped in the greasy dirt between the path's exposed roots. She rode one foot under the other and smoothly swung on a sapling next to the path. Hoyte paused. He followed the girl's motion, full of a new admiration.

"Are you comin'?" she asked.

"Yeah. What's your hurry?"

But again Cody didn't answer and as the path rose out of the dark gully, with its hoops of flood-exposed roots, Hoyte saw the boys where they had met the week before. Cody hooked her thumbs through the straps of her backpack.

Jerry, the one with the lean fox-like face, cropped hair, and sharp nose, stood with one shoulder against the old sycamore. The other two boys, Mike and Roy, were sitting on the bare length of a tree trunk turned into a bench. This was a gathering place not just for the boys. A charcoal heap circled by stones, burnt cans, and bottles was within sitting distance of the trunk. Cody still didn't know which was Mike and which was Roy, but one of them moved over when he saw Cody.

"You get expelled?" Jerry asked.

"No." Cody didn't take the seat.

"Heard that was a hell of a punch you threw," said one of the boys sitting on the trunk, the one with the black baseball cap and the wide lips. "Remind me not to get into a fight with you."

"It just sort of happened," said Cody.

"My cousin is half-Indian," said the other boy. He was heavier set with a butch haircut. "He can run like hell and's quiet as a snake goin' through grass. He's the best hunter in the family; and I know it 'cause he's Indian. You don't wanna mess with anybody got Indian in 'em."

"Nah," said Jerry. He gazed at Cody with narrowed eyes. "All it takes is gettin' a hard whoopin'." He waited as if for Cody to agree, but she didn't have to. "Get a good whoopin' and then you know how to whoop anybody."

Cody ran her tongue under her bottom lip, then looked away. The hook in her stomach wasn't fear.

"We gotta get goin'," said Hoyte, but Cody let her backpack slip from her back.

"You ever taste beer?" Jerry asked.

"No," said Cody, as if surprised he'd ask, but her smile was like a dare.

"Mike's got some beer."

Mike was already taking the beer out of his backpack. Mike was the boy with the butch haircut. Now she knew. Mike drew out a tall beer can.

"If your brother ever finds out you're stealin' those, you're gonna be the next one gettin' an ass-whoopin'," said Roy admiringly.

"I didn't steal it," said Mike, "I misappropriated it."

"You mis-what?"

"Exactly, Roy." Mike wiped the lip of the can with his shirt sleeve. "See? I'll be halfway 'cross the country before you two morons figure out what I said." Mike offered the beer to Cody and Cody might have taken just enough to taste but there was a bonding and sacredness in the offer. She lifted the can to her lips and took two swallows. Her eyes grew wide and she held the can away from her. She turned her head to the side, voiced the bitterness of the beer with closed eyes and a stuck-out tongue.

"Never had beer?" Roy asked.

Mike held out his hand.

"One more," said Cody.

"Don't you mess with her, Mike" said Roy with an eager smile.

Cody tipped back the can, this time letting the beer fill her mouth, tasting it, feeling the fermentation pop on her tongue, then momentarily held it in her mouth as she handed the beer back to Mike.

"So what do you think?" asked Jerry.

He made her shy. She wanted to please him. "I like it."

"You want a veritable beer, Hoyte?" Mike asked.

"Veritable?" asked Roy.

"Means the real thing," said Mike tugging up his pants.

"It does not," said Roy.

"It does so and you'd know it if you read books—spelled b-o-o-k-s. You might have heard of them."

Hoyte took the beer. He wouldn't have if not for Cody.

"I bet she leaves you alone now," said Mike.

"I bet she doesn't," said Cody.

"How do you know?" said Roy. "Seems to me like you gave her a pretty good whoopin'."

Cody shrugged. "Just don't think she's gonna."

"What's between you and her is your business," said Jerry, "but if she brings anybody else into it, you let us know."

"That's right," said Roy. "We'll nip in the butt."

"The what?" said Jerry.

"I said we'll nip it in the butt."

"It's bud," said Mike.

"Who's Bud?"

"Roy— Now, somebody outta hit you upside the head," said Mike. "It's not butt. It's bud. You nip it in the bud. Like a flower bud."

"Well that might work for a flower," said Roy. "But if somebody's up to mischief—if you're gonna stop 'em—then you gotta nip 'em in the butt. Who's gonna care 'bout some flower?"

"It's not a proper expression."

"Says who?"

"Idiomatic English," Mike persisted.

"Who?"

"I like butt," said Cody.

"I bet if you nipped somebody's butt that'd stop 'em alright," Jerry mused appreciatively.

"Philistines," said Mike.

Then they thoughtfully quieted as they imagined how that would sugar off, who would say what, and how their new pact would be invoked. From a nearby street the snarl of acceleration rattled their quiet.

"Jake Farnham," said Roy with an appreciative smile.

"That's a helluva pickup he built himself," said Mike. "I'm makin' one for myself."

"You and what mechanic," said Hoyte.

"You watch."

"I wouldn'ta wasted a motor like that on a pickup," said Roy.

"It's a sleeper," said Cody.

"I woulda put it in a Mustang or somethin' like that," said Mike.

"Can't even," said Roy.

"You even know what he's got in there?" Jerry asked.

"He's got a 427 Big Block," said Cody matter-of-factly. "And you could fit it in a Mustang. I saw it done."

The boys gazed at Cody. Stunned. "How do you know that?" Roy asked.

"I'm in love," said Mike.

"Just by listenin' to it," said Cody.

"You cannot," said Hoyte.

"Ask him if I'm right," said Cody with the flicker of a smile. She tilted her head back and stared Roy down.

Mike leaned back on the palms. "Give her another beer!"

"You know Jake?" Roy asked.

"I wouldn'ta put it in," Cody added.

"Why not?" Jerry asked.

Cody shrugged. "I'd of made it the way it was."

"You wanna work on cars someday?"

"I already done," said Cody.

"With who?"

Cody's expression changed, lips rolled shut. She shrugged. "My dad."

They talked for another ten minutes, then Cody swung her backpack over her shoulders and Roy crushed the empty can underfoot, digging it into the dirt. "Hey," said Jerry. He pulled a jar of peanuts out of his backpack. "These are to cover up your breath. Roy and Mike held out their hands and so did Hoyte and Cody. Jerry portioned the peanuts into each of their hands. Cody and Hoyte stashed theirs in their jacket pocket, then took the path that climbed the wooded slope to Soot Tabor's neighborhood. The other boys continued along the riverbank, their houses further along. Cody led the way, mindful to ration the precious peanuts.

"How you feelin'?" asked Hoyte.

"Okay."

"You feel it?" he asked.

"A little," said Cody, a slight wobble and lightheadedness in her step.

5

Cody and Hoyte helped Soot weed her garden and pick cherry tomatoes. When Cody's basket was full, she brought it into Soot's kitchen where Soot and Ada Byron were boiling them. Soot looked twice at Cody, then asked her to sit at the kitchen table. She turned Cody's chair so that they faced each other.

"How do you feel?"

Cody swallowed. "Fine!"

"You sure, sweetheart?" Soot studied the air above and beside Cody. She shook her head. "There's something wrong."

Cody's heart raced. She dug her hands into her jacket pocket, fingers tightening around the last peanuts. "I'm okay. I feel fine."

"Has a doctor looked at you since the accident?"

Cody shook her head.

Soot cupped Cody's cheeks in the palm of her hand. "And what happened to your face?"

"Had a run-in with a tree."

"That reminds me of my days climbing trees." Soot turned to Ada, dicing tomatoes next to the stovetop. "Were you a tree-climber when you were a little girl, Ada?"

"Oh, I loved climbing trees."

Soot turned back to Cody. "I remember the day my mother forbid me climbing trees. It was Pater Butterfield who was friends with my older brother, and he decided that day he'd climb trees with me while he waited for my brother, so I took him on a tour. He was a gentleman, you see, and insisted: Ladies First! I liked that. Boys didn't always let girls take the lead. Well, mother got wind of what was going on and called me in. Then and there she forbid me climbing any more trees and then went out and I don't know but poor Pater didn't show his face for a long while after that.

"Of course I had no idea but my mother said I was too old to be climbing trees. In those days we girls wore skirts more than kids nowadays. I had no idea why my mother threw such a fit but not too long after that I sussed it out. Naïve preteen me! He was climbing trees for the view alright. I stopped climbing in skirts after that, at least when boys were around; or at least I made sure it was the right boy.

"I think my mother had no idea I'd be horrified and titillated. A boy wanting to look at one-eyed me! I suppose my mother reasoned that if she'd told me why he was following me up the tree, I'd have gone out to show him more. But that's another story. All you need to know, Cody, is that somewhere in the waters of life, your frog-prince awaits, but those waters are full of sweet-talking alligators."

Cody knew she sat before the one-eyed witch. She sat like the guilty awaiting sentence; hands folded in her lap, feet tucked under the chair and lifted to the toes. Soot knew about the beer. Soot knew about the sweet-talking boys. Soot knew why there were peanuts in Cody's pocket. Guilt rang in her ears, thumped in her breast, sucked the breath out of her lungs.

"You look pale as a ghost," said Soot. "I have that effect on people. Sometimes while skipping stones I've been known to sink a toad or two."

Cody swallowed again, and suddenly solicitous, asked if Soot would like more tomatoes.

"How is Ratter doing?" Soot asked.

"She caught a mouse two nights ago."

"I suppose if you're a cat there's nothing so rewarding as catching a mouse," said Soot, and Cody decided then and there she had never met a sorceress so subtle or dangerous. Then Soot added: "I would love more tomatoes."

"Hey," said Ada, "I hear you're helping to build your mom's new house."

"When I'm not at school."

"You think your mom could help me build a tiny house when she gets better?"

"Soon as she's better she might."

"Tell her Ada Byron is ready to move out of Soot's second bedroom and strike out on her own. Tell her she wants to build a tiny house that will follow her wherever she goes."

After that Cody straight away returned to the garden and couldn't bear to look at Hoyte.

"You still feelin' that beer?" Hoyte asked.

"I'm fine." Cody dropped an extra peanut in her mouth.

6

In an act of generosity and magnanimity, as Cody deemed it, Soot said nothing to Arvid or Drew when they picked her up. Ada gave the children paper bags filled with zucchini, squash, and a handful of cherry tomatoes.

Halfway up the mountain, Drew turned in her seat, eyeing Cody. "Since when do you eat peanuts?"

"We got 'em at school."

"You'll eat peanuts but you won't eat peanut butter? You know you're the only kid in Vermont who doesn't like peanut butter— the only one."

"I'll eat peanut butter."

"You will?"

The words slipped out, panicked, meant to put her mother off the scent.

"Just how hard did that tree hit you?" Drew asked,

"It wasn't the tree." The beginnings of maturity is when childhood's neat and separate piles of beans, onions, carrots, and herbs are put into the soup and stirred. Cody saw how deception in one ingredient sets all the other ingredients awry, such that the wages of beer lead to a lifetime of peanut butter—and in the belly of an alligator.

It was a glum ride to the house.

But when they reached the driveway, Drew turned in her seat again. "Hey, babe," she said, "you see that bag between you and Hoyte. You wanna carry that in for me?"

"What is it?"

Drew swung around, lifted herself to one foot with a hand on the car roof. "It's a present for Virginia."

Cody followed her mother down the embankment. The shadows under September's late afternoon sun were longer and darker and a cold wind had followed the morning's rains. Cody drew her jacket tighter. "When are we puttin' the windows in?" she asked.

"Soon."

Virginia had taken down the sheets dividing Cody's old room from the kitchen. The couch was moved so that it faced the picture window and she had laid three boards over two cinder blocks to make a coffee table. Cody put the bag on the coffee table. Drew found Virginia folding the sheets in her bedroom.

"I got you something."

"For me?" Virginia paused.

Drew backed up, inviting Virginia to follow. "It's out on your coffee table."

Virginia neatly put down the sheet. "You certainly didn't have to get me a present." She went to the couch and pulled out the two gift-wrapped books. She glanced at both Cody and Drew as she carefully opened them.

"Just tear the paper!" said Cody.

"Did you have anything to do with this?" Virginia asked Cody.

Cody shook her head.

Virginia gently slipped the first of the two books out of the wrapping paper—a textbook on nursing; then the second—a resource manual. "Oh Drew! These are expensive books!"

Drew smiled, shrinking a little like her daughter. "I know."

"Well, I don't know what to say." Virginia's eyes grew damp. She stood. She carefully reached for Drew, one arm over Drew's shoulder and embraced her. When she let go, Drew still nodded and smiled; and it struck Cody that she hadn't seen her mother smile so freely since her father's death. "You too!" said Virginia, and she hugged Cody. "It's just so unexpected. These are expensive books!"

Drew shrugged, then said more intently. "Those are good books, right?"

"Yes. They're wonderful books."

"Good," said Drew softly, then relaxing. "Good."

"I'm going to have to build a bookshelf now. I suppose that shouldn't be too hard after building a house. And I suppose I should think about nursing, shouldn't I?"

Chapter 14

She smiled. Can you imagine?

You could say
She was a clumsy child, almost uncaring.
I never will forget that day she dropped
My mother's Doccia Plate. I could have cried—
I did. A Tulipano. Very rare.
The plate was what she wanted though. As soon
As I would leave she'd take it from the shelf,
Sit in her chair and turn it 'round. Whatever
She saw in it I'll never know.

My worst fear
Was that she'd break it. When she did, I told her—
I told her— I was not unkind but firm
You understand. She had so many toys
To play with— I was firm. One has to be
With children.

On the following morning, Sunday,
I called for her and called. She wouldn't come.
I thought, as she would sometimes do, that she
Ignored me. When I went into her room
I found her staring out the bedroom window,
Her hair was soaking wet, as were the sheets—
Why don't you answer me? I asked.

Look, Mother,
She said, she's tapping on the glass. See?
She keeps pink ribbons 'round each finger–nine–
A ribbon for each daughter that she has.
But see, she has ten fingers mother, ten;
And though I counted all night long, she has
Nine ribbons.

Dear, I said, that is the dogwood
And just a branch that scrapes the glass, the ribbons
Are its blossoms, nothing more. She turned.
I never will forget how green her eyes were.
Her lips were almost scarlet, as though the fever
Were only in her lips and eyes. The sheets
Were tangled in her arms and legs, the child
Was always restless.

     I helped her out of bed
I bathed her and I washed her hair. She had
The loveliest hair when she would let me groom it.
It started at her widow's peak and fell
Behind her ears before the bangs swept forward
To curl at the corners of her lips—
You've heard, I'm sure, when hair's described as heart-shaped.
Hers was like that.

     Mother, she said, all night
I saw her coming from the hilltop down
To stand outside my window. She wore a cape,
Black with silver threads. I could not find
Where any one began or ended; in
Her hair were burning candles, more than I
Could count, and even brighter was her face.
She said if only I would close my eyes
Then she would take me in the cape, the light,
She promised, would not be so bright. But mother
I would not sleep.

     My dear, I said, the cape
Was nothing but the field, the silver threads
The hillside birches and the candles in her hair
Were stars; and though you thought she stood outside
It only was the moon that rose behind
The hilltop slowly higher 'til you thought
She must have come to look at you.

     But mother, she said—
          I interrupted her. It's time
For breakfast. You have had a fever, dear,
And nothing more.

(You understand, in those days
You let a fever run its course. Whenever
Had mother or her mother—
They made do!

The roads were muddy troughs and on a Sunday?
No. That's how it was. What needed done
We did ourselves. We were that kind of people.
We always were.)

You need fresh air, I said.
I took her to the kitchen where I opened
The door. She backed away.

There's nothing there
I said, no one!

But, Mother, close the door
Please, she's whispering and whispering
To me.

It is the wind, I said.
*   But when*
She passes by her daughters, they will let
The flowers down they gathered in their tresses
And spill their aprons. Mother, see? She takes
Their flowers and she blows them from her hands
Into the door for me.

It is the wind,
I said, the wind; and those are not her daughters
But apple trees—the wind shakes loose their blossoms.
Come, stand beside me in the door. She did
And held my hand as tightly as she could,
As though it were the threshold frightening her.
There's no one here. I told her. No one. Is there?
I see, was all she said.

Of course, I answered.
She rubbed her eyes. She quietly looked again
And pointed.

There's the tree, she said,
That scrapes my windows: there, that branch. It bends
Around itself just like the curled up finger
Of someone knocking at the door. They want
To be let in. And there, out in the field,
The birch trees that looked like silver threads. They are
So slender, Mother, and so many, they
Are like a bird cage. If I were a bird
I'd never want to fly in them. A bird
Could never find its way back out; all day

It would just have to sing and sing and hope—
Because if no one hears birds they keep singing
Until their hope is gone. And look how when
The wind blows hard enough the apple trees
Can almost reach their branches to the ground,
As if they wanted back the flowers they lost—
But it's too late. Once they're gone, Mother, they
Can't be brought back. Isn't that right? They just
All blow away. Mother, stay here with me.
Please stay.

     I said—I have too much to do.
First to the cellar for your breakfast, then
We have to glue the plate together, then
I put you back to bed. I turned. She stopped me.
She pointed out the door and to the garden.
It's called a tulip, Mother, right?

     The flower?
I asked. Yes—yes dear.

     I was gone a moment,
You understand. Just to the cellar—
I found her sitting in the doorway, knees
Drawn up, head resting on her knees, her hands
And skirt bunched in her lap.

     I said to her—
I said—you have to cover up your legs.
I saw the breeze tussle her hair. You'll chill!
I said.

     And only when I knelt beside her–
I couldn't see (the sun was bright, too bright,
Reflecting in the doorway) – only then
I saw—held in her hands– that she had picked
The tulip!

     Dear, I said.
        She wouldn't answer.
Wake up, I said. You'll chill again. Wake up—

1

Over the next few weeks Drew taught Virginia how to hang a door, install windows, and rough-in wiring. Drew's mood lightened. If two hands weren't enough, then Drew leaned on her crutches or against the wall to lend a third. Her bones hurt less every day and the knots of bruised flesh were looser. For plumbing, Drew called in Barstowe, whose plumbing skills depended on what was being bartered.

The day of his arrival he leaned out of the truck and freed himself like a cork from a bottle. He wiped his brow. He went to the back of the truck, let the tailgate fall with a dusty *thunk,* and pulled out a scraped and dented metal toolbox. "Get's goddamn heavier every time I lift it." When he made his way into the basement, with Drew following, he said it again with extra emphasis. "Get's goddamn heavier every time! Why do you s'pose that is?"

"Sorry I can't help," said Drew.

"Not as if you could, anyway," he rounded the corner, opened the basement's newly hung door. "You know how it is, Drew. There's every tool besides the two you need. But sure as weather, leave one out and that'll be the one I need."

Barstowe briefly studied the framing. "And where's your kitchen?"

"Already drilled the holes," Drew pointed. "Hot. Cold. And gray water."

"Hell, Drew, I'll have that run before noon. You couldn't have schooled Virginia in the art of sweating pipes? And how's she doin'? You two gonna go into business?"

"Not if she has any sense."

"She don't look so much the type likes gettin' her hands dirty."

"Used to be a nurse."

"Used to be?"

"Her husband didn't like her workin'."

"Wish to hell I had a wife didn't like me workin'."

 "You'd need a wife first."

"Too much work."

"Work suits you."

"I suppose so," Barstowe grumbled, kneeling over his toolbox, sorting through it. "A man gets a reputation for hard work when all he's done is worked hard to avoid work."

"Good a career as any, George."

"I know, but it's the hardest one." Barstowe took out a saw and set to installing a Y in the plumbing stack. "Since you got nothin' better than stand there bein' a cripple, how is it worked out between you and Virginia?"

"It's workin' George. She gave us half the property. Was already subdivided by her grandad. Soon as we're done buildin' this place me and Cody are gonna build a new place."

"And that's alright by Cody?"

"That or we move into the truck," said Drew.

"I bet she wouldn't mind that."

"What's that mean, George?"

"Well now," said Barstowe, "she's got an eye for the mechanical. Haven't ya noticed? I've seen it. She don't give a damn one way or t'other for the buildin' trade, but put her in that old Ford of yours and I bet she'd have it polished and mint in no time."

"Yeah, she and Daryl." Drew's jaw clenched. She pushed her hand through her black hair.

"Don't grudge her that. You know that little car lot I used to have? There's most customers look at a rundown car and see a rundown car. But Cody shows up with Virginia and she's lookin' at those cars and seein' if she could make somethin' out of 'em. Didn't say a word. She didn't have to."

Drew leaned back. "We're not livin' out of a pickup truck at least."

"Hope it works out for ya, Drew."

"Virginia's okay, George; and I like it up here. Even just sellin' that lot downtown would get us enough to drill a well, run some power and build us somethin' we can start livin' in."

"You think Virginia's gonna want this place?"

"Who wants to know?" Drew asked with a prodding smile. "You seem awful interested in Virginia, George."

"Now don't you jump to conclusions."

"She's okay."

"Is she? Just?"

"Why are you askin' me, George?"

"Now I'm just bein' conversational but, you know, I remember her grandpap. He was a character. There's a story 'bout him when Brookway up and decided Slim's Pond ought to be designated a lake. The town council got together and announced there'd be a public hearing. Hugh Darby's farm abutted Slim's Pond in those days. He figured his property line didn't stop at the water's edge; and he was proud of his beach front property besides. He'd go to fish on Sundays. Every now and then the pastor would see him on a Sunday mornin' and let him know what he thought of that. Hugh would say that when fish went to church, he'd go there too.

"But anyway, Hugh got wind of the town meanin' to designate his pond a lake and bein' Hugh decided there was no good behind it. Changin' the pond to a lake was like takin' his property. If government by committee could change a pond to a lake, then there wasn't anything sacred. So on the day of the committee he tugged up his britches and drove his tractor into town bein' as his old Dodge was in no mood. And after that tractor was done with him, Hugh's mood was no better. He got up before the committee and set before them his argument. 'What damned fool committee,' he announced, 'with nothin' better besides, takes it as a matter of oath and consequence to change a pond to a lake?'

"Old Severance Shipley took exception to being designated a 'damned fool' committee and told Hugh so. Besides, he said, there was a public beach on Slim's Pond and designating the pond a lake might do to increase tourism and put a little extra in the pockets of local businesses.

"'Well,' said Hugh, 'what are these so-called tourists gonna think when they show up expectin' a lake?'

"'Well now, Hugh,' said Severence, 'I've known you to advertise farm fresh eggs as if they were a different egg from the mean. What other kinds of eggs are there in these parts? They're all farm fresh. And I've seen you advertise your corn as sweet corn and sugar corn as if all the rest of us didn't have more sense than to sell feed corn. But that's all we're trying to do, Hugh. We're just trying to gussy up Slim's Pond.'

"'Now look!' said Hugh; but Hugh, his store of wit less than his argument's acreage, sputtered to a stop. All that was left him was to set forth the facts as he saw them. 'By God that en't no lake! Why, I could piss halfway 'cross it!'

"That was enough for Mrs. Eddie Granger, who stood straight up and said to old Hugh, 'You're out of order, Hugh Darby!'

"'Damn right I am,' he said, 'if it wasn't for bein' out of order I'd piss all the way 'cross it!'"

2

Mrs. Santoff's full name was Julia Delilah Santoff. She was young and new to the office. She didn't sit behind her desk but took a seat opposite Cody, legs folded beneath her. She wore thick black glasses and habitually pushed them up the bridge of her nose. Cody, meanwhile, stared at her feet.

"You can call me Julia." Mrs. Santoff flashed a brief smile.

"I know."

"We can talk about anything."

"But you don't want to talk about anything," said Cody.

"Try me."

Cody continued to stare at her feet, fidgeted, pressed her lips together and stretched in her seat as if eager to discover the key that would unlock the room. "Do you believe in witches?"

"Okay. Sure. What kind of witches? You mean like the kind that wear tall black hats and ride brooms?"

"No."

"You mean like the witches in *Bewitched*?"

"Bewitched?"

"*Bewitched* was an old TV show about a guy who married a witch. Her name was Samantha. She looked like everybody else—was beautiful, blonde, and wiggled her nose when she cast spells."

"Sort of."

"So that kind of witch?"

"Yeah," said Cody, looking up from her feet, "what happened to her?"

"The first thing that happened was that her husband made her promise she wouldn't use witchcraft."

"Why?"

"So—" Julia paused. "Life is like rolling dice. Sometimes the unexpected is terrible, it's also what makes life surprising and wonderful. Imagine if you played a game with your best friend and she could always make the dice roll however she wanted?"

"That would be cheating."

"Exactly."

"But if she's a witch then it's not fair to make her not be a witch." Cody sat up, palms resting on the seat's edge, "It's like being really good at something, and being told you can't do it."

"So would you let your friend bewitch the dice?"

Cody considered that, saw the trap, and squirmed defiantly on the seat's edge. "No."

"You'd want her to play normal just like Darren wanted Samantha to play normal."

"But did her magic help him?"

"Many times."

"And he still didn't want her to use witchcraft?"

"He still didn't."

"But if it helped him—" Cody threw himself back into the seat, "then it's like she knew how to do somethin' he didn't. It's no different than if I was really good at somethin' and you weren't."

"Why wouldn't he want her to do something if she were good at it?"

Cody drew up her shoulders, swaying left and right, but no answer came forth.

"Okay," said Julia, "Let me ask this way—"

"Because he's mad," Cody interrupted. "Because when you're really good at somethin' and somebody else isn't, you get jealous and don't want to play anymore."

"Have you ever played games with somebody you couldn't beat?"

"Can't throw rocks as far as Hoyte."

"So did you quit?"

"No, 'cause I'm smarter than him and I'd rather be smarter than good at rock throwin'."

"Yeah, in life, it's not like you can just up and quit the board game, is it?"

"Some do," said Cody darkly.

Julia nodded, touching Cody's wrist. "You're right."

Cody let that simmer for a moment. "Some do and it isn't enough they just go away but they gotta change the rules and if that doesn't work they gotta pick fights, and if they can't cheat they gotta try'n knock the whole game off the table, and everybody with it."

"Why do you think people are like that?"

"'Cause if they can't win then nobody can. 'Cause it's like you're still makin' the rules. If you don't let anybody play how they wanna play and you don't let anybody win, then it's like you're makin' the rules and it's like you're still winnin'."

"So what would you do?"

"There's always gonna be somethin' somebody's better at."

"What if you were a witch?"

"Like in the TV show?"

"Sure."

"Well first I wouldn'ta married him."

"Why not?"

"'Cause I wouldn't want to not be a witch."

"So what about a friend?"

Cody sat back and kicked at the air. "They wouldn't be a friend if it bothered them I was a witch!" Then thoughtfully sitting up, her palms once again on the edge of the seat, elbows straight. "Why do people even care about what happened to me? I didn't mean for any of it to happen."

"So Darren and Samantha had an argument when she told him she was a witch," said Julia. "Darren didn't believe her. He said he had an aunt who believed she was a lighthouse. You know what Samantha said?"

"What?"

"She said that maybe his aunt really was a lighthouse, that Darren was the one who couldn't see the world the way it really was."

Cody sat with this for a while, turning the idea in her thoughts like a lovely puzzle. "And then what?"

"Well that's the point. We all think the aunt is crazy, but maybe it's all of us who are crazy?"

3

"Where were you this morning?" Audrey asked.

"Mom's truck broke down again."

"What happened?"

"Radiator."

"Don't you ride the bus?"

"Had to meet Mrs. Santoff early and the truck broke comin' down the hill."

Audrey traded peanuts for Cody's apple. "So when did you start likin' peanuts?"

Cody shrugged. "No reason."

"So what was it like?" Audrey leaned across the table. "Did you lie down on a couch?"

Cody wiped a peanut from her lips. "No— we talked about a TV show. About a witch."

"Seriously?"

"About why her husband wouldn't let her use magic."

"Why not?"

"'Cause maybe he thought it was like cheatin'."

"That doesn't sound fair if she's a witch."

"I know."

"And that was all you talked about?'

"Yeah," said Cody.

"I don't get it."

"So what if you had a friend who had special powers, like a witch?" Cody asked.

Audrey stared. "I do."

"Who?"

"You."

And it was then that the notion finally landed on Cody as to who she and Mrs. Santoff had really been talking about. She sat back and turned her new discovery around as if it were a new toy to pick apart. Then she leaned forward again. "Would you play cards with me?"

"Right now?"

"Knowin' I might read your mind?"

"Yeah, but there'd have to be rules about no cheating."

"So you wouldn't let me use magic?"

"That's not the same!" Then Audrey leaned forward, speaking conspiratorially, "So what was the TV show?"

"*Bewitched.*"

"Wanna look it up?"

"How?"

"On my smartphone," said Audrey. "I bet we could watch."

4

The next Saturday morning was Drew's day to get a walking boot. Cody was going with her and waited in the loft, reading; but when she didn't hear her mother calling, she finally rolled over, half slid, half jumped down the ladder. She didn't bother tying her sneakers. She stepped carefully down the embankment, avoiding the wet clumps of grass. Cody went to the sheet covering the doorway to her mother's room, then stopped.

"Just these," she heard her mother answer impatiently.

Drew peaked through the curtain. Virginia was on the floor. She had a little pill box in her right hand and was picking up pills under the bed. Her mother was sitting on the edge of the bed, the leg with the cast straight in front of her. Her crutches lay next to her.

"Why are you still taking these," Virginia asked. "You should have been off these weeks ago!"

"I'll quit when the pain quits."

"You've been crying."

"It's what you do when a piece of shit tries to kill you and your daughter."

"It's the withdrawal, honey."

"What do you know?"

Virginia didn't answer at first. She continued picking up the pills. "Well, there's more than one way to murder a spouse. My husband didn't have to drive me off the road; he just had to leave a middle-aged woman with nothing."

"Must be a real eye-opener," said Drew.

"I know. I'm nobody special."

"Give me the pills."

"Why?"

"Because it's my goddamn medication."

"This isn't your medication!" said Virginia. "Where did you get these?"

"It's none of your business."

"These aren't helping you."

"So how would you know what kind of help I need?"

"I used to see women like you every day. I probably should have said something sooner."

"You think I'm an addict?"

"You're dependent. Why are you taking these? Are you still in pain or scared?" she paused. "Maybe I should take one? If I go back to nursing I can get as many as I want. I know lots of nurses who took pain medications and more; and God knows I've lost control of my life." Virginia picked one of the pills from the pillbox.

"So you think this is all in my head?"

"It's that or you're still in pain," said Virginia. "Are you still in pain?"

"What are you doin'?"

"I'm taking one."

"Don't!"

"Why not?"

"You don't need it," said Drew.

"Give me one good reason."

"I don't see you on fucking crutches." Drew threw one of them at Virginia's feet. "Need it? It's yours."

"That's not a reason."

"Then what is?"

"Your daughter."

"I can look after my daughter."

"You're angrier every day."

Drew was silent. Ratter slipped between the curtain and jamb and Drew saw Cody. "C'mon, babe. Stop hiding. Come in."

Virginia was momentarily at a loss, then put the pills on the bedside table and left.

"Do you—" Cody hesitated.

"Do I what?"

"Do you still wanna go?"

"Why wouldn't I want to go?"

"'Cause it's almost eight."

Drew gestured to the clothes flung over the back of the chair. "Grab those, babe. Why didn't you get me?"

"Didn't know I was s'posed to."

"So you were just gonna sit in your loft?"

"No!" Cody passed the clothes to Drew. "I just didn't know I was s'posed to get you."

"While I listen to fucking Virginia?" Drew pulled on her top. "Jesus Christ, Cody."

"I would've if you'd told me!"

"You gonna spend the rest of your life havin' to be told?"

Cody looked as though she meant to say something but shoved her hands into her overalls and backed against the wall. She shrank into her unzipped hoodie.

"Cody, what's wrong with you? Get my clothes!"

Cody diffidently went to the chair and returned with carpenter pants and a t-shirt. "Why don't you wear a dress? It'd be easier to get on."

"Are you gonna help me or not?—Give me the crutch."

"Why are you so mad?"

"We're late."

"Do you want something to eat?" Virginia asked from their makeshift kitchen.

Drew buttoned her pants and hopped onto one foot, tipping the crutches under her. "We don't have time," said Drew but Cody took what Virginia offered, nibbling at the eggs and toast as she followed her mother's halting progress.

Virginia drove. Drew pushed back her seat as far as it would go, distractedly studied the passing landscape. Then she finally glared at Cody. "Really? Watching TV?"

"If Mr. Vine hadn't caught us nobody'd care."

"So it's only bad if you get caught?"

"Isn't it?" Cody asked defiantly.

"No!"

"Why not? If it's not hurtin' anybody, what's it matter?"

"What's it matter? You're there to go to school, not to watch TV. Did you think nobody was gonna notice?"

Cody crossed her arms. "How'd we know the school clock was wrong?"

"You were looking at a smartphone!" Drew jammed her cast into the floorboard and grimaced. "How could you not know what time it was?"

"It was full screen."

"Jesus Christ, Cody!" Drew glared at the cars ahead. "And how— That's not even the point! You shouldn't be watching TV when you're at school!"

"It was only because of Mrs. Santoff," Cody glowered.

"Mrs. Santoff?"

"Yeah. I didn't even want to go."

"So you're blaming her?"

Cody twisted in her seat. "That's not what I'm sayin'."

"You don't wanna go again? 'Cause it sure seems like you must'a had a great conversation if it made you wanna skip class?"

"I didn't mean to!" Cody's voice rose.

"You know why we're doin' this? 'Cause I got child protective services up my ass. You know what they're gonna do if they decide I can't take care of you? They're gonna find somebody else and there's gonna be nothin' I can do about it! You understand that? You wanna end up with Daryl's parents? Fuck, Cody, this isn't the time to turn into a teenager. You think you can hold off for just another year maybe? Maybe 'til we get the state off our backs? Jesus, babe, next thing you'll take up drinkin'."

"What about you?"

"What *about* me?"

Cody crossed her arms. "You're takin' drugs you're not supposed to."

Drew gazed darkly out the window. "Okay."

They sat in silence after that, then Drew finally asked: "So you gonna tell me what you were watchin'?"

"*Bewitched.*"

"Oh, I used to just love that show!" Virginia volunteered. "I couldn't get enough. The actress who played Samantha was such a dear! I wanted to be just like her, but I could never understand why Darren wouldn't let her be a witch?"

"See?" Cody blurted.

"Then I got married," Virginia nodded. "And I found out I was just like her."

"Why?"

"Well, I decided it was more important to be who he wanted me to be."

"Who did you want to be?"

"I wanted to be a nurse!" said Virginia. "That was my magical power, sweetie. But Lester wanted a stay-at-home housewife."

"So why did you give up what you wanted?"

Virginia gave a sharp laugh. "Because my husband was the devil. He promised me everything I wanted: a house, cars, lots of money. All I had to do was give up my magic powers."

"Your nursing?"

"My soul," said Virginia.

"Devil can't take your soul 'less you agree to it."

"Dunno, babe," said Drew flatly, "seems like you were a pushover for a little TV."

"That's not the same as sellin' your soul!"

"Selling?" Drew laughed. "You don't drive a hard bargain."

"Not like you even believe in the devil," Cody crossed her arms again.

"Grandpa used to say your soul's like a garden." Drew leaned into Cody. "You do good and all that good will grow like flowers. Problem is, life's full of rats too. If you're not careful, you'll be nothin' but weeds on the inside."

"We were just watchin' a show." Cody didn't budge.

"Jesus, but you're stubborn."

5

They were in a spacious room. Drew sat on a reddish brown exam table, one leg down, and the cast up. Large windows looked out toward Mount Mansfield and above a swath of rooftops. The nurse scissored through the cast's remaining fabric and pulled it apart. Cody leaned closer, studying Drew's leg. It was slack, shapeless, and covered in a film of dead skin. There were thick crusty scars around her ankle and the ankle itself looked like a bony fist. The nurse wiped Drew's leg with a damp cloth as the doctor came in.

"Can I touch?" Cody asked.

"You really wanna touch that?" said Drew.

"Yeah."

"Okay, babe. Suit yourself."

Cody leaned against the exam table and touched the intersecting scars behind and around her mother's ankle. She traced them with her finger's tip and stepped back. "Are you gonna be able to walk now?"

"Maybe" said Drew.

"Just a little," said the doctor. "Baby steps."

Cody decided she didn't need to know so much about walking boots. She went into the hallway and found Virginia talking to the nurses at a nursing station. "I'm going out front," she said and returned to the hospital's main entrance. There were a handful of tables and couches in a little waiting area. Outside the automatic doors, orange and yellow marigolds hung in pots. As Cody walked toward the doors, the flowers burst into a vapor of flames. The orange and yellow petals fell like spits of fire and spread along the doors, over Cody's head, flowing like a flood of fiery water across the ceiling. The doors automatically opened and the inferno vanished. October's leaves dryly scraped the sidewalk. Shards of sunlight reflected from the parking lot. Cody went to a stone bench outside and to the left of the doors. She leaned over, her forehead in her palms, and closed her eyes.

Someone sat next to her.

"Are you okay?" a girl asked.

"I have a headache," Cody answered.

"My dad gets them. Migraines." Another silence followed before the girl asked, "Is that why you're here?"

"No. My mom's getting a walking boot."

"Broke her leg?"

"Yeah."

"How?"

"In a car—" she started to say 'accident' but stopped herself, "—wreck."

"I was in a car accident once, but nobody got hurt. My dad was driving. It was snowing and he lost control. We went off the road and down a field. The whole car was turning in circles 'til we stopped on top of a stump. The car couldn't be fixed but soon as it happened, Dad checked if we were okay and started making jokes."

"Why?"

"'Cause he said grandpa used to tell him a story about when grandpa was little. Grandpa's dad was driving the first car in town 'cause he was a doctor and it was still horse and buggy. He was goin' down a long hill and the car just kept goin' faster and faster; and the faster it went the more he was yellin' at it like it was a horse. Kept sayin' 'Whoa! Whoa! Whoa!' But the car kept ignorin' him, goin' faster 'til it saw some grass it liked, took a drink in the creek, and bounced up the other side. After it stopped Grandpa looked at his dad and said: 'Why didn't you just use the brakes?' Grandpa said it was the only time his dad ever slapped him. Dad says life's full of unexpected potholes. You can slap who's with you or you can laugh."

Cody sat up, blinking. She glanced at the dark-haired girl and froze. The girl's right cheek, temple, and arm were mottled, and her fingers shrunken.

"It's okay. See?" The girl held up her hand, slowly opening and closing it. "Our house caught fire."

"So—" Cody hesitated. "I mean— Sorry."

The other girl shrugged. "My dad's inside getting stuff for my burns. I still don't like goin' out in the sun. It feels like a really bad sunburn."

Cody lowered her head between her knees. Then she willed herself upright. "I didn't mean it that way."

"Are you sure you're okay?"

Just beyond the portico, in a downhill circle of flowers and shrubs, there was a low granite ledge with the hospital's name carved into it. A crow landed on the top, hopping to a stop, seeming to glance at Cody. It opened its wings, stretching.

"Do you see it?"

"Yeah," said the girl.

"Every time I see it, it's like it's tellin' me I'm supposed to notice somethin'."

"Like about the future?"

"Yeah."

"There was a girl who predicted the hurricane."

"I know."

"Did you hear about her?"

"Yeah."

The other girl was silent for a moment. "Do you think she really did?"

Cody straightened, palms balancing on the edge of the bench. "That was me," she said, embarrassed.

"Really?"

"Yeah."

"That was you?"

Cody nodded.

"Can I tell you something?"

"Okay."

"When I was in the house— When it was on fire— I tried to get out but there was so much smoke I couldn't breathe. I was looking at myself on the floor and I heard this voice. I knew it was Grandma even though she'd died. She said to close my eyes and breathe. I didn't want to but she said if I breathed she would help me get out. I said it hurt in the smoke and flames but she said it would be okay and showed me my whole life saying the pain was just a little part. So I breathed and it was awful. She told me to stand up and to not let go of her hand no matter what."

"Did she pull you out?"

"Yeah."

Both were silent after that, then the girl spoke again. "I told my mom but she doesn't want to talk about it and Dad doesn't believe in stuff that isn't science." Now she was looking at Cody. "I think it really happened."

"I believe you."

"I believe you too." The girl paused. "You should figure out what the crow is telling you."

6

"Now this is a new recipe," said Soot, "They're made with white wheat and I added wheat gluten just to see. And I might have started with too much yeast."

"What is it?" Lydia asked.

"It's my grandmother's Apple Jam Bread. Just break off a piece."

As before, the women's writing group was gathered in the Apple House. Meredith waited for the tray to reach her with something like a scowl. She broke off a piece from the braided loaf, inspected it, and tried it. "It's okay," she said.

"Honestly, Meredith," said Lydia, "it's delicious."

"That's what I said," Meredith objected over a mouthful of bread.

"You said it was okay."

"Do you want me to elaborate?"

"I think it's high praise coming from Meredith" said Soot.

"Speaking of praise," said Ada, "did you write that poem, Virginia?"

"Are we a poetry group now?" asked Meredith.

"We're a meeting of literary minds," said Lydia. "And I think that can include poetry."

"No," said Virginia. "I think it must be a translation."

"It's based on a German poem," said Ada, "why did you bring it?"

"Well," said Virginia, "I thought— I don't know. I've never read much poetry but this one struck a chord. I identify with the girl and the mother. I think I've been both. Sometimes I haven't listened and sometimes I haven't been heard. I just—well, that's it."

"What's the German poem?" asked Lydia.

"It's by Goethe," said Ada. "About a little boy with his father on horseback. The poem begins: Who's riding so late through the wind and wild? A father on horseback with his child. And then the father asks the child: Why, when I hold you tight do I feel you shivering with fright? The child answers: Don't you see the Alder King's crown? Don't you see his midnight's cloak? And then the father says: That's only the fog among the oaks. Then the Alder King calls to the boy: Child, child, come with me! My daughters will dance and sing you to sleep. But the father says it's only the leaves in the willows. And then the child cries: He holds my hands and kisses me here upon my head! The father shudders and holds him tight. He races home as fast as he can, the courtyard gates swing shut but the child lies dead in his arms."

"That's awful!" cried Lydia.

"It's sad and beautiful," said Soot.

"Now what do you mean when you say you feel like both?" asked Meredith.

"Well, isn't that child still inside us? The dreaming part? The part we lose if we don't listen to it?"

Jessie Aymes, who had decided to attend the writer's group after several absences, held the bread dangling between two fingers, elbow on the table. She addressed Virginia. "I just want to say that your situation is the most peculiar. I can't imagine how you're managing up there—you, Drew, and Cody."

"I—" Virginia paused, gazed at the ceiling while collecting her thoughts. "I think I'd have to write a novel."

"What you're doing for that girl—"

"Let's stay focused," Meredith interrupted, looking over her glasses at Jessie.

Jessie bridled. "I think it's remarkable."

"I suppose there are a good many remarkable occurrences during and since Hurricane Irene. But we're not here to catch up on village gossip. Did you have anything to add as concerns Virginia's poem?"

Jessie glanced at the other women and straightened. "Yes, Meredith, I might start by observing that you once dreamed of being a journalist. Whatever happened to that ambition?"

Meredith put down her remaining bread, momentarily rubbed her fingers, letting the crumbs fall. "Fair enough. But if the mother had believed the girl? I have to wonder the point. What could the mother have done? Indulged the girl? How would that have saved her life?"

"She might have taken the girl to the doctor," said Lydia.

"For having a fanciful imagination?" protested Meredith.

"Yes," said Soot evenly. "Imagination is a sign of insanity. What animal daydreams? What animals build castles in the air? Imagination is a dangerous thing. Does a girl imagine flying a broom over the midnight moon? Take her to the priests. They'll burn the imagination out of her. What if truth or death comes in the shape of a crow, carries a girl out of herself, and shows her the world overrunning its banks? What if she returns to warn us that a flood is coming? Was that all just fanciful imagination?"

A brief silence fell after Soot's questions.

Lydia nervously glanced at the other women. "Good Lord, Soot!"

Meredith sat back in her chair as though chagrined, then straightened again. "I admit—" Meredith nodded and said evenly, "I admit that the girl's warnings were prescient."

"Oh dear," Virginia offered sheepishly. "I suppose, at the time, I might have been embarrassed by her comments. But how do you know when to take comments like that seriously? We can't predict the future, can we?"

"Truth is timeless," said Jessie.

"What is that supposed to mean?" But Meredith's question was more statement than question.

"I suppose you think I'm spouting banalities," said Jessie. "But I'll tell you what I mean. I mean that the truth is like a thread. It's tied to a button at the beginning of time and to another at the world's end. Every once in a while there's some who glimpse that thread. It's just seeing the truth—just the thread that's the same no matter where we see it."

"Wouldn't that be a fun story to write," said Ada.

"You should write it," offered Soot.

"You know," continued Jessie, pushing her long white hair out of her face, "that thread runs through us too."

"Well of course it does," said Lydia.

"But that's it, don't you see?" said Jessie. "I suppose that kind of sight comes on us when death is neighborly, just as it came to the girl in the poem. She saw the truth but spoke it in a language the mother couldn't understand—and didn't care to. So you ask if the mother had believed her? As I see it, stories are as close to the truth as we come. And if nobody understands, then it's like we've flown into the birches and never find our way back out. She had to keep singing. The mother's understanding was that girl's only way out."

"Well," said Virginia, who'd been standing since she'd read the poem and wanted nothing more than to sit down again, "Well. I had no idea there was so much to be gotten from that. Now I don't know whether I'm coming or going."

"But do you want to know?" asked Ada.

"I—yes. Yes I do."

"Poems want you to hear them. They can't find their way out of their bird cages unless you hear them."

Chapter 15

1

"Morning, babe."

Cody didn't answer. She squeezed by her mother who stood at the plywood kitchen counter, and went to the table where there was already a glass of cider.

"Are you okay, babe?"

"Yeah," said Cody.

"Is jam and toast gonna be okay?"

"Yeah."

Drew put a plate in front of Cody, then sat across from her.

"Aren't you gonna eat?" Cody asked.

"I'm not hungry."

"You didn't eat last night."

"I know. Mommy isn't feelin' too hot."

"Are you sick?"

"Yeah. You could say that."

"What is it?"

Drew studied Cody before answering. "Hey. It's not easy for me either."

"I know."

"And we're gonna make it through this."

"It's takin' forever."

"Listen, I'm sorry for bein' cross with you this morning. It wasn't you. But look, maybe we should build ourselves a set of stairs. You had enough of walkin' 'round outside the house?"

"You wanna do that today?"

"If you don't mind askin' Hoyte to come over?"

"Where's Virginia?"

"Gettin' groceries. You wanna get Hoyte?"

"I'll get 'im." Cody put on a jacket. Since Cody had taken up with Jerry and the other boys, Hoyte's friendliness had a rough edge to it which Cody had noticed. Cody still thought that if a boy could throw a stone over a tree, so could she; and if a boy could drink beer, so could she. She knew that girls her own age were meanwhile intuiting the hierarchies of boys and she wasn't sure she wanted or needed to. She didn't want to be the difference between Hoyte and Jerry and for once she wished she could read minds at will. She didn't go to Hoyte's with the same abandon. She wasn't sure how he took their friendship. Hoyte must have seen her coming. He opened the door before she knocked. Cody stuck her hands in her pockets. "Hey Hoyte."

"Hey Cody,"

"You wanna help build stairs?"

Hoyte's familiar smile gradually appeared. "Yeah."

"I could use your help."

Hoyte took his jacket from behind the door and Cody skipped behind him. "That's gonna be more like a real house when we get those stairs in," he said.

"I liked havin' the whole top to myself."

"S'pose I'd like that too."

"Mom's gonna move up into the bedroom upstairs and she just got a walking boot. We got some walls up last week. Virginia isn't so much afraid of a hammer and nail now and she's not so much scared of Mom. She's gettin' braver."

They broke out of the copse and into the brown, brittle remnants of Queen Anne's lace and wind-stripped goldenrod. By late October there were still pockets of color on the hillside—pale aspen thickets, tamarack stands and oaks unable to shake the leaves from their exhausted limbs. The field rattled underfoot. The cold was still a dry cold. Hoyte and Cody ran their fingertips over the hooded seeds of the shriveled wildflowers.

Drew was already waiting, sitting on one of the wooden chairs with her walking boot in front of her and her crutches on the floor beside her. She winced as she scooted back in her chair. "Okay, babe—" she paused, breathed, continued, "you remember how to use a skilsaw. Don't work behind the cut. If it's gonna kick, let it kick, but you don't wanna be behind it."

"I know," said Cody impatiently.

"You see that red rectangle snapped on the floor?"

"Barely."

"Yeah, barely," said Drew. "That was half a year ago. That's your cut for the stair opening. When you cut it, just let the plywood fall down into the basement. There's nothin' under it. You think you can cut those lines?"

"I can do it."

"Don't be on the plywood when you cut it."

"I'm not stupid, Mom."

"You don't think I make stupid mistakes, babe?" Drew leaned to one side and pulled up her shirt. "See that scar?" She pointed to a divot on the right side of her waist. "From a table saw. Kicked a piece of wood straight through me."

Cody sighed. "I can do it, Mom."

2

There were only two aisles in Kemp's General Store. Virginia was between them and on her way out when she heard a familiar voice. She quietly walked to the end of the aisle.

"What brings you up this way, Nora?" The store owner, Hugh Kemp, was easy and familiar.

"Oh, you know, have a visit up the hill."

"What can I get you?"

"Thought I'd have lunch before heading up. I haven't had one of your sandwiches for—how long has it been?"

"Since early summer, Nora."

"Might be a bit before I'm up this way again so make it a good one."

"Suppose that's good news in your line of work."

"Hope so, Hugh, but not to worry. I'll be up again for the sandwiches."

"Say, and just so you know, they'll be closing the roads for a couple days—more shoring up to do. You'll have to go 'round the long way if you come back."

Virginia didn't wait to hear the rest.

She hurried out the store and into the truck. She had bought a pastry for the drive but left that in the bag. She drove straight to the tiny house. Drew was on her crutches, standing above the stair opening. Stringers were in place and Cody and Hoyte were in the basement installing treads. "The state's coming."

"Who?"

"Child protective services," Virginia answered curtly, "or whatever you call it in Vermont. It doesn't matter. The woman— The woman who was here before. Nora. She was at the grocery store. I was just there. I heard her say she was making a visit. I don't know where else she could be visiting but you. She's going to come up and if she asks to be let in, you have to let her in."

Drew's expression darkened. "Why?"

"It's her job."

"They were liars that called this in—Daryl's parents—they lied."

"Water under the bridge!"

"Where are you going?"

"Downstairs," Virginia was already headed for the door and out and around, "to your room."

"To do what?"

"For God's sake, Drew."

Drew grimaced with frustration and swung her crutches around to follow Virginia. "Let me do it!"

"You don't have time!"

"You don't know where I keep it!"

Virginia stopped, turned, impatient. "Drew!" She glared. "You think it's none of their business, or mine. I know. But, well, is this the hill you want to die on? Do you think it's going to be a winning argument? All she wants to know is whether Cody is safe. That's all she wants to know."

Drew fingers opened and closed on her crutches. She nodded quickly and angrily. "Okay."

Virginia turned.

"What are you going to do with them?" Drew called after her.

"I don't know."

"Don't throw them out!"

Then Virginia was out of sight. Drew jammed her crutches into the floor. "You better stick around," she called to Cody. "She might wanna talk to you."

"We'll keep on workin'," said Cody from the basement as if none of it concerned her.

Drew was still navigating the step to the driveway when Nora pulled up. She breathed, straightened, and waited. Nora stepped out carrying a manila folder. Her face was round and her blonde hair drawn back tight. "Hi Drew," she said. "I see you've had your cast removed!"

"Just yesterday."

"You must be feeling so much better," Nora smiled. "I broke my leg skiing—must have been ten years ago—but I'll never forget those first few days. And what a relief to get that cast off!"

Drew glanced at her boot. "They got me doin' therapy now."

"Oh I remember that!"

"Yeah," said Drew. "Stretchin' and puttin' weight on it—just a little. Tryin' it and I keep tryin'."

"But overall you must be feeling better?"

Then Drew guessed the aim of Nora's conversation. If she wasn't suffering, she shouldn't need the drugs. "Just Tylenol for the swelling and backache."

"Good! Good. And look how far you've come on your house! Do you mind if I take a look around? Is Cody home?"

"Yeah. Yeah, she is," said Drew. She gestured around the side of the house. "We're just puttin' in the stairs. So if you want to visit Cody, you still gotta go 'round. "

"Mind if I look upstairs first?"

"Suit yourself," said Drew, then added quietly and quickly. "It's all good. You go take a look around."

"Thank you," Nora answered crisply. She stepped into the first floor, saw that windows had been put into Cody's loft, then leaned over the opening into the basement and saw Cody and Hoyte. "How do you do, Cody?"

Cody looked up, perplexed. "I'm okay."

"Let's take a look downstairs." Nora stepped back outside but paused to speak to Drew. "So tell me how you're doing." She had put on reading glasses to take notes then let them hang around her neck. "I'm happy to see that your little house has come so far. But how about you?"

"Like I said—"

"No, I know. You've got a walking boot. You're getting physical therapy, but how about the prescription pain medicine? Do you still need prescription medication?"

"No."

"When did the last prescription end?"

"A couple weeks ago."

"And do you have any left over?"

"I don't know. There might be some sittin' around. I don't know. I don't know if I used 'em all."

Nora offered a tight smile, returned her glasses to her nose and wrote on a card that she gave to Drew. "You know, there are all kinds of people addicted to opiates—not just struggling mothers. There's a pilot program launching in Burlington next year. I know one of the women starting it up. If you call her, give her my name."

3

"Well," said Virginia, "I think that went well."

Drew leaned over a cup of tea. She had experimentally loosened her walking boot and now stretched her leg under the table. After Nora had left, Cody and Virginia had moved the kitchen table to the first floor, along with Drew's bed, now in her new bedroom and filling half of it. They had also moved the hotplates upstairs and there was even talk of their little refrigerator.

"Drew, you're not addicted. You're dependent. It's awful. They give you all these drugs and they keep giving them to you. People become dependent. It's hardly surprising. And then they offer no treatment. Doctors just throw up their hands and say: We don't know! We don't know anything about dependency or withdrawal! I've seen them say it. They wash their hands of you. Honestly. They shouldn't be prescribing drugs if they can't treat dependency."

"I can do this myself."

"Well, I couldn't have built a house without your help. Just think! I know what a joist is, a cripple, a jack stud, a header—"

"Jesus, Virginia, it's not the same!"

"Well I'm not so sure, Drew. You saved my life. You literally saved my life. What would have happened if you hadn't been here? I couldn't have done any of this. God knows I would have had to sell. And then what? Well, I don't know—"

Drew's cheeks streamed with tears. "My back, ribs, and leg were broken. My daughter was drowning. There was nothing—nothing I could do. I watched her being murdered. Right in front of me. How is that like anything you went through?"

"It wasn't."

"Then what makes you think—"

"Because you don't have to break a bone to be broken. There are a thousand ways life drives you off a road."

Drew shook her head. "Must have been hard watching your bank account drown."

Virginia leaned back in her chair, her expression a momentary knot of unspoken words. "So now what?" she said. "Are you going to finish what your husband started?"

"What does that mean?"

"Well, because I've seen how dependency plays out. You need help. You should have been off these drugs a month ago. And for God's sake your mother shouldn't be supplying you!"

"Where did you put 'em?"

"It's the withdrawal," said Virginia. "That's why you're sitting there crying. It's why you're angry. It's the withdrawal. I know you can't sleep. I see you swing from one mood to another. You're probably suffering from depression."

"Where did you put 'em?"

Virginia ignored the question. "Have you tried a methadone clinic?"

"Two weeks. That's the soonest they can see me."

"So what have you been doing already?"

"Cuttin' the pills up."

"Then let's keep doing that. Let's cut them down a quarter at a time."

Drew tightened the straps of her walking boot and pushed herself upright. "Sure," she said with a wince. "Where are they? What'd you do with them?"

Virginia took the pill bottle from her pocket. "Not unless I give them to you."

Defiance momentarily twisted Drew's expression.

"Let me help you," Virginia insisted. "God knows I'd be homeless if it weren't for you."

"It's not the same."

"Hate me if it helps."

Drew smiled. "If it kills the pain."

4

Cody met Hoyte holding a piece of toast and pushing her other arm through her backpack. They had to meet the school bus downhill just as they had for the first week and they'd used the same path. But now all the leaves were underfoot and a canopy of mist dripped from the forest. The rivers had risen out of their beds in the cool air and Cody and Hoyte descended into them.

"So what happened with the woman?" Hoyte asked.

Cody shrugged. "Didn't seem like she was gonna do anything."

"So she's not gonna take you away?"

"I wouldn't go."

"Not like you have a choice."

"I wouldn't let 'em."

Hoyte leapt ahead but Cody wasn't content to follow. Now if Hoyte went left, she went right. If he swung himself over a fallen tree, she ducked under it. Hoyte stumbled once or twice. Cody raced ahead, leaping over the dry gullies and then in an instant the earth tumbled under her and she fell forward onto her shoulder. When she tried to push herself upright, she fell sideways onto her hip and elbow.

"You okay?" Hoyte knelt next to her.

Cody laughed uneasily. "I don't know. I'm dizzy." She rolled over onto her knees, holding her stomach. "Ow!"

"What's wrong?"

"My head. I don't feel so good."

"What did you eat?"

"Just toast."

"You wanna go back?"

"Hold on." Cody's dizziness and nausea subsided and then was as quickly gone. "I'm okay."

"You sure? Because you don't look okay?"

"I'm okay." Cody pushed herself to her feet and shrugged her backpack back in place.

"You wanna walk?"

"No, I don't wanna walk. Let's go."

Cody moved quickly, skipping lightly down slope, then was half running again. This time she was alert to anything like another bout of dizziness, but whatever it was had passed her by.

"So what's next on your house?" Hoyte asked, close on her heels.

"Paint."

"Gettin' kind of late to paint, isn't it?"

"Paintin' inside and we're gonna use milk paint."

"Why milk paint?"

"'Cause it's a lot cheaper than buyin' reg'lar paint."

The path became less steep and opened into wider slope out from under a stand of hemlocks and into a sugarbush. Here and there were sap buckets like crescent moons rusted half into the ground. At the bottom of the slope the dirt road gleamed with the damp air. Cody skipped ahead, both hands hooked under the backpack's shoulder straps. She jumped off the embankment, over the roadside ditch, and landed with a knee in the dirt. She jumped to her feet, holding up her silt covered hands. She went straight for Hoyte.

"What're you doin'?"

"Need to clean 'em off."

Hoyte backed away with a quick grin. "Don't even think about it."

Cody clapped the gravel from her hands and brushed off her knee. "We decided."

"Decided what?"

"What we're changin' our last name to."

"To what?"

"Devaux."

"Cody Devaux?"

"Everybody in my mom's family had French last names and that was hers."

"Aren't you, like, Abenaki?"

Cody shrugged. "Mom says nobody talked about it much in our family, she said 'cause it used to be that if they found out you were Abenaki they'd make it so you couldn't have babies. My great aunt couldn't have babies."

"What'd they do?"

"Doctors would operate on 'em sometimes without tellin' they were makin' it so they couldn't have babies."

Hoyte let that sit. That's not the kind of evil you let slip by without giving it its due. He scooted a little closer to Cody with his hands in his pocket. "If I could pick my own last name I'd make it something famous or from a story."

"Like what?"

Hoyte shrugged. "I don't know. Maybe like, Einstein."

"That's the dumbest idea I ever heard."

"Why's that?"

"'Cause then you'd always be dumber than your name."

"So if it wasn't Devaux?"

"I dunno," said Cody scooting a little closer to Hoyte, "but you gotta pick a name like buyin' shoes—somethin' you can grow into."

5

Cody had called to her mother before leaving but hadn't seen her. She had snatched Virginia's toast and had raced out the door. Drew lay on her side with Virginia sitting next to her. Drew's muscles restlessly twitching as she wiped tears from her eyes

"What's happening?" Virginia asked.

"I can't sleep. I can't stop crying. I'm fucking burning up on the inside."

Virginia put her hand on Drew's shoulder but Drew shrugged it off.

"I gotta get up." She rolled over, pushed Virginia out of the way, and sat up, cupping her knees. She swayed as if she wanted to throw up; then she unsteadily stood. "Have you ever gone through withdrawal?"

"I've been with patients just like you."

"How much longer?" Drew bent over with her head between her knees, arms locked around her legs.

"It's horrible. It's never easy; one morning you think you'll die and the next—well, you'll wish you were dead twice over. There's no easy way through. But Drew, listen, one morning the craving will go away. The withdrawal will end just like that; but until it does you'll want to do anything—anything at all to stop it. For the hell you've been through and are going through, there's a whole wonderful world on the other side."

Chapter 16

There's nothing left but overall
Remnants of what had once been fall;
Even where a week before
A leaf or two blew through the door
The dwindling days have turned to soot
The little traveling underfoot.
Snow will follow soon enough
Careening through the unmown scruff
Of jimson weed and bush clover,
Nothing apt to be covered over
With just a midday's squall—but soon
Winter will stay the afternoon.
Then who will afterward remember
The few days readied since September?—
The ghostly sighs of thimbleweed,
The bony knuckles of the reed,
Whole fields of startled hair turned white
Before the year end's stricken flight.
I wouldn't ask but that I know
It's not just seasons come and go.
When ice gives way to watercress
And all of April's loveliness,
Remember, though the days are few,
November has its flowers too.

1

The school bus was abuzz with rumors. They began with an abandoned barn that had been floated from its foundation by Irene's floodwaters, carried just a few yards downfield, and set down with all its corners twisted like a recalcitrant box. One of the children had it on good authority that the barn had belonged to a cape that had burned down decades before and it was the foundation of that old cape that the real rumor concerned itself with.

Bones.

Bones scoured clean of muscular dirt and stone by the floodwaters. And not just any bones, said the excited children. Human bones. They were pretty sure of it. This wasn't the kind of thing that should have gotten out, but was a banquet on a Monday morning's bus ride. "How do you they know there was human bones?" asked one child. "'Cause they seen a skull!" said another. "No they didn't," said another. "They were headless. Wasn't any skulls found. Just arm and leg bones!" "And ribs," said another. "Were too skulls!" said another. "They found two skulls!"

And as if that weren't enough, some of the bones belonged to a child. And that, coming as it did before Halloween, was all the sauce a banquet needed. "How old a child?" asked one. "Don't know," said another. "But wasn't a baby."

"Who'd it belong to?"

That question was passed around until it landed on a boy, Nate Barner, who was roughly connected to the discoverers of the bones and who was sitting in front of Cody and Hoyte. He looked over his shoulder nervously. "Way my dad heard it, it belonged to some family with the last name Todd. Said nobody hardly knew 'em and they used to keep to themselves."

"How's he know?" asked a girl.

"'Cause he talked to some old people who were alive then."

"What happened to 'em?" Cody asked.

"Don't know much 'cept the house burned down back before the war and some said, apart from Todd, there weren't anyways anybody livin' there."

"Did he murder 'em?" asked a boy across the aisle.

"Dunno," said Nate. "Everybody thought it was just Todd lived there. Family was gone down to Boston. So when the house burned down nobody thought much of it. It was the depression and people didn't have time or money to think about anybody else."

"Todd died a couple days after the house burned down is what I heard," said another boy. "Heard he tried to put the fire out but he wouldn't talk about it. I bet the bones belong to whoever he was tryin' to save but couldn't."

"I hear the cops came down," said a girl in front.

"Yeah, but them bones are old," said Nate. "My dad seen 'em. He says they're old bones and don't belong to anybody recent."

"How's he know?" asked the boy across the aisle.

"'Cause the sheriff asked him to come in and look at 'em before the state troopers come down."

"How old does he think they are?" asked Hoyte.

"Didn't say," Nate answered. "Just it wasn't anybody recent."

"You suppose the bones was murdered?" asked the girl up front.

"Why would he murder 'em?" asked the boy incredulously, then glanced at Cody and shrugged. "Sorry didn't mean it that way. Just sayin'. Seems like if there was somebody in the house he tried to save 'em but couldn't."

"If I was gonna murder the bones," said the girl. "That's how I'd do it. I'd murder 'em in the basement then I'd burn the house down to cover it up."

"There'd still be the bones," said the boy.

"And then I'd make up a story about them bein' in Boston," added the girl.

"'Cept he died right after it happened," added another boy.

"Might have been a broken heart."

"Might have been guilt."

2

Cody sat across from Julia Delilah Santoff once again, but this time she waited with a kind of eagerness. The older woman had a way of tricking Cody into revelation. Cody couldn't put a finger on it, only that the guile of the older woman was subtle and devious. Cody sat like a bird of prey, determined to spot which way the mouse scurried.

"It's been a week," Mrs. Santoff smiled.

Cody swayed on the seat's edge.

"And how has your week been?" Santoff asked.

"They found bones, human bones, down in a foundation where somebody named Todd used to live," said Cody. Then she eagerly awaited, as a child will, for the adult to share whatever grapes they've plucked.

"Where did you hear that?"

"On the bus."

"And what did you find out on the school bus?"

"Just that there are two sets of bones, a child's and grownup bones and nobody knows where they're from. Coulda been murder or just 'cause the house burned down."

"You should go to the graveyard."

"Why?"

"Because I bet you could find Todd's gravestone."

"Why would I do that?"

"Because then you'd know when he died, and who's buried with him, and you'd have a good idea when the house burned down."

Cody stopped swinging her legs to consider for a moment. "I'm gonna do that." And then, being in a questioning mood, she asked Mrs. Santoff about the puppets, cars, toys, and felt dolls on a shelf above the little room's couch.

"They help me talk to younger children."

"How?"

"Sometimes children find it easier to communicate through play rather than words."

"So you put on a puppet play?"

"Sort of."

"How does that work?"

"Do you like stories?"

"Yeah."

"What kind?" And that question stumped Cody because the obvious answer was good stories, and yet Cody knew a rabbit hole when she saw one. If schooling teaches a child anything, it's that all questions are ambushes, no answer goes unpunished and obvious answers are rabbit holes—sure as certain.

"My mom tells good stories," she said.

"About what?"

"Some I think she makes up and some she remembers from when she was little."

"Do you have a favorite?"

"She told me one last night."

"Is that your favorite?"

Cody thought about that. "Whenever she tells 'em they're my favorite."

"Okay. What was last night's?"

"About a time she visited her granddad and asked him, what does it mean— knowin' the truth? Grandad asked, about what? And she said, 'bout anything? And he said he had a neighbor who was married, had a lonely daughter and an old horse. He said his neighbor was gettin' old but no matter what happened, good or bad, his neighbor was always okay with it.

"Then grandpa said one night the coywolves were carryin' on and spooked the old nag so much she run off. And that was the only horse they had. They didn't know what they were gonna do. Grandpa thought that was an awful thing. He said it'd be like if your tractor got spooked and headed off down the road without ever comin' back.

"So he went over and said that was an awful thing and asked if there was anything he could do. His neighbor shrugged and said, you know how these things go.

"How's that? asked Grandpa.

"And his neighbor said, how do ya know it's a bad thing?"

"Grandpa decided his neighbor didn't have any sense. So then 'bout a week later the old horse came back with a bunch of other horses and all the sudden he was rich with horses. Grandpa thought that was the best news he'd ever heard so he went over figurin' he oughta throw a party for 'em, but his neighbor shrugged and said, you know how these things go.

"How's that? asked Grandpa.

"And his neighbor said, how do ya know it's a good thing?"

"Grandpa decided his neighbor didn't have any sense. So 'bout a week later the coywolves were carryin' on again and all the horses spooked. The neighbor's daughter went out to calm 'em down and they broke her leg stampedin' to get away. Grandpa thought there couldn't be anything good about that but his neighbor shrugged like always, you know how these things go.

"How's that? asked Grandpa.

"And his neighbor said, how do ya know it's a bad thing?"

"'Cause when the neighbor's daughter went to the hospital and got mended, she and the doctor fell in love. They got married, moved into her pa's place and had a big family. They'd of had none of that if that tired old horse hadn't run off."

"So they lived happily ever after?" asked Mrs. Santoff.

Cody was about to agree before it occurred to her that this was also a trick question. "You know how those things go."

3

Later in the day, Principal Reynard ordered Cody and Olivia into his office for a discussion neither girl wanted to have. Cody arrived after Olivia and closed the door behind her. There were three seats to the right of the door—opposite Reynard's desk. Olivia sat in the nearest seat and Cody took the furthest. Reynard momentarily studied them, sitting forward, elbows on his knees. "I'm not here to adjudicate," he said.

"What does *ajdoodicate* mean?" asked Cody.

Reynard took a deep breath. He leaned back in his chair, fingers and thumb constructing a temple in his lap. "It means I'm not here to judge who's right or wrong."

"Why not?"

"Miss Tippet," said Reynard but was interrupted by Olivia.

"Train up a child in the way he should go: and when he is old, he will not—"

"Olivia!" Reynard interrupted, face growing red.

"It's in the bible," said Olivia. "It says in the bible—"

"I know Miss—"

"She called me a mutt—"

"She punched me in the face—"

"Ladies!" Reynard leaned forward, one hand gripping the arm of his chair. "I could just suspend both of you." A threat that momentarily silenced both girls. "I do not want any more reports from faculty concerning your behavior. Both of you are going to resolve your differences."

"I didn't start it!" said Cody.

"She did!" said Olivia. "She goes around— she reads people's minds!"

"I don't do it on purpose!"

"Ladies!" Reynard interrupted once again. "Ladies. I am not going to litigate your disagreement. But I will suspend both of you if you can't come to an agreement by yourselves." And then Cody and Olivia glanced at each other for the first time in weeks. As the adage has it: Nothing makes friends like a common enemy. They both sat on their hands and waited for Reynard to finish. "I have another matter to see to," he said. "I'm leaving the office. You two are going to stay here." He glanced at his watch. "I'll be half an hour at most. That means you have half an hour to sort this out. If you can't sort it out, I'll find my own solution. In the meantime, Mrs. Levitt is right outside."

That was how Reynard left them.

And at first neither girl spoke. They sat in their chairs, gazing spitefully out the window until the awkwardness was unbearable.

"Seems like you've been awfully mad," said Cody.

"You too."

"Have a right to be."

"So do I."

"'Bout what?"

Olivia didn't answer. She let her legs swing slowly under her and held onto the edge of the seat. She looked down at the floor then wiped at her eyes. Cody glanced at her.

"What'd I do to you?" Cody asked.

Olivia shrugged.

"I didn't ask for any of this stuff to happen to me," said Cody.

"I know."

"So why are you so mad at me?"

"'Cause—" Olivia glared at the floor. "'Cause you're not a Christian."

"What's that got to do with anythin'?"

"'Cause God talked to you."

"I never saw God," said Cody. "Just saw stuff. And what's it matter anyway if I'm Christian or not? I don't know what I am."

"So do you wish you'd seen God then?"

Cody shrugged. "I don't know."

"Well it was like seeing God," Olivia persisted. "And why should God talk to you and not me?"

Cody let that soak in, in that way that adulthood first manifests in a child's mind. She began to work her way into fears and desires that weren't her own. "Are you sayin' God should only talk to Christians?"

Olivia shrugged.

"I don't see why he should," said Cody.

"What's the point of being Christian if just anybody can go to heaven and talk to God?"

"My grandma and grandpa think I talked to Satan."

"My mom thinks you talked to Satan," Olivia answered quietly.

"Do you?"

"I don't know."

"I didn't talk to God anyhow," said Cody. "Like I said: I just saw stuff."

"But maybe that's how God was talking to you?"

"Why's that make you so mad?"

"'Cause I quit believing in God."

"So how's that my fault?" Cody asked again.

"Because soon as I started not believing in God—" Olivia paused a moment, staring at her feet. "—it was like you saw him. And what if God really did talk to you—by showing you stuff nobody else would know? Does that mean I'm goin' to hell? Does that mean I have to start believin' again?"

"Why'd you stop?"

"Because—" Olivia wiped at her eyes. "Because of my little brother. Drowned. Everybody says it was God's will but if God wanted him dead then I don't believe in him. I don't believe in a God that wants people dead."

"Sorry."

"It's not for you to be sorry."

"So why are you always quotin' the bible if you don't believe in God?"

"I don't know."

"But why's that make you so mad at me?"

"Because I always wanted God to talk to me and he never did."

"How do you know?"

"Didn't you?" Olivia asked.

"Maybe he shows you stuff all the time, that's just how he talks—he shows you stuff every day, little things you're supposed to pay attention to—and you just don't know it 'cause you're expectin' him to talk like we're talkin' right now, only God's words are trees, stones, whole days, and people just bein' people."

"I hate readin' the bible."

"Maybe you don't have to stop believin' in God?" said Cody. "Maybe you can just stop believin' in other people's God."

"Is there any kind of God but other people's?" Olivia finally turned her gaze to Cody.

"Maybe," said Cody

"Reynard is a jerk."

Cody smiled.

"I mean, you should read his mind and totally freak him out."

"If he had a mind," said Cody.

And that finally was enough to make Olivia laugh. "I shouldn't have said all that stuff."

Cody turned her gaze to her feet. "I shouldn't have punched you."

"I'd have punched me if you'd said stuff like that to me."

Cody smiled.

"When's he supposed to be back?" Olivia asked.

"Half hour."

Then both girls were quiet before Cody spoke up again. "I'm goin' down to hang out with Jerry, Mike, and Roy. You wanna come along?"

"Yeah," Olivia nodded. "I'm really sorry 'bout your dad and what I said about you bein' Indian."

Cody sat with that for a quiet moment. "It's kind of like you."

"What is?"

"I don't believe in my dad anymore."

Olivia nodded then she moved to the middle chair, the chair next to Cody, and took her hand.

4

A little before their last class, Cody slipped into the desk in front of Hoyte's and asked if he wanted to come too, but Hoyte crossed his arms, leaning back in his seat. "You wanna do that again? How are you gettin' home?"

"Mom's gettin' us after physical therapy."

"What are you gonna do?"

"Hang out."

"Maybe you oughta be thinkin' 'bout gettin' caught with Jerry and Mike."

"Caught what?"

"Drinkin' beer."

"What do you care?" If Hoyte had anything to add, Cody didn't hear it. "Not like I ever made you drink anything." She spun out of the desk chair; and what exactly made her angry she couldn't put a finger on except that she felt betrayed.

Hoyte sprung from his desk but Cody turned on him.

"What?" she asked as though accusing him.

Hoyte didn't have time to work out what he meant. The simplest explanation was an apology that didn't come out any better. "Look," he said, "I mean, thanks for asking."

"Suit yourself," said Cody.

When Audrey met up with Cody after school, Olivia was there too. Audrey glanced uneasily at Olivia then at Cody and then at Olivia again.

"We made up," said Cody flatly.

"Seriously?" Audrey glanced at both girls. "Seems like all you guys wanted to do was kill each other."

Cody and Olivia both shrugged.

"Okay." Audrey leaned back on her heels appreciatively. "Just wow." She glanced at Cody's wrists, at the jade bracelet. "Is that new?"

"Grandma got them for me on my last birthday."

"I've never seen it before."

Cody was suddenly shy. "Never wore 'em 'til now, I guess."

"It looks Indian."

"Grandma said it was hers when she was little."

"Yeah, I'd be afraid of losing it."

And then Hoyte showed up, hands tucked into the pockets of his jacket, his gangly height awkward with the three girls. "You're coming too?" asked Olivia.

"Yeah," he nodded wryly, "guess so."

Cody didn't say anything but turned her back on him. They took the sidewalk for three blocks or so, then took to the berm, then the narrow dirt path that led through huddled sumac stalks into the taller grove of maple, ironwood and birch. The path wasn't so greasy as last time. They didn't have to swing from a sapling to balance through the scoured banks. The mud left in ribbed drifts and dunes had finally dried to a firm and fine-grained flour. There were only the fallen leaves to slip on, a yellow and brown carpet that was almost golden under the mostly jagged and stripped trees. The air was colder and they kept their jackets zipped.

"So what did you and Mrs. Santoff talk about today?" Audrey asked, following Cody.

"I told her a story Mom told me."

"About what?"

"How you can't always know if somethin's bad or good."

"What if you cut your thumb off?" asked Olivia.

"Depends," said Cody.

"How is cuttin' your thumb off anything but bad?"

"Suppose I cut my thumb off," Cody stopped. "And instead of Mom callin' Dad to take us into town, somebody took us to the hospital 'cause of my thumb. Then Dad never coulda tried to kill us and Mom wouldn'ta broken her back." And Cody said it with such conviction that Audrey and Olivia both stepped back to give the words some breathing room.

Finally Olivia said: "You'd give up your thumb for that?"

"Yeah," said Cody, suddenly shy.

Then Olivia added quietly, "But so then how do you know what actually happened was a bad thing?"

Now that stopped Cody in her tracks. She had an inkling as to what she ought to say but that wasn't what she wanted to say. Instead she jammed her hands into her overalls' pockets, gazed at her feet, and quietly shrugged. "I dunno."

"Yeah, me neither."

"I suppose dyin's the only thing there's nothing good to be said about."

"But didn't you die?" said Audrey.

Cody paused. It was true enough that dying wasn't what Cody expected—if she'd expected anything at all. She'd seen a world and inside that world her own with all its dandelions, seas and circling sun, like a marble in a velvet pocket full of marbles. "Wouldn't recommend it," she finally answered.

"But didn't something good come from it?"

"Don't know," said Cody, perhaps too near the terrible to see the good, or even want to. She stepped past Audrey and Olivia. They followed and Hoyte followed them—hands still in his jacket pockets. That was when Cody leapt up the next bank and the world spun out from under her. She fell to her side and slid back down on her hip. Audrey and Olivia giggled but their expressions changed when Cody had trouble standing. Hoyte had already moved between them and knelt next to Cody. "You okay?"

"Just dizzy." Cody leaned on one hand and pressed the palm of the other to her flinching forehead.

"My mom has migraines," said Audrey.

The pain receded. Cody looked up to see a crow among the torn leaves and silhouetted branches. The bird hopped from an ironwood to a nearby birch and softly trilled.

"Maybe you oughta sit for a minute," said Hoyte.

"I'm fine," Cody answered impatiently, shoving Hoyte away as she pushed herself to her feet. "Not any different than last time."

"Mom's migraines last whole days sometimes," said Audrey. Then once again they were following Cody. They sidled through the gully's understory of brush and sapling, the last leaves to go. The boys were there. They had only arrived moments before and were sliding the backpacks from their shoulders.

"Hey, Cody," said Jerry.

"Hoyte," said Mike with a nod.

Roy and Mike glanced over their shoulders, then parted to make room, both surprised to see Olivia. "I wanna go to the graveyard," said Cody straightaway. "I wanna see if I can find Todd's grave."

"Who's Todd?" asked Jerry.

"Name of the family whose bones they found."

"How do you know that?" asked Roy.

"Heard it on the bus," said Cody.

"So how are you gonna know if it's the right Todd?" asked Mike. "Suppose there's a whole bunch of Todds in the graveyard. And why would you want to anyway?"

"I dunno," said Cody, feeling challenged. "Can't know if you don't look."

"She's got you there," said Jerry with that sly grin. He nodded at Cody. "I'll go with you."

"Me too," said Olivia.

"You too?" said Jerry with that fox-like smile. "You and Cody make up?"

"Yeah."

"Will miracles never cease."

"You wanna go right now?" asked Mike.

"After the beer," said Jerry. "After the beer. Did you bring it?"

Mike guffawed. "Did I bring it, he asks me. Did I bring it? Fuck no. What do you take me for?" Mike made his way around the back side of the sycamore where there was a hollow in the massive old tree. "You think I'm gonna walk 'round all day with a beer in my backpack? What do you take me for?" He reached into the hollow and pulled out a bottle.

"That's all I was askin'," said Jerry.

"You asked me if I brung it," Mike said. "I didn't bring it nowhere. I put it here in the tree this morning. You'd know that if you'd walked with me this morning."

"I was late."

"You're always late."

"What does *indebliable*, mean?" Cody finally blurted.

"What?" asked Roy.

"*Indeblible*."

"Use it in a sentence," said Mike.

"Somethin' Principal Reynard said," explained Cody. "He said he hoped all our troubles had made an indeblible impression."

"Jesus, Cody," said Mike, tugging a bottle opener from his pants pockets. "That's not *indeblible*. That's in*deli*ble. He said *indelible*." The bottle hissed and foamed. "It means he hoped you wouldn't forget nothin'. And I got peanuts too."

Jerry took the beer from Mike's hands as he dried them off. "How is it you're stuffed so full of words but can't string a grammatical sentence together?"

"Readin'," said Mike. "And I can too string a sentence together."

Jerry took a drink and passed it back to Mike, then one by one, apart from Audrey and Olivia, they took a swig and sat on the makeshift stumps and log benches that surrounded the burn pit. "Aren't you curious?" Roy asked Audrey.

Audrey glanced at the others. "Not really."

"Beer's good!" said Roy.

"My dad let me taste some and it tasted awful," said Audrey.

"What about you, Hoyte?" Mike asked as if in disbelief. "You don't want any?"

"Not havin' any."

"You just here for my sweet company?" asked Mike.

"Just yours."

"I'm touched, Hoyte."

When the beer was passed back around, followed by peanuts, Olivia took it and held the can in both hands as if balancing it atop her closed knees. She studied it thoughtfully.

"You gonna have some?" Jerry asked.

She shook her head and passed it to Cody. Cody took two swigs this time, scrunched her nose, stuck out her tongue, and burped. Then Jerry had to burp, then Roy, and then Mike. When it came back around to Cody, she stood, tilted back her head and took four deep swigs of beer. That should have been all she remembered.

The beer can fell out of her hand and she weightlessly fell backwards. Mike and Olivia half caught her, laughing, then saw the pale gray of her skin and immediately began to shake her. Her eyes were half open and her head hung uselessly over Mike's arm.

"Holy Fuck!" Mike scrambled to lay her on the ground. "Cody!" He said, voice cracking, leaning over her, shaking her. "Holy fuck! Cody! Holy Fuck! Fuck! Fuck!"

"Quit saying that!" hissed Olivia, and she shook Cody by the shoulders.

"We need glasses!" cried Mike.

"Glasses?" Jerry hurriedly leaned next to him and turned Cody's blank gaze to his own. "What d'ya want glasses for?"

"Check her breath."

"Oh my God," Audrey stood now, hands opening and closing, backing away. "She's not breathing?"

Jerry turned on his knees, giving Audrey a sharp glance. "Can you run quick? Get help?"

Cody suddenly inhaled as if surfacing from the weight of an unseen ocean.

5

What Cody remembered was the crow. She saw it when she threw back her head and drank. She saw it above her on the heavy elbow of the sycamore's limb, the limb branching into many branches, like a black tear in the sky, as it reached over the burn pit and out into the further gully. She let go of the can, feeling weightless but not falling. She knew that Hoyte, Jerry, Mike, Roy, Olivia, and Audrey were scrambling to catch her. But she wasn't falling. She held out her hands to either side, fingers spread open, and rose, floating effortlessly into the spiraling tree.

6

"Wait!" Mike shouted at Audrey.

"Oh my God," Audrey paced back and forth, looking over her shoulder, then standing on her toes to peer over Jerry, Hoyte and the others. "Is she breathing?"

"Yeah, she's breathing."

Cody looked up at the children kneeling over her with the same expression of surprise, then she was limp again.

"I'm takin' her to Soot's." Hoyte would have picked her up but Cody was already pushing him away, trying to roll over, losing her balance. "I don't need help," she said groggily. "I'm okay. I don't need help."

"Take my hand," said Olivia.

"I don't—" But Cody's speech was slurred and uneven. This time she pushed herself to her hands and knees, head hanging down.

"You oughta just leave," said Jerry to Olivia. "You know what your Ma and Pa would do."

"You know what mine are gonna do?" cried Mike. "Man, I'm ruined."

Olivia reached over Cody, picked up the beer, and downed the little remaining.

"What was that for?" Mike's eyes were as wide as his mouth.

"I'm helping," Olivia answered flatly, then took Cody's hand and helped her stand with her other arm around Cody's shoulders. "C'mon, Cody," she said. "C'mon."

"You all comin'," said Jerry.

"Ah hell," said Mike. "Why are you even askin'? I'm gonna get my ass whupped but I en't a coward."

"Me neither," said Roy.

Hoyte picked up Cody's backpack, the others their own, and they followed Olivia and Cody. What Cody remembered were the wind-stripped branches, the smell of the river, the bruise of her bone and muscle carrying her, a house and then another, then George Barstowe sticking his head out from under the hood of the car he'd sold to Ada—Ada in the driver's seat. When she saw Cody groggily held by the other children, she hurried from the car and knelt in front of her.

"What happened?"

"She just sort of blacked out," said Olivia.

"C'mon then." Ada took Cody's hands.

The next that Cody remembered was sitting in Soot's kitchen with Soot in front of her, Ada behind Soot, the other children behind Ada, and Barstowe off to the side, leaning back with a watchful air.

"Cody? Hon?"

"Yeah?" Cody gazed at Soot as if still waking from a deep sleep. The back of her chair was to the table. Soot brushed Cody's dark hair out of her face.

"She was taking a big drink of beer and she just sort of passed out," said Audrey.

"Cody," Soot said again, "look at me."

"I'm okay," said Cody groggily.

"Oh, honey."

"Wasn't like it was a strong beer or nothin'," said Mike. "I've drunk strong beer and that weren't no strong beer. And that's not the kind of beer—" And Mike would have gone down that road a good several miles if Jerry hadn't given him a look.

"What's your name?" Soot asked Jerry.

"Jerry, ma'am."

"Jerry, I've got some orange juice in the fridge. Get it out. There are glasses in the cupboard to the left of the sink. Bring over a glass soon as you've poured it."

But when Jerry came back with orange juice Cody hesitated. "I en't supposed to drink orange juice."

"Hon, you aren't supposed to drink beer," said Soot. "Beer is what you're not supposed to drink. Drink the orange juice. I want to make sure you're not hypoglycemic."

Cody drank as the color slowly returned to her lips and cheeks. "So. Now," said Soot, "all of you tell me what happened."

They all started at once, but quickly quieted. "We were—" said Audrey, feeling suddenly alone in the crowded kitchen. "I mean, I wasn't, but everybody was passing around beer, just one beer, and it was like Cody tried to drink a lot at once and she passed out."

Each child nodded.

Then each told a little more of the story, all of them swinging on the same gate—that there had only been one beer between them, and that Cody must have blacked out from drinking too much at once. But none of them described Cody's expressionless pallor. None had seen fainting before and so this must be what fainting was—something like death—and so they said that Cody had fainted and that was all. They didn't say that they hadn't known what to do until she breathed again, until the color returned to her lips, until her eyes, neither closed nor open, finally recognized them again.

Soot eyed them with her one eye then asked them each for their name. After that she sent them home. All but Hoyte could walk home, and Hoyte said he'd go home with Jerry and call from there. That left Olivia, the last to leave, but she stopped, turned—shy and reticent. "I want to stay."

"Do you live far?" asked Soot.

"That's not it," said Olivia. "I just want to stay with Cody."

Soot sized up the girl, nodded. "No. That's alright. You stay and keep Cody company. Why not?"

Then just like that the two girls were alone. Barstowe had gone back out. "Prob'ly shouldn't leave a car wide open in the middle of the road," he said. Ada went upstairs to find a blanket for Cody's shivering. Soot only went so far as the room next door, looking for the phone to call Drew and Virginia.

Olivia pulled a chair around the table's corner, legs stuttering on the wooden floor. "You looked pretty bad."

Cody had bent over, head between her knees, hands around her ankles. "I en't ever gonna drink beer again."

"I drank some."

"Why'd you do that?"

Olivia leaned forward, elbows on knees. "'Cause it was sorta like takin' communion."

"What's that?"

Olivia shrugged. "Just a way of belonging to somethin'."

"Your mom and dad are gonna really, really gonna hate me now."

Olivia smiled. "I'm not tellin' 'em about you." Then she leaned over like Cody, her chest on her knees, whispering. "Is Soot a witch?"

Cody turned, eyeing Olivia and the room lest Soot walk in. "Why?"

"'Cause Mom and Dad say she's a witch."

"She is."

Olivia gave her a look. "Can she do magic?"

"I dunno," Cody whispered.

"Why's she only got one eye?"

"She gave her other eye to a sailor."

"Did not."

"So she could see when she was gonna die."

"She didn't even."

"Just a story I heard 'bout the one-eyed witch and I bet she's the one-eyed witch."

"All I care is if she's good or bad."

"It makes her so she knows stuff about you without you're havin' told her."

"Like what?"

Before Cody could answer, Soot returned telling the girls she had apple pie, freshly made, and that they should eat and that Drew and Virginia were on their way from the hospital. She put out plates and Ada returned with a blanket. Barstowe returned too, his large frame nearly filling the doorway. Ada put the blanket over Cody's shoulders, sitting next to her, while Soot filled a kettle with water. Barstowe sat with a satisfied exhalation, the chair creaking under him. "What're ya makin'?" he asked.

"It's a tea restorative," said Soot evenly.

"And what are we supposin' happened to Cody?"

"I'm not sure," said Soot

Ada rubbed Cody's shoulder. "Maybe it was a head rush. I used to get those; even blacked out once. I was stretching and next thing I know, I woke up on the floor."

"Don't think it was a head rush," said Olivia.

Because the backs of the chairs were to the table, Soot told the girls to turn around and then placed a slice of pie before each of them. "Look at you two," said Barstowe sniffing and wiping his nose with a handkerchief. "Don't think I ever seen two children dive into apple pie as morose."

"George," Soot scolded. "Let them be."

"I seem to recall you getting into some scrapes," Ada added.

"You warn't ever a child if you din't," said Barstowe. "And who still doesn't?"

"Every day," said Ada.

"Every day?" said Soot. "What have you done?"

"I write."

"That hardly sounds criminal." Soot dished some pie for Ada and Barstowe.

"Worse than criminal. Family, friends, acquaintances. Nobody's safe. Don't be friends with a writer. Take poor George Barstowe: I'm putting him in my novel; and you too, Soot. I'll have half the town in my novel before I'm done."

"And Meredith?"

"She's the troll in the commentary of my life."

"Don't know 'bout Meredith, but bein' fit between the pages of a book might be slimming," Barstowe patted his stomach, "and that'd suit me just fine."

"So, enough of that," said Soot. "I'm sure they're wondering what the future has in store for them. Have you girls ever had your cards read?"

The girls shook their heads.

"Tarot cards?"

"No, but I'll do it," said Cody and Olivia added a defiant, "Me too."

Soot eyed them both, as if to be sure they might not change their minds, then went to her desk and returned with a deck of cards wrapped in dark blue velvet. She dealt Olivia's cards first. Two cards to the left, one crossing the other, one in the middle, and two crossing on the right. "Your past," said Soot pointing to the first card dealt on the left, a heart pierced by three swords suspended over dark clouds. Roses bled from the wounds. "You've felt betrayed and hurt."

Olivia and Cody glanced at each other guiltily.

Soot gave a flickering smile. "Is that what you think? Let's find out what that something is." She tapped the card that lay crossways on top of it, a painted sun with flames curling at the card's edges. Soot nodded thoughtfully. "You're in conflict with your divine source. That's rough."

Olivia's eyes widened.

"Terrible to feel as if the divine has betrayed you. But what do you think the divine is? Do you know?" Soot turned the card upside down. "Do you see how the card is painted? It's clever isn't it? No matter how you turn the card, the sun is the same, but some people say you should turn the card this way, some that way, but no matter how the card is turned, the divine is unchanged."

Olivia nodded.

"The card in the middle is the bridge from the past to the future." Olivia saw a man in a winterish overcoat among nine slender birches. He was injured and leaned on one of them as if it were a staff. "This is the nine of wands," said Soot. "Trust in your own strength. Do you see how the tree he holds is coming into leaf? And do you see his footprints in the snow? He doesn't turn back. Have the courage of your convictions."

Olivia glanced at Cody again.

"Pay attention." Soot tapped the crossed cards to the right. "These are your future." The card underneath was a boy kneeling in grass and flowers, having planted a sapling. He held the birch in one hand and patted the dirt with the other. "That's the Page of Wands," said Soot. "Do you see the child planting the new tree? Rebirth? Renewal?" Soot glanced at Olivia slyly. "Maybe new friends? But do you see the card that crosses it?" She tapped the last card, an old farmer carrying a lantern. "You see?" Soot studied Olivia as though the meaning should be obvious. "The card is called The Hermit, but the card is reversed. The cards are warning you not to isolate yourself. The divine is in all things—and in friends especially."

7

Soot sent Cody and Olivia to sit on the porch swing while she cleaned up the apple pie. They sat in silence for a good several minutes until Olivia, her eyebrows a knot of concern, whispered the one certain conclusion she'd drawn from the experience. "She's a witch."

"I know it," Cody answered.

"She's the one-eyed witch."

"I told you," said Cody, "and she en't good or bad."

"So what are you going to do?"

"I dunno."

Another silence followed.

"Are you going to tell your mom about the cards?"

"I dunno. Are you?"

"No way." Olivia shook her head. She held her own five cards face down in her lap. "I'd have to homeschool for the rest of my life. I'm keeping them secret. Let's make them secret. Let's promise not to tell anybody."

"You won't?"

"Nobody."

"Then I won't either." Cody nodded.

"Can I see your cards again?"

Cody turned her own cards over and saw the second of the last two cards Soot had dealt—Death. Olivia uneasily rubbed her own cards with her thumbs studying it. Soot had painted the cards herself. She said that depending on whose cards she read, she might give them away; and reading Olivia and Cody's cards, she thought she should. "She doesn't look like Death," said

Olivia. "She looks like some kind of queen—like a queen of the night."

"She does to me," said Cody quietly.

In the center of the card was a slender woman in a black tunic and cloak. She held a birch staff in her right hand and the moon was curved like the blade of a scythe above her, seeming attached to the end of the staff. She looked directly at the girls. Her hair was like the crow's feathers and one hand was outstretched, as if inviting the girls to take it. There was the hint of a knowing smile in the woman's lips and eyes, as if she knew something the onlooker didn't know.

"I'd be more scared if she was a skeleton."

"I'd be less scared if she was," said Cody, "'cause then I'd know better and run away."

"Can we look at the last card again? The one that crossed death?"

Cody slipped the two of swords on top—a kneeling youth whose hood and dark hair covered his eyes. One guessed that his gaze was downcast or his eyes closed as he decided between the two swords, one in each hand and crossed above him. "You have a choice," was all that Soot had said, before she handed the cards to Cody.

"What do you think she meant?"

"I dunno."

"I think it's a girl, not a boy, and she's skinny like you. And who would choose death?"

"I dunno." said Cody again, and jammed her fists and the cards in her pockets.

Olivia leaned forward with her palms on the edge of the porch swing. "You think Soot knows more than what she was sayin'?"

"Bet she does."

Olivia was silent, then said, "I probably better get going. Take care, I guess."

"I guess," said Cody, "Take care. I'll see you tomorrow."

8

When Drew and Virginia arrived, Soot had come out to sit with Cody and hold her hand. The late fall's drifting sun had slipped around the back side of the house and a few loose leaves rattled over the fir planking. Virginia was first on the porch. She knelt in front of Cody, studying her eyes. Drew followed with a cane, swinging her walking boot awkwardly up the porch steps.

"What happened?" Virginia asked.

"I think I drunk too much."

"Drank," corrected Soot.

"Drank."

"How much did you drink," asked Virginia.

"I dunno," said Cody. "I chugged a bunch."

"Cody—" But whatever Drew had in mind to say was lost somewhere between anger, concern, and self-reproach. "How are you feelin' now, babe?"

"I'm okay."

"And before?" asked Virginia.

"Kind of dizzy. Like I was gonna throw up."

"Where's Audrey?"

"Went home," said Cody. "And everybody else."

"Everybody else?" said Drew. "Must have been one hell of a party."

"Olivia was there," said Cody, "she helped carry me. Just at first."

"Carried you?" Virginia asked.

"Just at first," said Cody, "then when I was walkin' I couldn't keep my balance."

"Was it worth it?" asked Drew.

"I en't ever gonna drink again."

"How many kids were there?"

"There were six," said Soot.

"And what was Olivia doin' there?" Drew asked. "You two gettin' into it again?"

"We're friends now," said Cody quietly.

"Yeah okay. Wouldn't expect that. Not with what she said. Not with how you decked her."

"We're friends, Mom. Okay? I'm not stayin' mad at her. I'm not like you. I don't wanna stay mad at people forever!"

Drew closed her eyes. "Yeah okay, babe. I get it. But you and me? Didn't we just talk about this? I mean, Jesus fucking Christ, Cody. If Daryl's parents find out about this—"

"I'm sorry, Mom."

"Yeah. You're sorry. How 'bout you not goin' off in the first place?"

"I think you should consider—" Virginia began, but Drew cut her off.

"Seein' a doctor?" Drew asked.

"Well, it's not normal to black out like that," Virginia's voice rose, "if blacking out is what it was. We don't know!"

Drew pressed both her palms against her forehead. "Really? And what happens when child protective services finds out I let her go off drinkin' beer?"

"You didn't."

"So take a chance?"

"It's not normal, Drew."

"I'm not gonna lose her over this!"

"Drew," Virginia almost shouted, "you need to take this girl to the hospital!"

"You feel like you need to go to the hospital, babe?"

Cody had moved to the edge of the swinging bench. "I'm okay, Mom."

"Drew," Virginia persisted, "she's a child!"

But Cody had already stood, her expression fixed, and was walking to the car. "Hey," said Drew, glancing at Soot. "Thanks for lookin' after her. I owe you."

"You're going to have a hard couple nights, Drew."

"Couldn't get worse."

But Soot's one eye remained fixed on Drew. "You know what I mean."

9

Cody sat in the back seat. She watched her mother's jaw clench and unclench; saw the sweat at her temples and the strands of hair, hair like her own, bead together. She hadn't gotten her father's dark waves but that suited Cody. Drew and Virginia had briefly argued at first but now sat in silence, Virginia driving; and that suited Cody too. But pulling into their driveway, Virginia had to circle around Kati's old hatchback. "Is that your mother?" she asked Drew.

"Yes," Drew sighed.

"Well," said Virginia, "I can just disappear."

Drew grabbed Virginia's wrist, stopping her from climbing out of the car, then turned, facing Cody, tears streaking her cheeks. "Don't think this means I'm done with you."

"I know," Cody's eyes narrowed. "You're mad and you're gonna stay mad."

"What?"

"Why are you cryin'?" Cody asked.

"I'm goin' through a hell of lot right now, babe."

But Cody didn't answer, looking out the window, hand on the door handle.

"Don't you open that door," Drew tried to turn in her seat but half cried out with frustration. "This isn't about me. You think you're gonna make this about me? You and me?—we are not done. Just 'cause Mom's here? You and me—" But Drew's rage was interrupted by Kati's call from the tiny house. The inside light of the house lit up the evening's early chill.

"Why can't you be happy?" Cody blurted.

"About what?"

"Drew!" Kati called from the tiny house.

"You haven't been anything but mad since Dad tried to kill us!" Cody cried, bursting into tears.

"I'm not s'posed to be mad about that?"

"What about me?"

"Drew?" Kati called again.

Drew turned to Virginia. "Can you—I don't know. Tell her I'm having a fucking moment. Will you? Give her a rum and coke. Tell her I can't talk to her. Hold her the hell off, can you?"

Virginia quickly nodded, briefly took Drew's hand, then Virginia was out of the car.

"You?" Drew turned back to Cody. "What about you? Let's see? There's people out there deciding whether I should even be allowed to be your mom. You decked a girl, made up, then went out for a beer. What part of that am I s'posed to be happy about?"

"It's not just about that!"

"About what then?" Drew shot back. "My husband tried to murder me and murder you!"

"My dad!" Cody sobbed. "My dad tried to kill me! He tried to kill me—"

Drew didn't answer but painfully turned a little more and reached over the seat, drawing Cody into a tearful and tight embrace. "I'm so sorry," she sobbed. "I'm so sorry, Cody. I'm gonna get better. I swear. But I haven't slept; I can't eat any more; and Jesus, I'm burning up inside. Just give me a chance. I'm so sorry, babe; I'm gonna get better. You don't deserve this."

Cody clung to her mother as a child will cling, shaking. "And he tried to kill you."

Virginia stood on the makeshift step to the front door. Kati leaned with one hand against the door jamb as though to step down but couldn't get past Virginia. "What's going on?" she demanded. "Is something wrong? I should go. Let me go."

"She and Cody just need a minute."

"What happened?"

"Well I'm sure Drew will tell you."

Kati looked over Virginia. "Look, who are you to stand here? I want to go down."

"Who am I?" Virginia took a deep breath and slowly shook her head, her red hair beginning to fall in strands. "Well, to start with, I would like to step into my house and have a rum and coke because I could really use a rum and coke, but here you are, in my way; and I don't know what I'm going to do if you don't get out of my way but we're both going to regret it because I frankly don't know what I'm capable of."

Kati gave a short laugh, almost like a snort, defiantly tossed her long hair and stepped back. "Go ahead. Go have your rum and coke."

Virginia stepped into the doorway but didn't go by. She glared at Kati, jaw clenched, then spoke. "I was an emergency room nurse. I got to see all sorts of things—good and horrible. But it makes you wonder what we are, Kati, because in an emergency room you meet people inside out—wounds like hideous butterflies and bone like green wood under all that tangled flesh. You ask yourself if that's all we are—just flesh on bone. I saw horrible things, gruesome, but the most horrific were the ones you couldn't see, inflicted a thousand times over with a word or gesture: the kind that makes a child despise herself; the kind that calls itself love but only loves itself."

"Who—" said Kati bridling. "Who are you to talk to me like that?"

"Give me the drugs," said Virginia quietly.

"That's none of your business!"

"Give me the drugs. I don't know where you're getting them. I don't care. What you're doing is illegal and Kati, for God's sake, Cody needs her mother! She can't eat. She can't sleep."

"Don't tell me what my own daughter needs!"

Virginia lowered her voice. "If you don't give me the goddamn drugs you'll be hearing from the police. Give me the drugs or I make life a living hell for you."

Kati's face contorted, but she was already digging in her satchel. "You'll call the police?" she said dismissively, hands shaking. "I'm sure you will. That's not a luxury everybody has, you know. No. You wouldn't know. Look at you. Why would you have a reason to be afraid of the police?" Kati shoved the pill bottle into Virginia's hands. "You don't know the last thing about what it's like living your privileged life."

"Those are Tylenol," Virginia continued to hold her hand palm up. "Give me the oxycodone." Kati glared with frustration but shoved the drugs into Virginia's hand. "Drew will survive the withdrawal," said Virginia, "but these drugs? They'll kill her."

10

"Who the hell does she think she is?" Kati asked. She was sitting at the small table in the upstairs kitchen. Virginia was downstairs. She ran her fingers through her long black and graying hair as if the motion were a nervous tick. Cody was in bed in the loft.

"Let it go, Mom." Drew was leaning over the small counter, carefully slicing an apple into thin strips and warily eating one after the other.

"You?" Kati scoffed. "You? Telling me to let something go?"

"Yeah," said Drew. "Me."

"Do you know how hard it is to get those?"

"They're not helping." Drew momentarily heaved.

"Look at you! My God! Look what that man did to you. And where's your father? You know, I tried calling him but he doesn't answer his phone. Just like him. I wrote him and who writes letters anymore? So you ask me why I think you need them? My God, Drew, you can't even hold down an apple. I'm your mother."

"My mom." Drew spread her hands on the edge of the table, head lowered between her arms. "Jesus Christ, Mom. Now you wanna be my mom? Now?"

"What are you saying?"

Drew swallowed, still trying to hold down the apple. "I'm sayin' you had a child, Mom. A child. I needed you when I was a child. And it was like you had no fucking idea that you'd had a child."

"You were better off. Look at the way parents spoil their children. I never spoiled you. You were better off without me running your life the way—"

"Parents are supposed to run their children's lives! That's what parents do! They run their children's lives!"

"Was I supposed to just devote my life to you?"

"Yes."

"Yes?"

"Yes! Jesus Christ, Mom. Yes! That's what you do when you have a child. What were you thinking?"

Kati laughed, glancing at her reflection in the dark windows. "You know what you were? You were— What were you? I wasn't thinking about you at all. You showed up in the middle of the night— I can almost tell you the time. You were my orgasm. And oh how I wanted that orgasm. You want to know what I was thinking about? That's what I was thinking about. An orgasm!"

"Jesus, Mom."

"You can't seriously tell me you're shocked. You of all people! You've never been shocked by anything in your life!"

"Do you ever think of anybody but yourself?"

"Do I? Let me tell you. Do you know what happened to your great aunt? I'm sure I've told you. Have you told Cody? They cut her open. The great state of Vermont cut her open and threw out her uterus like a filthy dish rag. They didn't even tell her. She was only thirteen years old, Drew. Thirteen! Just a year older than

Cody. And, you know, she always worried the same thing would happen to me and to Cody. Tell them you're Irish, she'd say. For years everyone would tell me that I was black Irish. That's what everyone would say. What do I know about the Irish? Nothing."

"Mom, I don't know if I can—"

"You asked if I ever thought of anyone but myself. I spent the first twenty years thinking of everyone but myself—I learned how to be invisible: the agreeable daughter; the obedient wife; the selfless mother. Who the hell wants to spend their lives being invisible? I wasn't the best mother but you must have learned something from me because I've never met a woman as independent."

"Because you weren't there," said Drew. "I had to be."

"And look what you've accomplished!"

"I feel like I'm dying, Mom," Drew breathed.

"I brought help but your new best friend confiscated the help."

"Mom!"

"I understand," Kati stood. "You're exhausted. I'll go."

"I'm sick."

"I know Sweetie," Kati kissed Drew on the cheek. "I know. But how can I help you? How long are you going to live here like this? I know the old house is gone, but maybe we can build a new one? If you can build a house for this woman you can build a house for us too?" Kati let the tip of her finger slide out from under Drew's chin. "Tonight's not a good night. I see that. I'm staying with Jessica again."

Cody watched Kati leave from her perch in the loft, her head poking through the short balusters, fingers curled around the edge. Cody's grandmother mesmerized her: how she moved, clothes, earrings, necklaces, bracelets and the long black hair that was somehow defiantly fierce. After she had gone, Drew sat at the small kitchen table with a long exhalation, staring at nothing for what seemed like an age to Cody. Then she finally leaned across the table, wrists thin and hands shaking, to take up the day's unopened mail. She sorted the envelopes then caught her breath. She hurriedly opened a legal-sized envelope before uttering a short cry or laugh, Cody couldn't tell; and seemed to heave.

"Are you okay?" Cody asked.

Drew looked up, straight up. She was crying but smiled. She waved Cody down. Cody rolled across the mattress and slid down the old orchard ladder. Drew waited for her, one hand impatiently outstretched, the other holding the letter. She drew Cody into a tight embrace. "They're saying—" she half whispered, "They're saying they're done. They're not gonna take you away, babe. They're all done." She took Cody in her arms and Cody couldn't remember her mother's embrace ever being so fierce or so strong.

11

Cody and Drew lay in Drew's bed, Drew with her arm around Cody's shoulder. They looked out the window at the foot of the bed with its muntins crisscrossing the stars and the passing moon. "You know you got a birthday comin' up, babe."

"Yeah," said Cody.

"Scorpio," said Drew, studying the windowed stars. "One of us wasn't enough."

"What are Scorpios like?"

"Like you and me, babe. Fearless, determined and if you cross us, nasty as hell."

Cody was silent a moment. "I like fearless and determined."

"So what kind of beer do you want for your birthday?"

Cody poked her mother with an elbow. "I don't want beer," she growled. "I'm never drinkin' beer again."

Drew smiled.

"You haven't smiled in a long time." Cody turned on her side. "Don't scare it away."

"I'm not," said Cody, suddenly serious. "I'm just sayin'."

"So what happened to you, babe?"

Cody shrugged. "I dunno."

"I oughta take you to the hospital," Drew said softly, sleepily.

"How come Grandpa hasn't come 'round? Was he like Daddy?"

"No." Drew shook her head. "No. He wasn't like Daddy." Then she sighed. "He was— Yeah, he broke my heart too, but not like yours. My dad was full of ideas. He was always makin' plans and I always figured I was in 'em that he loved me as much as I loved him, but findin' out his plans didn't have me in 'em broke my heart. I loved him, Cody; but, you know—the difference between him and your dad—it must of hurt him too. I still love him but he thought he couldn't give me or Mom what we wanted. Don't ever think bein' who you are, rich or poor, isn't enough. You're the most beautiful human being I know and any child you have is gonna fall in love with you. I'd of loved my dad no matter what but he figured he'd failed us. He got to drinkin', got angry, blamed me and Mom for his bein' angry, then decided he'd be better off without us and us without him. But you know that was his way of tryin' to do the right thing. It wasn't the right thing, babe, but life doesn't always spell it out."

"You still love him?"

"Yeah, babe. I guess I do. I kept thinkin' he'd come back one day; he'd throw me up in the air like when I was a little girl and everything would be the way it should've been and then the older I got the sadder the dream got 'til I hated it and hated him."

"But you—"

"I know." Drew smiled wistfully and shook her head again. "You'll see. Sometimes you hate the people you hate because you love 'em so much. Sometimes, babe. Sometimes."

"What'd you love about him?"

"He was just full of ideas and when I was a little girl he was like a magical being." Drew smiled again. "You know, he had a crow. I don't know if he tamed it or found it when it was a baby out of its nest. He trained it to sit on his shoulder. Mom hated it. When I was little I used to think he could talk to animals. I wanted to talk to animals too—just like him."

Cody rose onto an elbow. "What happened to the crow?"

"I dunno," said Drew wearily, beginning to fall into an exhausted asleep. "I dunno."

Cody didn't answer and in only a minute or two Drew was asleep. Cody dug out Soot's cards from her pocket. She had already arranged them from first to last. First was the Emperor, her father; then the Ten of Swords, betrayal; next was the present, the High Priestess and knowledge of divinity; next was the future—Death and the Two of Swords: choice. 'Not Death,' Soot had said, tapping the Two of Swords, "This card. This is the card that matters. Choice." But it was the image of death that captivated Cody.

"What are you looking at, babe?" Drew stirred.

Cody quietly folded the cards against her belly. "Nothin'."

"Somethin' botherin' you?"

"Can I ask you somethin'?"

"Yeah?"

"What's an orgasm?"

Chapter 17

from
  one end of night to the other—the crow
    stretches

1

Cody woke.

The moon was in the window's opposite corner and the window was open. She slowly sat up, rubbed her eyes, and shook her mother's shoulder. Drew didn't turn. "Mommy?" she said. "Mommy?" Then she gave a sharp cry. A woman was sitting in the window. She sat with her back against the right-hand jamb, one knee up and her other foot hanging down. She was beautiful—the woman from the Tarot. Her shoulder-length hair wasn't hair but like raven's feathers at midnight. She gazed at Cody with an expression both adoring and amused.

There was light.

The light was a brilliant thread shining around all sides of the bedroom door. Cody's hand slipped from her mother's shoulder. The light was like a song or laughter that Cody intimately remembered; hardly believing she'd ever forgotten it. Water came and went under the door as though waves washed through the threshold. Constellations tumbled over Cody's feet like seashells—the water as full of light as the night sky. She touched the doorknob, fingers closing around it before she recalled the woman in the window. The strange and beautiful figure already seemed like a distant memory but there she was again. Her amused expression hadn't changed. She pointed at Drew who was waking, turning as if to embrace Cody—

Cody screamed.

2

"Jesus Christ, Cody!"

Cody's eyes were wide. She sat up, gasping for air. In the window's corner claws clattered like little nails. A crow leapt from the window and into the early morning air. Cody swung into her mother's embrace, shaking, and clinging to her mother's thin cotton shirt.

"What in the hell, babe?"

"Nothin'." Cody's answer was muffled.

"Nothing?"

Cody shook her head quickly.

"A nightmare?"

"Just— Not all of it. Just—"

"And I thought I had a bad night."

"I want it to stop."

"What, babe?"

"Everything," said Cody. "All of it."

"What?"

"Bein' sick," said Cody. "You bein' sick and me."

Drew stroked Cody's hair. "What Daddy tried to do? It's over. That's all over. We're here. You. Me. We're here, we're hurtin' but we're alive and we're gettin' better."

"Did you see the crow?" Cody asked.

"What?"

"The crow!"

"All I heard was you."

"It was in the window," Cody looked over her mother's shoulder without letting go. "I saw it in the window. It was there!"

"Was it maybe in your dream?"

"It was in both."

"It was just a shadow, babe."

3

Hoyte ran to catch up with Cody as she walked to the school bus pick-up. She didn't turn when he caught up with her, gravel skittering under his steps. "Hey."

"Hi Hoyte."

"How'd it go, yesterday?"

Cody stared at her feet as she walked, hands in her jacket pocket, hood up. "Why do you want to know?"

"I mean—" he hesitated and shrugged. "I dunno. Just askin'."

"I en't ever gonna drink beer again."

"You find out what happened?"

Cody kicked at a stone. It rattled off into the ditching's drift of shriveled leaves. "Nothin' 'cept I blacked out."

"Just from that little bit?"

"Doesn't matter anyhow. I got caught is all you need to know."

"I don't care 'bout that."

"You did yesterday."

"I just wanted to know if you were okay."

"I'm okay."

"Why are you so mad?"

That question stopped Cody, stopped her walking, stopped her so that she stared at her feet and finally glanced at Hoyte. "That woman who came by from child protective services wrote and said Mom didn't do anything wrong."

"That whole thing was bullshit anyways."

Cody smiled and nodded. "Yeah it was." Then they picked up where they left off, kicking stones as they walked along. "But I'm not talkin' 'bout that anymore."

"I'm not askin'."

Once more they picked up side by side, both of them with their hands in their pockets. "Do you wanna go to the graveyard on Friday?"

"What for?"

"'Cause that's where Silas Todd's s'posed to be buried," said Cody.

"Which one is he in?"

"Old Town Cemetery."

"Isn't that down by Otter Creek?"

"They used to call it the Indian Road."

"The river?"

"Yeah," said Cody, then added, "And back before that Mom doesn't know what we called it."

"Wish they still called it that," said Hoyte. "What is it you wanna find out?"

"Just wanna know if there's anybody buried with him. If there en't then his family's probably those bones in the flooded cellar."

Then Cody and Hoyte were by the roadside. There had been a rain during the night. The edges of the asphalt and the bare limbs were still black with the visitation. Cody zipped her jacket to her chin and crossed her arms. "Aren't you cold?" she asked Hoyte.

"Nah."

"I am."

"Hey—" Hoyte was hesitant. "I got somethin' for you."

"You got somethin?"

"I mean—I didn't buy it. I found it. It's an old hunting knife. Maybe. I found it out in the woods, cleaned it up, sharpened it and made a new handle. You wanna see it?"

"Yeah," Cody answered warily.

Hoyte dug it from his pocket, offered it to her, handle first, carved cherry wrapped in leather cord. Cody took it, pulling it out of its homemade leather sheath. The blade was tarnished but clean. "I like it," she glanced sidelong at Hoyte.

"It's for you."

Cody flashed a brief smile as she cradled it in the palm of her right hand.

"Are you left-handed?"

"Yeah."

"You even write left-handed?"

"Yeah."

"Hey—" Hoyte paused.

"Yeah?"

"I mean, if you decide you wanna go do somethin' again with Jerry and Mike—"

"Well I en't drinkin' beer again."

"Just sayin' it's cool and I'd still come along."

After that, Cody and Hoyte ran out of anything to say that wasn't incriminating. Cody bit her lip, carefully sheathed the knife, and slid it into her coat pocket. She rose up and down on her toes. A mist was rising from the curling tumble of the brook, circling over the road. With the trees bare, there were only the white pine and hemlocks to stay the bristling mist. Cody gave Hoyte a sideways glance then unzipped her jacket like Hoyte's.

"I thought you were cold," said Hoyte.

"I warmed up."

4

A little before noon, Arvid visited Drew. "I brought you some food," he said. "I don't think you will want any, but you must try to eat even if just a little."

Drew's eyes were dark and hollow. She sat at the kitchen table like a woman in mourning, downcast and wrapped in a blanket. Arvid moved his chair next to hers and took out two mugs. "A little snert," he said. "We call it *erwtensoep*. It's really just pea soup with celery, onion, leek, some carrot, and potato. We also like to eat it with rye bread and then you put bacon and cheese on top of the bread. I suspect that would be too much for you."

Drew smiled.

"I think it is a good sign," said Arvid, noticing her expression.

Drew took a deep breath and wiped at her eyes. "It's like he's tryin' to kill me all over again."

"I know," Arvid pushed the mug toward Drew. "Try it."

"I don't think I can."

"I've gone through it," said Arvid. He patted his leg. "And I did not think I would survive."

"Addiction?"

"I worked as a peacekeeper for the UN during the Bosnian war and was in a helicopter when it experienced a mechanical failure. The crash crippled me but the cure almost killed me. I, like you, became addicted to the medication. At first I reduced the dosage little by little but— you know, I'll tell you a little story... When I was a boy my grandfather took me fishing, he asked me a question: If you had to cut off a dog's tail, which do you think would hurt more? Just a little at a time or all at once? Being a little boy, I thought just a little each time would hurt just a little, but to chop off a tail all at once? That must hurt terribly. So I said a little at a time. As you can expect, my grandfather offered to cut off my big toe just a little at a time. So, many years later, you could say that I was trying to cut off my tail a little at a time. I tried taking less a little at a time but I experienced what you are experiencing."

Drew leaned and smelled the soup. "Thank you."

"You should try some."

"So what did you do?"

"I didn't cut my tail off all at once," said Arvid.

"How quick?"

"It took me a month."

"Tomorrow," Drew said. "I'm not takin' anymore."

"All at once?"

"No." Drew tasted the soup and closed her eyes at the taste of it. "I've been cuttin' back already. But I don't know if it's the drugs or the rage eatin' me up inside."

"Anger is an addiction."

"It's gonna kill me all the same."

"It is as difficult, I think, as getting over a drug addiction," said Arvid, "and I would even say that anger is a drug itself. I have seen whole nations destroyed by the addiction to anger and revenge."

"I can't forgive him."

"There is no one to forgive, Drew. The man who tried to kill you is gone. He is like a character in a play who has come and gone. You know, we Europeans hold grievances that go back thousands of years. Once when I was in Ireland, a taxi driver began to complain about the English. The more he described their offenses, the angrier he became. And then, as we were some ways in the country, he pointed to a hillside and in a spitting rage said: Do you see that hillside? That hillside used to be nothing but oaks, the loveliest oaks you'd ever want to see. All gone. Not one left but the Brits took them. And we got nothing. Not one thing but a bare hillside.

"And so I asked him, when did this happen?

"He said, 'Bloody King James! That's who it was.'" Then Arvid smiled, adding: "The same King James, you know, who commissioned the King James Bible. And while I do not compare your anger to a taxi driver in Ireland, the man who did this to you is also gone. There is only the memory of him. It is for you to decide whether that memory will consume you like an angry wolf, or whether you will feed the wolf which brings you some hope for the future."

Drew sighed. "When will this stop?"

"Don't give up. If there's an easier way I don't know what it is, Drew. But one morning you will wake up and the craving will stop. It will be just another memory."

"Arvid," Drew paused, before tears fell from her lips. "Cody was drowning. I saw her drowning. I saw her dying. I couldn't help her. The water—I saw it going over her and I couldn't stop her from dying." Then she began to sob, wrecked, fingers twisting the canvas of her dungarees, sobbing the way a child sobs. "She's my daughter!"

Arvid leaned and embraced Drew with her fists pressed tightly against her mouth.

"She is still here," said Arvid softly. "Perhaps that wasn't the time when you were meant to save Cody, but now—today's Cody and tomorrow's. There is surely a part of her that is still drowning and that still needs you to rescue her."

"It's myself I can't forgive."

"What do you want? This evening, tomorrow, and into the coming months. Tell me, Drew, what are your dreams?"

"Cody gettin' her birthday party."

"And then what?"

"I want to build Cody a beautiful house—" Drew wiped her eyes and grimaced with the effort to calm her trembling. "I'm gonna build us both a beautiful house. She deserves that." She straightened and remembering Cody's words said: "I en't never gonna take painkillers again."

"You see?"

"We're gonna travel too."

"Where to?"

"I'm takin' her out west."

"You know, I've never been out west."

"I'm gonna get a runner—an old pickup that's a runner like my dad's." Drew tenderly lifted her ankle and straightened in her seat. "We'll put some sleeping bags in back, maybe a couple chairs for takin' in the views when we cross the plains and get into the Rockies."

"You know, you are already building her a beautiful house."

5

Mrs. Santoff was writing when Cody came into the office. Cody took the familiar blue seat. First she gazed at the felt dolls on the shelves then peered out the window.

"You want to be outside?" Mrs. Santoff finally asked.

"Yeah," Cody slid down in her chair, legs straight, hands jammed in her pockets.

"The days are getting shorter and shorter."

"I'm okay."

"And setting the clocks back."

Cody uttered another barely audible, "Yeah."

"So how are you doing?"

"They've stopped investigatin' us," Cody answered.

"Who?"

"The woman who came when grandma and grandpa complained."

"Oh." Santoff paused, "You mean Family Services?"

"Yeah."

"I'm happy that's been resolved."

"Mom didn't do anything."

"And you had a little adventure too," Santoff continued.

Cody leaned deeper into her seat and closed her eyes. "Do we have to talk about that?"

Santoff laughed. "What do you want to talk about?"

"I don't know."

"Isn't your birthday soon?"

"Yeah."

"What are you going to do on your birthday?"

"We're gonna try to finish the house," Cody sat up. "We're gonna finish it for my birthday. All we've got is to put in some cabinets, cover walls with board, and divide up the basement for Virginia, then paint everything."

"Are you doing that work?"

"Sometimes. Sometimes Hoyte comes over but mostly it's me and Virginia doin' it."

"She must have had some building experience?"

"Mom's been tellin' her what to do. At first when Mom was really hurt she'd just tell me and Virginia, but when Mom wasn't lookin' Virginia'd throw a fit and when Virginia wasn't lookin' Mom would throw a fit. And then Mom started doin' a little bit of buildin'. I think Virginia would rather be readin' her books on nursing."

"What about you?"

"I keep my fits to myself." Cody jabbed her foot at nothing. "Mom was gettin' better before she got addicted. Now she's tryin' to get off 'em. It's been makin' her sad and mad at the same time and makin' it so she can't sleep or eat. All she's got time for is bein' mad or sad. She can't do or help with anything."

"What about you? How are you doing?"

"I got headaches come and go."

"Have you seen the nurse?"

Cody squirmed in her seat. "Don't see why I need to see a nurse. And I keep havin' dreams where I see what's gonna happen and sometimes what should happen—or just see things—or almost. Like there's somethin' stoppin' me from seein' what I want to see." Cody paused. "But when I try and tell people they don't believe me. Or I forget what I saw."

"You feel like people aren't believing you."

Cody's hands grasped at the nothing in her pockets. "Sort of."

"Being believed is important," Santoff nodded thoughtfully.

"Yeah."

"But sometimes being believed means finding your own way to tell the truth."

"What do you mean?"

"If you were a puppeteer, you'd use puppets. Maybe you'll write poems and tell stories. Maybe you'll build houses like your mother."

"I en't gonna build houses."

"You never know."

"I know."

"Life surprises us."

"And what does buildin' a house have to do with tellin' the truth anyhow?"

"What do you think you'd like to do when you grow up?"

"Fix old cars."

"A mechanic?"

"I wanna fix old cars and sell 'em for new."

"Good for you!"

A motion in the shelves distracted Cody. The dolls stirred to life. She nervously glanced at Mrs. Santoff before they and the toys spilled like water onto the floor and desk. She pressed herself into the back of the seat. Outside the window, puppets appeared as if the windowsill were their stage. "Stop it!" Cody lowered her head in her hands, stiffening against the sudden pain.

"Hey!" Santoff had hurried from behind the desk. She knelt in front of Cody. "What's going on?"

"Nothing!"

"That wasn't nothing."

"I made it stop," said Cody. "It just— It happens when people are thinking really hard."

"When what?"

"When people are thinking hard about something."

"You should see the nurse."

"I'll be okay."

"Does it always hurt like that?"

"It didn't used to."

"I'm sending you to the nurse whether you want to or not."

"Now?"

"Yes, now."

Cody sighed and sat up, palms down, elbows locked as she swiveled on the edge of the seat. She stood, went to the door and paused again. "Sorry 'bout the letter."

"The letter?"

Cody glanced at her feet. "I oughta go."

"No, wait. What letter?"

"From the hospital. 'Bout whether you can have a baby—"

"How do you know about that? Who told you?"

Cody hunched her shoulders apologetically and shrunk against the door. "I just— it's what I've been sayin'." And then, as if disbelieving her own self, she looked away embarrassed. "Sometimes it's like everything in the world comes to life and shows me what somebody's thinkin'. It's like we don't really do our thinkin' in our heads but it's the world thinkin' through us. Our heads are just where the thinkin' comes out."

Mrs. Santoff sat back on her haunches. "That information is private, you understand?"

Cody quickly nodded.

"I don't know who's been telling you this—"

"Nobody."

"Or why—"

"You don't believe me," said Cody, her eyes moistening, her voice flat with anger. "You never believed me."

"That's not what I meant."

"No, but it's like you said—" Cody's hands tightened into fists. "Everybody has their own way of tellin' the truth."

6

By Friday the story of Jerry, Cody, Olivia, Roy, and Mike was already being transformed into myth as it was retold by children from one class to the next. Cody saw the glances, the mouths at ears as if she'd predicted a whole new calamity or had drawn the blood of another Olivia. Cody and the others had returned from a wilderness that was dangerous and tantalizing. One by one they were summoned to speak with Reynard and yet they somehow hadn't been banished. The sidelong glances were a mix of awe, respect, and even fear.

The new relationship between Olivia and Cody was observed in the way that children accept sudden realignments between friends and enemies. They assumed that whatever drew Cody and Olivia together was natural and inevitable; needing no more explanation than what children intuitively grasp—that to have a friend is to see the world through another's eyes, and sometimes that means the ruin of one world for a new and larger one.

Jerry, Olivia, Mike, and Cody met at the end of a line of school buses. They stood with their hands in their pockets, Cody back in her blue overalls and light green jacket, hood up—and all of them carrying backpacks. So late in autumn the sun never wholly dispels the long nights. The clouds are as heavy with shadow at noon as at evening, and the trees cast their stripped limbs across the roads as if to grasp for their own lost leaves—stick season in Vermont. When Hoyte joined them, they started their walk to the graveyard. "Audrey's not coming?" he asked.

"She was grounded," said Cody.

"And she didn't even do anything," Mike gave a sharp laugh and tugged at his pants. "Just goes to show. That's a life lesson right there—a life lesson. It's called karma. If you're alive, it means you're bein' punished for somethin'."

"That's not what karma means," said Olivia flatly.

"It is," Mike went on, "and I'll tell you what's more. The way people think 'bout karma's all wrong—all backwards. See, because every splinter, every time you stub your toe, every time you catch cold when you're not expectin' it, you're bein' punished. Most people think it's 'cause of somethin' they already did. But see, the way karma works is you're gettin' punished for somethin' you're gonna do, so the trick is figurin' out what crime you're gettin' punished for and go do it. That way you're not gettin' punished for nothin', you're just evenin' things up."

"That is the dumbest thing I ever heard," said Hoyte.

"Hoyte, it doesn't surprise me you'd say that. And frankly I'm hurt."

Hoyte shoved him off the sidewalk.

"Pearls to swine," Mike skipped back onto the sidewalk.

"I don't know," said Jerry. "I kind of like it."

"That's 'cause we're from the same side of the tracks," said Mike, "if you catch my meanin'. It lends a fixity to life 'cause you always know why bad things happen to you."

"It's karma for thieves," said Hoyte.

"Do you just sit around and think this stuff up?" asked Olivia.

"Just at school," said Mike.

"At school?"

"There's nothing else to do at school. 'Cause I always used to draw and the teacher'd always catch me drawin' so I figured she couldn't say anythin' if I did all my drawin' in my head, except that when you start drawin' in your head you start usin' words to color and drawings get to turnin' into ideas. See? And instead of makin' drawings you're paintin' whole stories with words. Cody. Hey Cody! See? She's smilin'. Cody knows what I'm talkin' about. Indians are story tellin' people. You know what I'm talkin' about, right Cody?"

"Sure," said Cody, suddenly reluctant. "I guess."

"So how about you," Jerry said to Mike. "You must'a got a good combin' out for stealin' beer?"

"I foreswore beer for the rest of my life," Mike continued matter-of-factly. "Said I'd never touch it again. Not for the rest of my life."

"You fore-what?"

"Foreswore, Jerry. As in I swore I'd never drink it again."

"So did I," Cody added.

"You did not," Jerry grinned.

"Jerry, I babbled like a brook. A man don't stand on principle when he's an island flooded by bad weather. It's why I walk here with you today."

Jerry shook his head, smiling, and the group walked silently for a moment.

"Hey Cody," Mike finally spoke up. "You know I'm just joshin' you right? I don't mean anythin' by it—about Indians and all that. I just say whatever gets into my head."

"I en't worried about it." Cody pushed off her hood and slipped the hair out of her face. The sidewalk to the Old Town Cemetery took itself through Brookway's old Victorian neighborhood, its brick and concrete cracked and buckled by maple and elm. Each house had a generous porch with faint blue ceilings to keep the wasps and ghosts away. Driveways led to barns connected by shed added onto shed until the house and barn met and married. The children took a shortcut between two of the houses and crossed to a narrower dead-end road whose cracks were tufts of grass, shortest where the occasional car travelled. On both sides hemlock collected the evening's early dark. The uphill road curved gently to the right until it ended just beyond the cemetery. The cemetery itself was bordered by low granite posts with a low chain slung between them.

"If it's all the same," said Mike, "I'm gonna wait right here."

"Afraid to go in?" said Hoyte with a skeptical smile.

"Do you even know what time of year it is?"

"That oughta make a difference?"

"Hoyte," said Mike, "you got the longest legs of anybody here—and I got the shortest. You got more brains than all of us put together. Me? I don't got any brains to spare. But whose brains you think they're gonna eat if it comes down to runnin'?"

"You don't got enough brains to worry about," said Jerry.

"I got what I need."

The entry was between two taller waist-high posts. The gravestones beyond were mostly old, cracked, or grainy sandstone weathered beyond reading. There were newer graves out from under the shade of the hemlocks. Olivia stepped past Cody, hands in the pocket of her knee-length coat, then turned. "What?"

"I just en't ever seen you with your hair up," said Cody.

"I wanna cut it short."

"How short?"

"I don't know," said Olivia. "I haven't ever cut it short."

"Why not?"

"Mom wouldn't let me."

"You wanted to?"

"Not 'til now." Olivia paused again, as if cornered, then answering flatly. "Mom and Dad are separating. Mom said it wasn't Christian for a girl to cut her hair short."

Cody chewed on that as they continued into the graveyard. "Hope it goes better than it did for me."

Hoyte and Jerry went to the back of the cemetery and to the oldest gravestones. Olivia and Cody strayed toward the newer stones from the 1900's. Some five minutes had gone by when Cody froze. She pressed the heels of her hands into both her eyes, welling with emotion. She fell cross-legged to the ground, sitting and bent forward.

"Are you okay?" Olivia hurried to Cody's side.

Cody shook her head and Olivia saw what Cody had seen—Daryl Tippet. Cody abruptly stood up, struck her hips with her fists, and ran out of the graveyard. She crossed the road and fell to her knees with her back to the graveyard. She knotted her fingers in her hair. Olivia and Hoyte went to her. Cody began to shake with long sobs.

"It's stupid," said Cody. Olivia knelt next to her, resting her hand on Cody's shoulder. Hoyte joined her on the other side. Cody wiped her nose with the back of her jacket sleeve. "It's stupid," she said again, her voice and breath beginning to calm.

"What do you want to do?" Hoyte asked.

"I'm sick of cryin' over him," Cody's voice was flat with anger. She stood up and wiped her eyes again. "I'm not cryin' over him or anybody else." Then she said under her breath. "Not even myself."

"You've got to sometimes," said Olivia.

"Not for him I don't. He made a stupid choice— It was his choice. Wasn't mine." Cody's fists opened into her hair again and she took a deep breath. "It was stupid."

Jerry and Mike stood a little behind with their hands in their pockets. "There's some can't stand the thought of anybody havin' somethin' better, even life itself," said Jerry. "They got one foot in the grave and there's only satisfaction in them knowin' both of yours got there first."

"It's more than that," said Cody quietly.

"It's believing in somebody your whole life and finding out none of it was real," said Olivia mostly to herself.

Cody rubbed her eyes and turned to Jerry and Mike. "Did you find his grave?"

"Yeah," said Mike. "I found it"

"Where was it?" Jerry asked.

"Right up front."

"Why didn't you say somethin'?"

"Well I was goin' to and then what with Cody findin' her dad's grave," Mike answered irritably. "Seemed like she had more pressing issues."

Cody went to Jerry and Mike then stepped between them when they parted. "Where is it?" she asked.

"There," Mike pointed. "It's there on the right and it's got writin' on it."

Cody steadied her resolve and walked to it. The chain separating the cemetery from the road was at her shins. She bent and wiped at her eyes again. The others stooped behind her.

"Silas Todd," Cody read. "Born 1900, Salem MA. Died 1938, West Brookway.

Beneath this stone
He lies alone,
Buried with the grief he bore.

Let Silas Todd
Go now with God
And let him grieve no more."

"What d'ya suppose they meant by that?" asked Mike.

"Somethin' tore him up," said Hoyte.

"And there isn't anybody buried with him or beside him." said Cody.

"Why's that matter?" Mike asked.

"'Cause if those bones in the old foundation were his family's then it'd make sense he was buried alone and it'd make sense why he died of grief."

"Why didn't he just tell 'em?" Mike asked.

"Maybe he figured it was his fault they died," said Jerry. "And he was grievin' too much to tell 'em."

"So now what?" asked Mike.

Cody straightened. "I dunno."

"So," said Hoyte, "you really okay, Cody?"

"I en't gonna die of grief," she answered coolly.

The others nodded.

Then Hoyte spoke his thinking aloud: "You found out what you wanted to find out."

Cody's gaze turned to her father's gravestone. She shook her head. "C'mon. Let's go."

My skeleton and I go out for walks,
Although he mostly likes it in the closet.
I'll hear him tap, tap, tapping
His skull for some conundrum; there are many.
It's no small thing for any skeleton
To think. His skull's a ruined house, its clasps
And door-locks long since gone.
            He teeters, grasps —
Ideas are fretful winds. They blow into
And through his vacant stare, emptily tumble;
Then out the way they came. He stands perplexed,
A sharp forefinger's bone upraised, his jaw
Aslant — he'd almost had it.
            So it goes
It's times like these that we go out. I keep
Our walks discreet though every now and then
We'll meet a passerby (my skeleton
And theirs will pay no mind). We pass a cape,
A woodpile covered by a sheet of tin,

And laundry—skirts and sheets. They billow ghostlike
Above the ruined dooryard.
                    He walks
With fingers laced behind his spine; looks
A little this way and a little that.
The dust recoils between his toes and smolders
At his heels. There's nowhere he'll stop
Unless it's where there used to be a house,
Midfield, where now there's just foundation stone.
He'll gaze with longing and he'll heave
And here and there a leaf snagged in his ribs
(And bones withal) will tumble down. They'll scrape
And skitter through and in between until
He stands in them.
                  He lingers. He'd share
A secret he kept in life; that now,
In death, keeps him. I never asked and yet
One day he pointed where the house had been
With such a trembling grief
He might have been as likely reaching to touch
Another's unseen fingertip.
                 A gust
Took from the cellarhole a crackling smoke
Of leaves. The sheets of the house nearby
Were chased into the field's conflagration
Of nettle, thorn and thistle. Too late
They fled but couldn't flee. The sudden gust
Confounded them — the mother and her child!
I saw them both. How like a mother's hand,
And like the daughter's where the small sheet clung
If only by a clothespin to the larger;
As if they'd change what was already done,
As if this time they'd reach his outstretched sorrow;
Undo, a hundred years gone by, the crows
That rise like startled ashes from the ruins—
Their screams dispersed into the neighboring hemlock
And birch.
                 His lowering finger curls beneath
Their rake of knuckles. The sheets lay motionless
Under a settling soot of leaves and wildflowers charred
By frost.
               He never afterward did more
Than linger. I'll not swear that what I saw
Was true, but then I can't be sure that I
Won't too, for guilt, regret, or for some sorrow
Dwell in your home.

You'll know me, if I'm there—
My bones, a few remains, shelved in a poem;
Willing, if just for company, to share
Your walk and should you need me to — your pain.

Chapter 18

1

Drew's old pickup hummed smoothly up Route 7's southbound straight stretch. Virginia took some satisfaction in her shifting. Drew sat in the bench seat next to her with her head back and eyes closed. She was pale and her skin glistened with sweat. Virginia was struck by how Drew and Cody looked alike, both hollow-cheeked, rail-thin, and seemingly fragile—nothing like the women of her own family.

Beyond her were the steep walls of the now familiar mountains. They rose out of the meadows and fields to the east. At the foot of the mountains, the patchwork of fields gently rose and fell westward toward Lake Champlain. To the west of Lake Champlain, the Adirondack Mountains once more lifted the earth out of itself. Their jagged opinions were snagged in each other's silhouettes, unlike the older, smoother Greens.

Another couple miles southward on Route 7 and Drew suddenly inhaled, eyes wide, reaching and bracing as if to keep herself from falling. Virginia swerved toward the center line, surprised by Drew's cry. "Jesus, Drew!"

"I'm sorry!" Drew swallowed.

"What's wrong?"

"Being there, in the water, trapped."

"You were dreaming about that again?"

"I can't stop."

"Well, you know, it's not surprising. I think you're suffering from post traumatic stress!"

"It's withdrawal."

"Feeling helpless when your daughter's drowning isn't something you just get over."

"I can't stop dreaming about it." Drew forced herself to relax. "Every time I fall asleep. It's the same. It's the same fucking dream."

"If nothing else you need a full night's sleep."

Drew wiped at her eyes with the backs of her hands. "I can't."

"Don't give up."

"Jesus-fucking-Christ," Drew's voice trembled. "How much longer does this last?"

"Have you taken any more?"

"No."

"For how many days?"

"I don't know." Drew glared out the window. "Maybe since almost a week now?"

"Well, some patients' withdrawal lasted just three or four days. It depends on the drug. The worst usually only lasts a handful of days—but they're terrible and awful days."

Drew was silent. She jammed her hands in her pockets, just the way Cody did, and closed her eyes again. "You know," she finally said, "you know how Cody says she saw what was happening?"

"You mean her out of body experience?"

"Yeah."

"She told me a little about it."

"There was—" Drew paused. "When we were trapped in the car, at first, the water was just coming in. Coming in and I couldn't move. The windows were busted. The current was sinking the truck. I blacked out. All I remember is the black. The floating—" Drew breathed. "Just floating. Nothing. There was no vision. There was no voice. There was no light."

"But you remember the black?"

Drew nodded. "Yeah. Yeah I do. I remember the black. And how wonderful it was."

"Do you want to know what I think?"

"What was I supposed to do?" Drew asked.

"What could you do? You were trapped. Your body was broken. You were drowning. You can't blame yourself for what you couldn't change. You have to stop, Drew. She's alive and you're alive."

Drew shook her head. "When you're a kid and your dad thinks you're the reason he's failed at everything, it's like he's driving you off a bridge; and the one person who's supposed to pull you out—doesn't."

"Drew!—"

"I'm not talking about Cody!" Drew interrupted angrily, then quietly. "I'm talking about me. Mom and Dad were the ones supposed to be pulling me out of the water, not drowning me in the wreckage of their own lives. I swore I wasn't going to be *that* parent."

"You aren't."

"Just once it would have been nice."

"Drew!—"

"For me," Drew continued. "Just once in my life!" She jammed her feet angrily into the floorboards. "If someone had been there for me."

2

Jerry and Mike had gone on. Cody, Olivia, and Hoyte sat on the curb, their backpacks on the sidewalk. Cody traced a figure eight in the street's pavement with the stem of a cracked leaf. Hoyte sat on one side and Olivia on the other. Hoyte picked up the pebbles, washed in a thin line against the granite curb, and flicked them into the center of the street. The school was across the street, the buses gone and the children too. Someone had put jack-o-lanterns at either end of the school's portico. They couldn't decide which was more haunted, an empty house or an empty school.

"Have you ever cut your own hair?" Olivia asked Cody.

"I did it with a bowl once," Cody smiled, glancing sidelong at Olivia.

"Really?"

"Yeah. And I didn't tell Mom I was doin' it."

"What'd she do?"

"She tried to guess what bowl I used."

"She wasn't mad?"

"Worse," said Cody flatly. "She couldn't stop laughin'."

"Will you cut my hair?"

"Punchin' you wasn't enough? You want me sorry for cuttin' your hair too?"

Olivia pulled a pair of scissors out of her pocket, sharp-tipped and shining in the gray daylight. She held them upside down between herself and Cody. "Not too short. I don't want any bangs. And still under my ears."

"I wouldn't—" But Hoyte stopped himself.

"Wouldn't what?" said Cody.

"Wouldn't wait too long," Hoyte tossed another pebble into the middle of the road. "Better do it before your mom shows up."

Cody took the scissors. She knelt behind Olivia, lifted the back of her hair, squinted, lined up the scissors with the sidewalk across the street, and cut. "Maybe nobody cared."

"About what?" Olivia asked.

"About Silas Todd."

"They put up a tombstone and wrote a poem for him," said Hoyte.

"Then pob'ly forgot about him," said Cody. She reached over Olivia's shoulder and handed her a clump of hair. "Figured that was as much as what they owed him. And what if those bones were his family's; what were they to Silas once he was dead? Or them? Prob'ly they just left 'em there, if they even knew 'bout 'em. They had other things to think about. Preferred forgettin' about 'em."

"Or something could've happened," said Hoyte. "It was the Great Depression and all."

"It's not like you need something like that," said Olivia.

"You think dyin' oughta stop the world," said Cody, handing Olivia another swath of hair, "especially if it's your own dyin', but the world keeps on like you were never there."

"So you're sayin' we don't matter?" said Hoyte.

"Those people in the graveyard matter to you?" Cody asked.

"Maybe not, but that doesn't mean what they did in life doesn't matter just 'cause you don't know about it. Maybe one of them built this sidewalk you're sittin' on. Maybe one of 'em built the house or cleared the property where somebody's livin'. Maybe if one of 'em hadn't done one little thing then we wouldn't be here. Sayin' that nothin' you do in life matters is like—" Hoyte threw another pebble. "It's like sayin' you can pull one thread out of a carpet without it fallin' apart."

"So you're sayin' we're all doormats?" Cody answered.

Hoyte's next pebble bounced to the other side. "I'm not sayin' we're doormats!"

Cody grinned. She handed another clump of hair to Olivia.

"So," Olivia paused delicately, "are you two— like boyfriend and girlfriend?"

"No!" Cody tugged Olivia's head for the next cut. Olivia cried out. Cody glanced at Hoyte, head down, askant, then snipped the next strand of hair. "I mean, we're friends."

"It's just that opposites attract. *Ow!*"

"We're not opposites."

"*Ow!* Stop pulling my hair so hard!"

"You want me to cut your hair or not?"

"Are you almost done?"

"Depends on what you say next."

"I just mean he's so together. You two would be a good fit— *Ouch!*"

"And I'm not?" Cody gave Olivia a final sharp tug before handing her a final snippet of hair. "I'm done."

Olivia exhaled with relief and stood up. She blew her hair from the palm of her hand, felt the hair around her ears, cupped the nape of her neck. "How's it look?"

"Like you prob'ly shouldn'ta paid for it," said Hoyte.

"Well I didn't."

"That's what it looks like," he cracked a smile, leaned back onto the sidewalk.

"It's not that bad," said Cody, eyes narrowed as if appraising artwork. "I could prob'ly cut a little more on the right side."

"You mean pull it out by the roots."

"It's uneven."

"Good."

"It's not gonna look right."

"Doesn't have to." Olivia bent over and shook her hair. "I'm sick of having to be perfect anymore."

"Wish I had that problem," said Cody.

"You're lucky."

"How am I lucky?"

"No, really." Olivia sized up Cody, unsure where they were headed. "You've got lots to feel lucky about."

"How am I lucky?" Cody jammed her fists in her pockets.

"I don't know. Do you *want* to be miserable?"

Cody glared, pressed her lips together, eyes cast down, fished for something to say, something to deny her misery and to also set forth all the reasons for it.

"You're lucky 'cause I like you," said Hoyte.

Cody glanced at Olivia but Olivia's corkscrew smile sent Cody wheeling around to shove Hoyte instead. "How is that lucky? That just makes me even more miserable!"

Hoyte playfully lifted his hands.

Cody crossed her arms, standing between Hoyte and Olivia, eyes downcast, lips in a thwarted curl, and seemed to study the designs made by the toes of her sneakers. She turned them in half circles. "Are you gonna tell 'em I cut your hair?" Cody asked.

"My mom? She'd be madder at you for cutting my hair than for punching me."

Cody smiled.

Olivia returned to the sidewalk's curb and picked up her backpack. "I'll see you tomorrow."

Cody nodded.

"You should come over," then Olivia added, "at my dad's new place."

"Yeah I will."

"So I guess I'll see you tomorrow," said Olivia.

"Hey. My birthday's on Saturday," said Cody shyly. "You wanna come up?"

"Yeah, I'll ask Dad if it's okay." Olivia began her walk home. Hoyte and Cody stood side by side, each abruptly unsure what to say, familiar conversation as altered as a half-travelled world in a changing season. "So," said Hoyte, finally, "how's your mom doin'?"

"She's okay," Cody answered, gazing at nothing. "She's addicted to pain meds."

"Is she tryin' to get off 'em?"

"Been tryin' since about a month ago."

"That's hard."

"En't been easy." Cody glanced at Hoyte, then smiled shyly, gazing at her feet again as she sidled sideways a little closer to Hoyte.

"Did you really know what motor Jake Farnham's rig was runnin' just by hearin' it?"

Cody smiled.

Hoyte nodded knowingly. "So how'd you know?"

"Me 'n Dad helped install it."

"So wanna come over for some ice cream?"

"Dunno if I can."

"We could make some." Hoyte stared at his own feet. "If you want. Got an ice cream maker. You and me if you want. And I won't tell anybody 'bout you guessin' car motors."

Cody inched a little closer.

3

"Jesus," said Drew, "remind me why we picked you up?"

"Hoyte's dad woulda done it," said Cody.

"You two are hitchhikin' next time." Drew adjusted her legs. Cody sat on Hoyte's lap between Drew and Virginia. She had drawn up her knees, feet between Hoyte's knees.

"I'm okay," said Hoyte.

"Nobody asked you, Hoyte." Cody's mood had turned dour.

"So you gonna tell us what you found out about Silas Todd, babe?"

"Nothin'."

"Nah. You gotta give me something."

"Dad was buried there."

"Yeah." Drew shifted uncomfortably. "Okay. That's something. What about Daryl Tippet's wife and kid? Buried with him?"

"No."

"See? You got somethin' to be happy about."

Cody's mouth twisted into a helpless grin before she quickly composed herself. "Silas Todd wasn't either. Means those bones they found are prob'ly his wife and kid."

"So now what, babe?"

"I think they oughta be buried with him."

"Hey," Drew turned, glancing at Cody.

"What?"

"Been awhile since you laughed. Missed it. I could use a little more. Don't hold it back."

4

Drew slept, then didn't. She sat on her bed with her knees drawn up. She paced or slumped at the kitchen table, startled out of sleep as she slipped from the chair. Cody was woken on and off and so was Virginia, who quietly spoke to Drew during the night. Cody fell asleep to their subdued voices and when she woke in the morning, slipping down the ladder, Drew's expression was haunted by exhaustion. She sat with her head hung down, hair over her eyes and lips, loosely fingering a cup of coffee. Virginia was up and bringing Cody half a grapefruit.

"Did you sleep alright, babe?" Drew asked.

"Yeah."

"'Cause I'm havin' a hard time. You think you can take the bus home today? No more adventures?"

"Oh, I could pick her up," said Virginia, "we're having another writer's-reader's group tonight."

"That's okay," said Cody. "I'm comin' home and makin' ice cream with Hoyte."

"And hey, you're gonna be thirteen tomorrow," said Drew.

Cody suppressed a smile.

"You're gonna have a good time. I'm gonna beat this and you're gonna have a good time tomorrow. I swear, babe, I'll take some pain meds if I have to."

"Isn't a doctor s'posed to be helpin' you?"

"They can put you on the drugs. They got licenses to put you *on* drugs, but don't have licenses to get you off 'em." Drew paused. "They're fucking useless."

"They shouldn't of put you on drugs," said Cody.

"They should treat dependency like every other disease," said Virginia. "My God, how many people have to suffer before they do something?"

"Just hope you never go through this." Drew pulled a sleeping blanket back over her shoulders. "One minute ice is in your veins and the next there's fire runnin' through 'em."

5

On the way to the reading group, Virginia pulled into Hugh Kemp's grocery store. She nosed up to the porch. The old lamp post flickered over the two pumps but the Kemps had hung Christmas lights from the porch's thickly painted eaves. Virginia leaned back, only meaning to momentarily close her eyes, then nearly cried out when she was awakened by knocking on her window. Barstowe stood outside, the knuckle of his right hand still raised. Virginia cranked down the window. "I'm so sorry," she patted her chest, "I must have fallen asleep!"

"No bother," said Barstowe. "Shouldn't of surprised ya like that."

"Oh my! Well," said Virginia, "you seem to be everywhere!"

Barstowe took off his hat and gave it a squeeze. "There's more of the river given' way upslope. Went to have a look. Gonna have to close the road again for a day or so. Saw you parked here when I drove by and saw ya comin' back 'round. Seemed I oughta make sure you weren't broke down."

"No," Virginia rolled down her window the rest of the way. "I just left the house a little early. Drew has it rough. I don't think the withdrawal, not as awful as it's been, will last much longer. It can't, but she's exhausted and so is her daughter. And I'm worried about Cody. Drew should have taken her to the hospital by now."

"Where were you headed?"

"A writer's group—really more an excuse to get together and gossip. We're supposed to meet at Lydia's and here I sit."

"What time?"

"Eight."

"Why it's not even seven o'clock yet," said Barstowe, still alternately releasing and squeezing his hat. "How would you like we had a cup of coffee. I'll drive you in."

"I can't leave my car here!"

"It's no matter to Hugh this time of night."

Virginia momentarily turned, gazing out the windshield, then grabbed her purse. "Why not?" She didn't so much as bother to lock the truck. She climbed into Barstowe's rig and he took her into Brookway and to the old brick train depot that had been turned into a little grocery store and café.

"What'll you have?" Barstowe asked.

"A cup of coffee and a cinnamon roll."

"I'm buyin'," said Barstowe and he returned with mugs and rolls for both of them.

"You know I used to know your grandpap."

"How old are you?"

"I'm not that old. 'Bout your age I suspect. I was just a boy when Pappy used to bring me along. We'd go there to help your grandpap with whatnot and then go down to fish in his pond. Used to keep his ponds stocked with sunfish, bluegill, catfish, and trout."

"I must have met him only once."

"He was a handsome fellow and had the best lookin' family around, half of 'em redheads, and when I first saw ya I thought you had the look of a Darby. But now tell me, you bein' the only Darby hereabouts—you plan on stayin'?"

"Well I don't know. There's so much up in the air."

"You've got a house now, don't ya?"

"Yes I do," Virginia protested, "but I really should have my own and so should Cody and Drew. She's had a terrible experience. And she and Cody need to restart their lives without me mixed up with them. And Cody's turning thirteen tomorrow!"

"I'll tell you what, Drew doesn't take to many people but she's cottoned to you."

"She puts up with me."

"Don't sell yourself short, Virginia. Puttin' *up* with is what we call a hard and fast friendship in Vermont. Some go so far as to call it a marriage. You two couldn't be more opposite but I suspect ya both give each other something the other needs."

"Needed?" Virginia straightened and glanced at her watch. "I'm needed in a writer's group and what have I written? Oh forget that. You know who gave us what we needed? You. You're a good man." Virginia touched his hand. "We built a house with everything you brought us."

"Well now I wouldn't go that far."

"But you did."

"Do you want a good story for your writer's group?" Barstowe leaned back, chin lifted, exhaling with his palms on his thighs. Virginia pushed a strand of hair out of her face.

"I don't know—"

"I'll make it quick. You ever hear of Moriah Havril?"

"Should I have?"

"No reason. But if you ever go down Newcomb you'll see there's a brick federal named after the Havrils. And a mighty fine building it is. Moriah inherited it from her father and all his millions too. She lived there with her second husband, Joad Bradley, for a good number of years. He was the most liked and decent fella in Brookway. And if you met him you couldn't help wonder if you mightn't have gone better if you'd had his looks, charm and common sense; but there wasn't a few who didn't wonder if they might not have been just as good-lookin' and charming if they'd married his wife's millions. So when Joad died early there was all kinds of fellas lined up to court Moriah's bank account.

"Moriah caught on quick. She was no fool, you know; but she was a decent woman too and didn't go chasin' 'em out of the parlor like she shoulda. She had a touch of the Victorian. She insisted a fella have a cup of tea when he'd come to visit, but then she started noticin' all those old timers couldn't hold a cup longer than a broke sap bucket. First thing they'd be askin' where the privy was. Now it didn't take long to put apples and sugar together. She went and hung up pictures of Joad Bradley over every toilet so as a man couldn't stand one way or sit t'other without Joad Bradley lookin' him right in the eyes. Joad smilin' just as friendly and charming as ever.

"Now there wasn't one of 'em could get down to business with him lookin' at 'em like you were tradin' apples and corn right there in the orchard. They'd go from one powder room to the next but there he'd be, and there they'd be, right back in that orchard. They'd come back down, excuse themselves and go runnin' fast as their legs could carry 'em—damn near ready to bust. The only way out was refusin' the tea but sure as rain you'd be drinkin' your second and third cup 'fore the clock struck noon. All those old grifters? Wasn't one of 'em kept chasin' her."

"Is a word of that true?" Virginia asked.

"As told to me by one of her victims," said Barstowe, then he drummed his fingers on his thigh. "If you don't mind my askin', how long has it been since breakin' up with your husband?"

"Mr. Barstowe," said Virginia. "Are you courting me?"

"Call me George. And, yes, I might be. I'm not sayin' I am. I'm not committin' to it, but if it's all the same; I might just be. The Darby's always were a good-lookin' bunch."

"Is that just a story too!"

"No it's not. And if you're writin' 'bout Vermont, then that Moriah was a Vermont character if ever there was."

Virginia momentarily smiled, gazed at her hands, then closed them with a business-like composure. "I'm late, Mr. Barstowe."

"George."

"We're late, George."

6

About an hour or so later Barstowe picked up Virginia from the writer's group and returned her to Kemp's Grocery. Neither Barstowe nor Virginia lingered, but Barstowe opened the door for her and saw to it that the pickup started. Virginia thanked him, promised that she enjoyed herself, and smoothly shifted Drew's pickup into the Greens. About halfway up, she slowed enough to let her hair down and study herself in the rear view mirror.

7

Virginia arrived at the tiny house to the smell of rancid milk. Cody and Hoyte were nearly finished painting cabinets, the ladder to the loft, and even the occasional floor board. The wood was a rainbow of colors. Each tread of the stairs going to the basement were a different color. Spices were opened. The kitchen counter spilled with spices—turmeric, cinnamon, paprika, mustard seed—whatever they could find to give the milk-paint color. Cody and Hoyte kept to their work, eying slantways and with the air of the guilty, unsure what Virginia's reaction would be. "Oh my!" she said. "Did Drew help?"

"She told us how," said Cody, "then she went downstairs and we did the rest."

"There'll be no lack for color this winter, will there?"

"We're almost done."

"How is your mom doing?"

"She's downstairs," said Cody, returning to her painting. "She didn't like the smell when we were strainin' the milk."

"Well, once it's paint you hardly notice," said Virginia.

After Hoyte had gone home, Virginia and Cody set about cleaning the kitchen and storing the left-over milk paint in the refrigerator, every color in its own mason jar. When Cody was done arranging them she turned to Virginia with a question: "Can you—" she hesitated. "Do you do math?"

"All the time," said Virginia.

"I mean, like, Algebra."

"Try me."

Cody did. She sat next to Virginia and after fifteen minutes of puzzling through homework, wanting it behind her before the weekend; she was leaning against Virginia with Virginia's arm over her shoulder.

"Do you believe in magic?" Cody asked.

"What?"

"Like in witches?"

"In black hats and riding broomsticks?"

"'Cept they don't look like they're witches," said Cody, "but you suspect 'em 'cause they do things that don't make sense—'cept by magic."

"I'm not sure that I do, sweetheart."

"Do ya think Soot is a witch?" Cody forged ahead. "Has she ever told your future with cards?"

"You mean tarot cards?"

"Yeah."

"Oh, that's just a game people play," said Virginia. "When I was in high school my friends and I read each other's tarot cards. They're like astrology. They were just something we did to entertain ourselves."

"You know how to read cards?"

"Oh I'm not a good enough storyteller. I really do think that's all there is to it. You need to tell a story that the other person wants to believe."

"What about magic?"

"Well, if you're ever a nurse, and if you ever save someone's life, you might decide that life is all the magic the world needs. Who you are behind those green eyes—there's nothing more magical than that."

"That's not magic."

"Well *that's* the kind of magic I believe in."

8

When Virginia went downstairs she found Drew sitting at her writing desk, a blanket over her shoulders and Ratter in her lap. She gazed out the dark window behind the desk, or at her own reflection in it. Her skin was pale and her black hair lay in wet strands against the nape of her neck. Dark rings were under her eyes.

Virginia knelt next to her and took her hand.

Drew didn't push it away. She held it. "Are they done paintin' upstairs?"

"I've been helping Cody with homework."

Drew nodded.

"Maybe it's time to go to the hospital," said Virginia.

Drew's voice was dulled by exhaustion. "Just one more night. For Cody."

"Sweetheart," said Virginia, "when did you take the last pill?"

"Five days ago."

"You were supposed to quit taking them a week ago."

"I couldn't."

Virginia hesitated, jaw clenched, wanting to say more. "Are there anymore?"

"I didn't think I was gonna make it," Drew's voice broke.

"Are they gone?"

Drew slowly nodded and held Virginia's hand more tightly.

"Mom?" Cody stood in the doorway.

"Hey babe." Drew straightened, trying to look better. "How'd it come out?"

"We painted everything."

"Everything?"

"We left some of the floorboards natural."

"All different colors?"

"All different."

"I hope they're all different. I'm comin' up to look at it."

"You don't have to."

"You sure? You're gonna be okay if I wait 'til tomorrow?"

"Yeah."

"C'mere, babe."

Drew took Cody into a slow embrace until she was holding her tight. "My little girl's gonna be gone tomorrow and I'm gonna have a teenager."

"It's still me," Cody answered flatly.

"Well," Virginia stood, "I'll guess I'll leave you two alone."

"No. Stay," Drew pushed herself to her feet. "I'm goin' up." She unsteadily climbed the stairs using the cane. Her walking boot was thinner and lighter now. Cody followed her into the small room that was tucked under her loft. Drew wheeled on her good foot, half collapsing onto the bed. She leaned back with an exhalation of relief, eyes closed, and patted the bed. "Lie down, babe. I could really use a little company right now."

Cody lay down next to her, arms crossed at first, then turned on her side, cheek on Drew's shoulder, facing her. "Are you still addicted?"

"It's awful, babe."

"I don't need a birthday party tomorrow."

"Yeah you do. And we finished the house! We gotta throw a party for that too."

"I'm tired of you bein' mad and sad and mad again."

"You and me both."

9

Cody didn't waken after falling asleep and Drew never fell asleep. She carefully pulled her arm out from under Cody and fled from the bedroom. She was crying. Her muscles twitched as if hooked by tiny barbs that tore against her every motion. She was driven to the kitchen's little sink by nausea. She slid down against the cabinets, first with her arms around her knees, then to her side, palms down, forehead pressed to the floor as she dry heaved. A bowl fell to the floor, breaking into shards next to her. Sweat dripped from her throat and blood thrummed behind her eyes. The sweat coalesced into goosebumps—cold and sweat and cold again. She was crying when hands gently lifted her upright.

Virginia sat on the floor next to her, embracing her.

Drew pressed her cheek against Virginia's shoulder just as Cody had. "You don't have to do this alone," said Virginia.

"I just wanna sleep."

"If it takes all night." Virginia knitted her fingers over Drew's shoulder.

"Oh God," Drew's voice wavered with a grateful sigh. "Can I feel sorry for myself now?"

"Jesus, yes."

"I can't do this another night."

"Maybe you won't have to."

"It's okay," said Drew. "We'll go—I don't know. Suicide by bridge? It's not— maybe it's not so bad. Maybe—maybe if I hit the gas a little sooner."

"Drew!"

Drew gripped Virginia's arms as if she were going to throw up. "Kidding."

"Honestly!"

Drew smiled before the nausea washed over her again. "Thank you."

For the next hour or two, Virginia held Drew as they sat on the floor. She sat next to Drew when they moved to the table and held her when she slumped and began to lean out of her chair with a sleepless sleep. She stood when Drew stood and slid down the wall next to her. Sometime before midnight, both of them on the floor with their backs to the wall, Drew lay her head on Virginia's shoulder and finally slept. When Virginia woke the next morning, Drew still slept under one arm and Cody had crawled under the other. Drew's breathing was easy and smooth.

Chapter 19

As on a sunny afternoon in May
When a wind through the open window takes
The curtains swirling after it to play,
Or summers when a strong gust shakes and shakes
The airing sheets until in letting go
They freely billow, there is never rest—
No sooner is the weathervane just so
Then comes a changing breeze as though in jest
Upending all that we'd been certain of;
That blows the leaves into the entry-hall
As would a child who plays at love-me, love-
Me-not until she's let the flower fall
And forgets—petals we try to catch before
We close our hands to see and see no more.

1

By midmorning Drew's color had returned. The sweating and the goosebumps were gone. Both Cody and Drew had slipped down so that their heads were pillowed on Virginia's lap. Cody slowly wakened as Virginia brushed her fingers through her hair. "Hey, hon," she spoke gently. "Wake up."

Cody rubbed her eyes and blinked. Virginia pointed to Drew's bedroom. "Go get a pillow, hon, and a blanket."

"Is she okay?" Cody asked hoarsely.

"I think it's over. It must be," said Virginia. "She fell asleep before midnight and hasn't woken since. She's going to be okay. She's made it. Run and get a pillow and blanket. Let's let her sleep."

Cody returned with pillows and a blanket. They lowered Drew to the pillows and covered her where she lay. Virginia stood and stretched, sore after an overnight on the floor. "Happy Birthday, hon."

"Where are you going?" Cody asked.

"Presents," said Virginia. "I left them in the truck last night."

Cody picked up Ratter—no longer a kitten but still slender with bones like tugged and pulled wires. The cat climbed onto Cody's shoulder and then behind her neck like an unsteady shawl. Cody went back to her mother and carefully knelt next to her, studying her face. When she heard Virginia's faint cry of surprise from outside, she carefully stood with Ratter still on her shoulders. She opened the front door. Virginia hurried inside with her shopping tucked under one arm. "Good Lord!" she said.

"What happened?"

"That animal! That coyote! Is it a wolf? Good Lord! I don't know what it is!" Virginia hurriedly closed the door behind her. "It was just sitting there. Right up by the rock, the boulder, the big stone. I didn't even see it! I could have reached out and touched it!"

"Was it the old one?"

"I don't know!"

"It's old and looks like it has a white beard?"

"I think so. Yes. Yes, and around its snout and its tail. Surely there's a way we can discourage it!"

"I seen that one," said Cody. "I'm goin' out to see if I can see it again."

"You will not!"

"Hey babe," said Drew, wakening. "What's up?"

"Virginia saw the coywolf."

"Yeah?"

"Are you done bein' addicted?"

"I slept," said Drew. "I slept, babe. I slept the whole night."

"I'm gonna go out and see if I can see it!"

"Stay here for a minute." Drew's expression eased into a smile. "I wanna look at my teenager."

"You feelin' okay now?"

Drew took a deep breath, scooted onto her back. "I think maybe I'm gonna be okay now."

2

The second Saturday of November, the day of Cody's birthday, began with mists nudging the slopes of the river valleys. The trees slowly coalesced out of the soaking and into the glittering light of midmorning. There was still green in the fields but the asters, goldenrod, and Queen Anne's lace stood over the grass like the thin bones of a vanished animal.

But Drew had slept.

The weariness of the last weeks wasn't gone but had changed. She had slept. She called Cody into her bedroom and sat back on the bed. "I'm gettin' dressed, babe," she said,

Cody looked at her blankly.

"I mean to get up and do something besides be miserable."

"What kind of clothes mean gettin' up?" Cody asked.

"Get my overalls," Drew leaned back on her elbows. "I haven't put them on since summer."

There was more than one pair but Cody knew where they were. She had helped put them away. She reached for the blue overalls—like her own. Drew shook her head and pointed. "Those," she said. She pointed at her old, light brown overalls, frayed at the seams and hips, and flecked with paint.

"These?"

"Yeah. Those. Got work to do."

"Today?"

"Yeah, babe. I'm throwin' you a birthday party." Drew sat up, gingerly unbuckling her foot from the walking boot. She pushed her flannel bottoms to her ankles. "Pull 'em off, babe. Help me get those overalls on." That took Drew pulling them over her hips, putting her walking boot back on, then leaning on Cody as she fastened the overall's straps. "How do I look?"

"Don't say anythin' to Olivia."

"She's your friend now, right babe?"

"Yes."

"Just askin'." Drew pulled her fingers across her lips like a zipper. "Not a word."

3

On the way to Cody's birthday party, Soot sat up front, hands in her lap, fingers knit together. Barstowe drove and Ada sat in the back seat. Soot was dressed in green tights with leaf prints, a red dress, a purple paisley jacket, and a midnight-blue scarf.

"That's an eye-catching outfit," said Barstowe.

"I do my best."

"Anybody'd see you a mile off this time of year."

"That's the idea," said Soot. "Some of us make up in foliage for what we lack in real estate."

"Well now, you've got me there." Barstowe pat his belly. "And I suppose that's the right kind of outfit for a birthday party."

"That's the most decent thing anyone's done for a long time," said Ada. "You giving all that building material to Drew and Virginia."

"Nice of you to say so, Ada"

"What got into you anyway?"

"Well now don't go ruinin' a good deed by askin' me the whys and wherefores. There'd be no such thing if every man and woman had to answer for doin' good."

Ada sat back, thwarted, crossing her arms.

"You'll just have to make something up," Barstowe added. "And on that subject, how's that book of yours comin' along?"

Ada blew hair out of her face, looked forlornly out the passenger-side window. "You should try it. Like pond fishing. Sit all day waiting for nibbles and every idea's too small to keep."

"Just throw 'em back in and they'll grow to something worth keepin' the next time," said Barstowe.

4

It suited Cody fine that Soot and the others showed up to see the house. She scurried away with Audrey and Olivia into the low-ceilinged loft where Hoyte was reading on his back, one knee over the other.

"Only you would read a book at a birthday party," said Audrey, seeing Hoyte.

"This is the coolest house I've ever seen," Olivia scooted to the windows that overlooked the valley, joining Audrey on her stomach and elbows.

"It's like being in a tree house," said Audrey.

Hoyte rolled onto his stomach. "You can see the Adirondacks on a clear day."

"Do you miss anything from your old house?" Audrey asked.

Cody rolled onto her back, gazing at the ceiling. "I was collectin' parts: chrome, mirrors, dash parts, stuff for old trucks."

"Do you ever think about if you'd been there? Like what you would have saved?

"I'd of carried out my mom."

Audrey rolled onto her side. "So what were you going to do with all that stuff for old trucks?"

"Fix 'em up." Cody still gazed dreamily at the ceiling.

"So why do you like cars so much?" Olivia asked.

Cody frowned, squirmed as she worked toward an answer, pressed her feet against the slant of the low ceiling. "'Cause it's like you're bringing' something back to life."

5

Sometime later Kati arrived. She swung into the cabin wearing a leather fringed shawl. A narrow braided strand of her long black hair was strung with beads. She studiously ignored

Virginia and went to Drew. She held Drew's wrist and cupped her cheek. "Let me see," she said. She turned Drew's face one way then the other. "You've lost weight—too much."

"I'm better, Mom."

"And where's Cody? How is Cody?" She let go of Drew and peremptorily searched the living room and kitchen. "Where's my birthday granddaughter?"

Cody was already climbing down the ladder.

"There you are!" Kati opened her arms wide, her bag still over her shoulder. "Give me a hug! You're getting to be just as big as your mother. I don't even have to stoop anymore." They embraced and then, just as with Drew, Kati held Cody at arm's length and studied her face.

"What are we going to do about that scar?"

"Mom," Drew said behind her, "can you give it a rest?"

"Nothin'," said Cody, crossing her arms. "I like it."

"Yes. Yes I know. I don't know why you do," Kati lifted Cody's chin.

"Mom!" Drew took hold of Kati's arm.

"Why do you wear Indian stuff?" Cody asked.

"It's our heritage!" Kati answered.

"My scar's my heritage."

"Ha!" Kati straightened, then she lowered her voice. "But you know our heritage isn't a wound? Of course you do. I understand what you mean. You see? You're already turning into a grownup. But you're not too old for presents." She turned to Drew. "Where are we putting Cody's presents? And have you heard from your father?"

"No, Mom."

"I'm not surprised." Kati glanced at Cody again. "He always adored you, Cody. Your birthday was the one day we'd hear from him—but maybe teenagers don't interest him as much. Who knows." Kati added her present to the others on the kitchen table. "You know he all but disappeared once your mother was a teenager."

"Mom!"

Kati patted Drew's arm. "But Cody still has her grandmother."

"Give it a rest, Mom!"

"Of course," Kati nodded in agreement. "Cody's old enough to learn about these things now, but I understand. Today's her birthday. No need to discuss it. Do you have any wine? Where's the wine?"

"We don't have any," said Drew.

"You can hardly call a house finished without wine in it," Kati took a seat at the little kitchen table and surveyed the other guests. Soot was seated opposite, hands folded in her lap, one knee over the other. She hadn't moved since Kati had come in.

"Did you travel far?" Soot asked.

Kati abruptly fidgeted under the gaze of one-eyed Soot. "I took— No. Not far."

"Drew must feel lucky to have her mother live so close."

"Yes," said Kati hesitantly, "I do my best."

Soot smiled. "Of course."

6

Shortly before noon Drew went downstairs to sit with Virginia on Virginia's bed. She bent over, cheek on her knees, eyes closed, arms wrapped under her legs. "I'll be okay," she answered with a sigh.

"You've done enough," said Virginia. "You put up the decorations. Cody opened her presents. She's had cake. She's having a good time with friends."

"Just for a minute..."

"I should think. And, well, the symptoms don't just end overnight. You're going to need time to recover. It could be weeks before you're completely back to normal."

"...A break from my mom."

Virginia was silent a moment. "I know it's not my place to say but I think your mother has behaved well. I wasn't so sure at first but I've been pleasantly surprised."

"She's scared of Soot."

"Of Soot?"

"Yeah." Drew pushed herself upright, hands on her knees, smiling as much to herself as to Virginia. "She's scared of Soot."

"Why?"

"'Cause Soot is Soot."

"I didn't think your mother would be scared of anyone."

"Soot looks straight through her."

7

A little before one or so Cody went downstairs for the goodie bags she had made. Halfway down the stairs she lost her balance. She leaned against the rail, then she sat on the stairs, unseen by the others, until the dizziness and nausea subsided. She went to the freezer where she had made popsicles and put them in the goodie bags. The dizziness, weariness, and nausea came over her again. She steadied herself, both hands on the lip of the open freezer; then, as if she had momentarily fallen asleep, she caught herself almost falling into the freezer. She took the bags from the freezer, forgetting what else she meant to put into them and returned to the stairs. She stared at each step, the bags in one hand and the handrail tightly in the other.

The nausea and fatigue returned. A darkness at the fringes of her vision began to close. She might have heard her name called by her mother, the sound of the bags falling down the stairs, the clamor of her thoughts and others that weren't her own, a confusion like the beatless pulsing of a dozen hearts.

The door was open.

She stepped through into the midday's light.

First there was silence, then the noise of a pickup truck pulling over the driveway's gravel ridge. It went a little ways down, stopping next to the stone marking the driveway's end. Her grandfather stepped out. His long hair and beard were a mantle of white. Cody ran to him, all else forgotten; and embraced him— eyes closed, cheeks pressed against the warmth of his chest, hearing his heartbeat. The nausea and lethargy vanished.

"Let me see," he said.

He held her, hands on her shoulders, and knelt. "Just like your mother. Just as beautiful. You look just like your mother when she was thirteen, except for your green eyes."

"Did Mom know you were coming?"

"Nope," he answered. "I wanted to surprise you."

He steered her with an arm around her shoulder so that they both sat on the stone next to the truck. "Now," he said, "Tell me everything."

"What do you mean? "

"How have you been?"

The first thing she wanted to tell him about was her dad, because everything that had happened began there. She wiped at her eyes with the back of her hand.

"Oh," said her grandfather, "that."

Cody nodded.

"I know all about that."

"You do?" Cody's voice cracked.

"Yes. That was terrible. You don't have to tell me about that. Let that go," he said, and Cody felt suddenly lighter and happier. "How's life treated you since then?"

Cody let a small smile cross her expression. "I got drunk."

"You what?"

"I got drunk and blacked out. That was after I punched out Olivia. Me, Mom, and Virginia built a house by ourselves. Virginia calls it a tiny house and Mom says it suits a big mountain. And I got mad at Hoyte." Cody momentarily smiled again. "He gave me a knife."

"You got drunk?"

"I blacked out."

"How much did you drink?"

"A bunch," said Cody, "I swallowed a bunch."

"Huh." Her grandfather considered that. "Are you sure you were drunk?"

"I know it," said Cody, turned serious. "I was drinkin' beer. Makes you black out if you drink too much."

"You've got strong opinions just like your mother," he smiled and looked out over the valley. "And you say you built a tiny house on a big mountain?"

"We built it."

"Yes. I suppose. Yes, we did."

"Me, Mom, and Virginia," Cody insisted.

"Oh. I see," he answered. "You think that house over there is what I mean." He shook his head. "You, Cody, are the tiny house and all this pain you've suffered is the big mountain. This story has been about you, Cody. You're the tiny house."

Cody considered that and leaned into her grandfather. "What do you mean?"

"Look around you." The old man gazed out over the valley and further mountains. "You are who you are because of these mountains: your bones, your voice, the way you walk. Your ancestors walked these valleys and mountains for twelve thousand years—they shaped them and you were shaped by them."

"Grandpa, I died."

"I know."

"Grandpa, I'm not scared of death."

"Want to know a secret?"

"What?"

"Neither am I."

"And I wish I hadn't punched Olivia."

"Why did you?"

"She was mad 'cause she thought I talked to God."

"Huh."

"But I didn't."

"Maybe she has and doesn't know it?"

"If it'd been me I'd know if I'd talked to God."

"You would? Huh. Then you know what God looks like?"

"No."

The old man let that sit for a moment. "Then how would you know? Maybe God is in that tree? Maybe in this stone? Maybe inside you? Or? Maybe sitting right next to you?"

"I'd know."

"Huh."

"And anyway you gotta die to see God."

"Is that so."

"Yeah."

"Then I have to tell you a secret."

"What?"

"Sometimes," the old man leaned into her, "you don't even know it's happened."

"I would."

"You think so?"

"I know so."

"You're sure?"

"I'm sure."

"I don't think you would."

"Grandpa, I'd know if I died."

The old man nodded as though corrected.

"Grandpa?"

"Yes?"

"Promise you'll visit from the spirit world."

"You're sure?"

"Just promise, Grandpa."

"But you're sure you know who you're talking to?"

"Promise, Grandpa."

"Okay." He took both her hands. "Consider it decided. I promise, cross my heart and hope to die, that I will visit you from the spirit world."

"And it won't be in some dream."

"Who says dreams aren't real?"

"I don't want it in some dream," Cody insisted. "And it better not be anything confusing so as I'm not sure it's you! I want to be able to see you just like now."

"I will sit beside you just as plain as day."

"Like right now."

"Just like this."

"And I won't forget any of it."

"Not a word."

"Promise?"

"I promise with every fiber of my being, and you know what else?"

"What?"

"Even when I'm not with you plain as day, you only have to wish me next to you."

"But nobody'll believe me."

"Hey," the old man shook his head. "You're the only one who has to believe."

"It's not the same."

"It's not?"

"It's like it never happened if nobody believes you."

"Huh." The old man considered this then turned Cody's gaze by the chin. "There's no believing in God until you believe in yourself, Cody."

Cody pursed her lips. "Grandpa, can I go for a ride in your truck?"

"Not today."

"It's my birthday."

"Nope." The old man shook his head. "You have to stay here. Now's not the time. And you'd be missed if you went with me."

Cody turned her gaze to the soil underfoot, rocking a little back and forth as if working out a way to change his mind. "But hey," he said, "I'll tell you a secret instead. It's a good one. Do you want to hear it?"

"I do," said Cody.

"Good." He leaned and whispered in her ear.

Cody smiled, her feet twitching excitedly. "Is that true?"

"You'll have to find out."

"What if nobody believes me?"

"Who cares?" he answered. "The secret's not for them. It's for you."

"You're really nice, Grandpa."

"So are you." The old man stroked Cody's hair. "And despite all the horrible things that have happened, Cody, you're loved beyond your wildest dreams. Take a look." He glanced at the house, inviting Cody to follow his gaze. She saw the tiny house and everyone gathered at the door.

"Who's that?" she asked.

"That's Soot," said the old man. "But go ahead. Take a closer look."

Cody wanted to see what everyone was looking at. She walked through a painted world until she could also see the dark-haired girl, rail thin and pale, lying on the stone at the front of the tiny house. She was dying. The older woman was doing something to her. Another woman, like the girl but older, was next to her with her hand on the girl's chest. She was crying, shouting at the girl, pushing and tugging at the child's clothes.

But the one-eyed woman didn't look at the girl; she looked at Cody. She moved her foot just a little to the side. There were cards underneath—the tarot cards—the first was death and the second was the kneeling boy, not a boy but a girl who was making a choice, whose hood covered her face, whose hair was like Cody's hair.

And Cody understood.

She spun around but the old man was already leaving, hands in his pockets, a crow on his shoulder.

'That's me!'

And thinking it was like saying it. Cody's eyes abruptly opened and she inhaled as if surfacing from the black waters of a well. She breathed. Virginia was above her.

"Cody!" her mother screamed. "Don't leave me! Cody!"

8

"Get out of the way!"

Virginia had shoved Ada, Kati, and Barstowe out of the way. She had seen Cody walk to the door, saw how she walked, saw her collapse in the open doorway. Drew was calling after Cody but Virginia was already there, leaning over the girl, steadying her bloodied head with one hand while lifting her eyelids with the other.

"Cody!" Drew screamed again. Virginia pressed a finger's tip to Cody's throat, then leaned with an ear to Cody's chest.

Cody suddenly breathed and tried to sit up.

She saw Virginia, Drew, Soot, Arvid, and then a shorter man she didn't recognize. He wore a leather necklace with a feather and his long hair was braided at his back.

"Oh thank God!" Virginia said firmly. "Thank God. Drew, call 911. Anyone! 911! Now!"

Drew bent over Cody as if the fear were filling her lungs, trapping her arms and legs, pulling her into an unseen and inescapable current. "No! God damnit, no!" She pushed Virginia aside and with a cry of pain lifted her daughter into her arms. "Like hell. I'm taking her. We can't wait."

"Drew!" Virginia scrambled to her feet. "Then I'm going to drive!"

"Like hell." She flinched as she carried Cody but didn't let her go until she reached the truck. "I'll drive. You help her if she needs help."

Chapter 20

There was a greenhouse where the March winds played. They left behind a seed and the seed became a daisy. For all the daisy knew, she must be very special.

April's lovers came and went with flowers in their hair. The daisy loved the brighter days, the shimmering nights, but lovers passed her by.

The bride and groom arrived in June. They went from flower to flower. The daisy dreamed of being gathered but only sorrow was her groom.

Girls toss petals to the wind and say he-loves-me-loves-me-not. The daisy wished they picked her petals— what else is a daisy for? But loneliness was all her answer.

September charmed the flower. She wanted petals dyed like leaves but the greenhouse keeper closed the doors; and though September knocked, the daisy bowed and let her petals go.

When the greenhouse keeper found the daisy: what a shame, he said. He took her out and just like that September carried off her petals!

Bless my soul! he cried.

With hands too delicate to see, and lips too soft to hear, the daisy's petals were kissed and gathered. And there was that, as large as the wind, that's the sound of laughter before December.

by Ada Byron

1

There are some happenings that are mysterious and inexplicable from the outside in. As far as Drew, Virginia, and modern medicine were concerned, Cody's survival was nothing short of a miracle.

To Cody, there was never any doubt.

She knew she would only be in the hospital for a day or two; that afterward the dizziness, headaches, and weariness would never return. She knew that from the moment the confusion lifted, as Drew stroked her hair in the emergency room. "Hey, babe."

"That's how Grandpa stroked my hair," Cody squinted against the overhead lights.

"Grandpa?"

"Yeah."

"What do you know about Grandpa?"

"He visited with his truck." Cody touched the bandage at her forehead. "It was all fixed up."

"Babe, you almost died." Drew's tears welled. "That wasn't Grandpa. That was Lou Redbear. He was an old friend of Grandpa's. Nobody knew where to find us 'til they found Lou. Grandpa died this summer."

Cody's fingertips moved from the bandage to the tender skin around it.

"You almost got stitches again."

"Feels like I did."

"You went headfirst when you blacked out."

"I wanna see it."

"I'm so sorry, babe. Virginia was tellin' me to take you to the hospital weeks ago."

"And I wanna see the truck."

"You will," said Drew. "You will."

"Are you awake?" Virginia asked, appearing between the curtains that enclosed the bed.

"I'm okay," said Cody.

"Oh thank God," Virginia exhaled. "I was sure you would be. Every sign was that you would be, but you can never be sure with these injuries. They're going to want to run a battery of tests."

Drew extended her hand. "Thank you, Virginia."

"I didn't do anything, Drew."

"You saved her life."

2

Lou Redbear stopped by the next morning. Cody was in her own room and Drew had slept in a chair next to the bed. Lou was a short and stocky man with a round face and deep crow's feet at his eyes. He wore the same feather necklace as the day before. The single braid down the middle of his back almost reached his jeans.

"Hey Lou," Drew stretched.

"I stayed in your house last night. It's a nice house." His voice was gentle and clipped. "I have to head back west. Can't stay. It's a long drive. Two days. There's a good rest area where I can sleep tonight."

"You drove all that way?"

"Your dad was a good man. Always helped. Didn't ask for anything in return; should have. He liked to talk about you and Cody. But that troubled him too. Said he was gonna fix up the Ford for you and Cody, but all he ever did was get parts. You know how he was. Always a dreamer. They're all in the back and other stuff that belonged to him. Figured he would've wanted you to have it."

"You didn't have to."

"Put in a remote starter switch. He hid the key. Didn't tell anybody where he put it. You'll want to put in a new ignition switch but if you're just driving on the property, she'll run just the way she is."

"Maybe we'll sell it," said Drew.

"We're not gonna sell it," said Cody flatly.

"Your mom told me everything that happened," Lou said. "You had it pretty rough. Seems like these days the women get it rougher than the men. But the way you picked up and carried Cody yesterday. Cody was lucky you were there."

"Have you seen Kati?" Drew asked.

"She's scared you blame her for what happened yesterday."

Drew began to speak but Cody rushed to finish the explanation. "It was a hematoma. It's when you hit your head and it bleeds on the inside. Everybody's sayin' I probl'y had it from hittin' my head when me and Mom went off the bridge."

"You're lucky to be alive," said Lou. "I had a cousin. He died 'cause of it. Got into a fight. But he was older and he was drunk. So maybe that's why. I would've told Kati about my cousin but it wasn't my place to argue."

"Where do you live, Lou?" Drew asked.

"Out past the Wind River Reservation. You and Cody ever want to visit—not much room but enough for you and Cody. If you keep driving you can see the Tetons on a good day. It's mostly good days. You'd like it there. I took your dad's fishing pole. Wasn't gonna tell you. But I like it. You can borrow it if you come out."

3

Two days later Drew drove Cody home. Drew was as happy to drive as to throw out her crutches and that meant Virginia was in the market for a new car. That suited Virginia. The first person she called was George Barstowe.

"What are your plans for it?" he asked.

"I need a job."

"I s'pose that means you'll be staying a while."

"What's that to you, Mr. Barstowe?"

"Well now if you'd like to come over for dinner, I'd be happy to explain."

"Can you cook too, Mr. Barstowe?"

"No, or so I'm told. The gesture will have to do."

But Virginia wasn't about to let Barstowe's cooking flavor their first date, and so Virginia cooked the first of many meals at Barstowe's, and though some of those meals turned into overnights, no one should be surprised that Virginia still insisted on her own house, a stick shift, and a pair of proper shoes for the weather. Just as she was settling into Vermont, Vermont was settling into her.

Around the same time, Soot invited Cody and Olivia to help bake a pumpkin pie. Neither needed convincing. Soot was already opening the door when they showed up. Soot guided Cody to the kitchen table with a hand at her back.

"Sit down," she said, as if impatient with having to say so.

Cody sat. Soot knelt in front of her, cupping Cody's cheeks. She turned her head to the left and right as if looking a little beyond her, touched the bandage on Cody's forehead, then offered a satisfied exclamation. Just as quickly she stood and pulled a rolling pin out of the drawer.

"What?" Cody asked nervously.

"Did you get a haircut?" Soot asked.

"Yeah."

"It suits you."

Cody's lips twisted with skepticism. She didn't for a minute believe that's what Soot looked at, but Soot tapped the rolling pin and gestured Olivia toward the pantry. "That's where the flour is," she said, "and we'll need butter, salt, evaporated milk, and vodka—among other ingredients."

"What's the vodka for?" an alarmed Olivia asked.

"For the crust," Soot answered matter-of-factly, as if the answer should have been obvious.

"You don't drink it?" asked Cody.

"Me?" Soot gazed at her, then busied herself with ingredients. Cody and Olivia glanced at each other as they rolled out their water and vodka pie crusts. They wordlessly concluded that Soot drank vodka.

"Is it going to taste like vodka?" Olivia asked.

"Of course not," said Soot. She raised her right hand, thumb to fingers. "When you bake the crust, the vodka goes *poof*!" Her fingers popped open like a vanishing puff of air.

Then Olivia finally worked up the nerve to ask the question: "You ever deal cards for people if they ask?"

There was a flicker of a smile before Soot answered. "It's called reading cards."

"So do you?"

"You expect I should read your cards again?"

That made Olivia shy. She glanced at Cody as if to say it was Cody's turn to risk whatever hex Soot might lay on them. "We were just wondering—" Olivia began.

"About the future?"

"I guess," Olivia answered weakly.

"Again?" Soot busied herself with a second pie before continuing her thought. "The future has a funny way of always being the future—" She stood on her toes, flattening the dough with half a dozen firm turns of the rolling pin. "—despite the best laid plans."

"But—"

"Fold it again. Press harder." Soot interrupted, one hand on her hip. "Do you want a flaky crust or not? Go get a chair so you can press down harder. You too, Cody."

That stopped the girls. Soon enough, Soot was happily humming, lighting the stove, setting the table, going in and out of the kitchen with decorations for Thanksgiving. The work of folding and rolling the dough quieted Cody and Olivia. Just when they thought the worst of their labor was done, Soot brought out the pumpkin halves from the oven. She divided the pumpkins into three bowls and set them to work pureeing.

"Don't you have a food processor?" Olivia asked.

"Or an electric mixer," Cody complained.

"How long is this going to take?" added Olivia.

"You're welcome to eat your pie now," said Soot. She stopped her own mixing, dipped a finger into her bowl, and popped the tip into her mouth.

Both Cody and Olivia stared, perplexed. "It's not pumpkin pie," said Cody.

"Yes it is," Soot answered.

Cody glanced at her own bowl. When she turned again, Soot was waiting with a wry smile. "Aren't you going to ask me where it is?"

"Where is it?"

Then Soot leaned over, gazing with her one eye. "It's in the future. Plain as day. And if I can see it with one eye, I bet you can see at least two more pies with two."

Cody stared back, speechless.

"Do you want to know the future?" Soot asked, her expression softening. "Or do you want to make the future? All you need are the right ingredients."

"Make it," Cody answered meekly.

"Good," Soot straightened, and with a ramrod posture she turned back to her own bowl. Cody and Olivia quickly turned back to theirs. When it was time to bake, Cody and Olivia helped Soot with canning projects, each beholding the future as they canned. Later, when the pies had cooled enough, Soot divided up her own, parsing out a slice to each of them. Cody and Olivia waited for Soot to begin. "Here we are," she said, raising her fork.

The children stared uncertainly.

"The future," Soot clarified as though her meaning should have been obvious. "Enjoy."

4

Olivia walked home, cradling her pie under a sheet of foil. Soot and Cody went to the front porch where they sat on the bench swing. The pie helped to keep Cody's lap warm. The sky was a diminished blue and the sun was low, but still lent a little warmth to the porch. Neither spoke at first, gently swinging back and forth. Every so often a breeze lifted Cody's hair. Though a bundle of nerves, Cody finally asked the question that was like a burning coal in her stomach. "Did you ever almost die?"

Soot turned, hands neatly in her lap. "How do you suppose I ended up with one eye?"

Cody let that sink in, looking at the empty porches across the street. "I don't even think Mom believes me."

"She believes in you," said Soot.

"I know."

"But you need somebody to believe you, am I right?"

"Yeah." Cody held her feet up as they swung. "Yeah," she sighed again. "Everybody says that, but it's not the same if it's just bein' nice. I had to do tests at the hospital and they were askin' me all kinds of questions. I told 'em 'bout bein' able to read people's minds without meanin' to and how, when I almost died again, I saw Grandpa. I mean, I think I saw Grandpa." But Cody was momentarily too shy to say any more. "They said it was because of where the bleedin' was—at the front of my head; that everything I saw was because of that, wasn't real, and would go away."

"And now you don't even know if you believe yourself."

"Yeah," Cody answered quietly.

"And what about that pumpkin pie we ate?"

"What about it?

"Where is it?" Soot asked.

"I ate it."

"And what if I don't believe you? Can you prove it was real?"

That gave Cody pause.

"And if nobody believes you," Soot said with matter-of-fact severity, "does that mean the pie wasn't real?"

"No. Just means I can't prove it," said Cody. Her feet rose and fell with the swinging bench as she worked out the intricacies of pumpkin pie. "Just means I can't prove it."

"It was a good pie, wasn't it?"

"I ate too much."

"Cody." Soot firmly took Cody's hand. "I believe you." Then she added evenly and with finality. "Life is a pumpkin pie. We know what we know, the two of us, no matter how many people have never stepped foot in our kitchen or tasted our desserts." Cody smiled, despite herself, then leaned into Soot. After that, they swung back and forth, together, once more holding hands.

5

"The pie smells good, babe."

"I ate too much." Cody miserably pushed against the truck's floorboards.

"So I guess you're not hungry for dinner."

"Why," Cody watched the houses go by, "what're we havin'?"

"You must not be all that miserable."

"I am."

"I don't think I've ever been so hungry," said Drew.

"What'd you do at the hospital?"

"They scanned my bones. I got a hairline fracture, prob'ly from carryin' you, but they're gonna let me start puttin' half my weight on my ankle."

"Does it still hurt?"

"Yeah, it still hurts, babe." Drew glanced at Cody. "How 'bout you and your head?"

"I'm fine."

"Did you and Olivia thank Soot?"

"Yeah."

"I don't know why but she's taken a real shine to you, babe."

Cody shrugged and smiled to herself. "I know. Ada maybe wants you to build a house for her."

"Good and we gotta talk about Grandpa's truck."

"I don't wanna sell it."

"We need the money, babe."

"What good's sellin' Grandpa's truck? We're just gonna need money again. I'd rather still need money and have Grandpa's truck than need money and have nothin'."

"What do we need another truck for?"

"I'll work on it."

"How? Who's payin'? Where? And when, babe, when?"

"I don't know!" Cody kicked the underside of the dashboard, "I don't know. But keepin' it means I can figure it out."

"Keepin' it where? That truck's been sittin' in a desert for fifty years. How long do you think it's gonna weather up here?"

"We'll build something to cover it."

"We will?"

"I'll help," said Cody, hands jammed in her pockets, "I'll help build it."

"We're not buildin' a house for an old beater."

"It's not an old beater!"

"We barely built one for ourselves!"

Cody crossed her arms, eyes watering, glaring out the passenger window. "I don't wanna sell it."

"I'll tell you what, babe. We'll look at it when we get home."

"Okay." But Cody's 'okay' was dark and reluctant. Neither Cody nor Drew spoke for the short drive remaining. November days are brief and the sun seems no sooner risen than setting again. There's nothing more companionable to November than a bleak mood. The towns huddle together while the distant farms hoard all but a little of the light that slips through their windows. The clouds that had billowed like towering sails are no more than thin gray sheets putting down snow over the field's bare and icy ribs. By the time they reached the turnoff, Cody had absorbed all of the evening's mood and shadows. "You've already decided what you wanna do," she said darkly.

"We're gonna look at it," Drew answered.

A warm square of light lit the path to the tiny house, some of the driveway and a swath of the truck. Lou had dropped it to the side of the driveway into the brown and tangled weeds. The old truck was out of kilter on the slanted bank, the wheels sprung higher on one side than the other.

"So you're gonna fix that up?"

"Yeah," Cody answered. "It was Grandpa's."

"I dunno, babe—"

"Fine," said Cody, fists shoved in her pockets. "He told me—" Cody hesitated. "He told me a secret."

"Who did?"

"Grandpa."

"When?"

"When he visited on my birthday."

"Babe—"

"He told me where the key was."

"Babe," Drew paused, "Grandpa was never here."

"Yeah he was," Cody answered, her voice full of hesitance. "Or maybe—" Cody's gaze fell to her feet.

"Or maybe what, babe?"

"Maybe he just looked like Grandpa so I wouldn't be afraid of him."

"Who?"

But Cody didn't answer. She abruptly turned. "He told me where the key was. I can prove it. Will you let me keep the truck?"

Drew gazed silently, biting her lip, then slowly nodded. "Yeah. Yeah, okay. No spending the rest of the night lookin', babe. You think Grandpa told you where he hid the key? Go get it."

Cody wiped at her tears and tugged open the old truck's driver side door. She climbed onto the bench seat on her knees. She took hold of the black shift knob and twisted but the knob didn't move. She crawled further into the truck, braced her hip under the glove box, feet against the floorboards, then felt her mother's hands over her own. "Is this what you want?"

They unscrewed the knob together until Cody held it in her hands. "It's *in* the knob!" she cried.

Cody wanted to run but waited for Drew.

Once inside, she rushed to the toolbox by the kitchen cabinets and took a hammer. She ignored Virginia's *good evening*, put the knob on the floor, and struck. It bounced as it spun. She centered it on the floor and struck it a second time. This time it cracked. The third time, with both hands on the hammer, the knob split open and the key, folded in newspaper, skittered across the floor. Cody looked at her mother, maybe as astonished as her mother, almost too afraid to smile.

Drew's hands rose to her hips.

"You promised," said Cody.

Drew nodded, gazing at the key. "You're right," she answered, agog. "You're right, babe. Jesus. I guess, Happy Birthday. He must of glued it in there somehow. Just like Dad to do that. We're gonna have to rig a cover for your truck before the weather moves in."

And that was all that Cody needed. She ran to her mother and embraced her.

6

Jerry, Mike, and Roy took a detour to Cody's house on the last day of deer hunting. They stood with Hoyte and Cody, crossbows slung over their shoulders, and took in Cody's truck. An unhurried snowfall tumbled over their shoulders. "I bet it's worth something already," said Mike, "just the way it is."

"It's gonna be," said Cody.

"Where are you gonna work on it?" Jerry asked.

"Dunno," said Cody, "but me and Mom are makin' a shed for it."

"Who's helpin' ya fix it up?"

"She can do it by herself," said Mike. "What makes you think she needs help workin' on it? She's smarter than you and me put together!"

"You and me en't much," said Jerry, his crooked smile rising slantways. "What do you know about fixin' up cars anyhow? Or me?"

"Just sayin'."

Jerry glanced at Cody again. "Hope you're better at fixin' up cars than drinkin' beer."

"It wasn't the beer," said Cody.

"And I foreswore beer for nothin'," said Mike. "If I'd waited, I coulda sworn off hematomas."

"You didn't foreswear nothin'," said Jerry.

"It's the principle."

"So when are you gonna start?" Hoyte asked.

"Summer."

Mike nodded. "What're you gonna do first?"

"Dunno." Cody wiped the snow and hair from her eyes. "Gonna stop it from rustin'."

"You know what year it is?" asked Roy.

"It's a '46."

"You're gonna be out of high school before you're done," said Hoyte.

"And it's gonna be a greenish-blue," said Cody.

"Turquoise," said Mike. "I'm in love." Silence descended and the boys imagined the old truck, shining somewhere between green and blue, on a shining road with a shining Cody driving.

"We better get goin'," Jerry finally said.

"Get any deer?" Cody asked.

"Got one downhill from here," said Roy. "Dad got it. An eight-point buck. Got three points on one side and five on t'other. Never seen one like it. Him and Jerry's dad are takin' turns carryin' it out."

Another silence followed as Jerry, Mike and Roy picked their way through November's scrub and descended downslope. "I'll tell you what," said Roy, as their orange hats disappeared over the ridge of leaves and ledge. "The day she tickles that project—"

"It's 'tackles'—" Mike corrected.

"Tickles," said Roy.

"Tackles," Mike insisted. "You tackle a project. You don't tickle it."

"Who'd go and tackle something?" said Roy, his words disappearing into the woods. "That's no way to get a thing started. You wanna tickle it."

"So help me, Roy—" said Mike and that was all that Cody and Hoyte could hear.

"You lettin' your hair get long?" Hoyte finally asked.

"Yeah."

"How long?"

"Dunno."

7

"What do you call it," Jessie asked.

"The Winds of March," said Ada.

"It's a sad story and lovely too," said Virginia. "But honestly, even if it's just a daisy, I don't know if I can stand any more tragedy."

"How is that poor girl Cody?" asked Meredith.

"She almost didn't survive," said Virginia. "If anything had happened to her—and to think of poor Drew. That would have been too much for Drew."

Meredith's husband backed into the small room behind the main office. He carried in a tray of tarts and a pot of coffee, setting them in the table's middle. "The Hawleys in the Arbor Room are complaining about noise again."

"Again?"

"Yes," her husband sighed. "I'd offer to move them but we don't have any vacancies."

Meredith angrily tapped the table with the tip of her pencil. "I don't know what people expect. They want to stay in an old farmhouse and are shocked to find out they're staying in a farmhouse!"

"What should I tell them?"

"Tell the room next door to quiet down," she answered. "You know what to do, John. Honestly." After he left, Meredith gazed at the others as if incredulous. "What does he think? Gut the hotel for a once a month complaint? We can't afford to soundproof every room."

"I could hardly do what you do," said Virginia.

"And on that subject," said Meredith, "I understand you saved that girl's life."

"I'm not so sure."

"Drew wouldn't have trusted anyone but you," said Ada. "If you didn't save Cody's life, then you saved Drew's."

"You've talked about going back into nursing," continued Meredith, "why don't you?"

"I am!" Virginia seemed caught by surprise.

"Wonderful!" said Lydia. "I've thought that's what you should do from the beginning! You've already done so much to get back on your feet. When will you start?"

"Well, I'll have to apply for a temporary permit and go through a re-entry program. It's been years but I should be able to begin nursing very soon."

"I'd shudder to think what would have happened if you hadn't been there." said Jessie.

"You know," Virginia paused to work through her thoughts, "I never gave it much thought. When you're a nurse, a patient arrives; there's an injury; there's a protocol; and, well, if a patient lives or dies it's because we could or couldn't do enough. The universe—" Virginia paused. "You learn to think of it as a machine; and the body too—a beautiful machine and how can you say that a machine is meant to live or die? A machine can be repaired or can't be. But then I think there must be a purpose—so many times I've been told by patients they were given a choice—and a reason to live."

"Are you an atheist?" Meredith asked.

"I think—yes, I think you could call me an atheist."

"One doesn't have to believe in God to have a reason to live," said Meredith. "And, you know, everything that happened to that poor girl has happened to countless others without the need to invoke the mystical."

"Good Lord, Meredith!" objected Jessie. "What harm is there in believing there might be a higher power or in a higher purpose to our lives?"

"A higher purpose?"

"Yes."

Meredith tipped her reading glasses down her nose, peering over them with a momentary grin. "Now ladies, I didn't say there's no such thing as God. Far be it for me to tell you what you should or shouldn't believe; only that one doesn't have to believe in God, that there are other explanations, and that it is incumbent on us to consider them. My niece, for example, who suffers from epileptic seizures—frontal lobe to be precise—

regularly hears voices, talks to the departed, and visits unearthly realms."

"Meredith," the older Jessie scolded, "must you trivialize everything?"

"Am I?" Meredith turned to Lydia. "What about your romances, Lydia? I don't recall there being any higher power dictating the fates of your lovers' lives? Who would want to read a story like that? If memory serves, your protagonists make their own decisions and reap their rewards. No higher powers needed."

"I wonder what Soot would say," said Ada.

"Well, she isn't here tonight, is she?" Meredith abruptly gazed at the papers in front of her as if they needed straightening. "You'll have to ask her this evening."

"What about her predicting the hurricane?" Jessie asked.

"Oh come now," Meredith replied, "predicting a hurricane during hurricane season? Do you know there are gamblers who place bets with higher odds than that? Some do quite well."

8

The day after Christmas, when enough snow had fallen that the evergreens lowest limbs slept under snow, Daryl's parents once more slowly pulled into the driveway. Virginia opened the door. Daryl's father, Wayne, stood with gifts under one arm while Marjorie, in a blue, knee-length coat, waited several steps behind. Wayne spoke hesitantly. "Merry Christmas. Marjorie and I— Kati, Drew's mother, told us what happened. We just wanted— are Drew and Cody home?"

"Yes."

But Virginia didn't need to call her. Drew was already standing behind Virginia in the short hallway. "Why are you here?"

"We—" The older man pulled Marjorie to his side. "Marjorie and I want to apologize."

"Okay."

"We would like to—"

But Drew didn't let him finish.

"Stay there," she said. She reached from behind Virginia and slammed the door.

"I can't tell you what to do," said Virginia.

"You want to."

"Well, I don't know!"

Drew glanced at Cody who gazed back from the kitchen table. "Fine."

"Tell me what you want."

Drew gnawed her lip in anger, but nodded. "Okay. Do I tell them to get the fuck out of my life and stay out, or— Fuck it, I can't think of another option."

"They lost their son."

"And I almost lost Cody. Twice. I don't owe them."

"She's their only grandchild."

"Yeah, and they tried to take her away."

"They lost their child."

"So are they gonna try to take Cody away again? And a merry-fucking-Christmas?"

"Drew, they can't do that."

Drew leaned against the wall, knocked the back of her head against it, eyes closed. Then she gestured at the door. "You think I should accept their apology?"

"Maybe for Cody."

"For Cody?"

"Yes, they're her grandparents. You don't have to like them and neither does Cody, but you don't need to punish them any more than they've already been punished."

"Would you give your ex a second chance?"

"No," Virginia shook her head. "No, I wouldn't."

"Then why should I?"

"Because it's not just about you, but Cody too."

"Who the hell just shows up?"

"Would you have invited them?" Virginia asked.

"That obligates me?"

"It's okay, Mom," said Cody. "You can let them in."

Drew glared at nothing for a moment. "Okay. But so help me God..." She left the threat unfinished and opened the door, reluctantly inviting Daryl's parents inside. Wayne unbuttoned his jacket. Marjorie kept her coat zipped, arms crossed, and lips drawn tight. They sat at the table. Wayne touched Marjorie's arm and she hesitantly lowered them. He put the presents on the table, wrapped in red paper and gold ribbon. "We wanted to apologize," Wayne's voice already cracked. "It's been hard on us."

"And us," said Drew.

"No. You're right. Compared to what you've gone through— And we don't want sympathy. We just— Drew, we want to be a part of Cody's life. We don't expect you to throw open your arms, but we want to do our part to help Cody and to help you."

"Why did you report us?" Drew asked angrily.

The older man turned to Marjorie who took a breath, straightened, and drew an envelope from her coat pocket. She pushed it across the table. "This is for you, Drew," then added. "I'm so sorry."

Drew hesitantly took the envelope. Opened it. Momentarily gazed at the check. "I don't want this from you."

"It's for us too."

"What are you saying?"

"We're saying—" Marjorie finally spoke, her voice unsteady and weak. "We're saying that Daryl hurt us all." She wiped at her eyes with the palm of her hand. "He betrayed us all, Drew. That's what we're saying. What parent wants to admit their child could do this and do this to their own child? Cody is all we have left. And you. We're begging you, Drew, please don't let Daryl destroy that. Whatever you decide, this check is for you and Cody; and regardless, you don't owe us anything. We think that's what you would have made in a year if our son hadn't tried—hadn't tried to kill you and Cody."

Virginia placed her hand on Drew's.

"We're expectin' money from FEMA for the house in Brookway," said Drew.

"Then this will tide you over," said Wayne.

Drew leaned back in her chair, looked out the window, considered what to say. "Okay."

"We won't intrude any further," said Wayne. Both he and Marjorie stood. Marjorie clasped her hands as they left, turned as if to say more but didn't. She followed her husband to the door.

"Where are you stayin'?"

"At the Apple House," said Wayne. "Just until tomorrow. We only wanted— we wanted to see you in person. We wanted to apologize in person."

9

In late June Cody and Drew pulled up to Lou Redbear's. His was among other trailers and double-wides along a straight stretch to the west of the Wind River Reservation. Lou's house was a trailer with an added cabin. To the north and south, the gently sloping mountains reminded Cody of the Greens, but the alpine forests and meadows were nothing alike. These forests were interspersed with meadow and dry scrub, favoring the slopes and valleys. Lou was already stepping out of the cabin as Cody and Drew climbed out of the truck. Drew flinched at first, then more easily made her way around the front of the truck.

"You look better," said Lou.

"I'm just stiff from sittin' so long—can't sit like I used to."

"Come on in. Susan is inside. She's making stewed venison."

The inside of the cabin was dark paneling and no wall was without shelves. There were rows of matryoshka dolls, each a little different from the next, arranged from smallest to largest.

These were interspersed with porcelain dolls in elaborate dresses, European and Indian.

"Susan collects them," said Lou, noticing Cody. "Her sister's husband works on drilling rigs. He has friends who are Russians. Follow me. I'll show you your bed. You'll have to sleep together, but it's a comfortable bed."

Not long after that, Cody and Drew sat down with Lou and Susan to eat. Susan's black hair was long and fell over her shoulders. "Your cheeks are like your grandfather's," she finally said to Cody. Her dark eyes peered inquisitively and with an intelligence that made Cody squirm.

"Thanks."

"Lou told me a lot about you. He says you had a vision that saved a lot of lives."

"I don't know if I did."

"He says you're famous; that you were in the news."

"Just once."

Susan nodded. Discussion changed to what life was like in the northeast, what the people and weather were like, and what the house was like that Cody, Drew, and Virginia had built. After finishing, Susan announced that she and Cody would be cleaning up. "I decided not to have children," she said, bringing the plates to the sink. Her manner of speaking was like Lou's—brief, plain-spoken thoughts. "I don't regret it. It's beautiful here but it's hard on the kids. It can be violent, especially for women and girls. There aren't many kids who make it out and there's no work for the men. But I wonder what it would have been like to grow up in Vermont." And then after that thought passed she added, "Tell me all about your vision." Cody was shy at first, but Susan was unembarrassed. She wanted to know about Cody's vision, then about Cody's friends—Hoyte, Olivia, Barstowe, Virginia, Soot Tabor, Jerry, and Mike. She asked about their character and if Cody thought they were good people. She especially wanted to know about Soot and sat Cody down while she took to drying the plates.

"I think she's a witch," said Cody.

"Maybe she's a shaman?" Susan paused, waiting for Cody's reaction. "Now you're thinking about her differently. I can tell by your face. Even though 'witch' is maybe just another word for shaman, you think about her differently."

"I don't think she's a shaman."

"Because she doesn't look like one? You said that she could see your spirit. Only shaman's can see spirits. But then I think that maybe you're meant to be a shaman too. Maybe what happened to you was meant to happen—so that you could have the visions."

"I didn't mean for any of it."

"Sometimes it's like that," said Susan, carefully arranging the dried plates on shelves. "You don't choose it but it chooses you. That's what happened to my grandpa. He was hit by a car when he was a child. He said he died when the car hit him and had a vision of another lifetime when he was killed buffalo hunting. In that other lifetime, he thought he had escaped before he saw his own corpse. When he saw it, he returned to his corpse and waited to be buried. When his joints fell apart he decided it was time to leave. He said being run over by the car was like being killed by the buffalo. At first he didn't know he had died, but then he saw himself and knew. Before he returned to his body a powerful spirit wearing the skin of the buffalo that had killed him in his earlier life appeared and told him that this time before returning to his body he should blow on it to return the breath of his spirit to its lungs. After that, when he returned to his body, he lived. And after that he was able to come and go from his body whenever he wanted."

Susan arranged the last plate, then opened the top drawer in a set of drawers. "These were grandpa's moccasins," she said, holding them up so that Cody could see them. "He never wore them. He liked them too much, he said. They were perfect and he couldn't bear to ruin them." She smiled and glanced expectantly at Cody, as if to know that Cody shared the joke. "That made Grandma furious. She made them herself and she berated Grandpa and swore she wouldn't make him another pair if he didn't wear them. So now, whenever I give Lou a gift, I make sure it's a little broken. If it's shiny, I scratch it. If it's straight, I bend it a little. If I make something, I make it a little too long or too short. He doesn't complain. But then when he thinks I don't notice, he will fix whatever I've given him. Then he's proud of himself. Then whatever I've given him becomes his favorite possession."

Susan put the moccasins back in the drawer.

"I think that's the way God makes us. He scratches us so that we're not too shiny when we're born. He bends us if we're too straight. He makes our memories too long or our tempers too short. He makes us like the taste of things that aren't good for us. He makes sure we're flawed so that if we fix our flaws, we'll be proud of ourselves; we'll feel that we're who we are because of our own effort; we won't be afraid to wear ourselves out fixing our flaws."

"Some people don't fix 'em," said Cody.

"They'll be born with the same flaws in their next lives. God is in no hurry. He will let you take as many lifetimes as you want; and will always have more patience than you. Eventually you will stop blaming God. A flaw is like a thorn. Some blame the world because they think that life has strewn thorns in their paths. Others stop what they're doing and pull the thorn out of their foot."

"That's what I'd do."

"It's never as easy as you think, but the thorn only works its way deeper into your foot the longer you put it off; and then it's as painful to take it out as leave it. But you have to do it. I don't know what your flaw is. You're still young."

Cody stuffed her fists in the pockets of her overalls and stretched out her legs. "I'm gonna keep all my flaws," she said defiantly, "like a thornapple, so as everybody'll leave me alone."

Susan smiled. "When your experiences are extraordinary, sometimes it's easier for you and for everyone else to make them ordinary."

10

That night, because Drew still wouldn't buy her a smartphone, Cody wrote two letters, one to Olivia and one to Soot. To Olivia she wrote:

Dear Olivia,

Sorry for punching you. Sorry for the haircut. We're out west now but we haven't seen the Tetons yet. Mom really wants me to see the Tetons. There's some other mountains here but they aren't anything special. They're like our mountains except more self-important because they don't like it having so many trees on them. And it's awful quiet out here. The wind blows and fills your head with dust and wind.

They don't have towns out here. All they got are graveyards. It's a sorry place to live. Out home the woods grow over a graveyard. Out here all a graveyard's got to compete with is a desert. Don't know which is deader. There was one by where we spent the night. I copied down a poem from one of its gravestones. It's kind of old fashioned but probably everything was old fashioned those days. I liked the poem and ought to maybe collect them. Here's what it said:

Lutetia Sue Plover
Born 1862 - Died 1923
Whoever you may be, grieve not
Because my stone is small
Or seems thus but an afterthought.
What need have I for more than this?
I loved the world withal

And yield rather with a kiss.
Though we are passers-by today
(Bless you who've come to call)
Be in no hurry. If I may,
Don't think of me as being gone
Say rather: 'Twas time that I move on.

When I die, and that's supposing I stay dead next time, I want to leave something behind. Don't know yet what I should, but something that returns the favor of being born.

P.S. The poem was too big for the grave stone so they had to wrap lines around the back and squished it at the bottom.

And then Cody wrote to Soot:

Dear Soot,

The starlight is really bright out west. That's something to be said. And being in the desert at night is like being on the ocean. You can see far off lights like you can see ships and they could be five miles away or twenty and you'd never know. Those far off lights might be just one house in a world of darkness and if they don't move like a ship I suppose the people in them are journeying just the same even if they don't consider it like that.
Doesn't matter if you're on land or water.
Susan Redbear is Lou's wife. She says I look more Indian than not and said she heard some Indians had blue eyes because of when the Vikings used to fish up our way a thousand years ago. Then she wanted to know about all my friends, and Vermont, and we talked about you. She says she thinks you're a shaman. I'd never have the nerve to ask in person, but being we're a thousand miles apart—Are you a shaman?

Love,
Cody Devaux

P.S. Mom is telling me stories again.

Chapter 21

Drew woke Cody before sunrise the next morning.

"Where are we going?"

"I'm showin' you the mountains, babe. We're gonna see 'em with the sun rising on 'em."

Cody pulled the cover over her head. "I've seen the mountains."

Drew pulled it back down. "Not *these* mountains."

"What mountains?"

"The Tetons"

"Can't we wait 'til morning?"

"It is morning."

"It's still dark out!"

Drew yanked the cover off and triumphantly stood with it. She shook her sore ankle as if to shake loose the stiffness, then yanked the blanket away before Cody could snatch it back.

"Mom!"

"Mom's faster than you again." Drew grinned with satisfaction. "Get used to it, Buttercup."

"What're we havin' to eat?"

"No time. Pack an apple."

Cody glumly rolled out of bed and slipped into carpenters and her favorite blue jacket. The drive west, over the last rise before descending into the valley to the east of the Tetons was veiled in darkness. Cody barely saw the ridges of the nearest mountains feathered by moonlight before she fell asleep under her borrowed blanket. She was in the middle of a dream about a long road like the road they travelled under a river of stars which was like another road.

"Hey, babe," Drew shook her awake. "Take a look."

They had parked. The air was cold enough to frost the windshield and through the haze Cody could see the first inklings of a reddish apparition far above the horizon. She leaned forward to scrape the glaze of ice and finally saw it, the topmost peak— that light.

The author wishes to revise
The late summer's riotous plot—
The gourd, the liquored grapes, and flies
Besotted where the apples rot.

There's hesitance at first and yet
There always comes the killing frost;
And then not one forgiving stet
To spare so little as the moth.

It ought to be enough to live
And let the season have its say,
Accepting what the short days give
And what the long months take away;

And yet there's something in me burled,
Counter to the grain, knowing
Whatever expurgates the world
Might well choose me the next one going.

Change will come but I'll always prefer
The crass defiance of the crow
Plopped on a spit of long-dead fir—
A quarrelsome smudge condemning the snow.

About the Author

PATRICK GILLESPIE lives in Vermont with his wife, dog, and cat. A February thaw is melting the brook's ice and he listens to Schubert. He's thinking about his own near death experience, at the age of eleven, and wonders if he'll ever grow tired of telling the story.

He took up carpentry after a Master's Degree in Children's Literature, wrote poetry, and founded a blog called Poemshape where he discusses poetry and publishes his own poems there. *Tiny House, Big Mountain* is his first published novel. He's in his mid-fifties, and has already written a second novel in the same mythical town of Brookway, Vermont.

He's cut back on his carpentry and is devoting all his time to writing—more poetry, a third novel, and articles for his blog. He has a writing cabin in his back field. He built it himself. He now lets his grass grow into a field of wildflowers and scythes it himself—summer and fall. It's a good way to keep fit after writing all day. If he's not in Vermont, you might him in Berlin, Germany, his place of birth and (when not happily in the Green Mountains) the city he loves the most.

www.ingramcontent.com/pod-product-compliance
Lightning Source LLC
Chambersburg PA
CBHW020232260626
47156CB00002B/652